CRY IN THE WILDERNESS

ALSO BY REBECCA HARTT

The Acts of Valor Series

Returning to Eden

Every Secret Thing

Cry in the Wilderness

Rising From Ashes

Braving the Valley

CRY IN THE WILDERNESS

ACTS OF VALOR, BOOK THREE

REBECCA HARTT

Book and cover design by eBook Prep
www.ebookprep.com

March 2021
ISBN: 978-1-947833-93-7

Rise UP Publications
644 Shrewsbury Commons Ave
Ste 249
Shrewsbury PA 17361
United States of America

www.riseUPpublications.com
Phone: 866-846-5123

ACKNOWLEDGMENTS

I may have written this novel, but the final product isn't fully mine. Without my editors Julee Schwarzburg and Sydney Jane Baily, this story would never have gained its luster. Even then, readers would have come upon many a typo if it weren't for my proofreaders, Elizabeth, Deborah, Wendie, Jeanne and especially Penny. These lovely women have transformed raw material into a finished product, and I am so very grateful!

This book is dedicated to my wonderful friend Rachel Rowe. You stole into my life like an angel and taught me how to be a better writer. I owe you a debt of gratitude I have never repaid. I'm so sorry I can't be at your side anymore. But I have named my heroine after you in your honor. I love you, and I always will.

PROLOGUE

he sound of Ethan's voice cracked through the air like a whip, bringing Rachel's head up from the design magazine she'd smuggled into her bedroom in her brother's home in Virginia Beach. Given how his voice was coming through the ceiling, Ethan had to be up in the attic, lecturing eleven-year-old Liam yet *again* for not doing his homework.

"I'm not sending you to private school so you can turn out like your mother."

Rachel had grown accustomed to her older brother's snubs. At times, she believed she deserved them. After all, at thirty years of age, she had yet to pursue an occupation. She'd married her high school sweetheart right after graduation. Making her and Blake's house a home and raising their son had been her life's work.

She certainly wouldn't still be living with Ethan more than two years after her husband's death if she were a go-getter like her brother, would she?

Tucking a strand of light-brown hair behind her ear to better hear, Rachel listened for Liam's reply.

"No, please. Don't!"

At her son's horrified cry, Rachel stuffed the magazine under her pillow and rushed out of her room. In moments, she was ascending the narrow staircase to the large, unfinished attic where Liam had chosen to sleep. He suffered the heat that rose to the third story during summer months in return for the view through two round windows into the trees outside.

As she raced up the creaking treads, Ethan's words reached her ears.

"There. Now you won't be distracted from your homework. You'll never be a lawyer if you keep taking in every hurt animal you come across."

"I don't want to be a lawyer!"

Rachel had never heard her son's voice raised in hysteria before. Like her, he was meek and abhorred confrontation. She crested the stairs to find him with his fists balled, his face white and tight with rage.

Her gaze cut to Ethan as he took a threatening step toward his nephew. "You'll change your mind," he said, sending a chill up Rachel's spine.

A vision of Liam dressed in the uniform of a Navy lawyer and wearing the same smirk that rode his uncle's lips formed in her mind. *Never!*

Ethan stepped back, nearly bumping his thinning head of dark hair on an exposed beam, giving Rachel her first glimpse of the birdcage Liam had set before the window. The door hung open. The cardinal Liam had been nursing back to health lay in a scarlet heap of feathers on the floor.

It was dead—her brother had killed it.

Rachel felt something inside her snap. Indignation rose, empowering her to hold Ethan's belligerent gaze as she marched toward her son and slid her arms around him. Liam's frame quaked. Nearly as tall as she was, he remained rigid with emotion.

"You should go now," she told Ethan in a voice she scarcely recognized.

2

CRY IN THE WILDERNESS

His expression registered amazement at her tone. But then, taking in the two of them allied in defiance against him, he broke eye contact and looked over at the cage.

Considering it a moment, he said in a voice devoid of remorse, "I'm sorry, Liam. I overreacted. Take a thirty-minute break outside, and then you'll be ready to study. All right?" He went to ruffle his nephew's hair, but Liam shrank from him.

"Just go," Rachel commanded.

Ethan's eyes narrowed at her uncharacteristic temerity. She could see the usual belittling words forming in his mouth, but because Liam was watching, he bit them back. He could not repress the dismissive *humph* that made his beaked nose twitch, however. Spinning on the soles of his polished shoes, he headed toward the stairs.

She waited for the door at the base of the steps to shut before she released her son. Liam sank onto the bed as if his quivering knees couldn't support him. His gaze fell to the bird with its broken neck, and his face crumpled.

"I was going to release him tomorrow." Tears of lament rose in the dark-blue eyes Liam had inherited from his father.

Rachel sat next to him. To her dismay, he shifted away, reminding her forcibly of Blake and the way he used to fight for poise, dashing the tears from his eyes.

"I'm so sorry," Rachel blurted as guilt ambushed her.

Liam leveled a glare at her. "Why do we live here?" he whispered on a furious note. "I hate this house. I hate Uncle Ethan!"

Astonishment kept her mute for a moment. "I thought you liked him."

Her son's face twisted with incredulity. "Like him? How could anyone like him?"

Rachel blinked, reshuffling her reasons for putting up with their living arrangement. She had thought she was providing Liam with a father figure. Ethan had always taken such pride in his nephew.

When Blake's parachute failed to deploy and their whole world had imploded, Ethan had been their rock, stepping in as executor of

Blake's estate. Then, one year after her husband's death, when the Navy forced them out of base housing, Ethan had offered them a roof over their heads. She'd been so grateful not to have to house hunt when it was all she could do to get out of bed in the mornings.

Liam's pointed question jarred Rachel's assumptions. *Have I been blind all this time?* Apparently, she had been. Her son, forced to attend a rigorous private school and to apply himself like a scholar when he would rather be outdoors communing with nature, was as mistreated as she was.

"Oh, Liam," she whispered. Fear gripped her as she envisioned what she secretly desired: freedom for both of them. More than once, she'd fantasized about picking up and leaving, but roadblocks were *everywhere*. "It won't be easy to leave. We'll have to save up money."

"What about Dad's life insurance?"

She swallowed down the guilt that rose in her. "Your uncle invested it all into your college fund." As executor of Blake's estate, he'd had every right.

"What about the social security money?"

She was astonished Liam even knew about that. Currently, it went into a bank account co-owned by her brother, who'd set it up that way so he could deduct their rent and food.

"We still have that." She intended to contact the Social Security Administration and arrange for her monthly benefits to go into her personal account.

"I don't understand why he thinks he's in charge of me. He's *not* my dad."

Shame seared her. If grief hadn't put her in a depression so deep she'd needed to be hospitalized, Ethan would never have assumed so much control. "I'm sorry. I'll take care of everything. We'll find our own place." Saying the promise aloud made it real.

Liam went still a moment, visibly picturing the future. He met her gaze suddenly, his eyes wide with fear. "What if he won't let us leave?"

The question mirrored Rachel's own fears. "He'll have to. He doesn't own us."

4

Or did he? Her thoughts went to the paper he'd made her sign when she was hospitalized. It was a legal form meant to give him temporary custody. That paper hadn't made him Liam's legal guardian, had it?

"Listen," she added, wanting to encourage herself as much as Liam. "God's going to help us. He helped me get strong again. He'll help us find our own place."

She'd been introduced to the Word of God for the first time when she and Blake attended a church together mere months before his death. The comfort of knowing her husband lived on in the afterlife had allowed her to put the pieces of her shattered heart back together —at least so it beat again. Then, during her treatment for depression, faith-filled counselors had assured her God still had plans for her, plans to prosper her. She'd rallied from despair to live out her intended purpose—and this was so not it.

"I'm going to pray about it," she insisted. "God will show us the way out."

Liam heaved a sigh. "How long is that going to take?"

His despairing tone plucked at her heartstrings. Clearly, her son had lost faith in her. He still believed in his father, though, whose memory he revered. In Liam's eyes, Blake could do anything. "Your dad's going to watch out for us," she comforted. "He's an angel in God's Army now. He'll show us the way."

A suggestion of hope appeared in Liam's defeated expression. "Yeah." He nodded.

Rachel glanced past him to the cage hanging open. That open door was a sign, wasn't it? The time had come for them to break free.

Dear God, help us. Her gaze went to the dead bird lying at their feet. If they didn't leave soon, they might well end up broken, just like that cardinal.

CHAPTER 1

ONE YEAR LATER

*C*hief Petty Officer Saul Wade shoved his way into the Trial Services Building in a rotten mood. He'd been operating in Mexico for the past eleven months and had barely settled in at home when he got news requiring him to pack his bags again and leave. His stepdad had died, making him the heir to the ranch on which he'd been born and raised, the place he'd never wanted to go home to.

The dark-skinned security guard on duty lit up to see him. "Hey! How you doin', Chief? I ain't seen you here in months!"

"I'm good, Hewitt. You?" Saul slapped the envelope he'd brought onto the X-ray belt and surrendered his cell phone, which was not permitted in the building. Stripped of both his phone and the weapon he'd stowed in his car, he suffered a sense of vulnerability.

I'm not in Mexico, he had to remind himself.

"Where you been? Oh, wait. Guess you can't tell me that."

"Somewhere hot," Saul replied—which had to be obvious given his savage tan and the copper streaks in his mahogany hair. Thanks to his

Native American ancestors, he had blended in well with the Mexican population, but he'd had to cut his long hair short. The sacrifice had been well worth it.

"How many bad guys did you kill this time?"

"Classified." Saul thought of the three dead *narcos* he'd added to his list of terminated targets, bringing the total to nineteen. His code name in Spanish, *El Segador*, had become a part of Latin American folklore. To his teammates, he was called The Reaper—as in The Grim Reaper, the ultimate symbol of death. He was America's top sniper and a proud member of her most elite Special Operations force, SEAL Team Six.

Stepping through the metal detector, Saul's gaze went straight down the hall to the doors of the courtroom where a court martial last year had ended in the vindication of the accused, Saul's teammate and newly appointed executive officer, Jonah Mills. The FBI had promptly arrested their corrupt commander, Daniel Dwyer, who'd been sentenced to life in prison.

But Saul didn't picture that when he looked at the doors. He pictured, instead, Rachel LeMere, the widow of his best friend, Blake. She'd attended the trial because her brother, the prosecuting attorney, had apparently forced her to come. Saul had thought of her every day since he'd seen her there, as thin and sad as a wraith. Blake's death had all but killed her, too.

"What's the matter, Chief? You don't seem so chipper today," Hewitt needled, drawing Saul's attention back to him.

"I am never chipper," he said, half-joking, half-serious.

"Jolly then." Hewitt's eyes danced.

Saul directed a pointed look at the man's tubby midsection. "You're the one who's jolly, Hewitt. I thought I suggested you lose some weight."

The man chuckled. "You said to lay off the donuts. You didn't say nothin' about no honey buns," he added, gleefully.

Saul snatched his folder off the X-ray belt as it reappeared. "No empty carbs at all, Hewitt. And no pop either." He indicated the can of Coke near Hewitt's hand.

"Pop?" The guard made a face. "Who talks like that? This is a Coke!" Hewitt snatched up the can and drained it as if to prove his point.

Saul simply shook his head and walked away. After all these years, he still said *pop* instead of *soda*. *You can take the boy out of Oklahoma, but you can't take Oklahoma out of the boy.*

Stalking down the hallway, he searched the plaques on the doors for the name *Spenser*. All he needed was for Spenser to accept the document he carried, an agreement to represent the Navy SEAL third class who'd cracked a few heads at the waterfront while breaking up a fight.

With a mutter of annoyance that his job at home amounted to babysitting and paper-pushing, Saul located Spenser's door only to find a note stuck to it saying the man was in a meeting. A drawn arrow suggested Saul might find him farther down the hall. He continued on, through an open door into a waiting area and drew up short. There sat the woman he'd just been thinking about, lifting her gaze from the magazine she'd been poring over.

"Saul!" Her gray-green eyes widened with wonder, lending beauty to an otherwise unremarkable face. Her hair was longer, hanging in a mousy brown curtain to her shoulders. He was glad to see a little color in her cheeks. She'd also gained some much-needed weight since the prior year.

"Rachel." Guilt struck Saul swift as a rattlesnake's strike. Blake had been like a brother to him. Yet not once after his death had Saul checked in on Blake's widow to see how she was faring. "What are you doing here?"

Her gaze shifted toward the closed conference room. The silhouette of two men behind a pane of milky glass had him guessing Spenser was in there talking to her brother, Captain O'Rourke.

"Studying," she said rather stiffly. "Where have you been?"

Had he heard a hint of accusation in her tone?

"Out of the country." He turned his attention to the magazines, all open to scenes of handsome dining rooms. "You redecorating?" he asked, hoping to ease the tension between them.

"No." She eyed the spread before her. "No. This is what I'm studying, interior design."

He glimpsed something like defiance in her eyes. "That's good." He was glad to hear she'd found interest in life again.

"Yeah," she agreed, but her soft mouth firmed.

Unwilling to know what she was thinking, he gestured with the envelope at the conference room. "Spenser in there?"

"Yes. With Ethan."

He could hear her brother now, his tone as condescending as it had been during Lieutenant Mills's trial the year before.

Saul sighed. "How much longer do you think they'll be?" He didn't want to sit down and have a heart-to-heart with a woman who'd had to be hospitalized following her husband's death. He didn't have that kind of skillset.

Rachel shrugged. "I don't know. Half an hour maybe?"

He pictured the work he still had to do before he took off. "Can you do me a favor?" Guilt stung him even as the request left his mouth. What had he ever done for her apart from escort her and her kid to her husband's funeral?

"Sure."

He held out the envelope. "Can you give this paperwork to Spenser for me?"

She stretched out a slender hand with pretty but unpainted fingernails. "No problem."

"I'd give it to him myself but I'm leaving town this weekend, and I have a million things to do."

Her gaze jumped to his. "You're leaving again?" She sounded incredulous.

"Yeah, my stepdad died last week. I gotta go settle his estate and sell the land he left me."

"Oh. I'm sorry for your loss," she said sincerely.

No loss, Saul thought. "Thanks." A beat of silence followed his terse reply. "It was good seein' you," he added, hating himself. "You look like you're doing well."

"Do I?"

Irony this time. The woman's complex emotions discomfited him. He backed away. "Take care." With shame nipping at his heels, he turned and hastened away. The silence that followed had him glancing over his shoulder to gauge her response to their meeting.

What he glimpsed only deepened his guilt.

Rachel sat with a hand over her mouth, staring down at the magazines, tears rimming her lower lashes.

She's missing Blake, Saul rationalized, while sensing there was more to it. Rachel LeMere was battling demons, but he didn't want to know about them because he couldn't begin to help her—not when he had demons of his own to contend with.

Disappointment gouged Rachel's heart. When she saw Saul Wade coming toward her, her soul had soared. Having dreamed for months that Saul would somehow rescue her, she had thought, *This is it!* He would ask how she was doing and offer to help, somehow.

Yet, he hadn't. Sure, he'd expressed polite concern for her, but then he'd promptly distanced himself, clearly unwilling to involve himself in her life.

So much for him rescuing her.

Would it have made any difference if she'd explained what she been through, how she'd taken her brother to court and lost? Incredibly, the judge had denied her petition to regain sole custody of her son. Worse than that, the man had humiliated her in court and extended the length of Ethan's guardianship right up to Liam's eighteenth birthday.

It wasn't until a month later that Rachel found out Ethan and the judge had gone to law school together.

The prospect of appealing her case before a different judge was unimaginable. She couldn't do it, not when she lived in Ethan's house, subject to his belittling comments, his scorn, his absolute conviction that he was the best substitute for a father Liam could ever have—better, even, because Blake's commitment to the Teams had taken him away so often.

Rachel had given up solving her situation by legal means. Only God was big enough to handle the mess she was in. Either He came through for her, or the next six years of her life would be a living hell.

Gripping her hands together, she bowed her head and prayed fervently. *God, if Saul is really supposed to help me, You're going to have to convince him.*

In his second-story bedroom tucked into the eaves of his bungalow-style cottage, Saul filled his duffel bag with what he would need for two weeks of leave. It would take at least that long to settle Cyril's estate. Who knew in what sad shape his stepdad might have left the ranch?

Standing halfway between his dresser and his bed, Saul lobbed the clothing he'd only recently put into his drawers back into his duffel bag—jeans, T-shirts, and an extra pair of cowboy boots. All the while, he was aware of Duke, his chocolate Labrador retriever, watching him with his head on his front paws, ears flattened.

"Don't look at me like that."

Duke gave a long groan, and Saul put his hands on his hips. Why couldn't he take his dog with him? Poor Duke had already spent eleven months without him, staying with Lieutenant Mills's family, who had a golden retriever. It wasn't fair to Duke—or to that family—to leave him there again.

"You want to come with me, boy?"

The dog's broad head popped up.

"Want to go to Oklahoma? It's a long drive."

The Lab's eyes brightened. He cocked his head.

Saul pictured the woods and the stream where he grew up, "Heck, you might like it so much you won't want to come back." As if privy to the pictures in Saul's head, Duke's tail wagged.

In the blink of an eye, Saul's memories went from good to bad. He pictured his mother on the front porch holding the squalling baby. "Cyril, stop it!"

Cyril held Saul by the scruff of his shirt. Ignoring his wife's pleading, he flung Saul into the door of his new Ford F-150 pickup truck. The bone in Saul's nose cracked. Hot blood gushed out, running over his lips.

His thoughts fast-forwarded to his senior year of high school. This time it was Puca, Saul's full-blooded Muskogee Creek grandfather, standing on the porch, blocking Cyril's racist friends from entering their home.

"Leave." The paralyzed half of Puca's mouth made him difficult to understand, but the proud way he'd held his frail body got the message across.

"Out of the way, old man." Cyril shoved him to his knees.

With a roar of rage, Saul went to punish his stepdad for his cruelty. Puca's protest, immediate and unquestionable, was the only thing that stopped him.

"Violence is not the way," he said to Saul as he helped his grandfather to his feet.

With a mutter of annoyance, Saul flicked off his memories. He could not believe ol' Cyril had gone and left him the ranch. It was probably mortgaged to the eaves, and this was his last bid, even from the grave, to torture his stepson.

If Saul's real father hadn't bought the ranch in the first place, Saul would have met with the estate lawyer online and found a Realtor to sell the property for a reasonable price. He'd never intended to go back home. But Saul's daddy had bought the ranch before Saul was even born. It was Wade land, not Lawson land.

"So, suck it up," he ordered. Duke cocked his head again.

Saul was stuffing his socks in the bag when his cell phone rang.

Recognizing Lieutenant Mills's extension, he answered quickly. "Yes, sir."

"I know you're trying to leave, Saul, but did you get that paperwork over to Spenser yesterday?"

Saul pictured the document he'd left with Rachel LeMere. "Uh, yes, sir. Well, I left it with someone who was going to give it to him."

"Could you make sure Spenser actually got it? Potter still hasn't heard from him yet."

"No problem, sir." Except he didn't have Spenser's number, so it sort of was a problem.

"Listen, don't call me back unless there's an issue. I know you're busy. Drive safe and take your time. We got everything covered for you here. If you need more than two weeks' leave, just let me know. I'll get the new CO to approve it." Jonah Mills had held the Team together until a new commander was found to replace the disgraced Dwyer.

"Thank you, sir." Saul ended the call, then sat and stared at his phone. He could look up Spenser's number, or he could just call Rachel—assuming her number hadn't changed. He'd been thinking about their strange encounter for the past twenty-four hours anyway.

Picturing her exquisite eyes, he pressed her number and then braced himself for the sound of her voice.

Rachel's brow knit with concentration as she answered the last questions on a quiz in her online class, History of Interior Design. The test was timed. With a documented disability, she could have had the time limit waived, but Rachel never made use of her accommodation. Doing so would give Ethan one more reason to point out her incompetence.

The question had four possible answers, two of which seemed right. Rachel could sense the seconds ticking away as she reread every word, making sure she understood. The buzzing of her cell phone— unusual at any time of day—shattered her focus.

With a huff of annoyance, she glanced at her phone, and all concern about her quiz vanished.

Heavens, it was Saul! Her pulse spiked. Had God answered her prayer already?

"Hey," she answered on a breathless note. At the same time, she selected one of the two answers and submitted the quiz with only one second left.

"It's Saul."

She pushed to her feet, heart pounding. "I know." Was he finally going to ask about her situation? Was he going to help?

"Did you ever get that paperwork to Spenser for me?"

Her expectations nose-dived. The call wasn't personal at all. "Um, yeah, I put it right into his hands yesterday."

"Okay. Great. Thanks. We just hadn't heard from him yet, so..."

She could sense him about to hang up. "Not to worry." She kept talking in the hopes of breaking through the barrier he kept between them. Blake hadn't been exaggerating when he'd described his friend as the strong, silent type. "Lawyers are notorious for taking their time. But he did get the paperwork. I watched him read through it as he walked back to his office."

"Cool. Thanks again."

"Where is it you're headed, exactly? You said you were headed home."

"Oklahoma."

"Oh, that's right. You're from Oklahoma." He'd made no secret of his Native American ancestry, wearing his hair long and dressing in cowboy boots—wait! A sudden idea sparked. Oklahoma bordered Texas. That couldn't be a coincidence. "Are you driving or taking a plane?"

"Driving."

Her idea solidified into a certainty. She'd been searching for months for a way to get to Texas without Ethan tracking her. "How... how long does it take?"

The sound of the garage door rumbling open signaled Ethan's

arrival home. Rachel heard Saul's answer but didn't take it in. Desperate to speak with him, to broach the possibility of her electrifying idea, she knew she couldn't do it now, not with Ethan in the house.

"Listen." She threw caution to the wind. "I need to talk to you about something really important before you go. Can you meet me?"

Her question met with sudden silence.

"There's a park in my neighborhood," she persisted. "You know where First Colony is, don't you?" The upscale neighborhood was known to most people. "Can you meet me there, within an hour?"

"I have a lot to do before I leave."

"I'm sure you do, but this is really important. Please. It won't take long." She held her breath waiting for his answer.

"What time exactly?" he finally asked.

Relief made her head spin. She glanced at the time on her phone, realizing Liam's bus would deliver him from school at any minute. It was three thirty.

"What about four o'clock?"

Another silence. Then, sounding as if the words were pulled out of him, he said, "All right," before hanging up on her abruptly.

With a sharp exhalation, Rachel put her phone away. Hope pounded through her. Downstairs, the garage door rumbled shut. Ethan would go straight into his study and seclude himself for at least an hour, sipping on scotch and sorting through his mail.

With her heart racing, she returned to her desk and opened the email client provided by her online school. With a tremor in her fingers, she composed a quick message. *I may have found a safe way to Dallas! I will know more by this evening. Say a prayer!*

Closing down her laptop, she got up and searched for her tennis shoes.

She tied them off, then straightened and stared with dismay at her reflection. Perhaps if she took more care with her appearance instead of wearing Blake's old sweatshirt over a pair of skinny jeans, Saul would be more inclined to help her. But ever since Blake's death, she hadn't cared what anyone thought of her. Her hair hung straight and limp to her shoulders. She rarely wore makeup. Hearing Liam's bus approach, however, she surrendered any thought of changing.

She slipped from her bedroom with her stomach churning. This had to be what God wanted, the reason why He'd put all those dreams about Saul into her head. Saul was *meant* to give them a ride to Dallas. But could she convince him of that?

Tiptoeing down the broad, curved staircase, she kept a nervous eye on Ethan's study door, praying it stayed shut. It opened suddenly as she stole across the foyer. Quelling her startle reflex, Rachel faced her brother with a carefully neutral expression.

"Where are you going?" His eyes narrowed with suspicion. She wasn't permitted to go anywhere without his knowledge.

"I thought I would take Liam to the park for an hour or so. He studies better when he's had a chance to play."

"Nonsense. He has PE at the end of the day. He doesn't need to go to the park."

A cold sweat breached Rachel's pores. She couldn't afford to let this opportunity slip through her fingers.

"You're right," she pretended to agree. "Just for half an hour then, so you can have some peace and quiet."

"Hmph." Ethan finally shrugged his bony shoulders in agreement, then stepped back into his office, freeing her to exhale.

As she exited the house, a small white bus from Norfolk Academy drew alongside Ethan's manicured lawn. As one of a dozen or so children from their wealthy neighborhood, twelve-year-old Liam enjoyed door-to-door bus service. He stepped down from the bus, moving like an old man, his expression somber.

Rachel's heart ached to see him so depressed. It had been over a year since she'd promised him they would move from Ethan's house. Not once in the intervening months had Liam asked what had happened to that promise. Smart boy that he was, he must have guessed her battle in court had backfired.

But none of that would matter anymore if Saul helped the way she hoped he would.

"Hi, sweetheart." Rachel met Liam in the middle of the yard. "What do you say we go to the park for a while?"

Attuned to the nuances of her voice, he searched her face, then glanced at the house. "You sure we're allowed?"

"I'm sure. Go put your backpack by the door. It'll be fine there. Hurry." She didn't trust her brother not to change his mind.

Liam ran and shook off his pack, then the two struck out toward the park several blocks away. As they walked, Rachel asked Liam about his day, then struggled to take in his reply as she asked herself whether Saul might stand her up.

He couldn't. For weeks, she'd been searching for a means to get herself and Liam to Dallas undetected. Public transportation wasn't an option, as Ethan would immediately track them down and force them to return. If he caught her, there wasn't any question he would use her actions as an excuse to seek sole custody. After her recent loss to him in court, Ethan seemed capable of taking her son away from her completely.

But he couldn't track them down if they got a ride with someone Ethan didn't know. That had to be what God intended. That had to be how Saul would save them.

Saul nosed his cobalt-blue Camaro into the parking lot at First Colony's neighborhood park. He sat a moment, marveling at how big it was. The castle-like clubhouse was flanked by no less than three swimming pools—one for babies, one for older kids, and one for the swim team or adults doing laps. Amenities included two tennis courts, a soccer field, and the enormous playground in front of him. With a climbing wall and a zip line, it called to mind the obstacle course behind his Team building, only that didn't come with a thick bed of mulch to cushion the men when they fell or even shade trees like the enormous live oaks encircling the play area.

Why am I here? This place was for privileged children and their white-collar parents, enjoying the cooler weather of this first week of autumn. It was a whole different cosmos from the world of trafficking and conspiracy that Saul lived in.

As well it should be.

All at once, his gaze collided with Rachel LeMere's. She stood by herself under one of the trees, staring at him, one arm across her chest like a shield, the other raised to shade her eyes. Even with the distance between them, her vulnerability tugged at him. He couldn't begin to imagine what she wished to talk about—probably something to do with Blake.

She'd better not cry. He pushed out of his vehicle.

Pulling his baseball cap over his eyes, Saul attempted to cross the playground without drawing attention to himself. That wasn't easy to do, not with his brawny physique, dark goatee, and gold hoop glinting on this left earlobe. For once, he was glad he'd hacked off his hair.

Aware that several mothers were tracking him with their eyes, no doubt viewing him with suspicion, he headed for a bench in the shade of the live oak and sat on it. Rachel would join him when she was ready. Taking inventory of the kids scrambling over the equipment, Saul searched for Blake's son—what was his name again?

At last, he found the boy wearing a white button-up shirt and gray slacks, sitting on a swing and staring down at his loafers.

Concern bored into Saul's consciousness. Blake's son hadn't grown much since the funeral three years ago. Like his mother, he looked thin and pale. And melancholy.

Not my problem. In that same instant, Saul remembered the boy's name—Liam. Blake had talked about him constantly, his face glowing with pride.

Rachel, having circuited the playground, finally joined him, sitting on the other end of the bench with her back to him. It was obvious she didn't want anyone thinking they were talking.

"Thanks for coming," she said in a voice loud enough for only him to hear.

"Sure."

In the subsequent silence, he could sense her gathering the courage to tell him something. He knew an urge to get up and run.

"I need to ask you a favor," she finally said, staring down at her clenched hands. "When you leave for Oklahoma, take us with you, Liam and me."

Saul stared at her back in mute surprise.

"I've been needing to get to Dallas, but I can't take public transportation. Ethan would find us. If we went with you, he would never know."

Her words confirmed what he'd only ever suspected, that her brother was a tyrant who controlled her every move. And she was afraid of him. "What's in Dallas?"

She hesitated a split second as if wondering whether she ought to tell him.

"My birth mother lives there. She's offered us a place to stay. Ethan doesn't know I've found her. He would never think to search for us there." She peeked over her shoulder to gauge Saul's response.

His incredulity mounted. "Who cares if Ethan finds you, Rachel? You're an adult. You're Liam's mother. You can go anywhere you want."

Her face contorted with grief as she shook her head and averted her face once again. "No. He has shared custody."

"What?"

She gulped in a breath and stared back down at her clenched hands. "When I went into the hospital, he got me to sign a paper giving him custody. I thought it was only temporary. When I found out it wasn't, I took him to court to get his custody stricken. Instead, the judge awarded him guardianship until Liam turns eighteen. I can't stay with Ethan that long. Saul, you have no idea."

No, he didn't. And he had liked it better that way. How on earth had Ethan convinced any reasonable judge he should have guardianship over his nephew?

"I don't understand this," Saul muttered.

"Because it doesn't make sense. The judge went to law school with Ethan. I never had a chance to win. I found that out later."

"Then go back to court."

"No." She swung around suddenly, giving up the pretext of not conversing. "Ethan knows the law too well. He'll win every time. I have to leave the state. I have to get to Dallas. Please, Saul. Take us with you as far as Oklahoma. I'll find a way from there."

The hope shining in her eyes kept Saul speechless. She was dead serious.

"Maybe you're wondering how we could get in your car without anyone seeing," she continued, tackling logistics before he could use them against her. "I've thought it through. We're going hiking with Liam's Boy Scout troop at First Landing State Park tomorrow, early afternoon. There's an overflow parking lot no one ever uses. Tell me what time to be there and we'll meet you. No one will see us leave."

"Rachel." He tried to cut her off. What she was saying was impossible.

"We won't take up much room. We'll only pack one small bag. Please, Saul. For Blake's sake, say yes."

"Don't do that," he shot back. "Blake was my best friend. I would have died for him, but what you're asking is insane."

The word *insane* turned her complexion ashen. Her time in a mental hospital must have sensitized her to the term.

"Sorry. What I mean is simply get yourself a better lawyer. You don't need to run off without telling Ethan where you're going. That's just..." He caught himself from saying the word *crazy*.

Lowering her gaze, she went perfectly still.

Regret stitched through Saul, followed immediately by guilt. Not only had he ignored Rachel and her son after Blake's death, but now when she was asking for his help, he had to refuse it.

"I'm sorry," he grated, stretching out a hand to touch her shoulder. He could feel her trembling.

To his dismay, she refused to look at him, to say another word. A long, pain-filled silence fell between them.

"Take care, Rachel." Removing his hand, Saul stood and walked away. Relief vied with guilt. It took all of his determination not to cast a backward glance. He didn't want to see the devastation in her posture. But she'd asked too much of him; she had to know that.

Agitated by the mere idea of what lay ahead, the last thing he needed was to make his impending trip any harder on himself than it was going to be.

CHAPTER 2

*S*aul jerked awake with his heart still racing. He found himself in his bed with the moonlight peeking like a concerned mother through the parted curtains at his window. Blake, of course, was gone.

Just a dream. But he could still sense Blake's presence, as if he'd actually been standing at the door, raging at him.

Peeling off the sheet sticking to his sweat-bathed skin, Saul rolled out of bed and crossed to the large window to part the curtains farther and crank the pane open, admitting cool night air. Duke, sleeping in his doggie bed, raised his broad head to regard him.

As the air flowed in, wicking the sweat from his bare limbs, Saul gazed down at his small front lawn, half-expecting to see Blake's truck parked behind his Camaro, but it wasn't. He looked back at his door and pictured Blake as he'd been in his dream, hands on his hips, eyes flashing with anger. He had yelled at Saul for walking away from Rachel that afternoon.

"I expected better of you, Saul Wade."

Puca had taught Saul to pay attention to his dreams. They were a source of spiritual guidance, he used to say. Goosebumps rose on Saul's forearms. He rubbed them away, then shook his head.

"No, I'm not going to do it. I'm not a hero." He was a loner, the dark horse, who followed his own crooked path.

That's bull. You're not a loner, you're a coward, echoed Blake's voice.

Duke rose suddenly from his bed and crossed to where Saul stood. The moonlight caused his eyes to shine.

"Not you, too," Saul muttered.

The dog didn't move a muscle.

"Do you realize what you're asking?" Saul spoke to Blake through his dog. "If O'Rourke is the kid's legal guardian, you're asking me to kidnap him. I could go to jail for that!"

Duke cocked his head, seeming to say, *So what?*

The words Blake had raged in his dream came back to him. *"You're my best friend, Saul. If you won't help Rachel, who will?"*

With a shuddering breath, Saul closed his eyes and dragged his fingers through his shorn hair.

"Fine." He reopened his eyes and glared at his dog. "I'll do it. I'll take them with me. You happy now?"

Duke's tail wagged, sweeping the hardwood floor.

Bemused to have made a decision born of a dream, Saul turned and stalked into the adjacent bathroom. If he intended to whisk Rachel and Liam out of Virginia with him that same afternoon, he needed to start his day early and come up with a fail-proof plan.

Rachel plodded along the dirt path at First Landing State Park, numb to her environment. Since her failure to convince Saul to help them, she'd stumbled about in a haze of self-doubt. How could she have been so wrong about interpreting God's will? She had been *so sure* her dreams about Saul had been a sign. But then he'd flatly turned her down and walked away, making her question her faith, even God's love for her.

She shook her head, no. *He does love me.* God had rescued her from the deepest of depressions. He had plans to prosper her—she knew that.

But a glance at the overflow parking lot seemed to suggest that wasn't true. Saul's car wasn't in the empty lot. They weren't leaving for Dallas, after all, which made the backpack she carried, stuffed with a change of clothes for both of them, her favorite Bible, and toothbrushes saved from a trip to the dentist, not only superfluous but seem as insane as Saul had said. Plus, it hung hot and heavy on her back.

As she and Liam trailed his troop leader deeper into the forest, despair threatened to swallow her. She fought depression's ravenous pull, fearful it might drag her into the same void that had consumed her after Blake's death.

"Look, Mom." Liam directed her gaze to the tiny reptile blending in against the bark of a tree. "It's a gray tree frog."

Rachel mustered a smile for his enthusiasm. "I see." She put her face near his, struggling to seem interested as Liam explained how to tell it apart from the squirrel tree frog.

Like his father, Liam adored the outdoors. The wilder the terrain, the better. First Landing State Park, situated in the heart of Virginia Beach, hardly qualified as remote, but its nearly three thousand acres offered campsites, a beach on the Chesapeake Bay, and nineteen miles of trails.

Liam's scout troop was hiking the most arduous of the trails. Through a maritime forest, along the cypress swamp, and on raised walkways through a saltwater marsh, they tramped in a quest to earn their hiking merit badge. Ethan intended for Liam to become an Eagle Scout, so much so that he'd signed himself up as a parent volunteer. Outdoor hikes were not Ethan's cup of tea, however, so he'd arranged for Rachel to take his place. Liam could not have been happier to be both outdoors and spending time with his mother.

If Liam is happy, then so am I.

An hour into their hike, her phone buzzed. Saul? Hope flared in her before she snuffed it out. Of course it wasn't Saul. She pulled her phone from her pocket and frowned. The number texting her was unfamiliar. But the words of the text stopped her in her tracks.

Fall behind the others. Wait for me at the second footbridge.

She blinked at the message, doubting herself, scarcely breathing. Maybe this was the scout master texting her, but why would he say fall behind when he was far ahead of them? It had to be Saul.

A tremor of hope shot through her. With clumsy fingers, she typed, *Okay.*

Her heart pounded. "Liam, wait!"

Her son turned around. Seeing her expression, he peered toward the other scouts, then ran back to her, his smaller pack bouncing.

"What's wrong?" he demanded, out of breath.

Rachel reached for him with both hands. "Do you remember Daddy's best friend?" She held his dark-blue gaze intently.

"Yeah. He was at the park yesterday."

His observation surprised her. "Yes. I asked him to help us leave Uncle Ethan."

Liam's eyes grew enormous. "We're leaving?"

"I think so." She pitched her voice lower lest someone unseen overhear them. With an anxious glance all around them, she showed Liam the text messages. "We've crossed the first footbridge, right?"

Liam nodded.

"So, we keep on going until we reach the second one." The plan sounded far too nebulous, even to her.

"It's around that turn," Liam said, still breathless. "What happens then?"

"I don't know." She kept hold of his skinny arm. "Let's go, just not too fast."

They continued along the path, following its sloping course through the thinning trees, before coming abruptly upon a marsh basin. The odor of mudflats greeted them. The rest of the boys and their leader were filing off the footbridge on the other side. As they disappeared into the forest, Rachel and Liam started cautiously forward. An osprey shrieked overhead, startling her gaze upward.

Saul was going to help them get away. He was actually helping!

"That's him!"

Rachel bumped into her son and followed his pointing finger to the camouflaged canoe gliding toward them. She would never have seen Saul if she weren't expecting him. He sat in the center of the canoe, wearing colors that blended in with the marsh grass, a baseball cap pulled low over his eyes. She knew him by his dark goatee. Euphoria flooded Rachel. Tears of gratitude stung her eyes. *Thank You, oh mighty and merciful Father!*

With a swish of his paddle, Saul guided the canoe alongside the bridge and grabbed hold of the railings.

"Rachel, climb in front," he instructed tersely. "Liam, you're going to take this seat. I'm moving back."

With a glance at each other, Rachel and Liam clambered over the railing while Saul moved back to distribute the weight. The canoe wobbled precariously until they were all situated.

"All set?" Saul pushed them into the sluggish current. Rachel heard his paddle sluice through the water as he propelled them swiftly from the bridge toward a bend in the creek that would take them out of sight, thanks to the tide being low.

"All technology has to be thrown into the water now," Saul instructed. "Cell phones, Fitbits, iPods, anything."

Rachel had known she would have to get rid of her phone. She'd memorized the numbers she needed. Her pictures of the happy years spent with Blake were safely stored up in the Cloud. Pulling her phone from her pocket, she dropped it over the side of the canoe and watched it sink out of sight.

"What about Liam?" Saul asked.

"I don't have a phone yet," Liam said in a small voice.

Glancing back at him, Rachel found him gripping the sides of the canoe, his eyes wide and watchful.

Behind him, their reluctant rescuer kept a steady stroke on the paddle. "No iPad or electronic games either?"

"Not with me."

"Good." Saul paddled harder.

Directing her gaze forward, Rachel searched for impediments to their escape. Saul kept them close to the mudflats, paddling with such stealth she could hear fiddler crabs scuttling between the reeds. A blue heron froze on the shore as they glided past it, so close she could see the webs on its raised foot. The creek widened as it headed toward the Bay.

They came abruptly upon a pier and a fisherman, who lifted his gaze from a crab pot to greet them. Saul's rhythmic paddling faltered. Rachel sent a panicked glance back and caught Saul tugging the brim of his hat lower.

He answered the man's greeting in a natural voice, then plunged his paddle deeper and whisked them out of the stranger's sight.

They were almost at the mouth of the bay when he turned their craft sharply toward shore. A minute later, he drove their prow onto the sand and wedged his paddle into the mud to keep it there. The bark of a dog drew her gaze to a familiar blue Camaro concealed behind bushes. Saul's forethought amazed her, causing a portion of her fear to abate.

"Hop out," he ordered.

Rachel stepped quickly out of the boat, then stabilized the canoe so Liam could join her. Together, they tugged the canoe farther ashore as Blake had taught them previously.

"Thanks," Saul said, climbing out.

She and Liam looked on in confusion as Saul flipped the canoe over. He then crossed to a nearby tree, reached behind it, and produced an ax.

Liam stepped toward her, then visibly relaxed when Saul hefted the ax and swung it at the bottom of the canoe, splitting the wood with a swift downward stroke. His intent became clear when he repeated the action twice more, turned the canoe back over, and dropped the paddle back in. Then he shoved the damaged boat hard into the creek.

They watched a moment as it coasted away, taking on water. With the ax still in his hand, Saul turned and regarded them.

Rachel could tell by his expression he couldn't believe what he'd gotten himself into. Pivoting toward his parked car, he popped the trunk and laid the ax inside it. In the stuffed trunk, Rachel glimpsed a hunting rifle, duffel bag, and first-aid kit before he shut the trunk and moved to the passenger door. Opening it, he flipped the seat forward.

"Back," he growled at the dog about to leap out. With a submissive nod, the big brown Lab scuttled backward. Saul met Liam's wide eyes. "You'll have to share a seat with him."

"That's okay." Liam ducked into the back with enthusiasm. "Hey, boy," he crooned.

Saul pushed the seatback into place and gestured for Rachel to get in.

"Thank you," she whispered as she shrugged off her pack and slipped inside.

"We're not out of the woods yet." He shut the door quietly behind her.

Seconds later, with a glance at her and Liam's seatbelts, he backed them down a rutted track with speed and competence that had Rachel holding her breath. She'd believed only Blake could drive like that. Arriving at a clearing, they reversed direction, then took off again.

The dirt track turned into a gravel one before it spit them out into the overflow parking lot. "I used to fish back there," Saul explained in response to her wondering expression. "Blake joined me once."

That was why he'd chosen the remote spot to put them into his vehicle. The overflow lot housed two busses now, one of them unloading a group of children. She shrank down into her seat to avoid being seen.

They exited the park and merged smoothly into traffic on Shore Drive. Rachel sat up higher in her seat and wiped her sweaty palms on her shorts.

Saul's gaze went from her bare legs to the pack on her lap. "You bring something with you?"

"A change of clothing and two toothbrushes."

He made a thoughtful sound in his throat and accelerated, speeding them through a yellow light. "What made you think I'd even show up?" His tone betrayed an element of self-directed anger.

"I didn't think you would. I should have had more faith."

Her answer received a frown and a sharp glance.

Rachel shifted in her seat to regard Liam. He was hugging the dog who seemed a willing recipient of his affections.

"What's the dog's name?" she asked.

"Duke."

"He's wonderful." Rachel faced front again. The dog would be good for her boy.

Saul speared a glance into his rearview mirror. His expression seemed to soften, but he had nothing to say to either of them.

Letting her head fall back against the seat, she released a shaky breath and relived what had just happened—nothing short of a miracle. She couldn't believe what she'd suggested yesterday had come to pass.

I'm sorry I doubted You, Father.

Mr. Hale, the scout leader, was probably just noticing they'd fallen way behind. How long until he notified the authorities? Or Ethan? Her stomach knotted.

"We're not going to stop anywhere, are we?" she asked, betraying her fear.

"Nope." With a muted roar, Saul's Camaro swept them up an entrance ramp and onto the highway that would lead them north and west, toward the Blue Ridge Mountains and beyond. In just three hours or so, they'd be in the western half of Virginia, far from the search that would be taking place for them at First Landing State Park. Then she would breathe a whole lot easier.

"Do you think that fisherman will be a problem?" she asked under her breath.

To her deepening concern, Saul didn't answer right away. "He wasn't there when I set out. If he had been, I would've turned around."

In which case, she never would have known he'd intended to rescue her, after all.

She licked her lips. How could she convey the depth of her gratitude?

"I promise you won't...regret this," she finished, forcing the words through a tight throat.

Rachel was certain he'd heard her, but he didn't answer—probably because he already did.

For the next few hours, very little was said. Saul, like Ethan, had XM Radio in his car. First, he played commercial-free classic rock, switching over to country as the foothills of the Blue Ridge Mountains loomed on the horizon. Rachel longed to ask if they could search for Christian radio, as the songs played would ease her tension and reassure her of God's protection. K-LOVE radio, which had played at the psych hospital, had been so helpful in reminding her she and Blake had become Christians together. He was still alive in heaven, and God wasn't letting go of her, either. She wasn't about to ask Saul to change his station, though, not when he was doing so much for them already.

Her thoughts went to her birth mother, whom she'd emailed the previous night with the disappointing news. Shannon deserved to know Saul had come through, after all, and that Rachel and Liam were on their way to Texas. But with her cell phone lying at the bottom of the creek, she would need to ask Saul if she could borrow his to make that call. She flicked a glance at his tense profile.

I'll ask him this evening, she decided, too leery of his taut expression to speak up.

Chasing the sinking sun, Saul drove at barely over the speed limit so they reached the Blue Ridge Mountains in three hours flat. The cooler clime was starting to make the trees turn, but it would be another two weeks for autumn to flaunt its full glory. As the sky turned violet over the rolling terrain, Saul finally broke the interminable silence.

"Gotta love the mountains," he drawled.

"They're beautiful," Rachel agreed, relieved he had said something friendly. With every passing hour, the fear that Ethan would catch them diminished, but Saul's brooding presence had kept her from relaxing.

Even so, when he veered off the highway onto an exit ramp, Rachel shot him an uncertain glance. "Where are we going?"

"Get a bite to eat." His laid-back reply further eased her concerns. She'd been hoping for a bathroom break, and Liam had to be hungry. Plus, here was her chance to borrow Saul's phone and call her birth mother.

They drew up to a fast-food restaurant with several cars outside. Saul lowered the windows, letting sweet mountain air drift in before cutting the engine.

"I'm gonna walk the dog. You two run in and use the restrooms. Don't buy anything with a credit or debit card."

"I have cash." Rachel had been hoarding it for months. "Can I get you something?"

He considered a second, then nodded. "A burger and a sweet tea would be great."

"And could I borrow your cell phone to make a quick call?"

With visible reluctance, he reached into the compartment between the seats. Punching in a code, he handed her an Android.

"I'm only going to make one call," she assured him.

"Keep your eyes down and don't talk to anyone if you don't have to," he added. "Bring your food back to the car. I'll leave it unlocked."

They scrambled out of the car as Saul snapped a leash on Duke. Once in the restaurant, Rachel sent Liam into the restroom, then dialed the number she'd memorized, aware that Saul was keeping an eye on her through the window between them.

"Hello?" Her birth mother's voice, now familiar to Rachel, helped to relax her further.

"It's me." She talked quickly and quietly so no one overheard her. "He came. He actually showed up, even though he said he wouldn't. We're on our way!"

Shannon gave an exclamation of joy. "Yes! I love this man! Oh, Rachel, I'm so happy. Everything is ready for you."

"I still don't know how we'll get to Dallas from Oklahoma, but I'll figure that out," Rachel promised her.

"I know you will."

Shannon's confidence in Rachel wasn't something she was used to. "I can't wait to see you in person."

"I can't either. This is amazing. Your dreams really were a sign from God."

"I know. I can't talk long. I just didn't want you worrying about me when I didn't reach out."

"How long will it take for you to get here?"

"I don't know exactly—two or three days? I'll call again when I know more."

"That sounds great, honey. Take care of yourself. Do you have everything you need?"

"I think so." Catching sight of Saul walking Duke along a row of bushes, she added, "We're in good hands."

"It certainly sounds like it. You're sure Ethan has no idea where you are or where you're headed?"

"I'm sure." The hardest part had been keeping the details from her son. Remarkably, Liam hadn't pestered her with questions these past few hours. He had to have been wary of Saul, just as she'd been.

"All right, hon. I'll wait to hear from you again—from this number?"

"Probably. Bye, Shannon. I can't believe this is happening." Calling her *Mom* didn't feel right yet.

"Me neither, darling, but I'm so glad it is. Be careful."

"I will. I'll call again soon."

Liam emerged the instant she thumbed the call to a close.

"Who'd you call?" Her son's frank gaze demanded honesty.

"Someone who can give us a place to live. I can't tell you more than that—not until we get there."

He searched her gaze. "'Cause you're afraid Uncle Ethan's going to catch us," he guessed, astutely.

She hushed him, shooting an anxious glance at a family sitting close to the restrooms. "Wait for me right here, honey. Then we'll go get our food."

Within ten minutes, they were back in the car with their burgers and drinks. Rachel put Saul's phone back in the compartment between the seats. Saul returned to the car to put Duke in the rear and to feed him kibbles from a bowl. As the dog wolfed it down, Saul got back behind the wheel, and they took off again, eating their fast-food dinner.

Rachel managed to finish only half of her burger. She offered the rest to Liam who declined it.

"Duke will eat the meat," Saul told her.

She separated the bread from the patty and offered it to Duke, who took it so gently Rachel was moved to pet his head.

"I've always wanted a dog." She had been too busy with a young son and a husband who was often away from home to consider getting an animal to care for. But Liam, she knew, would love a real pet.

Saul glanced at her but didn't speak. Two hours later, they passed the first exit for Roanoke. By then, it was nightfall. Above the jagged backs of the Appalachian Mountains, the sky had turned an indigo blue, shot with stars.

Saul snapped off the radio, which was cutting in and out because of the mountains' interference. "We'll stop at the very western edge of Virginia, in Bristol."

Rachel's muscles, tense and taut for hours now, ached for lack of mobility. "Would you like me to drive for a while?"

"I'm good. Thanks," he tacked on.

"How far away is Bristol?"

"Two more hours."

Liam's quiet moan in the backseat echoed her own dismay. The day seemed interminable, and it still wasn't over. If only they could drift asleep like Duke, who was snoring lightly, his head in Liam's lap.

"How many days does it take to get to Oklahoma?" Rachel asked, thinking she ought to have packed a book or electronic game to occupy her son. But, then, she hadn't actually expected Saul to rescue them.

"Two more days after today," Saul said shortly.

Two more days. She'd known the busses to Dallas took over twenty hours, but that was because they drove through the night, she realized.

Liam finally voiced one of the questions she'd been expecting from him. "Why are we going to Oklahoma?" he asked, his voice hesitant.

The uncertainty he had to be feeling made Rachel reassess her reasons for keeping her birth mother a secret. Did she really think Ethan would catch them somehow? No. God hadn't gotten them this far only to let them get caught. So why not give Liam some answers?

She twisted in her seat so she could see him, a small silhouette in the back.

"Saul grew up in Oklahoma, and he has some property there. He's giving us a ride out west because Texas is just to the south, and we're going there."

"Why?" Liam asked again.

"You know I was adopted, right?" She had already implied as much to Saul when she'd told him about her birth mother.

"Yeah," Liam said with a question in his voice.

"Well, I found my birth mother this past year, and I reached out to her."

"Doesn't she live in Russia?"

The question broadsided Rachel. "No, honey. Did Uncle Ethan tell you that?"

"Yes."

Rachel sighed. "That was something he used to tell me, too, when I was little. I don't know why he made that up. My mother was a teenager from Texas who gave me up for adoption so she could finish school. Of course, I didn't find that out until I reached out to her."

"What about the other stuff Uncle Ethan told me?" Liam asked on a hard note.

"What stuff?"

"That you were born with some kind of syndrome because your mother drank alcohol and that's why...it's hard for you to learn," he added delicately.

Stunned by Ethan's dishonesty and imagining he hadn't been half as delicate as Liam, Rachel took a cleansing breath.

"I don't know why Ethan told you I had fetal alcohol syndrome. That's simply not true. My mother's name is Shannon Johnson-Brown, and I was born in Arlington, Texas, a month premature. She was a teenager, not an alcoholic. And, yes, I have dyslexia, but I'm not stupid."

"I know," Liam said on an apologetic note.

"Shannon's a nurse now in the neonatal clinic. That means she—"

"Takes care of babies," Liam finished.

"That's right." Rachel sent her son an approving smile. "She lives in Dallas, Texas. She's divorced, and her twenty-year-old son, Ryan, goes to college now, so she says she has plenty of room for us."

Giving Liam time to process what she'd told him, Rachel sat back in her seat and cut a self-conscious glance at Saul. In the uncertain light, he appeared to be scowling. Ethan had made a bad impression on all the SEALs in Team Six at Lieutenant Mills's trial the previous year. Liam had likely just confirmed Saul's impression that her brother was twisted.

For the next two hours, Saul scarcely spoke a word.

By the time they pulled up to a roadside motel outside of Bristol, it was 9:00 p.m. Saul parked the car in the darkest part of the nearly deserted lot. There was nothing around them but a road and pine trees. "Don't move." Saul shook off his seatbelt.

Rachel went to hand him a wad of money to cover their room. Every month for the past year, she'd withdrawn a modest sum and hoarded it. The rest remained in her account, so it didn't seem as if she had planned a getaway.

"Save it. I'm only gettin' us one room. I'd have to pay for that anyway." He shut his door quietly and headed around the building for the main entrance. Watching him glide through patches of light and shadow, Rachel remembered Blake telling her Saul's footsteps were practically silent. A shiver coursed her spine as she considered what he did for a living.

"He's kind of scary, Mama." Liam's murmured words betrayed thoughts similar to her own.

"He was Daddy's best friend, honey. Daddy trusted him, so we can, too."

"How do you know Daddy wanted us to go with him?"

"I dreamed it." Their voices seemed disembodied in the dark car. "I dreamed it over and over again, like it was a vision from heaven."

Liam absorbed her words without comment.

Minutes later, Saul reappeared, popping out of the exit at the side of the building to open Rachel's door.

"All set." He thrust an electronic room key into her hand as she got out, lugging the backpack that had rested under her calves. Flipping her seat forward for Liam to get out, he ordered Duke at the same time to stay back. "Go on up," he instructed her. "I'll be right there."

Realizing Saul intended to walk the dog again, Rachel glanced at the number on the small envelope. She reached for Liam and escorted him up the outer staircase to their room on the second floor. Saul had no doubt requested a room adjacent to the stairs in case they needed to make a quick getaway.

"Here we go." She unlocked the door and opened it. After flicking on the light, she stepped into the room with her son, relieved to see two queen-sized beds. "Well, this is different," she said, striving for an adventurous tone. "When's the last time we stayed in a motel?"

"When Daddy was alive," Liam said solemnly.

Grief wrung her heart at the memory of their last summer vacation. A month later, Blake died in a tragic parachuting accident.

"That's a good memory." She did what she'd been taught in the hospital. Framing memories she cherished and labeling them as good kept her from succumbing to sorrow. "Maybe this will be a good one, too," she murmured, although she didn't see how.

Knowing Saul would want the bed by the door, she chose the one closest to the bathroom, dumping her backpack on it as Liam fired off a question.

"Are we ever going back?"

She faced him again. His worried, earnest face made her wonder how long it would take before he smiled again. "You can always go back once you turn eighteen." She hoped that knowledge encouraged him.

He blinked at her thoughtfully, his long, spiky lashes the image of his father's. "What about my rabbit? And my ant colony?"

She wasn't surprised he'd mentioned his animals before his PlayStation.

"I'm sure Uncle Ethan will free the rabbit in the yard and set the ants free, too." More likely, Ethan would toss the ants' plastic terrarium into the trash bin. But the rabbit he would let go. Closing the space between her and Liam, she rested her hands on his shoulders, now an inch higher than her own.

"It's going to be okay, sweetie. God got us this far." She let herself marvel at their near-miraculous getaway. "He's not going to let us get caught. We are *never* going back to live with Uncle Ethan," she added with resolve.

Beneath her hands, she could feel Liam's rigid frame relax. A soft knock on the door signaled Saul's return. Rachel identified him with a peek through the peephole, then let him in. Duke, freed from his leash, barreled in first. Saul, with a duffel bag over one shoulder, shut the door behind them and dropped his bag under the window.

"I was told there's a Walmart close enough to walk to." Bending over, he pulled Duke's bowl out of his bag. "Gonna run over there and get us what we need. Any requests?"

"Oh, yes." Rachel retrieved the forty dollars she had just tried to give him. "What do you think, Liam? Do you want a book to read or one with puzzles?"

Liam shrugged. "Either one's fine with me."

"Maybe we should come with you." Rachel doubted Saul would have the vaguest idea what a twelve-year-old boy would want.

"Not yet." Saul assessed her son. With visible reluctance, he took the money she thrust at him and slid it wordlessly into his front pocket. "Where's the room key?"

She took it from her pocket and handed it to him.

"I'll be back in half an hour. Someone knocks, don't answer. And, Liam." He addressed her son for the first time.

"Yes, sir?" Liam's voice held a note of uncertainty.

Saul held the bowl out. "You mind filling this with water for Duke?"

"Sure." Visibly relieved, her son took the proffered bowl and headed for the sink at the back of the room.

As Saul met Rachel's gaze, she sent him a grateful smile. His deep-set, hazel eyes betrayed a hint of his Native American ancestry, as did the strong cheekbones and the dark mahogany color of his hair. His gaze drifted over her, making her prickle with awareness as he seemed to note every detail of her appearance.

"Set the chain behind me." He swiveled abruptly and let himself out, closing the door soundlessly.

As Rachel crossed to the door to engage the safety chain, she pondered the look Saul had given her. Blake once said Saul was the most honorable man he knew. Surely he hadn't been thinking less-than-honorable thoughts just then, had he?

Turning, she drew up short at the sight of Liam down on one knee, rubbing Duke, who lay on his back with a rear leg kicking with joy.

"I found his tickle spot," her son announced, scrubbing the dog's ribs with vigor.

The smile on Liam's face was all the reassurance Rachel needed. Her son was already healing from the past.

CHAPTER 3

*S*aul pushed a cart briskly up the quiet aisles at the Walmart in Bristol, Virginia. His heart beat swiftly, the way it did when he operated deep in enemy territory. He refused to regret what he had done, freeing Rachel and Liam from Ethan O'Rourke's control. It felt like the right thing. But the prospect of losing his job, of being jailed like a criminal, made his gut churn.

He could lose everything he'd made of himself. No one else in the USA—perhaps even in the world—could claim to have eliminated nineteen terrorists. He had saved countless lives—men, women, and children who would have died at the terrorists' hands had they not been methodically dispatched. He was becoming legendary, at least among the Teams. Why risk jeopardizing all he'd worked for?

On the other hand, Rachel and Liam still needed him, not only to get them closer to their final destination but to teach them how to hide once they got there.

Saul knew the art of blending in. The first thing Rachel and Liam had to do was change their appearance before someone recognized them. With that object in mind, he picked out two graphic T-shirts for Liam, whom he'd only ever seen wearing a Boy Scout shirt and a button-down polo. In the ladies' department, Saul grabbed two flouncy tops off their hangers and picked out matching leggings, size small. The waif wearing her husband's old sweatshirts needed to vanish.

With their immediate wardrobe needs taken care of, Saul pointed his cart toward the electronics department, knowing books were displayed nearby. The sudden buzzing of his cell phone spiked his pulse. He pulled it from his pocket and his stomach tightened to see Charlotte Patterson-Strong, newly married to his teammate Lucas, was calling him.

"Charlotte," he said, bracing himself. The six-foot-tall redhead hadn't called him since she, Saul, and Lucas had all gone hunting for evidence last year to clear Lieutenant Mills and implicate their commander. "What's up?"

An employee stocking shelves glanced his way, then went back to work.

"Hey, where are you?" came the innocent-sounding question. Charlotte was obviously fishing for information.

"Headed for Oklahoma."

"Yeah, Lucas said you headed out west today. Sorry to hear about your stepdad dying."

"Thanks." He remained terse so she'd get to the purpose of her call.

"I'm calling to see if you'd heard the news."

His pulse accelerated. "What news?"

"Rachel LeMere went missing today, along with her son."

"No kidding," Saul said after a beat of silence. "Was that on the news?"

"Not yet, but it will be. Saul," she added on a note of warning, "tell me you didn't have anything to do with their disappearance."

He'd almost forgotten Charlotte was training to become an FBI special agent. She had contacts in law enforcement, giving her the inside scoop.

"What makes you say that?" He wondered if she would turn him in if she knew.

Halfway down the book aisle, a young-adult thriller caught his eye. He'd seen the movie made of it and figured Liam read well enough he would enjoy the book. Snagging it on his way by, he lobbed it into the cart and moved toward the grocery section.

"Look, I know she means something to you. I saw the way you reacted to her situation last year." Charlotte's tone gentled. "I wouldn't blame you for wanting to help her. I'm just saying...," she paused for a moment. "Be careful."

Her warning informed Saul she was on to him, but she wasn't about to get him into trouble.

"Always," he assured her. "Gotta run now." Hanging up on her abruptly, he snatched up a box of breakfast bars. As he charged toward the checkout lanes, a shelf full of beauty products had him making a quick right turn. Rachel needed to change her hair and to start wearing makeup. That way she was less likely to be recognized by someone who'd seen her picture in the news.

Within twenty minutes of his departure, Saul was striding back to the motel with two bags clasped in his right hand. As a southpaw, he kept his left hand free should the need arise to reach for the concealed SIG riding against his hip. Sudden doubts about leaving Rachel and Liam by themselves goaded him into a trot. If she turned on the TV and witnessed herself mentioned on the news, she might panic.

The quiet parking lot at the motel reassured him. All the same, he took the concrete steps two at a time, approached the door of their room, and put his ear to it. The television wasn't even on. With a steadying breath, he used the card key to let himself in.

Dialing down his intensity, Saul entered the room and assessed the situation. Liam was in the bathroom. The dog rested by the sink. And Rachel was sitting on her bed reading a Bible she must have brought with her as it didn't look like a Gideon Bible.

Conscious of her watchful gaze, he dropped his purchases on the bed closest to the door, lifted his T-shirt, and removed his holster from his belt before he laid both the holster and the pistol under his pillow where Liam wouldn't see them.

A glance at Rachel told him the sight of his gun hadn't freaked her out. She had stopped reading, showing interest in his purchases as he upended them on his bed.

"Shirts for Liam. He needs to ditch the scout uniform and change his appearance." He tossed them onto Rachel's bed.

She picked up a shirt, checking the size surreptitiously. "These are perfect."

"Some clothes for you, too. Same reason." He handed her both of the youthful outfits, while noting her startled expression. Wordlessly, she put them on the bed next to Liam's shirts. "And here's the book I picked out. Hope it's not too hard for him."

"Oh." She brightened as she took the book. "I'm sure it's not." She leafed through it. "He reads well above his grade level."

"Granola bars for breakfast. And this." Watching her reaction closely, he held up the box of hair color. He had chosen a sunny blonde hue, figuring it would change her look dramatically. "You need a different look."

Rachel regarded the box with obvious surprise, then eyed him uncertainly. "I was blonde as a kid."

"Then it'll suit you. We need to cut Liam's hair, and yours, too."

"Okay." Her tone was becoming uncertain.

"I got you some makeup, too. Put on a little mascara, eyeliner, and lipstick, and you'll turn into a whole new woman." He tossed all three items onto her bed.

Rachel glanced down at them, disguising her reaction. "Did you have enough money for all this?" she finally asked.

"Plenty." Turning his back on her, he fetched his duffel bag by the door, set it on the bed, and pulled out the hair-trimming kit he took anywhere he went. He could feel Rachel watching him as he crossed to the sink with it. He proceeded to lay out his tools—sharpened scissors, electric trimmer with seven different head sizes, a comb, fresh razor, and a tarp. The kit had seen him transform from one being to another, whatever disguise aided him to blend into the local population.

"Liam," Rachel called when the sound of running water stopped.

"We need to cut your hair, honey."

Her announcement met with a startled pause. "Coming."

Saul turned and met her gaze. "Go ahead and color your hair now. I'll cut yours next."

She examined the box uncertainly, then headed toward the small desk in the room with a mirror over it. Realizing she had likely never dyed her hair before, Saul pulled a rolled towel off the rack and lobbed it at her. "Head's up."

To his surprise, she caught the towel easily, bringing back the memory of a Thanksgiving banquet with the Team. Friends and family had thronged the event, coming together after the feast for a game of flag football. Blake had used Rachel as his secret weapon, tossing her the ball and allowing his team to score.

Smiling at the memory, Saul turned his attention to the boy who edged out of the steaming bathroom with his pants back on and his scout shirt hanging open.

"Hey, partner, we gotta change your appearance."

Liam studied the tools on the counter with reservation. "Okay." He glanced at his mother to see if she agreed.

"You can trust Saul, honey. He used to cut your dad's hair."

"I know."

Saul laid the small tarp on the floor, then indicated Liam should stand on it. "I need you to take that shirt off. Sorry, but we gotta throw it away." *Burn it,* he amended silently.

Liam stared at his reflection for a solemn second, then shrugged out of the shirt and tossed it aside, almost with relief.

Throwing the poncho over the boy's narrow shoulders, it was hard for Saul to see how Liam would ever get as tall as his father. Blake had stood at six one, a full inch taller than Saul was.

Saul plugged in the trimmer, snapped on a size-two head, and powered on the tool. Liam looked on with interest as his brown curls dropped away. Saul buzzed his hair into a military-style high and tight. In ten minutes flat, Liam was transformed.

"What do you think?" Saul asked, dusting off the boy's neck.

"It's okay," Liam said politely, although the tilt of his eyebrows suggested it would take some getting used to.

Saul removed the poncho, shook it onto the tarp, then spilled the hair clippings into the trash. He then went to check on Rachel's dye job, discovering she had saturated most of her hair.

"You missed some in the back." He picked up the applicator and applied the noxious mixture himself. She held perfectly still, reminding him of a doe frightened into stillness by a predator. "Let it sit there twenty more minutes, then you can rinse it out."

"It smells terrible." She wrinkled her nose.

"Oh, cool!" Liam had found the book Rachel had left on the bed. "This was made into a movie."

With heartening enthusiasm and a quick smile at Saul that forgave him for shearing him like a sheep, Liam threw himself down on the bed and started reading.

"I'm gonna shower real quick." Saul fetched fresh clothing from his pack and shut himself into the bathroom, where he searched on his Android for news from back home. The article appearing on his screen hit him like a punch in the gut.

LOCAL WOMAN AND SON MISSING. ABDUCTION SUSPECTED, NOT CONFIRMED.

He skimmed the article with his breath held, then expelled it with a silent curse. Sure enough, the fisherman whom they'd paddled past had testified he'd seen the missing pair in the company of a bearded stranger. Saul was grateful, at least, the man couldn't begin to describe his features, apart from his having a goatee, which he would have to shave off.

It took a steaming shower to calm his agitation. By the time he emerged from the bathroom, Rachel was hovering outside the door, eager to rinse out the dye.

"It's burning my scalp," she told him.

There'd been no time for a patch test. He hoped she wasn't allergic.

"Watch your eyes." He stepped aside as she headed into the bathroom. "You need help?"

"No, I got it. Thanks."

It took her fifteen minutes to emerge. By then, Saul had taken the clippers and then his razor to his facial hair. He eyed his clean-shaven face with a twinge of regret. He'd rather liked how intimidating he looked with a goatee. The skin around his mouth and on his chin was lighter than the rest of his tan face. Oh, well. A little sun would fix that.

Rachel stepped out of the steaming bathroom with a towel around her head, wearing yoga pants and an oversized T-shirt—another of Blake's, by the look of it—for sleeping. She drew up short at the site of his clean-shaven chin.

"You too?"

He aimed for a casual shrug. "I was gonna shave it anyway. How's the color?" He gestured to the towel on her head.

"I don't know yet." With eyes fixed on the mirror, she unwound the towel and tossed it under the sink. Dark golden hair now hung to her shoulders, brightening her complexion. "It doesn't look that different," she said, sounding worried.

"It will when it's dry and after I cut it."

She visibly swallowed.

"Not as short as Liam's," he promised with a smile.

"Okay," she said in a small voice.

Her submissiveness irked him. It made him want to punch Ethan O'Rourke in the nose.

"You can trust me." He tossed the poncho over her shoulders, recalling the happy, playful woman she'd been in Blake's company. At least, he hoped she could. He'd never cut a woman's hair before.

He began by lopping off five inches. Rachel's eyes got bigger the shorter her hair got.

"Don't worry, I'm gonna style it." He didn't know if he was reassuring himself or her.

"I'm not worried."

He snorted. That was so obviously a lie.

"How'd you learn to cut hair?" came the nervous question.

He smiled rather cynically and met her gaze in the mirror. "No barbers in the places I go. I've cut my hair and the hair of other guys on the Team for years now, but never a woman's," he admitted.

"I have faith in you." She sent him a reassuring nod.

He hoped she wouldn't be disappointed.

"Where were you this past year?"

The question made him pause in mid-snip.

"You know I can't tell you that," he replied, then began shaping the short mass into the beach-cut look he was envisioning. He wasn't sure if he could pull it off, but he'd give it his best try. Couldn't be much different than whittling, which he was good at.

Her soft lips pursed together. "I know. It was just...frustrating. God kept telling me you were going to help us, but you weren't even around."

At her surprising words, he lopped off a good inch more than he'd intended. His gaze darted to the mirror to see if she'd noticed. "What do you mean, God told you?"

"I mean, I dreamed it, over and over again." Her face turned pink. "So, I assumed God was telling me something."

He wanted to tell her, first off, that God didn't acknowledge his existence, so that was unlikely. Secondly, dreams had nothing to do with reality. But then he recalled all his dreams of her he'd had the entire time he was in Mexico, and a chill swept through him. Maybe God had been trying to tell him something? If not God, then at least his deceased best friend.

"What made you change your mind, Saul?" Her green-gray eyes met his in the mirror, demanding honesty.

"Blake," he said, hoping he didn't sound crazy. "He chewed me out in a dream last night."

Her eyes grew luminous, and a sad, sweet smile touched her lips.

"Isn't that amazing?" she marveled in a voice coated with emotion. "It just blows my mind that he's still alive—just not here, where we are."

Saul quailed at the possibility—not of Blake being alive, but of all the men he'd dispatched from this world waiting for him in the next.

"You need to hold still." He wanted her to stop talking.

When she obediently shut her mouth, he kicked himself for ordering her around like her brother. But she didn't seem to take offense. Her brow knit with concern as he made his way around her head, doing his best to layer as he went.

At last, he turned her to face him so he could work on angling the hair on her forehead. Standing as close as they were, he was aware that the chemical perfume of her hair dye didn't completely cover up her natural scent. It was still there, soft and feminine, and overlaid by the scent of soap. He caught himself drawing a deep breath.

"Okay." He made one last clip, ruffled her hair with his fingertips, and stepped back. "All done. What do you think?"

Rachel faced the mirror and took in her appearance with obvious interest.

"Wow."

Wow was right. He couldn't believe he'd pulled it off. Her hair framed her face in a short spunky cut that totally suited her.

"I look totally different," she marveled.

"That's the point." He unsnapped the poncho.

"Thank you." She laid a hand briefly over his.

Her light touch went clear to his toes, which made him pull his hand away.

"No big deal." Why in blue blazes did she have to appeal to him? He had no business feeling anything for his best friend's wife, whether Blake was dead or not. It was one thing to help her and Liam since Blake wasn't around to do it. It would be something else entirely to want to take Blake's place.

You are the lowest form of vermin, said a voice in Saul's head. It sounded just like his stepdad talking.

~

As Saul applied himself to tidying up their mess, Rachel approached the bed where Liam was already pages into his book.

49

"What do you think?" she asked him.

Liam lifted his gaze and his jaw dropped. "Do I know you?" He employed the same kind of humor his father used to have.

"You can still call me Mom," she quipped, playing along.

His quick grin faded. "Will we have to change our names, too?"

She had given it extensive thought. "I think that would be best, don't you?" She was conscious of Saul pausing in the act of pushing the balled-up poncho into the trash bag, along with Liam's scout shirt.

"You should," he advised.

"Can we pick any name we want?" Liam asked her.

"Maybe we should take my birth mother's maiden name, Johnson, since there are so many of those, and just come up with new first names."

Liam glanced back at the *Maze Runner* book he was reading. "I like the name Thomas," he declared, clearly taking it from the story he was reading.

"Well, Thomas is a great name," she countered, "but I think you should pick a name that sounds like Liam, so you'll turn around when people call you."

"Maybe Lee," Saul suggested as he wiped down the sink. "That's a good Texan name."

"Or Ian," Rachel proposed.

Liam wrinkled his nose at the name Ian. "I like Lee better. What about you, Mom? What name sounds like Rachel?"

"Well, there's Raquel." She mentioned the only name she could think of.

"Too similar," Saul commented as he rinsed out a hand towel.

Rachel pondered his input. Raquel was rather similar to Rachel. If Ethan saw the name, he would certainly pay attention to it. She needed a name that looked nothing like Rachel but still sounded like it.

"Angel," Saul suggested suddenly, then turned to assess her reaction.

"Angel?" Her stomach gave a funny flop as she met his deep-set gaze. "What do you think, Liam? Does Angel sound enough like Rachel?"

Liam nodded. "I think it's perfect. You look like an angel with your hair that color."

"Aw, thanks," she said, touched by the compliment. "Then it's set." She liked her new name. "I'll be Angel Johnson."

"And I'll be Lee Johnson," Liam echoed. His expression turned anxious. "Do you think Uncle Ethan's searching for us right now?"

From the corner of her eye, Rachel tracked Saul as he crossed to the desk and picked up the bottle and box she'd left there.

"I'm sure he is, honey. But he's not going to find us. Saul got us away without a trace."

Saul stepped toward the door, saying over his shoulder, "I'll be gone about half an hour. Gonna burn a few items and toss the rest. When I get back, we need to sleep. We're heading out early."

The door locked behind him with the softest click.

"He knows what he's doing, doesn't he?" Liam asked.

Rachel nodded. "Yes, he does. That's why God picked him to get us away. We're going to be okay." She patted Liam's knee. "Now, let's brush our teeth and get ready for bed. We don't want to give Saul any reason to wish he'd left us behind."

Ethan O'Rourke collapsed behind the desk in his study and leveled a baleful glare at the detective making a slow circuit of his private sanctum. "You're telling me you have nothing," he summarized. The police had combed the entire state park, questioned the scout leader, all the boys, and the single witness who claimed to have seen Rachel and Liam in a canoe with a bearded man. Still, there were very few leads.

Detective Mooney scarcely glanced in his direction.

"So far," he agreed, unperturbed by Ethan's biting tone. "We'll drag the creek tomorrow, though nothing indicates they might've drowned.

We'll pull up satellite images and question the witness again. Who knows what leads might turn up?" He had picked up Liam's latest school photo, framed and sitting on one of Ethan's bookshelves. "He's a fine-looking boy," he commented, then turned to Ethan for feedback.

It occurred to Ethan this man had not completely dismissed *him* as a suspect, which was completely preposterous, considering he was the one who'd called the police the instant Mr. Hale informed him he'd lost Rachel and Liam. At first, Ethan hadn't panicked. Knowing Liam's love of the wilderness, he'd figured they'd strayed off the path and gotten lost. It wasn't until a stranger, noting an effort underway to find some missing persons, came forward with the shocking announcement he'd seen them leaving the park in a canoe with a stranger that Ethan had started to worry.

Since then, he had wracked his brain as to who that man might be. He'd cooperated utterly with the police, sharing any and all information that might help them locate his family members. He'd been shocked when his demand for an AMBER Alert was denied.

"I'm sorry, but this case doesn't fit the criteria because the boy is with his mother," Mooney had explained.

Ethan promptly informed the detective that Liam's mother was incapable of caring for her son. That was the reason why the pair lived with him in the first place. Given Mooney's scrutiny of his study now, he seemed to find their family dynamics peculiar. He put Liam's school picture back on the shelf, then casually asked, "Are you sure Rachel LeMere didn't leave the park under her own volition, taking her son with her?"

Ethan had already answered that question. Articulating clearly so the man would hear him this time, he replied, "I told you, she doesn't have the mental capacity to pull off a disappearing act. Why would she leave?" He spread a hand to encompass his whole house. "She has everything she needs here."

"What did your sister do with herself during the day, Mr. O'Rourke? Did she work? Did she have any love interests? I understand her husband died three years ago."

"No and no. Her husband was her everything. She could scarcely live without him. She had to be hospitalized for several months following his death."

"Yes, I remember you telling me that. That's when you got joint custody of her son. Is she any better now?"

Ethan shrugged. "Somewhat. You asked what she does with herself. Against my better judgment, she takes online classes in interior design. I think she's hoping to be like one of those HGTV personalities who buy up abominable houses and transform them."

The detective cut him a curious glance. "Are these college-level classes? And she's enrolled right now?"

"Not a real college, mind you. Trade school. And, yes, last time I checked, she was taking a class."

Mooney's gaze dropped to Ethan's monitor. "Does she use your computer for that?"

"No, she has a laptop of her own."

"I'd like to see it. There might be an indication in her emails or browser history to suggest who the man in the canoe was. She might have left with him willingly."

They were back to that, were they? "I'm telling you, she would never leave. You checked her bank activity, didn't you?"

"Yes, and there were no recent withdrawals. That and the fact, from what you've noticed, she didn't take anything with her, both suggest she wasn't planning a trip, but we ought to consider all options. It's the nature of investigating," he added with a small, hard smile. "Now, if you'll be so kind as to take me to her room."

Stifling a groan, Ethan rose from his chair and plodded out of the study, knowing the detective would follow. As he climbed the stairs to the second story, he was struck by his home's echoing silence. It stirred an ancient memory in him, one he didn't care to revisit.

After thrusting open Rachel's bedroom door, he stepped inside, then flicked on the lights. The sight of her possessions, still in plain view, reassured him. If she'd planned to take off, she would have packed some if not all of her belongings, like the sketchbook still sitting on her desk, her laptop, her big books of fabric swatches and colored tiles.

"This is beautiful." Mooney came in behind him. "I can see she's got an eye for design."

Puzzled by the comment, Ethan decided the bohemian mishmash of repurposed furniture might look appealing to someone as uncultured as the detective.

"Here's her laptop," he said, unplugging it. "Do you need the charger, too?"

The man inspected the hardware. "Uh, yes please. I'll tag it and pass it on to our forensic team." He started rifling through her desk drawers. "No chance she left her cell phone here?"

Ethan cut him a sharp glance. "You said yourself the phone must be destroyed because it's not pinging her location."

"Oh, yes, I did say that," Mooney mumbled absently. He had opened Rachel's closet and was sorting through her wardrobe. "Not many clothes for a woman."

Ethan narrowed his eyes at the man. "What else?" he demanded tersely.

Mooney turned away from the closet. "I'd like to see where the boy sleeps."

Ethan nodded reluctantly. "Just so you know, he has a perfectly good room on this level, but he prefers sleeping in the attic."

The detective cocked his head. "Oh, why's that?"

Ethan searched within himself. "More room for his creatures, I suppose." Leaving Rachel's room, he headed for the steep stairs to the attic.

"Creatures?" Mooney echoed as he followed him.

"Strays. Injured animals. He takes them in without my permission and nurses them back to health."

"Sounds like a nice kid."

Ethan's heart gave a pang as he flicked the light switch. "Yes. Smart, too. He'll amount to something one day."

As they climbed the stairs to the third story, the smell of cedar chips grew stronger. A hollow ache formed in Ethan's chest as his head cleared the floorboards. The naked light bulb cast Liam's large room into relief. The birdcage still stood empty and broken in front of the dark window. The dead bird was gone. A wild rabbit shuffled about in another cage reeking of soiled cedar chips, which he was determined to empty as soon as the detective left. By Liam's high single bed, the disgusting ant farm crawled with tiny little ants busily tunneling in the dirt.

Feeling Liam's absence as keenly as a knife blade, Ethan crossed to his desk to finger the backpack from school left open atop it. He lifted out the books from inside. Liam always had homework over the weekend. How would he get it done if he wasn't here, where Ethan could oversee his work? Tears of loss pricked his eyes.

Where are you, my boy? Don't worry. I'll find you. I'll help you navigate this life.

"Mr. O'Rourke."

Realizing the detective had been calling him, Ethan turned around. "It's Captain."

"Sorry, Captain, sir. Do you see anything missing?"

Ethan let his gaze drift over every surface.

"No," he choked out. "Just my nephew."

Mooney's expression softened at Ethan's show of emotion.

"Well, that would suggest, like you said, their disappearance wasn't planned. Unfortunately, that leaves foul play as the likely scenario. As you may know, there's a high rate of human trafficking in coastal towns. It's possible they were kidnapped."

"By the man in the canoe," Ethan finished. His hands curled into fists. "I want you to find whoever took them," he exhorted through his teeth. "Find my family," he pleaded, "before they come to harm."

The detective nodded, then kept quiet for a moment. "Considering his mother might have also left against her will, I will issue an AMBER Alert."

Ethan closed his eyes a moment and released a shuddering sigh of relief. "I would appreciate that."

CHAPTER 4

*S*aul awoke as the first hint of sunlight framed the motel's closed curtains. Goaded by an instinct to keep moving, he swung his feet to the floor and plucked his cell phone off the adjacent table. One glance at his screen confirmed his instinct was right. His heart started to trot as he absorbed the text message sent to every cell phone in Virginia:

AMBER Alert Virginia Beach 8 hours ago. White male, age 12, abducted with mentally impaired white female, 31. No vehicle description. Last seen at First Landing State Park in company of unknown white male mid 20s-30s.

Mentally impaired?

Saul regarded the occupants in the next bed. What the heck kind of distortion was that? Rachel had admitted to being dyslexic, but Saul knew she didn't lack in intelligence. If anything, she'd outwitted her brother. But that lie Ethan had told his nephew about Rachel having fetal alcohol syndrome and her mother being born in Russia—what was that about? Why would any brother make up such gross untruths in the first place, let alone tell it to his nephew?

The puzzle only confirmed Saul's decision to help them was the right one.

Rolling quietly out of bed, he swiftly dressed. From his place by the door, Duke watched him with one eye open. The occupants in the other bed slumbered in peace. Having heard Rachel get up several times during the night, Saul decided not to waken her until after he'd walked his dog. He clipped his holstered weapon back onto his belt, snapped the dog's leash to his collar, grabbed up the card key, and let himself out, all without disturbing his traveling companions.

Brisk mountain air sharpened his five senses as he scanned the area for a threat, perceived none, and proceeded to take his dog for a run.

"Hup," he said to Duke, and they dashed down the stairs and across the parking lot to jog down a street devoid of traffic. He hated to take time out for a run, but the exercise would keep the dog placid on the long car ride. Plus, it would exorcise some of the urgency pulsing through Saul's own blood. They had to get out of Virginia, ASAP, and hope the search for Liam and Rachel didn't go national.

Should he tell her about the AMBER Alert? Not only was it insulting to her personally, but she was running scared as it was. Picking up his pace, he pushed himself to run in one direction for ten minutes, then turn and go back. With his mental clock ticking, he beat his return time, getting back to the motel in just nine minutes and forty-two seconds.

The sky had warmed to the color of butter by the time he and Duke climbed the stairs to their second-story motel room. Pausing at the door, he took five seconds to slow his breathing and then unlocked it with the card key and let the sunlight pour in.

"Time to get up," he said brusquely.

Rachel and Liam jerked awake with identical startled expressions.

"Sorry," Saul apologized, "but we need to go."

Rachel threw back the covers, offering him a glimpse of slender, shapely thighs. He jerked his gaze away, then watched from his peripheral vision as she gathered up one of her new outfits and scuttled into the bathroom.

"I'll be right out."

Saul kept an eye on Liam's preparations while feeding the dog and making sure all of their hair had been wiped away. Removing all traces of their DNA was impossible, but it didn't need to be obvious there'd been three people staying in room 202 instead of one.

"Have a breakfast bar," he offered the boy, who sat on the end of the bed clutching his backpack and waiting for his mother to emerge.

"Thanks." Liam took the breakfast bar and tore into it, while watching Saul eat a second bar. With quavering bravado, the boy added, "Are you saving one for my mom?"

"Of course," he said, reminded of the way he'd felt for his own mother. "She can have two and so can you." He tossed Liam a second bar.

In that moment, Rachel emerged from the bathroom in her new clothing. As she regarded herself in the mirror, Saul and Liam stopped eating and stared.

She turned and faced them. "I look different, huh?"

Uh, yeah. The flouncy flowered shirt paired with leggings made her seem ten years younger.

"You look like a girl," Liam commented.

Woman, Saul corrected mentally. The snug-fitting leggings revealed curves he hadn't realized she had. He forced himself to focus on her face and realized she hadn't yet put on the makeup.

"I thought I'd do the rest in the car," she explained.

"Sure." He handed her the remaining breakfast bars. "Eat up while I rinse off."

Ten minutes later, they piled into the car and pulled away from the motel in Bristol.

With Rachel applying makeup in the seat next to him, Saul consulted his digital map to get them to Route 11 West, a less-traveled roadway crossing into Tennessee. He would breathe a heck of a lot easier once they put Virginia behind them.

"How'd I do with the makeup?"

Rachel's question had him glancing over and doing a double take.

Her eyes, lovely in the first place, were a punch in the gut once enhanced with pencil liner and mascara. The rose-colored lipstick he'd bought made her mouth look suddenly...kissable.

"Perfect."

His terse reply made her stare at him a second, then zip up her pack and place it wordlessly at her feet.

Regretting his gruff tone, Saul considered mentioning the AMBER Alert to explain his tension. Rachel sat with her hands gripped together, eyes averted as she gazed out the window. Her graceful neck, clearly visible now that her hair was short, struck him as elegant.

"Look at the stream, Liam," she urged, keeping Saul from saying anything.

Liam peered into the woods on their right. "Do you see any deer in there?"

"Nope, but I just spotted an opossum."

Saul decided again not to tell her anything. They were almost at the border between Virginia and Tennessee anyway. AMBER Alerts were nationwide, but only residents of Virginia had seen the alert sent out overnight.

Ten minutes down the road, he realized Rachel was going to find out anyway.

"Shoot," he hissed, stifling the curse that would have singed his companions' ears.

Rachel followed his gaze toward the blue lights flashing up ahead. "What's that?"

"Roadblock," he said through his teeth.

She immediately braced herself as if they were going to crash straight through it.

"Easy," he said when her face paled with sudden fear.

"For us?" Her voice had risen an octave. "Are they looking for us?"

"Listen to me." Saul employed the voice he used on junior SEALs when coaxing them out of the plane on their first nighttime HALO jump. "The worst thing you can do is appear afraid." He met Liam's wide gaze in the rearview mirror. "Liam, I want you to pretend you're sleeping. Turn your face away from me. Rachel." He put a hand on her knee and gave it a squeeze. "I want you to smile."

"Smile," she repeated, darting an unsettled glance at his hand.

He released her in order to open his glove compartment for proof of registration, slowing at the same time behind the line of cars in front of them. In less than five minutes, he'd be talking to a state trooper. He could be staring down the end of a rifle in a matter of minutes.

Don't think that!

"What if they ask for my ID?" Rachel's voice betrayed her rising panic. "All I have is my Virginia license which will tell them exactly who I am."

Saul could see the color slipping from her cheeks. In desperation, he flipped down the visor in front of her. "You tell 'em you didn't bring it with you. Look in the mirror. Is that Rachel LeMere?"

She studied her reflection, swallowed hard, then shook her head. "No."

"It's how you wear the concealment that counts," he added, easing them forward. "You got nothing to worry about, just so long as you play the part. Understand?"

Rachel drew an audible breath. Then, to his astonishment, she propped a sneakered foot up on the dashboard, leaned her head back against the headrest, and sent him a relaxed smile. "You mean, like this?"

He caught himself staring. She had gumption in her yet, he was pleased to realize. "Exactly like that."

He dragged his gaze forward again, assessing the demeanor of the state troopers as they bent to address the vehicles ahead of them. They seemed bored, like they didn't expect to find a kidnapped kid so far from where he was taken.

"Let me do the talking." He took his wallet from his back pocket.

Finally, it was their turn. Saul reached back and nudged his dog. "Duke, speak." He lowered his window, and the Lab started barking. *Woof. Woof.*

"Morning," said the state trooper.

"Howdy," Saul replied, mustering a smile.

"License and registration, please." The trooper took a quick step back as Duke shoved his snout through the opening behind Saul's headrest.

Woof. Woof. Woof.

Saul handed over the requested items. "Hush, Duke," he ordered, only Duke didn't know that command.

The trooper examined Saul's documents. Then, careful to avoid the dog, he gave them back, along with a flyer. "We're looking for this boy and his mother, who disappeared from the Virginia Beach area yesterday." He had to raise his voice to be heard over the obnoxious dog.

Woof. Woof. Woof.

"Yeah, I got a text about that. Jeez, sure hope they find the pair." Saul frowned down at the pictures on the flyer, same as the ones online, except this time there was a sketch of the suspect—a man with a hat brim covering his eyes and hair covering his jaw. The detail about Rachel being mentally impaired had been omitted. *Interesting.*

The trooper tried to peer at Saul's passengers. He caught sight of Rachel, who sent him a friendly smile, then peered in the backseat at the boy who faced away from him.

"Sound sleeper," the trooper commented.

Woof. Woof. Woof.

"Always has been," Saul agreed.

The man focused back on him. "Where are you headed?"

"Knoxville. My sister-in-law's place."

Woof. Woof. Woof.

The trooper had enough of them. "Y'all be safe and enjoy yourselves." He stepped back and waved them on.

As Saul eased forward, telling Duke to be quiet and accelerating at an unhurried pace, Rachel snatched the leaflet off his lap. He cringed in expectation of her reaction.

"Oh, no," she cried, staring aghast at the photos. "They think we were kidnapped. They've issued an AMBER Alert!" She lifted huge eyes at him. "Oh, Saul," she added with heartfelt regret. "I had no idea it would come to this. I swear!"

Her remorse was all for him, he realized with amazement.

"You can drop us off at the next bus station if you want."

"That's not happening." He countered her panic with calm reassurance.

Her eyes narrowed suddenly. "Why aren't you upset? Or surprised?" she added with suspicion.

He decided to come clean. "I got the AMBER Alert on my phone this morning. They issued it overnight."

"Why didn't you tell me?"

He shrugged. "Didn't want you to worry."

"But you were worried," she realized, no doubt thinking back to his terse behavior.

He didn't bother to deny it.

Liam, who'd been listening in the backseat, asked in a tentative voice, "Is an AMBER Alert a state thing or a national thing?"

The question was pretty astute for a twelve-year-old. Glancing back at the boy, Saul said, "It's a national thing, but only the Virginians got the alert."

"We're in Tennessee now, right?" the boy asked.

"Yep, we just passed the sign for it."

"Phew." Liam blew out a breath of relief so exaggerated Saul and Rachel both laughed.

The worry that had cinched Saul's stomach since yesterday eased. He'd done it. He'd gotten Rachel and her boy away from Ethan O'Rourke without anyone the wiser—with the possible exception of Charlotte Patterson-Strong. But Charlotte wasn't going to turn him in as a suspect, so they were good.

Now all Saul had to do was get them closer to Texas, put them in an Uber, and trust they would be okay without him.

"You're a sniper, aren't you?"

Liam's question came just as Saul slid his gun under the pillow at their second motel, situated on the outskirts of Memphis. He'd thought the boy too busy watching the fishing show on television to see him remove his holster. With Rachel in the shower, Saul had no choice but to answer.

"Yep."

"That means you kill people, doesn't it?" Liam's tone was unmistakably disapproving.

Saul supplied the line that had sparked his imagination in the Navy recruitment office.

"I protect the interests of the free world." He then sat on his own bed, kicked off his shoes, and put his back against the headboard, hoping his crossed arms signaled to the boy their discussion was over.

Liam went back to watching the show, and Saul was about to relax when Liam quizzed him again.

"You're a hunter, too, aren't you? I remember Dad and you went on a hunting trip together."

Memories panned through Saul's mind of the great fun he and Blake had enjoyed, stalking a buck with hunting bows.

"That's right." He would never hunt with his friend again. His heart wrenched with a familiar loss.

"Do you hunt ducks, too? Is that why you have Duke?"

They both regarded the Labrador retriever who, on hearing his name mentioned, looked up from his spot by the door.

Saul chuckled. "Naw. Duke's mouth's not soft enough to hunt ducks."

Liam turned a puzzled gaze at him. "What's that mean?"

"Means he chews 'em up. I can't eat duck that's been mauled, so there's no reason for me to hunt them."

The boy nodded his understanding and went back to watching the show. Saul figured the interrogation was finally over when Liam regarded him again.

"Aren't you part Indian?"

"Native American," Saul supplied the correct term. "My mother was a Muskogee Creek."

Liam's face lit up. "I just learned that at school—the Indian Removal Act and the Trail of Tears."

Saul wasn't surprised Liam knew more history than most adults.

The boy continued to stare at him. Growing self-conscious, Saul tried to focus on the fishing show.

"I never met a real, live Native American before." All trace of Liam's disapproval was gone.

"Half. My daddy was white."

"Do you know how to live in the wilderness?"

Pictures flashed through Saul's mind. "Sure, my grandfather taught me."

Liam wriggled onto his side, the show forgotten. "Taught you what, exactly?"

"How to set traps, build shelters, start fires, track deer."

"Can you start a fire without a match?"

"If I have to." Saul started to warm toward the memories flooding back.

"What kinds of animals live in the Oklahoma wilderness?"

The kid liked saying the word *wilderness*, Saul mused. "The usual: raccoons and squirrels, badgers and jackrabbits, eagles, owls, egrets, and three-toed box turtles. Those are my favorite."

Liam's eyes brightened with interest. "How much land did you live on?"

"The ranch is about fifty acres." Saul pictured it in his mind's eye. "Most of that's forest and pastureland. We used to raise cattle in the pastureland. There's a creek you can wade in when it gets too hot." An unexpected excitement quickened in him at the prospect of seeing it again.

"Did you ever tame any animals?"

"Tamed a bobcat once, when it was still a kit. It would come when I called it."

"You can't tame a bobcat," Liam said doubtfully.

"Did once."

"No way."

"Truth." Saul drew an imaginary cross on his chest. The big fish on the screen caught his attention. "Hey, he got one."

They went back to watching the show. As the angler showed off his enormous catch, Liam focused back on Saul.

"Can I visit your ranch?"

Saul remembered the plan and shook his head. "Sorry. Remember what your mama said? You're heading for Texas as soon as we get to Oklahoma."

The boy's face fell. He faced the TV again, but it was obvious he'd stopped watching.

What would it be like if Rachel and Liam came to the ranch with him, if only for a little while—until the search for them died down? One thing Saul was sure of: Ethan O'Rourke would never think to search for them in Broken Arrow, Oklahoma.

Forget it. Saul clicked off the picture in his head. He had fulfilled his duty where Blake's surviving family was concerned. He didn't owe them anything more. Plus, his attraction for Rachel was unsettling. The sooner he put her and her son inside an Uber and sent them on their way, the better off he'd be.

He would face the memories waiting for him all alone. Having Rachel with him wouldn't make his homecoming any easier.

~

Rachel awoke trembling and covered in goosebumps. In her dream, Ethan had somehow found them and forced his way into their hotel room with the police on his heels. They had tackled Saul to the floor, intending to arrest him for kidnapping.

Turning her head, she sought the reassuring shape of Saul in the next bed over. Light from the parking lot framed the closed curtains and shone on his empty bed. Fear had her sitting up abruptly. He wouldn't take off without telling them, would he?

Liam mumbled in his sleep as she vaulted off their shared mattress.

The sight of Duke sprawled before the door immediately reassured her. Saul would never leave his dog behind. That meant he was somewhere close, but where?

Crossing to the drawn curtains, she lifted one to peer outside and startled back as a silhouette loomed outside. It was Saul, standing with his back to their third-story window to avoid the downpour. With a glance down at the nightshirt she wore to sleep in, she decided to join him. Nudging Duke out of the way, she let herself out, then kept the door from locking behind her by swiveling the security latch.

She faced Saul and caught him glancing at her bare legs. It was all she could do not to gape at his bare chest padded with muscle, tan skin, and just a faint line of hair beneath his naval. A pair of gray sweatpants hung low on his hips and his feet were bare.

"Hey," he said.

His reflective tone invited her to join him. She put her back to the space next to him. Rain splattered off the railing and landed in droplets near their feet.

"What are you doing out here?" A glance at him left her with a snapshot of his high cheekbones and pronounced shoulder muscles. Her pulse ticked upward. Blake had been stockier and hairier than Saul. And Blake hadn't had any tattoos either, certainly not like the skulls inked into Saul's thick upper arm.

"Couldn't sleep," he replied, on a note quite different from the terse tone he'd used for the past two days. "Why are you awake?"

"Same reason." She checked the impulse to talk about her dream, lest it come true somehow.

To keep from staring at his chest, she stared at the rain instead. The light coming from the lampposts found reflection in each individual raindrop, making them glint like shards of glass.

"I've been thinking," Saul said on that same reflective note.

The statement brought her head around. Instead of looking at her, he seemed to be picturing something only he could see.

"Running away from your brother is one thing. Living off the grid is harder. I don't know if you've thought it through."

"Of course, I have," she said, taken aback. Did Saul think she was stupid, too?

Her sharp tone brought his gaze to hers. "You can't collect social security money anymore."

"I know that. I don't need it. I can work for a living."

"How? Any employer's going to ask for your tax ID, and you'll pop up in a database where the law can find you."

"I'm going to work for myself, staging houses," she said with determination. "I'm not going to file taxes. I know that's illegal, but what else can I do?"

Saul dragged a hand through his short hair. "So, you'll resort to living like an illegal immigrant," he muttered, "afraid to go to the hospital or to call the police if something goes wrong."

"Shannon will call for us. Look, as long as Liam and I are free from Ethan, I don't care about the sacrifices."

Saul released a breath and finally met her gaze. "Why does he treat you like he does?" he asked, clearly mystified.

"You mean like I'm…inferior?" She let her bitterness show.

"Yes."

Rachel searched her memory and shrugged. "I'm not sure. He was twelve when I came along. I guess I stole the limelight or something. I was small, not very healthy, and, of course, with my dyslexia, my parents had to spend a lot of time helping with my schoolwork. Maybe he felt neglected."

"Where are your parents now, the ones who adopted you?"

"They retired to Florida years ago. They're both in their eighties, and Papa's got a heart condition."

"Why don't you go to them for help and live with them, away from Ethan?"

"They suggested it, actually. But I knew I'd be an imposition on them. The community in which they live doesn't allow children, so they would have had to move. Papa didn't need that kind of stress.

Then, too, I wasn't ready to live far away from Blake's grave. I used to visit it every day."

"But you're ready now?"

Loss swept through her momentarily, but she pushed it away. "Blake isn't in the cemetery. I came to realize that. He's in Heaven, watching over us. We wouldn't be with you right now if he weren't."

Thoughtful silence followed her words.

Saul stared out at the rain for a while, then asked her, "What made you sign that document?"

"The one giving Ethan shared custody?"

"Yes."

She shook her head, overcome with the regret she'd carried with her ever since. "I assumed it was temporary. I was in the hospital, not long after Blake died."

"I remember," Saul said softly.

"Ethan told me to sign the document so he could take Liam to the doctor if he happened to get sick. I didn't realize I was giving him custody."

"I can't believe that crooked judge sided with your brother."

"He probably owed Ethan a favor," she replied.

"I'm sorry. I wish I'd known what you were up against. Maybe I could have helped."

Without thinking, she put a grateful hand on his arm, finding it smooth and dense, a pleasure to touch.

"Thanks, but I doubt you could have helped." She let her hand drop.

"I could have," he insisted, gruffly. "I could have been a witness or something when you went to court."

"You weren't even in the country," she pointed out with a hint of bitterness.

"Listen." He stopped and visibly struggled to get his next words out. "What do you think of visiting my ranch for a few days before you head to Texas?"

The offer was uttered with so much difficulty, she waited for him to immediately rescind it.

"Why?" she couldn't help asking. Was he speaking out of guilt?

He shifted to better face her, and Rachel had to fight not to stare at his bare chest.

"There are things I can do to make your new life easier."

"Like what?" she asked, intrigued.

"There's an old truck listed among the goods Cyril left to me. I could fix it up, and then you'd have a vehicle to drive."

She realized Cyril was the stepfather who'd recently died.

"Are you serious?" Having a vehicle would be a tremendous help. "But I wouldn't have a license I could use." She frowned.

"I can get you one." He sounded more committed by the moment. "I have a contact who makes IDs for Black Ops. Not only do they look real, but they'll stand up to a certain level of scrutiny."

The prospect of owning an ID that passed as real intrigued her.

"Both of those things would be great, Saul, but you don't have to. You've done enough."

He gave a self-directed chuckle. "Yeah, that's what I told myself before bed. But then I couldn't sleep thinking about you trying to get by with no vehicle and no documents. What do you say? Want to come with me to the ranch, and I'll fix up the truck for you?"

Rachel hugged herself against the damp chill and considered his offer. On the one hand, she was eager to meet her birth mother and get started on her new life in Dallas. On the other, continuing their journey alone without Saul terrified her. She opted to postpone their necessary separation.

"Sure. Why not?"

"Why not?" he repeated. "You're cold," he added, as she quelled a shiver. "Why don't you go on back in? We've got an early start tomorrow."

Sensing he wished to be alone a moment longer, she nodded. "I don't know if I've thanked you enough." She gazed deeply into his eyes. "So let me do it now. Thank you *so* much. We could never have left without your help. It means everything." Before she lost courage thinking about his terse behavior up to that point, she stepped closer and hugged him.

One of his arms went around her, pulling her against his bare chest, enfolding her in his warmth.

For the barest moment, Rachel enjoyed a sense of complete security—something she hadn't experienced since Blake's death.

With reluctance, she moved away from him. Feeling flustered, she turned and slipped into the dark motel room.

Memories of slow dancing with Blake, their bodies plastered together, hit her with nostalgia so bittersweet tears flooded her eyes.

She went into the bathroom and let her tears fall. Her grief had a different feel to it than it had in the months directly after Blake's accident. There was more acceptance, less denial. Acceptance tasted bitter, like medicine you didn't want to swallow but knew you had to if you wanted to get well. She blew her nose with toilet paper and mopped her face, trying to pinpoint what else felt different.

A vision of Saul's ranch, which she'd never seen, formed in her mind's eye, complete with an old truck that was hers for the taking.

Hope, she realized. Tonight, her grief was infused with hope— something she hadn't experienced in a long, long time.

Standing on the walkway outside the motel room, Saul reeled at what he'd done. He'd gone from vowing he was going to put Rachel and Liam in an Uber to inviting them to join him at his ranch. Why?

He shook his head, not understanding himself. Even Rachel had assured him he owed them nothing more. But first, he hadn't been able to sleep, thinking of the difficulties they would face trying to live off the grid. Then he'd considered all the little things he could do to improve their chances. Next thing he knew, he was inviting them to stay a few days, maybe a week, with him in Oklahoma.

What was I thinking? He shook his head again, perplexed by his behavior. In any case, he realized he didn't regret his spontaneous offer. If anything, he felt like he could finally sleep. When Liam and Rachel took off for Texas, they would be better armed to face the future.

Just don't get attached in the meantime.

That hug she'd given him was nice. Real nice. Ever since his childhood when his schoolmates called him Half-Breed, he had kept to himself. But he'd never really felt alone because he'd had his family and the land. But then every member of his family except for Cyril died, and loneliness became his only companion.

It wasn't until he joined SEAL Team Six that Saul found a new family. His SEAL brothers loved and accepted him unconditionally. Even so, because of what he did, or because he knew the darkness owned him, he remained isolated, apart. But he didn't feel quite so detached with Rachel and Liam for company.

With his mind made up and his worries eased, Saul went back into the motel room, locked the door, and soon fell into a peaceful slumber.

CHAPTER 5

$\mathcal{T}$he following morning, Rachel dialed her birth mother on Saul's Android while he took Duke for a morning run. Liam, who had just learned they were going to Saul's ranch first, bounced on his bottom at the end of Saul's bed, watching curiously as she spoke to the grandmother he'd only recently heard about. Rachel put the call on speaker so he could hear Shannon's voice.

"Rachel, honey, I've been so worried. How's it going?"

Her birth mother's concern was gratifying. "We're fine. We're in Memphis right now, only about a day away, but...I wanted to let you know there's been a change in plans."

"Oh?"

Rachel took in Liam's bright expression as she elaborated. "Saul's going to take us to his ranch first so he can fix up a truck for me to drive."

"Okay." Shannon's tone was neutral.

"Saul says I can keep the truck or sell it and buy something newer. Plus, he'd like you to keep an eye on your mailbox. You're going to get some documents for me and Liam, a driver's license for me and two birth certificates with our new names on them. I'm going to be Angel Johnson and Liam's going to go by Lee."

"How on earth can he do all that?"

"I'm not sure. He has connections because of his job," Rachel answered vaguely.

"Wow."

Liam bounced harder, making the coils in the mattress creak.

"I know. Anyway, we're doing great, and we'll be there soon enough. I couldn't turn down a potential vehicle, nor a way to have new paperwork giving us new identities."

"No, of course not."

"Liam says hi," Rachel relayed. "I finally told him about you, and he's sitting right here listening to everything we're saying."

"Aww. Hi, Liam."

He stopped bouncing. "Hi."

For the next few minutes, Rachel listened as Liam replied shyly to Shannon's questions. She wanted to know if he preferred a turtle as a pet or a fish.

Minutes later, Saul returned from his run. Seeing the expression on his face, Rachel took Shannon off of speaker. "Hey, we have to go now. I'll call you in a day or two with an update."

"Sounds good, honey. Bye, Rachel. Bye, Liam."

As Rachel hung up, Saul put down a bag of breakfast food from McDonald's and removed the dog's leash. "Y'all eat up while I take a shower. Then we leave."

Within twenty minutes, they were back in Saul's car, pulling away from their second motel.

"How long is today's trip?" Rachel prayed their drive would be shorter than the previous two days.

"Seven hours."

"*Okay.*" For Liam's sake, she infused the word with enthusiasm.

Since his offer to take them to his ranch, Saul himself was back to being terse and quiet. Rachel hoped he wasn't regretting the offer he had made them.

She was just resigning herself to hearing nothing but country music for the next seven hours when Saul broke the silence.

"Broken Arrow," he said, as if they were in the middle of a conversation. "That's where my ranch is." He cast her an inscrutable glance.

She nodded her encouragement. "I've heard of it." All she knew about Saul were things Blake had told her. Maybe he would finally tell her things about himself.

"My dad bought the ranch when he was still single. He met my mother at a Native American festival—said it was love at first sight. Must've been since I was born less than a year later. Puca, my mother's father, lived with us, and he and I were tight."

"Puca?" Rachel repeated. "That's a cute name."

"It's Creek for *grandfather*."

Liam piped up from the backseat. "Saul can build a fire with his bare hands!"

When had Saul imparted that particular information? "Sounds like you enjoyed your childhood."

Saul nodded, but his mouth firmed. "I did, 'til my father fell off a ladder and broke his neck. Died instantly."

Rachel gasped in horror. "Oh, Saul. I'm so sorry."

A minute of silence followed before Saul continued talking. "I guess my mama couldn't handle the ranch on her own, not even with Puca's help, so she hired Cyril Lawson to do it. I reckon she was lonely. Anyway, she married him when I was fourteen."

His voice had hardened as he mentioned Cyril's name.

Rachel eyed his frowning profile. "I take it he wasn't very good to you."

"Used to work me like a rented mule," he agreed darkly.

She pictured Saul slightly older than Liam, toiling under a hot sun, and pity brought tears to her eyes.

"'That's why God gave you that red skin, boy,'" Saul drawled, obviously imitating his stepdad's voice.

Rachel gasped at the racial slur. "He said that to you?"

"Yep." Saul grimaced. "Cyril didn't like people who weren't white. Only exception was my mother. I think he found her pretty enough since he asked her to marry him." Disgust laced Saul's words. "She was beautiful, up until she got sick. Hanta virus," he continued in a gritty voice. "Comes from rat droppings, which she came into contact with from sweeping the barn. Unfortunately, she was pregnant, and the baby got sick, too."

"Oh no," Rachel exclaimed.

"Blessing only lived about two months. Then my mama died, mostly of a broken heart."

The story appalled Rachel. Glancing back at her son's face, she could tell it disgusted Liam, also. She couldn't begin to wrap her mind around the devastation Saul must have felt losing both parents when he was still a boy. Wanting to console him with a touch, she nonetheless kept her hands in her lap. She could still feel their hug from the night before.

"Please tell me your grandfather was still around."

"He was."

Rachel breathed a sigh of relief.

"That's when he taught me most of what I know about survival and tracking. That knowledge came in handy during SQTs."

SEAL Qualification Training, Rachel recalled. Blake had struggled through several of the courses.

"How long did your grandfather live?" she dared to ask.

"Unfortunately, he, uh…" Saul had to clear his throat to finish. "He had a heart attack when I was in high school, and it paralyzed him on one side. Died the second semester of my senior year."

Rachel closed her eyes to absorb the blow. Apart from the abuse Ethan had heaped on her during her early years, she had enjoyed a relatively happy childhood.

"Soon as I graduated," Saul plowed on, "I threw what I needed in my old beater and drove straight to the Navy recruitment office. Couldn't wait to get out of there."

"Wait, so this is your first time going back?" Rachel deduced with surprise.

"Yeah."

Regarding his set expression, she tried to remember how old he was now. Blake had been younger than Saul by two years, so Saul had to be at least thirty-four.

"Then it's been, what, sixteen years since you've seen the ranch?"

"Sixteen and change." He lapsed into silence that grew more and more brooding with every mile.

As Liam went back to reading, Rachel passed the time gazing out the window. They stopped for lunch just inside the Oklahoma state line. After that, the land became relentlessly flat and sparse. She'd never visited America's heartland before. The horizon was the limit of her sight, and every tree they passed grew bent toward the east— pushed over by a constant wind blowing from the west, mostly likely.

Bit by bit, the terrain grew lusher, with occasional hills and large trees. They crossed a river and bypassed Tulsa, with its skyscrapers reflecting the bright afternoon sun. At long last, after what had seemed like an endless car ride, they were cruising through Broken Arrow, a suburb of Tulsa.

The downtown area, comprised of two- and three-story saloon-style buildings, suggested a colorful history. Rachel spotted signs of a vibrant cultural community and evidence of growth everywhere.

"Sure has built up," Saul commented with a frown of concentration. "I don't recognize half of it, except for that grain elevator." He pointed it out to her.

All at once, the town fell away, and they were zipping up and down hills on a narrow country road. At a lonely intersection, Saul turned right. They went about a mile before he slowed at a mailbox, sitting by itself at the edge of the road. Drawing a visible breath, Saul turned left onto a gravel driveway.

Overgrown trees pressed in on either side. Rachel identified the trees that also grew back in Virginia —scrub oak, sassafras, and persimmon. The driveway itself was riddled with potholes.

Glancing at her silent companions, Rachel found Liam pressed against her seat, peering through the windshield with an eager expression. Saul, by contrast, appeared to be clenching his jaw. Dappled sunlight flickered on the dashboard as he adjusted his steering to avoid the larger potholes.

A hundred yards up the driveway, the trees gave way to prairie grass shot with towering sunflowers and smaller, reddish-orange flowers she'd never seen before. The driveway curved, revealing a cabin-style home with wooden siding, a stone chimney, and a covered porch. It stood in the field of prairie grass, flanked by a once-red barn and shaded by a mammoth pecan tree. Beyond the tree stood a small brick enclosure.

Focusing on the house as they parked in front of it, Rachel noted the weeds choking the steps to the porch. A window on one end of the house was broken, leaving a hole that resembled a black eye. At least the building itself was standing and appeared intact, although several shingles on the roof were missing.

Saul cut the engine and stared at his home with visible dismay.

"Is it in worse shape than you thought?" she asked him.

"It's pretty run-down."

His gruff words prompted another wave of compassion.

"I can help you fix it." As the offer came out of her mouth, she knew it was meant to be. After all, she'd been studying interior design. "I know a lot about houses."

Saul tore his gaze off his home to contemplate her. All at once Liam gasped.

"Hey, there's someone running toward the woods!"

Following his pointing finger, Rachel spotted a man tearing through the tall grass and headed for the tree line. It was obvious he had exited the house via a back door.

Saul jumped out of the car with impressive speed and flipped the seat forward. "Get him, Duke!"

Duke shot out of the car. Whether he'd seen the man flee wasn't clear to Rachel, but he took off in the direction Saul indicated, tearing across the yard in what looked like hot pursuit. Saul reached under his car seat to retrieve the pistol he'd stored there for the last leg of their drive. Her pulse quickened as he removed it from its holster.

He ducked to speak to them. "Stay put." Shutting them in his car, he headed toward the house with his pistol pointing at the ground.

"Keep your head down," Rachel instructed her son, even as she slid lower in her own seat.

"Are we in the Wild West?" he whispered, clearly unafraid.

Rachel had to smile. "No, silly."

"What was that man doing here?"

"I don't know, honey. Saul's going to find out." Time came to a standstill. Could Ethan have discovered their destination and set a trap for them? Surely not. Ethan would have had the police waiting for them, not merely one man, who'd run at the sight of them.

At last, Saul returned to the car, looming by her door before she'd heard his approach. He let loose with a shrill whistle that could have been heard for miles.

"House is clear." He opened her door. "It was just a squatter hopin' to lay claim to an empty building. He left a mess behind, but I doubt he'll come back. Come on in. We'll bring in our stuff once we've cleaned a little."

They exited the car and trailed Saul up the porch steps. Ceramic pots of every shape and size cluttered the large area, most of them still serviceable. Some previous occupant liked to garden as much as Rachel did. Saul's mother, perhaps?

"You still have a key?" she asked as Saul opened the screen door. The inner door hung ajar.

"Cyril's lawyer sent it to me."

A musty odor greeted them as they stepped into a dark interior. "Electricity should've been turned on by now. I paid the bill online." Saul pulled the heavy drapes back from the front windows, and light flooded in.

Rachel's eyes widened. The main room boasted a stone hearth, a cathedral ceiling with exposed beams, and a plush but filthy carpet. At least the heart of pine floor beneath it looked to be in good shape. .

"Oh, this is nice." She noted an ugly oil painting over the fireplace. The rest of the once-white walls stood bare.

"Kitchen's a mess," Saul apologized, gesturing toward it.

The great room flowed seamlessly into a kitchen boasting outdated countertops of sky-blue laminate and appliances that looked like they might not work anymore. Dirty dishes lay piled up in the sink, wrappers cluttered every surface, and a garbage can overflowed with trash. All the same, Rachel saw promise in how the kitchen was laid out.

"Ew, it stinks!" Liam pinched his nose.

Saul was already gathering up the litter and stuffing it into the trash can. Rachel went to help him, brushing his hand by mistake as they both reached for the same discarded box of a TV dinner.

"Sorry." She snatched her hand back. For the second time, touching Saul sparked unexpected pleasure. He felt it too, given the way his gaze jumped to hers.

After pulling the trash bag out of the can, he turned and carried it toward the back door. The screen slammed shut behind him, but the door remained open, prompting Rachel to cross the kitchen and peer outside.

This had to be the door from which the stranger had fled. The big, old barn with its flaking red paint stood twenty or so feet away, with a window up top and a pulley for lifting bales of hay into a loft. Saul set the bag of trash at his feet and freed his right hand to open one of the double doors while hefting his pistol with his left. She knew from the football games played at the Team get-togethers Saul was a lefty.

Plumbing the dark barn with a suspicious gaze, Saul finally put his gun away and disappeared inside, taking the trash with him.

In the barn's dim interior, Rachel caught sight of the truck Saul had mentioned. Her eyes widened as she pictured herself driving a vehicle built for a working man, not a petite woman. *I can't afford to turn it down.* She would take the truck and be grateful.

"How long are we going to be here, Mom?" Liam recaptured her attention.

She turned to find him putting a bowl of water down for the dog, who still hadn't returned from chasing the squatter.

"I don't really know, sweetie. I feel like I should help Saul fix this house so he can sell it. It's the least I can do after all he's done, don't you think?"

She expected Liam to balk at roughing it in a place that didn't even have electricity, but he shrugged and said wholeheartedly, "I think so."

Relieved her son seemed happy, Rachel turned to find Saul scowling as he reentered the kitchen. "What's wrong?"

The question seemed to surprise him. His expression cleared.

"Nothing. Truck's locked and I don't know where the keys are, but I expect the lawyer has them." Stepping up to the sink, he washed his hands, then shook them dry as there were no clean towels or even paper ones. Then he tipped his head toward the rest of the house.

"Shall we tour the place?"

"Sure."

Liam joined them as they crossed the living room and entered an L-shaped hallway. The odor of cigars and stale liquor floated out of an open door to the only bedroom facing the front of the house. Saul alone was brave enough to step into the room from which the odor came.

"This used to be Puca's bedroom," he stated in a gruff voice. "Cyril turned it into his office. He slept in here after my mama got sick."

From her vantage at the door, Rachel watched Saul assess the damaged window first. The twin bed in the corner of the room had clearly been occupied by the squatter.

Saul eyed the contents of the cabinet with a look of consternation.

"Is something missing?" she guessed.

"Nope. There are more now than ever."

More what? Rachel braved the stench to see for herself. Her eyebrows shot up to find the cabinet full of firearms. Some were rifles. A few were shotguns.

Saul scratched his chin. "Wonder why the squatter didn't take and sell these."

"Because the cabinet's locked?" Rachel suggested.

"He could've just broken the glass."

True enough. They all turned to assess the rest of the mess. A large desk, piled high with magazines and pamphlets, occupied one wall. Liam lifted one such pamphlet off the desk.

"Honey, don't touch anything."

Liam handed her the pamphlet wordlessly, his eyes enormous.

Rachel scanned it and blinked. "Saul, was your stepfather a white supremacist?"

"What?" He took the pamphlet she passed to him, read it, and balled it up with disgust. "Wouldn't surprise me if he was." He lobbed it onto the bed. "Come on. Let's get out of here."

Back in the hallway, they were faced with a double door for a laundry closet and three more rooms.

"This here's the main bathroom." Saul toed the door open.

The small window over the toilet illumined stained vinyl flooring and worn cabinetry. The toilet, tub, and sink seemed serviceable, however.

"This was my room." Saul visibly braced himself as he opened the opposite door. The stunned expression that came across his face had Rachel peering past him. Liam, however, went right on in.

A bunk bed took up one of the tan walls. Mismatched furniture lined the other three. But even with blinds filtering out the sunlight, Rachel could see the room was filled with knickknacks.

"Look, Mom!" Liam was holding a life-sized squirrel.

Rachel slipped past Saul to see better.

"Oh, it's carved out of wood," she stated, when Liam put it in her hands.

"Whittled," said Saul from the hallway.

Rachel marveled at how real the sculpture seemed, right down to the chips of glass for its eyes. She put it back on a shelf. There were other carvings—a bear, a tree with an eagle on a branch, and a beaver with a hatch-marked tail.

"Did you collect these?" She turned back to Saul, who still stood stiffly in the doorway.

"I whittled them. Puca taught me how."

"You *made* these?" Liam ran a hand over the beaver's smooth back.

"They're amazing," Rachel stated.

"Can't believe Cyril held on to 'em," Saul muttered.

"Of course he did. They're priceless."

"Oh, cool!" Liam found a replica of a rattlesnake, coiled on itself with just its rattler sticking up. "I want to sleep in this room." He looked to Saul for permission.

But Saul wasn't at the door anymore. Leaving Liam to explore on his own, Rachel stepped out of the room to find Saul opening the door of the last bedroom, clearly wary of what lay inside.

Rachel scented mildew and the faint essence of perfume as she stepped up alongside him. One glance at the double bed with its ornate headboard, antique dressing table, and matching highboy, and she knew.

"This was your mother's room."

"Yes," Saul replied, but he didn't go inside.

"May I?" she asked.

He stepped aside, letting her in.

Rachel walked up to the bed and looked around, taking note of the dated, adjoining bathroom. "I'm surprised your stepfather kept it like this." It still resembled a woman's room with a patchwork quilt on the bed and family portraits atop the highboy. Drawn to the photos, Rachel identified Saul's mother immediately. Her coloring was darker than his, but their noses and eyes were identical. She was as beautiful as Saul had described her. Saul bore more resemblance to his father, a muscular redhead with dancing blue eyes and a big smile.

Heavens, was that roly-poly baby in the strapping man's arms Saul?

"Is this baby you?" She spun toward the door, and her smile faded to see Saul gone. Poor man, the memories here were clearly too much for him to take.

"Mom!" Liam appeared at the door wearing knee-high moccasins. "Check these out."

"Honey, you need to ask Saul first before you help yourself to his things. Take those off and put them back where you found them."

With a pout of disappointment, Liam returned to Saul's old room. Hearing Saul's voice outside, Rachel headed for the living room just as he and the dog came in together. Duke pranced at his feet, seeming pleased with himself.

"What'd you find, Duke? Did you get him?"

Unless Saul could read the dog's mind, there was no telling whether Duke had even chased after the squatter.

"Good boy. Come on, let's get some water." Saul showed Duke the bowl of water Liam had set out for him. Then he turned and caught Rachel's eye.

"You two can have the bedrooms. I'll sleep on the couch."

She swung a dubious glance at the worn leather sofa, then remembered SEALs could sleep anywhere.

"You mind stripping the beds? I'm going to head into town," he explained brusquely. "Need to stop by Oneida Power and ask why the electric's not on. I'll get food and cleanin' supplies on my way back."

She pictured the squatter returning. "You want us to stay here? Alone?"

"Duke will protect you. You want my gun, too?" He started to reach for it.

"No, no." Rachel waved him off. "That's okay. We'll be fine."

"Didn't Blake teach you how to shoot?" Saul sounded incredulous.

"He tried." She smiled wryly at the memory. "I, uh, I put a bullet into the fender of his truck, which wasn't even close to the pile of cans I was aiming for."

Saul let loose with a rusty laugh. "That was you? Aw! He made up a story 'bout bein' shot at for driving on the beach in Rodanthe."

"He didn't want to make me look bad."

Saul laughed again, then sobered suddenly.

"I'll be back as quick as I can, before dark." Pushing outside, he collected their meager possessions and left them just inside the door. "Lock up behind me."

Crossing to the screen door, Rachel watched Saul get behind the wheel of his Camaro and execute a swift U-turn. He roared down the driveway, kicking up dust in his haste to get there and back quickly. Or was he hurrying away from the memories that haunted him at the ranch?

Turning to regard the house's dim interior, Rachel felt like eyes were watching her. With a shiver of concern, she stepped back and closed the heavy inner door, locked it as Saul had advised, then went to lock the rear door in the kitchen, too.

~

Standing in line at the Walmart Neighborhood Market, Saul felt like he was fifteen years old again, buying food for his mother who was too sick to get out of bed. The intervening years had compressed into nothing, as if no time at all had passed. At that moment, he was still the vulnerable, disillusioned, and angry teen he used to be.

Shifting on his feet, he glanced to his left and his right. As of yet, no one had recognized him, not even at Oneida Power where he'd been told a work truck had been dispatched minutes ago to take care of the issue. Broken Arrow had grown up so much since Saul had left, he had yet to glimpse a familiar face. Several of the buildings down on Main Street housed the same businesses, including Tim & Louie's barbershop, a family law firm, and the same dentist's office. The city's growth was more to the south of the tracks, extending into what was once pastureland.

With his shoulders so much broader and his hair cut short, Saul figured he might just get by with a week or two of anonymity.

As he lined up his purchases, which included half a dozen cleaners, a large pack of sponges, and an even larger pack of paper towels, he considered Rachel's offer to help him fix the house up. He'd only brought her there to give her the truck, but considering the shape the house was in, it would take all hands on deck to get it clean enough to sell. He couldn't afford to decline her offer, could he? That meant she and Liam would likely stick around a few more days than he'd intended. He wouldn't mind that one bit.

"Saul Wade, is that you?"

Heads turned, and Saul winced. The woman's voice was unmistakable. He knew before turning around it belonged to Tami Goodner, his mother's best friend and next-door neighbor. Her dark hair had turned silver, her blue eyes had receded into the soft folds of her face, but her welcoming smile was still as warm as it had ever been.

With a welling of affection, Saul eased out of the line to greet her. "Hey, Miss Tami."

"Oh, Saul!" She threw her arms wide and went up on tiptoe to give his cheek a resounding smack. "Just look at you, darlin'! Who knew you could have grown so big!"

He'd been as skinny as a twig in high school, with long hair he wore in braids. Little wonder his classmates had kept their distance.

Putting him at arm's length, Tami beamed up at him.

"I was hoping you'd come back and claim your property. Any chance you're going to stay?"

"No, ma'am. Plannin' to fix up the place to sell it."

"Sell it!" Her smile faded. "Why can't you just quit the Navy and come on home?" she asked on a plaintiff note.

"Uncle Sam owns me for another year, at which time I'll probably reenlist."

"Well, you must really love what you do." She eyed him uncertainly. "There was an article in *Tulsa World* recently that named you America's top sniper now that Chris Kyle's no longer alive, God rest his soul."

Saul darted an uncomfortable glance at the people openly eavesdropping.

"I can't confirm that."

"No, of course you can't." She looked annoyed with herself, then brightened. "Why don't you come over for dinner? Mark would love to catch up with you!"

"How is Mr. Mark?" Saul asked, hearing his western dialect thicken.

"Same ol' cowpoke he always was. Well? Can you make it tonight?"

Saul pictured Rachel and Liam waiting for him back at the ranch.

"Not tonight, ma'am. I just arrived, and I gotta lot of cleanin' to do. But I'll be sure and stop by some time."

"You'd better." She gave his chest a pat as if to make sure his muscles were real. "Your mother would be so proud of how handsome you've turned out." Her eyes misted over. "Do visit soon. Just drop in on us or call first if you want. Our number hasn't changed."

"Yes, ma'am." Feeling curious eyes on him, Saul went back to pay for his purchases. Just like that, the anonymity he'd been enjoying was gone. He would bet the contents of his wallet that by the next morning everyone he'd ever known, from his teachers in elementary school onward, would have heard Half-Breed Saul Wade was back in Broken Arrow.

Tami Goodner was as informative as the local newspaper, which meant Rachel—Angel—would need to keep a low profile for as long as she remained with him.

∼

"Liam!" Rachel called her son's name louder, only to be answered by silence. She'd been stripping the beds and loading the linens into the washing machine. Hopefully, the appliance would run after Saul checked with the power company.

"Liam?" Rachel peered into Saul's old bedroom and found both Liam and the dog gone.

With growing consternation, she hurried to the front door, finding it unlocked and wide open. Liam had obviously gone outside.

"Liam!" Pushing through the screen door, Rachel bellowed his name from the porch. The sun, having dipped behind the trees, threw long shadows across the sweet-smelling prairie grass.

"I'm over here." Liam's voice sounded muffled.

"Where?" she called back, hearing her own relief.

"In the cemetery."

She'd just determined his voice was coming from the small brick enclosure she had spotted upon their arrival. *That's a cemetery?*

Leaping off the porch, Rachel ran past the pecan tree toward her son. The enclosure wasn't more than ten-by-ten feet, with a wrought-iron gate on one side that hung open. As she slipped through it, she spotted the dog sniffing in one corner and Liam down on his knees pulling grass out by the roots.

"Honey, what are you doing?"

"There's another one here on the ground, and the grass is growing over it."

Hearing his concern, Rachel let him continue his pruning. Her gaze went to the three headstones rising out of the grass. She could already guess who was buried there. All the same, it came as an unpleasant shock to read their names.

"Jessie Hawk Henderson," she read. "1934–2004."

"That's Puca." Liam glanced up from his earnest labors. "The other two have to be Saul's parents."

With a weight on her chest, she read their names out loud.

"Leonard James Wade and Melody Henderson Wade." Eyeing the years they'd lived and died, she was struck by how Saul's mother had died within a day of her first husband, exactly four years later.

"Melody," she repeated, thinking the name suited the pretty brunette in the photos she'd just admired. Her gaze slid to the marble slab Liam's efforts were exposing. "That must be for the baby."

"Blessing Lawson," Liam read, "January to March 2003."

Eyeing all four markers, Rachel was struck by the number of staggering losses the younger Saul had suffered.

"Mom?" Liam's soft voice drew her attention back to him.

He clambered quickly to his feet and threw his arms around her in a way he hadn't done in years.

"You're not going to die too, are you?"

"What?" She pulled back to regard his pale face. "Of course not, honey. What makes you say that?"

"Saul's dad died first, and then his mom."

Rachel drew a sharp breath as she caught on to Liam's logic. "That doesn't mean I'm going to die next," she soothed, rubbing a hand over the top of his shorn head. The angle of the sun lit the depths of Liam's dark-blue eyes.

"God's not done with me, remember?" They'd had this conversation after she'd come home from the hospital.

"Was God done with Daddy?" Liam countered.

At the defiant question, Rachel grimaced. "I don't know, honey. I don't have all the answers. All I know is God gave people free will and, as a result, bad things happen. That doesn't mean God wants them to." She pictured Blake's executive officer, Jimmy Lowery, who at Commander Dwyer's behest had done something to Blake during parachute training. He'd lost consciousness after jumping from the plane. The chute had never been deployed, and Blake had died on impact.

Liam broke eye contact and fell solemnly silent.

"But think of it this way," Rachel urged. "If Daddy hadn't died, I would never have gone through his journals and found out what Commander Dwyer was up to. He never would have gone to jail for what he did. So, at least something good came of something bad."

Seeing Dwyer hauled off in cuffs by the FBI had been the only good thing Rachel could think of resulting from Blake's death.

"Come on, sweetie. It's getting dark, and Saul told us to stay inside in case the squatter comes back."

As Liam moved away to grab the dog, Rachel directed her gaze beyond the walls of the enclosure, seeking any sign of the squatter. He could be lurking in the woods, watching them.

As they hurried toward the house, Duke lifted his nose to the air, scenting something. Rachel's anxiety rose abruptly.

"Come on." She urged Liam into a run. However, lights flared suddenly in the windows as they approached, countering Rachel's unease.

"Great! The electricity's back on. Now I can wash the sheets."

What she really wanted was for Saul to return from his trip into town. Being alone with her son in the middle of nowhere with a stranger potentially spying on them wasn't the sanctuary she was craving.

~

Petty Officer Marcelino Hewitt looked up to see Captain O'Rourke leaving work for the day. O'Rourke had been absent for the past two days, following the disappearance of his sister and nephew. Marcelino had read all about it in *The Virginian-Pilot*.

He'd never much cared for the captain, even though, as everyone knew, O'Rourke was the best JAG at NCIS Oceana Naval Air Station. Marcelino would have had to be heartless, however, given the man's long face, not to feel sorry for him. The captain's black tie was askew. He stood more stoop-shouldered than ever.

"Have a good evening, sir," Marcelino called as the captain went to exit the building. "I'm very sorry to hear about Miss Rachel and her son." According to *The Virginian-Pilot*, they'd most likely been kidnapped.

O'Rourke's dark-as-ink eyes took a bead on him. "You knew her on a first-name basis?"

At the quiet question, Marcelino took a small step backward. "She...asked me to call her Rachel," he reassured the JAG swiftly.

"Really? But then she had to wait outside my office for a ride to school. You must have struck up a conversation with her."

Marcelino didn't know what to say to that. Was the man implying he had flirted with his sister? Clearly, he was out of his mind with grief.

O'Rourke backtracked on his stork-like legs until he stood across the X-ray belt from Marcelino. "Was she friendly with anyone else? A man with a goatee, perhaps?"

Marcelino realized with a shiver it wasn't grief clouding the captain's eyes. It was something colder, something unhinged.

"A goatee, sir?"

"Are you hard of hearing, Petty Officer?"

"No, sir."

"Have you ever seen Rachel with a bearded man?" O'Rourke articulated each word.

Marcelino, who felt like he was sitting in the witness box, swallowed hard. The only bearded man who'd come into the Trial Services Building lately was Chief Saul Wade, the Navy SEAL who always teased him while his hazel eyes glinted with affection.

"No, sir," Marcelino said. Chief Wade would never have to resort to kidnapping to get himself a woman.

"No?" O'Rourke cocked his head. "Why the hesitation, Petty Officer"—he had to consult Marcelino's name patch—"Hewitt?"

Saul Wade not only knew Marcelino's last name, he also knew his first—and gave him a hard time about it, all with that same gruff affection.

"No reason, sir."

"I see." The JAG's shoulders sagged, and his mouth drooped. Without another word, he swiveled on his polished shoes and stalked through the exit, straight into a downpour.

Marcelino found himself thinking of the last time Chief Wade had come into the building, just a few days earlier. Miss Rachel had been here that day, too. She used to sit outside O'Rourke's office waiting for him to drop her off at school. She'd admitted her brother had sold her car without her permission while she was in the hospital.

An intriguing possibility entered Marcelino's head. What if Miss Rachel had been bullied by her brother, and Chief Wade had found a way to set her free? A smile tugged at his lips and grew.

Chief Wade and Miss Rachel together, huh? He rather liked the idea. It suited him better than the alternative suggested by the newspaper.

CHAPTER 6

The thumping on the roof abated suddenly, causing Rachel to pause in the act of mopping the kitchen floor. Keeping her ears pricked, she continued her labors, bringing a muted shine to the old vinyl flooring, even though she would advise Saul to replace it. A new floor comprised of laminate planks that resembled real wood would be her first choice. But if he replaced the flooring, he should also get rid of the kitchen cabinets and the blue laminate countertop. In her mind's eye she pictured stainless-steel appliances and pale-gray cabinets topped with white granite that was flecked with gray and gold chips.

The rear screen door yawned open, interrupting Rachel's daydreaming. Saul strode in, then drew up short.

Rachel pointed. "You can walk on that side."

He picked his way to the sink and stuck his thumb under running water. Suspecting an injury, Rachel propped the mop against the counter and joined him to assess the damage.

"Hammered it," he informed her in his terse manner.

She could tell as much, for his nail was already turning purple.

"Can I get you some ice?"

Her question brought his gaze around. She found herself the focus of his hazel eyes. The way he regarded her made her pulse quicken.

"No, thanks." He turned off the water. "There's an easy way to get the blood out." He turned his whole body this time, so they stood face-to-face, mere inches apart.

Rachel tried to step back, only she was wedged between Saul and the corner of the cabinetry. Not wanting to seem like a scared rabbit, she stood her ground.

"I'm afraid to ask," she finally replied.

"Got a small drill lying around?"

"You've got to be kidding." She sent the thumb he was cradling a horrified glance.

"I don't kid much."

"I know. I'm sorry." The urge to brush back a lock of his mahogany hair that had fallen over one eyebrow made her grip the counter next to her, instead.

He cocked his head. "Sorry for what?"

Rachel licked her dry lips. "For everything you've been through," she answered honestly.

His eyes, dark green shot through with brown highlights, seemed to peer deeply into her soul. All at once he broke away, tossing over his shoulder, "My whittling kit."

Watching him glide toward the bedrooms, Rachel admired the breadth of his tan shoulders made all the more apparent by his sleeveless T-shirt. His growing appeal so dismayed her she snatched up the mop and went back to cleaning the floor.

What would Blake think of her if he knew?

She realized with deepening confusion Blake would probably approve. But Saul wasn't her type. He was a sniper, for heaven's sake. He used his deadly aim to end people's lives—bad people, she amended. Then she sighed.

I'm just lonely. God certainly didn't intend for her and Saul to end up together. The mere notion was...unsettling.

Saul returned, carrying a small wooden box. He walked around the spot she was mopping to set it on the table by the back door. Taking a seat, he opened the box and proceeded to paw through it.

From the corner of her eye, Rachel saw him plug what looked like a tiny electric drill into an outlet. A high-pitched whirring affirmed her guess.

"Still works," he said on a note of satisfaction. In the next instant, he set his right thumb on the table, placed the tip of the drill on his nail, and promptly drilled a hole in it. Blood gushed out.

Swallowing a cry of dismay, Rachel hurried to tear some paper towels off the roll. She carried them to Saul, who'd unplugged the drill and with a grim, satisfied smile took her offering.

"Thanks." He made a quick makeshift bandage, wrapping his bleeding digit, and lifted his gaze to her.

Feeling lightheaded, Rachel sank in the chair next to him.

"Squeamish?"

"Not usually. I've just never seen anyone do anything like that, especially without disinfecting it first."

He peeked under the paper towel. "Blood washes out the infection. Now the blood's out." He went to show her. "Much better than having it throb for twenty-four hours."

"I guess." Her gaze went to the black-ink tattoo on his shoulder. With surprise, she realized it wasn't a random depiction of skulls. One was obviously a male. Another one had long braids. The third was clearly a woman, and the fourth was a baby.

With her breath catching, Rachel realized she was looking at his dead family members. He took them wherever he went.

"Looks good in here. You've done a lot already."

His comment forced her to find her voice.

"Yeah, I wanted to talk to you about your plans. You say you want to sell this place, right?"

"Yes." His tone was girded with determination.

"Okay, well, I don't know the real estate market here, obviously, but I'm sure if you invested about twenty-five thousand dollars into renovating the kitchen and bathrooms first, it would sell much faster, and you could recoup all of your investment and more by raising your asking price."

Saul studied her for a second, then turned his gaze out the window through which Rachel could just make out Liam's spiky head over the tops of the prairie grass. Her son claimed he had found an animal's lair in the backyard and was sitting in wait for the critter to return so he could identify it.

"Where would I get twenty-five thousand dollars?" Saul finally asked, turning his attention to his injury.

"You could open a home-equity line and pay it all back when the house sells."

He inspected his thumb with a growing scowl, although it had stopped bleeding.

"I have no desire to stay here and oversee a renovation," he said in a flat voice.

"I understand." She gave one last push. "Maybe you could find a trustworthy contractor."

"Maybe." He balled up the bloodstained paper towel and tossed it into the trash. "Thanks for cleaning, though. You really don't have to."

"But I want to. This is our deal. You helped me. Now I'm helping you."

"Just until I get the truck running. You don't owe me anything." With that definitive statement, he pushed the chair back with his knees and went outside again.

Rachel sat a moment. Was Saul as physically aware of her as she was of him? After all, he had to be as lonely as she was—even more so —with his family dead and gone.

She put a swift end to a vision of them kissing and stood as the thumping on the roof resumed.

That is never going to happen, Rachel promised herself.

~

At six o'clock that evening, the sky outside the kitchen windows had blushed to a pretty shade of mauve. Rachel, Liam, and Saul sat at the kitchen table, finishing their supper.

"I'm all done." Liam put his napkin on the table. "Can I go back out now?" He had expressed his plan to put a grasshopper in an old mayonnaise jar, so he could inspect it using a magnifying glass he'd found in Saul's bedroom.

Rachel glanced at Saul, who dabbed at his remaining spaghetti sauce with a piece of bread.

"Stay close to the house where we can see you," Saul chimed in.

"And take your plate to the sink, please," Rachel added as Liam leaped to his feet. He did as she asked, then darted outside with the jar Rachel had found in one of the cabinets.

"You gonna finish that?" Saul gestured to Rachel's half-eaten dinner. Despite his protests that he hadn't brought her to his ranch to cook for him, he hadn't turned down the dinner of spaghetti and meatballs she'd whipped up using groceries he'd bought the previous night.

She slid her half-full plate in his direction. "Help yourself."

"You don't eat enough," he commented, taking her plate all the same.

Blake used to say the same thing before he gobbled up her leftovers. Now, Saul was doing it.

"Is Liam safe outside once the sun goes down?" She deflected his focus onto her son.

"Around here?" Saul's gaze went out the window. "Sure he is."

"What about the squatter?"

Saul twirled the spaghetti with his fork. "He won't come back as long as he sees people in the house."

"Liam mentioned bobcats, though. Would they ever attack a little boy?"

"Mmm-mn." Slurping up noodles, Saul shook his head. The hoop in his earlobe glinted. He chewed and swallowed. "Wild animals know to avoid humans." He reached for his iced tea. "Adult animals."

"I've heard you tamed a bobcat." Liam had shared the story with her that afternoon.

He put his glass down with a thud. "Yep."

"Was it a baby bobcat or an adult?" She tried to catch him in a lie.

"Baby," he admitted, catching her eye and smiling. "But you can tame just about any animal if you're patient enough."

His steady regard did funny things to Rachel's insides. For a heart-thumping moment, she thought Saul might be flirting with her. But then he turned his ear sharply in the direction of the front door and the moment was over.

"You hear that?" Vaulting from his seat, he started toward the living room.

Rachel followed him and discerned the sound of a rumbling motor.

Saul crossed to the big picture window, while waving Rachel out of sight behind him. Peeking around him, she peered past the porch, over the tall grass toward the source of the sound, and spotted an older-model El Camino stalled where the driveway curved. Half-concealed by the sunflowers and the prairie grass, its headlights were extinguished. It was hard to tell in the twilight whether the car was white or yellow, but Rachel could make out two occupants in the cab. Rather than approach the house, they kept their distance.

"Go get Liam."

Saul's serious request startled Rachel into motion. She turned and raced for the back door, wondering wildly if Ethan had tracked her down already. Impossible. Ethan wouldn't be caught dead driving an old beater like that one.

"Liam!" she called, searching for her son in the tall grass.

"What?"

Following the sound of his voice, she found him on his knees near the wall of the barn with his hands cupped. "Sweetie, you have to come in right now."

"Why?" It was clear he had caught a grasshopper and was about to put it in the jar.

She snatched up the jar and grabbed his arm at the same time. "Someone's out front, and we don't know who it is."

Liam let her draw him back to the house while managing to hold on to his catch.

"Stay right here." She took the lid off the jar and left him in the kitchen before returning to Saul, who stood exactly where she'd left him. The car still loitered. Every few seconds, its motor revved as if the driver were issuing a threat.

"Who could they be?" she whispered. "Why are they doing that?"

"Don't know yet."

The cold quality of Saul's voice made her reassess him. In the fading light, his profile reminded her of an old daguerreotype of an unsmiling Native American.

"Why won't they leave?" she whispered, gazing back to the interlopers.

"They will. I need you and Liam to go stand in the hallway, away from the windows," he added, without taking his eyes off the vehicle.

Reading between the lines, she realized he intended to take the fight to the intruders—of course, he did. SEALs never let themselves be intimidated. The hallway would protect her and Liam from any bullets that might fly.

"Be careful," she ordered, then went to get Liam from the kitchen. Her son had put his insect in the jar and was puncturing the lid with a knife. "Come on, honey. Saul wants us to stand in the hallway while he chases off the visitors." She kept her tone as casual as if she were asking him to brush his teeth before bed.

Liam's face reflected sudden fear. "Is it Uncle Ethan?"

"No, no. Come on." She grabbed his sleeve and hurried him past Saul, who waited by the front door with an impassive expression. Once they were safely in the hallway, Rachel heard the door creak open.

Disobeying Saul, she inched forward until she could peek through the picture window. Saul leaped off the porch and dashed toward his car with his head low. He ducked into the passenger seat, his upper body disappearing momentarily. In the next instant, he withdrew, stood with his pistol in hand, and fired it.

Crack.

From where she stood, it sounded as though he'd shot out one of the old car's headlights. The intimidation tactic clearly worked. In the next instant, she could hear the car backing away.

She ducked out of view as Saul came inside, shutting and locking the door behind him.

"You can come out now." He drew the curtains over the big front window.

As Rachel emerged with Liam behind her, she noted the butt of Saul's pistol pushing out his T-shirt. Apparently, he was going to keep it on his person now, in case the interlopers returned.

"Pull down the blinds in the kitchen," he requested, then moved past her, heading into his stepfather's study.

Rachel glanced at Liam's tense expression, knowing she needed to distract him.

"Hey, let's look at your grasshopper." Both the jar and the magnifying glass lay on the kitchen table. Once she'd pulled the blinds —picturing light-filtering cellulose blinds instead of the clunky wooden ones—she joined Liam, who'd pulled the jar close to him and was eyeing it through the magnifying glass.

"It's so cool," he exclaimed. "He has jointed limbs. You look."

She took the chair next to his and, taking the lens he handed her, expressed her fascination. All the while, she wondered what Saul was up to. At last, she left Liam drawing a sketch of his specimen in a notebook and sought out Saul. He was sitting at his stepfather's desk, leafing through the contents of a file folder.

When she paused in the doorway, he regarded her with a dark scowl.

"What did you find?" She was afraid to ask.

"Just tryin' to make sense of all this paperwork. These pamphlets" —he gestured at the piles on the edge of the desk—"were published by a group calling themselves the Fists of Righteous Americans, or FOR

Americans. It's a hate group, as you guessed, comprised of white supremacists advocating the violent removal of anyone whose skin isn't white—like me," he added with sarcasm.

"I'm sorry," Rachel said, not understanding the motive for such hatred.

Saul picked up a pamphlet, skimmed it briefly, then read out loud, "'They have usurped the white man's hard-earned positions in industry, corrupted the English language, and lowered the standards in schools,'" he quoted. "What's more, it appears that Cyril was one of their elected officials. At least, that's what this paperwork states." He slapped shut the folder he'd been leafing through. "I'm guessing our recent visitors were his followers."

"Really? Why would they come here? They know Cyril is dead, right?"

"They know." Saul nodded at the large cabinet against the wall. "My guess is they're after those."

Rachel pivoted toward the gun case. A shiver of foreboding raised goosebumps on her forearms. "Maybe you should get rid of them."

"I will. As soon as you and Liam leave, I'll turn them over to the police."

"Why not before then?"

"'Cause the police might want to scour this place searching for evidence of something illegal." He got up from the desk. "You and Liam don't need that kind of scrutiny." Crossing to the locked cabinet, he gave the doors a shake.

She watched him turn toward the desk, pull open a drawer, and feel up inside of it. "Same place he used to hide it." He came away with a key.

Unlocking the cabinet, he reached for a shotgun. Handling it with casual precision, he checked it for ammunition, and four shells fell into his palm.

"Loaded," she murmured with dismay.

Saul's scowl made him frightening. "This isn't any place for a child," he muttered as he pocketed the shells. "Never was," he added to himself.

Putting the shotgun back, he reached for another.

His words caught Rachel's attention. Was he saying he wanted her and Liam to leave? She was just starting to warm to her task of fixing the house up.

The second shotgun was also loaded. With a shake of his head, Saul emptied it of ammunition and put it back. He pulled out a rifle this time. It, too, was loaded, with shiny bullets that glinted in his palm.

This is going to take a while, Rachel realized. Moreover, watching Saul handle weapons with such practiced ease was nearly as upsetting as his statement about children not belonging there.

"I'm going to go check on Liam," she said.

Saul didn't even acknowledge her as a bullet from the fourth rifle clattered into his palm.

Ethan slurped the last suggestion of scotch off the ice cubes in his tumbler before he lowered it with a thud onto the glass-covered surface of his desk. He realized he'd begun the habit of inebriating himself each evening in his home office, and he didn't like it.

I won't find my family if I'm drunk.

His cell phone gave a shrill ring, sobering him instantly. He picked it up and groaned. His mother was calling him again. But what did he expect? She'd been Rachel's mother, too, so he deigned to answer.

"Hello, Mother."

"Ethan. I'm glad you answered. Is there any news on Rachel and Liam?"

Ginger O'Rourke's anxiety reminded Ethan they were in the same boat. Maybe his mother was also drinking too much.

"There's news," he articulated his words carefully, "but it's not helpful."

"What is it?" she prompted, eager for anything.

"When they dragged the creek, they found a canoe, probably the one used in their kidnapping. It had been sabotaged so it would sink, making it harder to collect any DNA evidence. Tire markings suggest Rachel and Liam were put into a car and driven from the park. The police have requested satellite imaging so maybe we can learn the make and model of the vehicle."

"Oh. Yes, that would be good." Ginny's voice quaked with the effort it took to talk.

"How's Dad?" Ethan asked, in order to distract her.

"Oh, he's hanging in there."

The doctors had said Eddie O'Rourke was near death. The old man could have chosen a better time to clock out.

"Is there anything else? Have the police found anything on Rachel's laptop?"

Ethan had badgered the police that very afternoon. "They're working on it. We don't know Rachel's passwords. They've got a hacker helping them."

"I see. Well, call me if anything changes."

"I will."

"Good night, darling."

"Good night." Ethan severed the call with a press of his thumb.

Darling? He'd never felt like his parents loved him. They'd done their duty, though, he had to give them that. They'd been superlative parents—far better than the ones he'd been born to.

With a sneer, he summoned his earliest memory. His father—his real father—had thrust him into the arms of an orphanage staff member. Ethan, who couldn't have been more than three, shrieked and pleaded with his father to take him back. Ivan Yostoff—the name on Ethan's birth certificate—had taken one last look at him and walked away.

Feeling tears slide down his cheeks, Ethan dashed them away and rose unsteadily to his feet. The need to feel a connection with the father he hardly remembered had him weaving toward his file cabinet instead of heading upstairs to his room. He pulled open the drawer that archived matters A – L and located his birth certificate, filed alongside Rachel's, under Important Documents.

There it was. His mother, whom he could not recall at all, was Tatiana Yostoff. He had overheard his adoptive parents discussing her once. Contrary to the Russian stereotype of a father drinking and running off, it was his mother who'd been the drunk. She'd apparently left his father for another man. Unable to care for Ethan, Ivan Yostoff had surrendered him to the orphanage.

It wasn't Rachel who'd come from Russia, it was Ethan. But she'd never been told the truth by their adoptive parents. In fact, he doubted Rachel even knew Ethan was also adopted. Their parents had been absolutely circumspect about where they came from. Their reticence to talk about the past had aided Ethan's lie—at least until Rachel required her birth certificate to get her driver's license. Her birth mother's very American name had tipped her off.

Studying his own exotic birth certificate, Ethan stared at his father's name and summoned a vague memory of a tall man with brown hair. A feeling of great loss rose within him.

"I would never give up my son." He addressed his long-lost father. "You are as weak and pathetic as the wife who left you." He shoved the certificate back into the file next to Rachel's and slammed the file cabinet shut. As he headed out of his office, his gaze alighted on the framed photograph of Liam. Ethan veered off course to pick it up.

"Don't worry, son," he said to the sweetly smiling boy. "I will never stop searching for you."

~

Rachel awoke the next morning, surprised to find the sun shining brightly behind the lace curtains at her window. Disturbing dreams had kept her fitful all night, causing her to oversleep. She stretched in the old double bed, content to believe her dreams of Ethan bearing down on the ranch and driving an El Camino would never manifest into reality.

Sleeping in Saul's mother's bed gave Rachel an affinity for the woman. Turning her head, she met Melody Wade's dark gaze in one of the framed photographs. She and Melody had several things in common. They had both lost their husbands at an early age. They had both been left with sons to raise. Gazing at the cherubic, slant-eyed infant on Melody's lap, it was hard to see any resemblance between Melody's baby and the Navy SEAL who had rescued her. Saul had looked so innocent, so harmless.

Her thoughts flashed to the practiced way he'd emptied the array of weapons of their ammunition. Life had a way of hardening people.

Thinking of Saul made her feel guilty for lying in bed so late when she ought to be fulfilling her promise to fix up the house for selling. Rolling out of bed, she reached for the robe she had found in the closet, along with other clothing and a beaded, suede purse Saul said she could have, and went in search of him.

A peek into his old bedroom told her Liam was still sleeping. Saul wasn't in the living room where he'd spent the past two nights. His blanket sat neatly folded atop his pillow. Duke lay before the front door, the way he had at the motel when Saul had gone out.

He's running chores. Or maybe he was turning in all those rifles and shotguns, despite what he'd told her the night before. Backtracking to the office, she braved the creepy atmosphere to peer at the gun cabinet. It still held an arsenal of weapons, although none of them were loaded anymore, thank God.

Where had Saul gone? Rachel wandered to the kitchen and found a note sitting under the empty jar. Someone had set Liam's cricket free, but next to the jar was a sheet of paper with an elaborate sketch of the insect.

Picking it up, Rachel admired the lifelike drawing and remembered Blake telling her Saul was an amazing artist. He certainly was. Moreover, he seemed to care about the cricket's life, having set it free. A message had been written at the bottom of the sheet in a stylistic cursive she never would have expected from him.

· · ·

Gone to meet with the lawyer handling Cyril's estate. Back by noon. Don't work too hard. -S

She intended to work her very hardest. Putting down the drawing for Liam to see, she turned to eye the kitchen. Apart from a total renovation, she had done all she could do to make the kitchen more appealing. Half a dozen more projects awaited her in other parts of the house. In the walkup attic, there were household goods that needed to be sorted through, with the majority disposed of. Then, too, there was the living room where years of fires had left a layer of soot on the hearth's stone façade. Figuring a blackened fireplace could turn away even the most interested buyers, Rachel decided the attic could wait. She would tackle the hearth first.

Maybe her efforts would put a smile on Saul's face. Despite what he did for a living and despite his terse speech and his often-frightening demeanor, he was every bit the decent soul Blake had discerned him to be. Making Saul's life a little easier was the least she could do for him.

Sitting across from Cyril's estate lawyer, Saul read with jumbled emotions the letter the man had just handed him, along with the keys to Cyril's truck. The letter was written in Cyril's crude print.

Dear Saul,
I know you don't have fond memories of me. But a man comes to a point in life where he realizes the mistakes he made. I was told by my doctor I only have a few weeks to live. Death makes a man look back at all he's done in his life. I didn't treat you good, and I didn't do right by your mama neither. I'm sorry for all that. To make up for my wrongs, I'm leaving you the ranch because it belonged to your daddy first. It's only fair you should have it. I'm also leaving you anything and everything that's on the property. As for liquid assets, you're

the only son I ever had, so you get what's left in my bank account. It ain't a
fortune, but it's better off going to you than to my so-called friends who would
use it for evil. I just want you to know I'm sorry, and I hope you can forgive me.
Your stepdad,
Cyril

Saul looked up from the letter, still reeling.

"Let me guess. These so-called friends of his were white-supremacists."

The lawyer shrugged. "Couldn't say, though he was known to hang out with some real knuckleheads."

Saul pictured the names listed in the FOR Americans' documents.

"Cyril had me hold onto his truck keys so they wouldn't drive off with it the minute he died." The lawyer nodded at the set of keys in front of Saul.

Saul picked them up and pushed them into his pocket. "How much did he leave in liquid assets?"

"After subtracting my fees, there's about twenty-five thousand in cash. That's nontaxable in the state of Oklahoma."

Astonished, Saul remained mute. Twenty-five thousand was exactly the sum of money Rachel had estimated it would cost to renovate his home. Talk about coincidence. She wouldn't find out about it, though, lest she volunteer to oversee a renovation herself. While he liked having her around—liked it way too much—the best thing he could do for her was to get Cyril's truck in working order and send her on her way. Thanks to Cyril's association with the FOR Americans, Saul's home wasn't the safe place Rachel and Liam deserved.

Saul stared down at Cyril's letter, marveling how the man who'd ruined his teenage years and belonged to a hate group had requested his forgiveness. And he'd realized his racist cohorts weren't really friends. *"Death makes a man look back at all he's done in his life."*

"Where is Cyril buried?" Saul considered paying his respects.

Apparently, there'd been no room left for him in the tiny graveyard on his land.

"Park Grove Cemetery. Don't know if you knew this, but he was a veteran of the First Gulf War. The VA paid for his burial and gave him full military honors."

Saul had known. Cyril had reminded him of it constantly. *"You got it easy, boy. When I was hardly older'n you are, I had to walk through minefields in Iraq and watch my friends get blown up."* It occurred to Saul, with no small amount of irony, that he and Cyril had something in common, after all. He, too, had seen friends killed in battle.

"Do I need to sign something?" Saul asked, suddenly eager to leave.

The lawyer slid a packet of paper across his desk. "Everywhere there's a sticky note, I need your initials. Full signature on the last two pages."

Fifteen minutes later, Saul left the building relieved he'd gotten that task behind him. All that was left was to get the truck titled in his name—then make certain it was in fine running shape so his houseguests could start their new lives.

His thoughts went to Cyril's letter, tucked into the folder he carried. *Am I going to be like that, old and dying and regretting everything I've done in my life?*

Pushing into the Department of Public Safety minutes later, he was relieved to see only a handful of people present. Taking a ticket, he hoped he'd be called up soon, and then he lowered himself onto one of a dozen plastic seats in the waiting area.

As the man who'd come in after him went to get a ticket, Saul noted the policeman's uniform with an uneasy feeling. The cops in Oklahoma didn't get AMBER Alerts from Virginia, did they? He was thinking of leaving and coming back the next day, when the man turned around and noticed him. His face lit up with recognition.

The weight on Saul's chest increased.

"Holy cow, is that you, Half-Breed?" Andy Cannard came toward him with a welcoming smile and his hand extended. All five people in the office turned to witness their reunion.

CRY IN THE WILDERNESS

All Saul could do was act like everything was normal.

"Sure is, Duck." He tossed back Andy's junior high nickname, when students discovered *canard* meant "duck" in French. Then pushing to his feet, Saul received Andy's hearty handshake. Noticing the man's rank of sergeant, he couldn't help ribbing him.

"Since when did they let guys like you onto the force?"

Andy let loose with the same boisterous laugh Saul remembered. Popular with the girls and a total jock, he and Saul had moved in different circles. But Saul had plenty of teammates back home who reminded him of the policeman.

"Guys like *me*? Since when did they let guys like *you* into the SEAL Teams? That's what I want to know."

Saul cringed and glanced around to see if others were still listening.

"Oh, sorry," Andy said, seeing his reaction. "I forgot that's supposed to be a secret." He brushed his blunder aside and helped himself to the seat next to Saul's.

With an inner groan, Saul sat down, too.

"Now, let me guess." Andy pitched his voice thankfully lower. "You're here because old Cyril Lawson died."

Ten minutes later, Saul heard his number called. Dismayed by Andy's natural ability to make a person talk, he showed his former schoolmate his ticket and stood. Little wonder Andy was now a detective with the Broken Arrow Police.

"Nice talkin' to you."

Andy pointed a finger at him. "I'll be down to the ranch in a couple of days."

"I need three days at least to make the place presentable." Saul was already regretting having mentioned the squatter and the FOR Americans' literature. Now he had to hope Rachel and Liam would be safely on their way to Tulsa before Andy showed up at the ranch.

Shouldn't be a problem. In a few minutes, he would have the truck titled in his own name. Then he'd stop by the auto parts store on his way home and pick up what he needed to get the truck up and running that very night.

Heck, Rachel and Liam might be headed for Texas by the same time tomorrow. Strangely, the prospect of their departure in no way pleased him.

CHAPTER 7

"Whoa."

Saul's astonished expression when he walked through the front door made Rachel's herculean effort worthwhile.

She flushed with pleasure and stepped back to appreciate her own work. "Makes a huge difference, doesn't it?"

"Sure does. I can't remember the fireplace ever lookin' that clean." His gaze swung to her face, and a rare smile transformed his features. "Well, hey, Cinderella."

Realizing she had likely smudged her face, Rachel lifted a self-conscious hand to her cheek.

Saul promptly threw his head back and laughed, a sound that made her stomach cartwheel.

"You just made it worse." He shook his head and chuckled again. Then, faster than she would have liked, his humor faded. "Time to take a break."

He held up a brown paper bag clutched in one hand. In the other, he held a manila envelope.

"I brought us some of the best barbeque sandwiches you'll ever eat. Where's Liam?" he added, peering past her.

"He's still in the bedroom."

As if on cue, Liam wandered out of the back hall carrying a wooden box. He held it up for Saul to see. "Are these tools for whittling?"

Rachel tried to gauge Saul's reaction to her son digging through his stuff.

"Yep." A pained expression crossed his face. "Puca gave me those."

"Put the box back where you found it," Rachel instructed, certain Saul considered the contents too precious to be played with.

"But I want to learn to whittle," Liam protested, his shoulders falling.

"Not today." She started toward her son when Saul's words made her stop.

"If you help me get the truck running after lunch, I'll show you how to whittle afterward."

"Cool!" Liam's face lit up.

"Thank you," Rachel said, touched by his willingness to indulge her son. "We'll put the box here on the hearth for now." She took it from Liam. "It's time to wash hands. Saul brought us barbeque."

"Awesome. I love barbeque!"

As Liam scampered toward the bathroom, Rachel tugged the rubber gloves off her hands and followed Saul into the kitchen. He'd laid their bagged lunch and the envelope on the counter.

"So, you got the keys to the truck?" Oddly, the thought of continuing her journey to Texas did not excite her as much as she'd believed it would. She sought to rationalize her feelings. *I just hate leaving projects unfinished.*

Saul pulled a set of keys from his pocket and laid them by the envelope. "Yep. Cyril left them with his lawyer to keep his *so-called friends*—his words, not mine—from stealing it." He washed his hands at the sink. "Apparently, when Cyril found out he was sick, he had a lot of regrets, including who his friends were."

Rachel made a thoughtful sound. "That's got to make you hate him just a little bit less."

Saul stilled in the act of drying his hands. "I was thinking of visiting his grave some time. You know, pay my respects." He glanced at her for her reaction.

She smiled encouragingly. "I think you should."

Saul gestured at the envelope. "The title for the truck's in there. I went and signed the back already, figuring you'll want to trade it in for something more appropriate."

A sudden worry occurred to her. "You realize we're leaving a paper trail. If Ethan finds me, the title will lead him right to you."

Saul sent her a small, tight smile. "I pretty much accepted that risk when I picked you up at the park."

Guilt pinched the tops of her shoulders. "I don't think I understood what I was asking of you. I was just so focused on getting away. I'm sorry."

Saul's smile softened. "I'm not sorry."

With those touching words, he grabbed up their lunch and carried it to the table.

Ethan snatched up the phone ringing on his desk at work and snapped, "Captain O'Rourke, JAG Corps." Expecting a work-related call, it caught Ethan off guard to recognize the distinctive voice of Detective Mooney, Virginia Beach Police.

"We believe we have a lead," the man stated after identifying himself. "Your sister used the email client offered by her university to communicate with a woman named Shannon Johnson-Brown."

"Shannon Johnson-Brown," Ethan repeated, thinking the name sounded vaguely familiar.

"Any idea who she might be? Old school friend, perhaps? College roommate?"

"Rachel didn't go to a four-year institution. She married right out of high school. The name does sound familiar, though. I just don't know why."

"If you remember, give me a call right away."

Ethan could tell the man was about to hang up. "Can't you track the woman down by her IP address?"

"We did. Geolocation data suggests she's in Dallas, Texas. Did Rachel ever live in Dallas or visit someone there?"

Ethan cocked his head. "Not that I know of. When will you know more?"

"We're waiting on a court-appointed order. Google is proprietary and won't share their customer's information without an order."

"As soon as you know more, call me," Ethan exhorted, eliciting a slight pause on the other end.

"And you do the same, Captain." Mooney promptly hung up.

Ethan dropped the phone receiver gently in its cradle, then dragged his long-fingered hands over his face. *Shannon Johnson-Brown.* Why the devil did that name ring a bell?

Liam watched Saul tighten down the bolts keeping the new battery in place. Afternoon sunlight blazed through the cracks of the barn's western wall, laying a stripe of gold across the man's scarred knuckles.

"You ever work on your dad's truck, Lee?" Saul used Liam's new name.

Liam reflected on the past. "No," he admitted, but he was finding automotive work sort of interesting. Standing atop a footstool, he'd already helped Saul remove the old battery and put a new one in its place. When his hand slipped, he'd expected Saul to snap at him like Uncle Ethan used to do, but he hadn't done that—not yet, anyway.

"Truth is," Saul gave one last tug on the wrench and made a wry face, "this truck is older'n you are. It won't keep running if it's not maintained. That's gonna be your job," he added gravely.

Liam swallowed and sent a nervous glance at the components under the hood.

"So, let me teach you what you need to know." Saul put a grease-covered finger on a big round thing shaped like a cake. "This here's the carburetor."

Caurbraitor, Liam repeated the word in his head the way Saul pronounced it.

After unscrewing the nut on top of the carburetor, Saul lifted the lid and showed Liam the insides.

"This is the carburetor filter. Old filters get clogged. All this black stuff gums it up, and the engine can't breathe. When it starts to cough, you spray the filter with this." Saul bent toward the plastic bag at his feet and came up with a can. It had a thin straw stuck to the lid. Saul popped the straw into the spray hole, then gave the can a shake. He pointed the straw right at the filter and sprayed a light layer over it. "Here, you try." He handed the can to Liam. "Spray around the whole thing, but not too much."

Even standing on the footstool, Liam had to go up on his toes to reach the far side of the filter.

"A little more right there," Saul prompted instead of yelling at him. "Good job. Now, listen up." He held his hand out for the can and put the straw back on the lid. "I'm gonna put this filter cleaner in the tub behind the seat of the truck along with some other supplies and a tool kit."

"Okay." Liam watched Saul walk to the cab of the truck and flip the seat forward.

"Now, let's check the oil." Saul returned to stand before the engine. He twisted off a black cap and pulled out a long metal stick. "This is how you check if there's enough oil or if you need an oil change."

Liam stared with perplexity at the stick. It dawned on him Saul was saying "oil" and not "all."

"This old truck burns oil, so you gotta check the oil level at least once a week. Like this." Saul snatched up the rag that lay nearby, swiped the stick, then stuck it all the way in and out again. "The oil level ought to be between these marks."

He showed the stick to Liam. "What do you see?"

"There's not enough," Liam guessed.

"Right—10W-40," Saul stated, grabbing another item out of the plastic bag. He showed Liam the bottle, pointing to the number and letter combination he'd just said. "I'll leave this bottle plus an extra one behind the seat, along with the other stuff."

"Okay." Saul poured amber liquid through a funnel into the oil tank. As it went *gallup, gallup, gallup,* Liam slid his gaze up Saul's deeply tanned arm to his bulging bicep, made evident by his cut-off T-shirt. He remembered his father's arms being roped with muscle, too. But Daddy didn't have any tattoos.

Peering closer at the tattoo on Saul's upper arm, Liam realized the skulls were really skeletons wearing flowing clothing. And the one with long black hair was holding the littlest skeleton. His thoughts flashed to the graveyard sitting a few yards away, and suddenly he knew what the skeletons' names were.

"Something you want to ask me, Lee?"

Liam jerked his gaze up and met Saul's steady regard. Was he mad? Was he gonna yell at him?

"No, sir."

Saul stared at him with eyes that reminded Liam of the forest, all green and brown.

He licked his lips nervously. "I was just wondering if you missed your mom when she died."

Saul averted his face. It took him a while to answer.

"Sure, I missed her. Felt like a part of me was gone." When he looked back at Liam, his eyes were wet. "But nothing's gonna happen to your mama, Lee." He said it with so much certainty that Liam nodded in agreement. "And nothin' should've happened to your father, either."

At the mention of his father, Liam's throat ached.

"Blake was the best friend I ever had," Saul added quietly.

Tears pricked the backs of Liam's eyes. As Saul swallowed hard, it occurred to Liam that here was a man who knew exactly how it felt to lose a parent.

Clearing his throat forcefully, Saul put the oil stick into the hole one more time and showed it to Liam, who nodded his approval. Then Saul put the cap back on and tightened it. He reached into his pocket, then pulled out a key ring and extended it to Liam.

"Go ahead and start it."

Liam's eyes flew wide. "I've never done that before."

"There's a first time for everything. Use the key with the square head."

"Okay." With his heart beating faster, Liam stepped down from the footstool and went around the engine to climb up into the driver's seat, keeping the door open.

"Give it a turn," Saul called out, "and hold it there 'til the engine stays on."

Liam stuck the proper key into the ignition. With a held breath, he turned it the way he'd seen in movies. Both his parents' vehicles and Uncle Ethan's had push-button ignitions.

The engine gave a stuttering rumble before issuing a throaty roar. Liam snatched his hand from the ignition. *Cool.* A sense of accomplishment rushed through him. But then his heart sank. The truck was running, which meant they would leave for Dallas soon.

He didn't want to leave. Sure, it had been a little scary when they'd first arrived, with the stranger running out of the house and finding the little graveyard. But since then, Liam had thoroughly enjoyed himself. The sky was bigger here, and it was so quiet he'd heard a hawk screaming way up high. And in the evening, when the sun set and the whole sky turned orange, the prairie grass seemed like it was on fire.

No one demanded he read for hours and write until his fingers cramped. His mother didn't walk around looking half alive. The only scary thing here was Cyril's office. Liam hadn't ventured inside it since he'd picked up the pamphlet on the first day. Still, the thought of leaving for Dallas made his stomach hurt.

But then he remembered the previous night when Saul had chased those intruders away. He and his mom wouldn't be safe here unless

Saul stayed, too, and Saul couldn't do that. He worked for the military, just like his dad had.

With a shake of his head, Liam accepted the inevitable.

~

As Saul taught Liam how to whittle, Rachel went through the rooms of the house decluttering. People didn't realize it was hard to sell a house that looked like it belonged to someone else. The secret was to get rid of all personal items, making it possible for prospective buyers to imagine themselves living there.

With reluctance, she set the framed photos of Saul's family in a small box for him to take to Virginia Beach with him. Once decluttered, the house seemed a little better, but it was a long way from being staged. She had to reconcile herself to leaving the work she'd started here unfinished.

After storing other extraneous items in the attic and placing giveaway items outside in the barn, Rachel poured herself a glass of iced tea and went to stand at the screen door to watch Saul and Liam whittle on the stoop.

The setting sun had turned the sky a palette of colors, including gold, peach, and a beautiful violet hue. Between the sky and the red flowers—Saul called them Indian paintbrush—the view from the front of the house was downright picturesque. But the breeze wafting through the screen hinted of a chilly autumn, reminding her she needed to continue on her way to Dallas so Liam could enroll in a new school. Hopefully, his fake birth certificate would pass for a real one.

"Done." Liam held up the result of his handiwork. "Hey, Mom!" He sprang up the steps and brought it to her.

Rachel knew from eavesdropping earlier that Liam had been aiming to whittle a bobcat on his first go around.

"Aw, he's cute," she said, thinking privately the stumpy-legged creature resembled a woodchuck more than a bobcat. "Good job. And this was only your first try. You're going to get as good as Saul if you keep it up."

"Not if I don't have tools." Liam went suddenly still, staring down at his carvings. "We're leaving tomorrow, aren't we?" he demanded on a dejected note.

Rachel's chest tightened. Liam seemed even less eager to go than she was.

"I don't know, honey." Her gaze went over his shoulder to where Saul still sat on the steps, one ear cocked to their conversation. "Saul and I have to talk about that first."

"Can't we stay until I've seen a bobcat?"

"That's not a choice we have, honey." She pitched her voice low, unwilling for Saul to feel obliged to host them any longer. "Why don't you take your shower now, and then you can sit on the porch tonight with a flashlight and search for animals. Can I keep your carving?" She held out her hand.

He plopped it onto her palm and headed wordlessly into the house.

With a silent sigh, Rachel turned to finalize plans with Saul.

"Can you turn out the porch light?" he requested as she pushed open the screen door.

"Sure." Wondering why he wished to sit in the dark, she reached back in and turned off the light, then joined him on the steps, sitting in the spot Liam had vacated. The box of tools between them kept them two feet apart.

Saul was staring up at the darkening sky.

"Are you looking at the moon?" she asked, glimpsing the platinum disk just above the trees.

"Stars. Keep your eyes peeled," he said in a relaxed voice she had rarely heard him use. "This is the only place in the world where they blink on all at once. It's gonna happen any second."

Intrigued, she gazed up at the darkening heavens and waited for the first sign of a twinkle.

"Now," Saul said.

A second later, the light of a thousand stars pierced the denim canvas to spangle the expanse above them.

"Wow," Rachel exclaimed with astonished pleasure.

"Yeah."

"It's so beautiful here. Don't you think?" She hoped he would give his home a second chance before selling it.

It took him a long time to answer. "Reckon it is."

"You were right about Liam liking it here."

Out the corner of her eye, she saw Saul's head turn. "What about you? You like it, too?"

Was he asking for a reason? "I feel safe here. Apart from that hate group wanting to get the firearms in Cyril's office." She wished she hadn't mentioned them as Saul's gaze went to the curve in the driveway where the El Camino had idled.

Silence fell between them, interrupted only by the symphony of crickets that increased in volume as the sky darkened.

Saul broke in abruptly. "You ever wonder if you're gonna regret your whole life when death comes knockin'?"

The question startled Rachel until she realized where it came from. "You said that's what happened to your stepfather."

"Yep." Saul stared up at the night sky. "He wrote me a letter and left it with the lawyer. Said he was sorry for the way he treated me."

Rachel tried to gauge Saul's reaction. "Isn't that a good thing?"

His thoughts seemed a million miles away. "Yeah. Makes me wonder, though, if I'm going to be like him one day."

The fear underlying Saul's words kept Rachel quiet a moment. "I hope you never regret helping me and Liam get away."

Turning his head, Saul caught and held her gaze. "No. That's one thing I know I won't regret."

As they exchanged smiles, warmth flowed through Rachel. "Should we leave tomorrow?" she asked, saddened by the prospect.

His own smile faded. "The day after. I want to show you something first."

"Show me what?" she asked, intrigued.

"A place in the woods, a special place with lots of cedar trees. Liam could find himself a big hunk of cedar to take to Dallas with him. Not many cedar trees there, I don't imagine."

The comment depressed her. "I'd better buy him some whittling tools, then."

"No need." Saul patted the box between them. "He can have these."

"But they're your tools, Saul. Puca gave them to you."

"I want Blake's son to have them."

Before she offended him with her refusal, Rachel leaned over the box and kissed Saul's cheek.

"Thank you," she whispered, startled by her impulse but not regretting it.

He regarded her, frozen. Then he abruptly stood and started off the stoop.

"Gonna take a walk," he tossed over his shoulder.

Watching his silhouette retreat down the driveway, his head bowed, his fingers in the pockets of his jeans, Rachel asked herself if her chaste kiss had upset him or whether he was still pondering his stepfather's letter. Or was he still worried about regretting his whole life when death came knocking?

Putting herself into his shoes, she shuddered to imagine how it must feel to have snuffed out so many lives, whether ordered to or not. It wasn't like he'd been personally motivated to murder his targets. Eliminating threats was his job. He did it to keep his country safe. Surely God would take that into account when Saul finally went to meet his maker.

Help him make peace with You, Father. Then she stood up with the toolbox and headed back into the house with it. At the door, she flipped on the porch light so Saul could find his way home.

CHAPTER 8

"Shouldn't Duke stay here and guard the house?" Rachel asked as they started down the steps the following morning. Liam ran ahead of them with Duke on a leash.

Saul glanced over at her. "No one's going to break into the house with my car parked out front," he said, reading her mind.

Liam slowed and turned around. "Which way from here?"

"Just wait for us," Saul called back. "I'll take this," he said to Rachel before lifting the backpack she'd filled for their picnic off her shoulder.

"Thanks."

As he slung it over his own shoulder, her gaze alighted briefly on the flexing muscles of his deltoids. Wresting her gaze from the muscular SEAL to her son, she found him hopping up and down, eager to get to the secret spot Saul wanted to show them. The grin on Liam's face made her glad she'd agreed to stay another day.

Saul had given her son a small saw to carry. Over breakfast, they'd discussed the best wood for harvesting. Even though green wood was optimal because it was softer, Saul explained they couldn't go lopping off parts of living trees without hurting them. They would search for a felled limb and cut it down to size.

Saul pointed as they neared the boy. "Head toward those trees."

Following Saul's cue, they left the driveway to walk through the tall grass. The midmorning sun shone warmly on Rachel's back. The rustle of prairie grass as it brushed their knees seemed to whisper words of freedom. Savoring the feeling, she identified the trees by their leaves as they approached them.

When they stepped into the forest's shade, Rachel was struck by the silence. Cooler weather had thinned the canopy so sunlight broke through here and there, casting golden pools on the forest floor. She'd experienced a similar atmosphere in an ancient cathedral in Rome, which she and Blake had visited on their honeymoon. Sorrow tugged at her, as she remembered thinking they had their whole lives ahead of them.

Focusing back on Liam, Rachel caught him trying to imitate Saul's gliding walk. No doubt her son wished he could walk in boots without making a sound.

All at once, Saul stilled and put a finger to his lips. Then he cupped his ear.

Rachel strained to hear something. "A creek?" She detected the rippling sound of water.

Saul nodded, then continued making his way toward it. They followed immediately behind him, eyes peeled for something special. Duke kept his nose to the ground.

A carpet of ferns sprang up beneath their feet. The trees thinned up ahead, and the rush of water grew louder. Abruptly they came upon the creek, rippling over red clay and gray rock. Only ten feet across at its widest point and maybe two or three feet deep, it fed the thirsty roots of the bald cypress standing at the water's edge surrounded by its own knobby knees. Its leaves had turned a rusty color, matching the clay of the streambed.

"Over here." Saul waved them over to a large, flat rock that jutted into the water. It provided the perfect vantage for basking in filtered sunlight.

Rachel examined the clearing with wonder, as both Liam and the dog leaped onto the rock.

"Can I go in?" her son asked her.

Rachel checked to see whether Saul might object.

"Sure. Take the dog off the leash first. He won't go anywhere."

"Awesome!" Liam freed the dog, then plopped down on the rock to wrestle off his shoes.

Duke stepped boldly off the rock and into the water. It went up to his shoulders, letting Rachel know the water wasn't deep.

"Best keep an eye out for crawdads," Saul warned as Liam whipped his shirt off. "They'll pinch your toes if you step on 'em."

Liam's confounded expression made Saul chuckle.

"You mean crayfish?" The boy put a tentative foot down.

"Out here, they're crawdads."

"Oh, it's cold!" Liam hugged his scrawny chest while wading toward the middle of the stream.

"You goin' in, too?" Saul stepped back ashore to set the backpack by a tree.

She was tempted to. Part of her wanted to revel in this little slice of heaven, splashing in the shallow creek with Liam, Duke, and Saul. But something deep inside insisted it was time to withdraw emotionally. She didn't want to feel even a portion of the loss she had felt upon Blake's death.

"I think I'll just watch from this rock."

He sent her a searching gaze. "Suit yourself."

As she lowered herself onto the smooth sandstone, Saul removed his gun and holster, then stripped off his belt with a fluid tug. As he peeled off his shirt next, her mouth went dry at the sight of his broad, tan back. Then he turned around. Having only seen his chest in dim lighting, it came as a shock to note the array of nicks and scars marring his smooth muscles. The reminder of his dangerous career sobered her instantly. His world and hers would never collide again after tomorrow, would it?

She tore her gaze away to watch Liam stalk some small creature in the shallows. Duke was out of the water now, snuffling on the far bank.

"You're gonna get hot there." Saul waded into the water.

"I know." She could hear in his voice the invitation to join him. But she couldn't, not without leaving behind a piece of herself. She couldn't afford that. She had fought long and hard to strengthen her self-reliance. Starting tomorrow she would be facing the world on her own, with no Saul to lean on. The thought alone terrified her. *God will see me through. He always has.*

"I'll be fine here," she insisted.

Saul waded into the chilly water. Why did Rachel feel the need to keep aloof? He could only surmise she was worried about leaving the next day. Honestly, she wasn't the only one. When he pictured what it would be like working on the house all alone, panic gripped him. Hadn't he asked her to stay another day just to avoid being alone?

"Whatcha got there?" he asked as Liam waded toward him with his hands cupped together.

"It's a fish." Liam came closer. His eyes glinted with mischief, reminding Saul suddenly of Blake. "Gotta keep him wet. See?" The boy's hands sprang open.

Saul flinched as chilly stream water sprayed him.

As Liam threw back his head and laughed with glee, Saul gave a mock growl and flung water back at him. The boy's shriek brought the dog plunging back into the water, dousing all of them, even Rachel who gasped and moved to a dry spot.

The horseplay continued for several more minutes. Then Liam clambered from the stream and put his shoes back on. "I'm going to go look for wood," he declared.

"You want me to come with you?" Saul asked him.

"Nope. I gotta find it by myself this time."

"Okay," Saul said, struck by the boy's resolve.

"Stay within sight of us, honey."

"I will." Liam snatched up the saw and began combing the shoreline for fallen limbs. Duke regarded him a moment, then decided to follow.

Rachel lay across the rock on her stomach, trailing her fingers into the water, then scooping out a handful to dribble it on her neck. The curves of her body filled Saul with sudden longing. He suffered a crazy impulse to lie down next to her.

All at once she lifted her head and caught him staring.

"If you forgive your stepfather," she picked up their conversation from the previous evening, "then your own sins will be forgiven."

He stared at her, perturbed to learn his sins were weighing on her mind. "How do you know that?" In lieu of lying down next to her, he sat on the rock, not far away.

"It's in the Bible." She gazed out at the water as if thinking of the exact words. "'For if you forgive men their trespasses, your heavenly Father will also forgive you.'"

As he pondered the passage, she seemed to wait for his response.

"What if you don't forgive men their trespasses?" Memories of all the hurtful words Cyril had unleashed on him, all the hardship he'd been forced to endure, panned through his head.

Rachel swallowed and put her head down. "I think you can figure that out," she said, softly.

Saul ran his fingertips over the smooth surface of the rock next to him. He would have preferred to run them over the soft line of Rachel's back. Her shirt had ridden up at the waist, exposing an inch of cream-colored skin that made him want to discover if it was as soft as it looked.

"You should forgive him," she prompted with her eyes shut.

He absorbed her recommendation with a deep breath, then let it out. What would happen if he did forgive Cyril?

For fourteen years, following the two and a half years it had taken to become a SEAL and then a sniper, he had set his crosshairs on a target and pictured Cyril's face. Without that hatred still burning in his gut, could he even pull the trigger?

Perhaps not. And then what? He was The Grim Reaper, after all, a man whose destiny it was to walk the crooked path. If he didn't terminate *narcos* and deadly terrorists, what would he do instead? Become a rancher like his father? Hardly. The thought of beating his blade, so to speak, into a plowshare was ludicrous. Not even God could forgive Saul's sins as easily as that.

"Hey, I think I found something!"

"Okay, wait. Don't cut it yet," Saul called back. Glad for an excuse not to have to justify himself to Rachel, he pulled his feet out of the water and went to put his boots back on.

~

"I love it here," Liam declared, half an hour later.

The unguarded statement robbed Rachel of her contentment as the three of them sat together on the flat rock enjoying their picnic of sandwiches and apples. Saul and Liam had come back with a large hunk of cedar cut from a sheared limb. Liam kept it on his lap throughout the picnic, using it as a tray.

"I like it here, too," Rachel agreed with her son. "Thank you, Saul, for asking us to stay another day."

He nodded and turned away.

Rachel's stomach tightened with concern. Since urging Saul to forgive his stepfather, he'd lapsed into a brooding silence. Perhaps she had overstepped her bounds. It was none of her business whether he chose to let go of his tragic past or not. And yet, with her whole heart, she wanted Saul to be happy, to experience the peace that came from knowing he was forgiven and loved. There was only one way to do that, as far as Rachel knew, and that was to forgive and forget, as she'd done regarding the men responsible for Blake's death.

But telling Saul how to come to terms with his past wasn't her place. That was something he would have to realize on his own. Given his withdrawal since mentioning forgiveness, he wasn't about to take her advice anytime soon.

"We should probably head back to the house," she announced as their picnic petered to a close.

"Aw, why?" Liam protested.

Her heart hurt for her son. If only he could return to this place whenever he felt like it.

"I have to write a list for Saul about what still needs work before he puts the house on the market."

"And I gotta get to Lowe's and buy a new window for the office," Saul said, backing her up.

"Can I go with you?" Liam asked him.

They both looked to Rachel for permission. Picturing the El Camino rolling up while they were gone she answered, "If that's okay with Saul, but Duke stays with me."

"Deal," Liam said, like it was his decision.

Bemused and a little worried that Liam's evident attachment to Saul would make their departure even harder, Rachel started to put their things away. Liam clipped the leash back on the dog as Saul slid his belt back on, reattaching his gun and holster.

"All right, Lee," Saul said, giving the boy a nod. "See if you and Duke can retrace our tracks. Go on ahead of us."

Liam lit up at the challenge. "Okay."

"You can do it, honey," Rachel added, confident he would find his way. She quickly zipped up her pack.

Saul, looking at her like he wanted to say something, caught her arm.

Facing him squarely, her pulse quickened at the realization they were suddenly alone in this idyllic setting. Her thoughts flashed back to the kiss she'd planted on Saul's cheek the previous evening. He wasn't thinking of following it up with a less-than-chaste one, was he?

With the realization she hoped he was going to do exactly that, she wet her lips with a dart of her tongue.

Saul lifted a hand, catching the side of her face with a gentleness that surprised her. Rachel's breath hitched. As he stroked the curve of her cheek, she could feel the calluses on his fingers that came from cradling a rifle.

"I'll never forget this day," he told her in a gruff voice.

Her eyes began to sting. "Me neither," she whispered.

His jaw muscles jumped as he worked to form his next statement. "And thanks for caring about my immortal soul," he added with quiet intensity. "But I'm pretty sure it's past redemption."

The words affirmed what she'd guessed earlier. Dismay tugged at her. "No, Saul. There's no such thing as past redemption."

He sent her a cynical smile. "If you say so, Angel."

With that, he dipped his head and dropped the world's gentlest kiss on her lips. While still chaste, it nonetheless conveyed a deep-seated hunger.

"I'll keep your advice about forgiveness in mind." Releasing her chin, he then took the pack from her motionless fingers, flung it over his shoulder, and took her free hand.

Bemused that Saul was holding her hand and clearly didn't intend to let it go, Rachel fell into step alongside him as they left the stream behind.

We're friends. We'll always be friends, regardless of how many miles stand between us.

Wishing things could be different, that they could stay there with him forever, was a waste of time. Saul was going back to the Beach when his leave was over. She and Liam were headed to Dallas tomorrow.

But she would cherish the memory of this day for the rest of her life.

∼

With Liam sitting in the seat next to him, his short hair ruffling in the breeze that blew through the open windows, Saul pointed the old Ford toward town while listening to its engine for potential issues. They roared up the country road, trailing a spume of smoke behind them. The truck burned oil, all right, but it would get Rachel to where she wanted to go.

His stomach hollowed out at the recollection they were taking off the very next day.

I should not have kissed her. He eased off the gas at the edge of town. People and cars were out in full force on this early autumn evening. Yet he felt lonelier than ever, even with Liam riding shotgun.

He'd just wanted her to know how special she'd become to him, like a beacon of light in his bleak and stormy existence. His angel, not only Blake's widow.

Still, tomorrow, he would send her and Liam off to beat back the wolves on their own. He couldn't protect them forever as he wished he could. Uncle Sam owned him, at the very least for another year, maybe five if he chose to reenlist again. Twenty years of service gave him benefits for life.

There was no way around it. Tomorrow, they would say good-bye.

As they neared Lowe's, Saul's gaze alighted on a cell phone store across the street. Verizon was the company he used for his own cell service. Rachel ought to have a mobile phone of her own, not just to make traveling safer, but to keep in touch with him. *Yes.* The ability to do that eased the weight pressuring his chest.

He parked the old truck and took the boy into the store with him, where he relied on Liam to identify the type of mobile Rachel had carried before she dropped it over the side of the canoe.

By the time the two of them returned to the ranch with a cell phone and brand-new window, the sky was dark. Rachel, Saul was glad to see, had drawn closed the curtains in the living room. He hurried into the house with Liam on his heels, only to be greeted by Duke like they'd been gone a month. With a spurt of worry, Saul called Rachel's name.

She emerged from the back hallway carrying a pen and notepad.

"That took longer than half an hour."

"I know." He regretted the time spent away from her. "I'm sorry. Any issues?"

"No, just checking my list to see if I forgot something."

Saul handed Liam the box with her new phone in it and gestured for him to give it to his mother.

"What's this?" she asked as Liam held it out to her.

"Open it," her son urged, grinning.

Rachel lifted the lid and gasped. "It's a cell phone!"

"I put it on my plan so we can stay in touch," Saul explained.

"But..." Her eyes clouded with concern.

He knew what she was thinking. They were leaving a paper trail for Ethan. He honestly didn't care.

"Thank you," she said, swallowing her objection. "It's the same model I used to have."

"I picked it out," Liam informed her proudly. "It has unlimited data, so we don't need to find Wi-Fi. Maybe I can download some games from the app store," he suggested hopefully.

"Of course we can," Rachel answered, exploring the phone's features. She lifted her gaze abruptly. "You're already in my contact list."

Saul had entered his information first thing. "That okay with you?" His face heated.

"That's perfect. Thank you. Having this will really help me launch my business. Speaking of which—" She held up the notepad she'd written on. "I'd like to go over my list with you."

"Fire away." He stepped close enough to tell she'd washed her hair. The yellow sundress she was wearing must have come from his mother's closet, although he couldn't remember her ever wearing it.

Rachel showed him the notebook. "There are two columns. This one is for the quick and dirty version, the other for a total renovation."

"Walk me through the first list," Saul replied, earning a grimace of acceptance.

As she walked him around the kitchen, telling him what appealed to buyers and what didn't, Saul trailed behind her, inhaling her clean vanilla scent and memorizing the graceful way she gestured as she spoke.

"...after you take down the blinds in the kitchen windows."

"Wait, what's wrong with them?" Saul realized he'd missed whatever she'd said.

"They date the kitchen," she said apologetically, "as do the cabinets, the counters, and the floors. Still, if you're not doing a total reno, at least give buyers a view of the land through the windows."

"Ah." He acknowledged her point, but as long as the skinheads were lurking, the blinds would stay put.

"You'll want to oil the faces of these cabinets, too, but most importantly, you must replace this sink."

Saul eyed the lime-stained metal sink. She had a point.

"Wait, I'll show you what the new one should look like." After pulling the new cell phone from the pocket of her dress, she typed with her thumbs as she spoke to him. "Search for a farmhouse sink with an apron front. It looks like...this." She showed him a picture she'd found online.

"That would fit well in here."

"It does cost a bit, though," she murmured with a frown. "Maybe Lowe's sells them cheaper."

Guilt burned in Saul for not mentioning the twenty-five thousand dollars sitting in his bank account. He considered telling her, then changed his mind, knowing she would push for a total renovation. He didn't have the time for that, nor the patience to hunt down a local contractor he could trust. Instead of fessing up, he trailed Rachel into the living area where she encompassed the rest of the room with a wave.

"This area is your selling point. You'll want to repaint the room and resurface the floor. Then steam-clean this rug and all the others in the house. You can rent cleaners at most hardware stores. Last but not least, buy four throw pillows in the same rich burgundy that's in the rug." She pointed toward the mantel. "And put a big mirror up there instead of that oil painting. You can find good but affordable ones at consignment shops. Most importantly, though, tell your Realtor to strike a fire in the hearth before showing the house, so it looks all cozy in here."

He pictured a fire in the hearth and Rachel snuggled up with him on the sofa. *Never going to happen*, he realized, sadly.

"Now the bedrooms," she declared, unaware of his thoughts.

Fifteen minutes later, Saul could not deny Rachel had an eye for details that would serve her well in her intended field. He could picture each room as she described it, with the walls freshly painted and the rugs more vibrant. Since the day of their arrival, his mother's room had been slowly transformed.

The framed family photographs had been boxed for him to take home. A pastel comforter found up in the attic had taken the place of the dusty quilt. A pair of flowered prints matched the antique pitcher and bowl that graced the antique washstand by the bathroom door. Atop his mother's mirrored bureau, a silver tray held a pink perfume atomizer that unified the color scheme. It didn't feel like the same room at all, a fact that made it easier for him to linger longer than five seconds.

"So, you'll work on the short list at least, right?" She handed him the notepad.

He weighed the list against the time he still had left of his leave. "I'll try."

As their gazes caught and held, she sent him a sad smile. "I'm really going to miss this place."

I'll miss you, too. The words stuck in his throat.

"Excuse me." With those whispered words, Rachel hurried from the room.

Saul watched her go. Did she merely feel scared about leaving for Dallas or had she perhaps developed feelings for him? Was that even possible? She had loved Blake with every fiber of her being. She couldn't possibly have feelings like that for a rough-edged loner like himself.

We've gotten used to each other. Once she's gone, I'll get used to that, too.

CHAPTER 9

*R*achel awakened to the now-familiar crowing of the Goodner's rooster. Her first thought as she turned her gaze toward the sunlight shining through the lace curtains was, *Today we leave for Dallas.* The realization kept her paralyzed in bed, strangely reluctant to get up.

From her first phone call with her birth mother, she'd known they were meant to reconnect. God had planned it all along. So why, now that the day had finally come for them to meet, was she filled with trepidation?

A passage from the book of Joshua came to mind, even though she couldn't remember it exactly. *Be strong and courageous! Do not be afraid or give up for the Lord your God is with you wherever you go.* Feeling encouraged, she tossed back the covers and got out of bed.

It took them all morning to pack. Saul had gifted them the two rolling suitcases brought down from the attic. He had encouraged her to fill the larger one with anything of his mother's that had caught her fancy. Liam, too, had been told to take as many memoirs from Saul's old room as his mother agreed to, including several of Saul's carvings and the knee-high moccasins.

As they crammed more and more items into their bags, Saul busied himself with replacing the window in Cyril's office.

It was just after noon by the time Rachel realized she was putting off the inevitable. Using her new cell phone, she let Shannon know they were on their way. Her birth mother's excitement provided some much-needed motivation. All the same, Rachel's feet dragged as she pulled her suitcase into the hallway and paused to gaze upon the room she'd slept in for the past week. Sunlight lay in a bright triangle across the comforter.

She forced herself to turn away. "Honey, are you ready?"

Peeking into Saul's old bedroom, she found Liam sitting disconsolately on the lower bunk and staring at the dog, who slept on his rug. Without a word, Liam stood, grabbed the handle of his suitcase, and pushed past her, tugging it toward the front door. The dog scrambled up and followed him.

A glance into Cyril's study showed a brand-new window admitting sunlight into the previously dismal office. *Much better.* Now all Saul needed to do was throw out the piles of propaganda and paperwork— why he hadn't done that yet confused her. He also needed to turn the firearms over to the police and clean the stained rug.

Trailing Liam and Duke through the living room, she spotted Saul, who'd avoided her all morning, peering under the hood of the truck as the engine rumbled. He'd parked it beside his Camaro, its front end pointed down the driveway.

Liam went down on his knees at the door to hug Duke good-bye. He raised bloodshot eyes at her.

"Can we come back here and visit sometime?"

The question caught Rachel off guard. "Um, I don't know, honey. Saul wants to sell this place."

"Why?"

The answer was too complicated to explain. "I really don't know."

After climbing to his feet, Liam grabbed his bag and thrust through the screen door, dragging his bag behind him. Rachel followed more sedately, while keeping the dog inside.

As they emerged, Saul shut the hood of the truck with a *clang*. With a closed expression, he crossed to the stoop and grabbed Liam's suitcase, swinging it to the ground for him. Scowling, Liam snatched it back and lugged it over the gravel toward the vehicle.

Saul watched him a second, then came up the steps to help Rachel with her suitcase. As they walked to the truck together, she glanced sideways, searching him for signs of the same emotions she and Liam were both feeling, but Saul avoided eye contact. He heaved her suitcase into the truck bed while Liam struggled on the other side to do the same with his.

As Saul went back to the porch for the toolbox, Rachel stepped up into the driver's seat and put her new cell phone in the cupholder. Liam slammed shut the door next to him. Saul appeared at his open window and stuck the toolbox through it.

"Put this at your feet."

Liam wordlessly complied, and Saul spun away. As he walked behind the truck, kicking the rear tires, it dawned on Rachel that perhaps he was hiding his true feelings. He had to be dreading staying here alone without them.

Dwarfed by the size of the truck, Rachel adjusted both her seat and all the mirrors. No thanks to her brother, it had been over a year since she had driven any vehicle, and never a truck as big as this one.

Saul appeared at her window. "You want to take a test drive first?"

"No, I think I'm okay." *Just rip the Band-Aid off.*

She shifted her gaze past him to the porch and the pots she had meant to fill with flowers.

"You remember what I said about the oil level and the carburetor, Lee?" Saul asked her son.

Liam stared at his knees and nodded.

With a sigh, Saul shifted his attention to Rachel. Her breath caught at the banked emotion in his eyes. Their departure was distressing him, too.

"I overlooked the porch when I made my list," she said, postponing their departure another minute to instruct him on what to do. "You

137

should buy several chrysanthemums, all different colors, and put them in the pots. It'll make the entrance much more welcoming. Buyers will love it."

"Okay," he said without even glancing behind him.

"Wouldn't hurt to buy a couple of Adirondack chairs, too, if you can afford them. You'd have to get them delivered since you won't have the truck."

It had to be obvious she was stalling. He stuck his arm through the window, drawing her attention to the dash.

"So, the gas tank's full." He pointed to the gauge. "You shouldn't have to stop for gas. It's only a four-and-a-half-hour drive. The PikePass right there on your windshield will get you through the tolls. I just linked it to my debit card."

She shook her head, amazed by his generosity. Moreover, his thoroughness touched her.

"Thank you," was all she could offer.

"You're welcome. Keep an eye on the temperature indicator here. The truck burns oil, so if it's running hot, that means you need more oil. Lee's gonna check the level every week." He earned a glance from her son. "Do you have the title?" He returned his attention to her.

"Yes." She'd put it in her suitcase.

"Good. Don't be afraid to sell her and get yourself a smaller ride."

"I won't," she promised.

"Gonna use your cell phone for navigation?"

She plucked it out of the cupholder and showed him the open app. "Waze says I'll get there in four hours and twenty-five minutes."

"And your mom knows you're coming?"

"I just called her. Told her I'd be there before six."

"All right then." He thumped the side of her door and stepped back. "Drive safe, now."

So, no good-bye kiss. What did she expect, especially in front of Liam? Nevertheless, she was disappointed. She wanted to memorize Saul's appearance so she would never forget him. A hank of hair fell over his deep-set hazel eyes.

"Can I take your picture?" She blurted the question, adding, "so I don't forget you?"

SEALs didn't like their picture taken.

Saul's eyebrows pulled together. "I guess." He gave a jerky shrug.

Sensing her question had made him uncomfortable, she snapped a quick succession of photos with her new phone, wondering all the while if she would ever see him again. He'd been Blake's closest friend. It almost felt like she was losing Blake all over again. A lump swelled in her throat as she put her phone back in the cupholder.

"Good-bye, Saul."

He nodded his reply.

With a tug on the gear shifter, she put the truck into drive and transferred her foot to the gas pedal. The truck lurched forward with a throaty rumble. The wheels churned over gravel. Tears stung Rachel's eyes as she pulled away. At the curve in the driveway, her gaze went to the rearview mirror. Saul stood where the truck had been, watching them leave.

In that moment, she realized this had to be even worse for him than it was for Liam and her. For the first time since his homecoming, Saul would be all alone with no one around to distract him from his memories.

Comfort him, Lord.

CHAPTER 10

Saul stashed his SIG under the seat, stepped out of his Camaro, and strode toward the police station, eager to turn over the rifles and shotguns now lying in his trunk. He'd wrapped all of them, save the small hunting rifle that had belonged to Cyril, in a blanket, making it feasible to carry them together, but he couldn't walk into the station with an armful of firearms. Someone with authority would have to come out and collect them.

Tamping down the loneliness that welled in him in the wake of Rachel and Liam's departure, he pushed open a heavy glass door and found himself in a foyer buzzing with activity.

Unwilling to join the line of people standing before the information desk, he decided to locate Andy and enlist his help. Spotting Cannard's name and room number mounted to a placard, Saul ventured down a hall in search of his office. At the end of the hallway, he realized he must have passed the room and turned around. His gaze lit on a billboard covered in BOLO—Be on the Lookout—flyers and a terrible thought occurred to him.

Saul slowed his step. Surely the same flyer he'd been handed at the border between Virginia and Tennessee hadn't been disseminated all over the country, had it? He searched the dozens of posters, not seeing anything that struck him as familiar until, suddenly, there it was. Rachel and Liam's old photographs were right there for anyone to see, along with the composite sketch of himself, the man wanted in association with their disappearance.

Not good. Saul's heart began to thud. He glanced around to see if anyone was staring at him. Several people walked by him without paying him any attention. All the same, he reconsidered what he was about to do. He hadn't had a goatee as a teenager. His hair had been much longer. But what about his mouth and his nose? The sketch depicted both perfectly. He'd grown up in this town. The people here knew him. Even with his eyes concealed by his cap, they could hazard an accurate guess as to whom the sketch depicted. He considered ripping it off the billboard, but someone might see him do that. Plus, there were always cameras in police stations.

With his mouth dry, Saul made the decision to turn around and walk casually out of the building. He turned around and strolled back down the hall, running smack into a woman as she stepped out of an open door.

"Excuse me," he said, intending to keep on going.

Her eyes flew wide with recognition. "Saul Wade? Is that you?"

He blinked and stared, trying to come up with a name.

"Bethany Sauers," she supplied, summoning the memory of a plain, freckled girl who'd knocked out a bully on the playground once. "We went to high school together."

"I remember. Sorry, you look different," he said, justifying his memory loss.

"I hope so," she drawled with an eye roll. "What brings you here?"

"I was just leaving, actually." He could still see the composite sketch of himself in his peripheral vision.

"Andy told me he'd run into you. Why don't you come in and say hi to him?" She gestured toward the doorway from which she'd just emerged.

"I, uh, I can't right now. But could you pass along a message to him?"

"Of course." She perked up, eager to get all of it.

"Let him know he's welcome to come by my place and check out the, uh, the propaganda and paperwork I told him about."

Her expression turned quizzical. "Okay. I'll tell him right now. You're sure you can't do it yourself? His office is right here in the Command and Control Room."

No wonder Saul hadn't been able to find it. "No, I gotta run. Just remembered I forgot to leave water for my dog."

"Okay." Given her expression, she didn't believe his lame excuse.

Saul didn't care. He turned and headed for the exit as fast as he possibly could without raising suspicion.

Holy cow! His likeness was hanging on a billboard in the Broken Arrow Police Station.

Thank God, though, that Rachel and Liam were gone and no one but the folks at the phone store had laid eyes on Liam. He, himself, would be gone in a few more days, after he put a respectable dent in the list Rachel had left for him. That reminded him—he needed to stop by Lowe's again to buy several gallons of paint.

"My cedar!" Liam cried out, suddenly. They were the first words he'd spoken since leaving the ranch twenty minutes earlier. "I left my cedar on the porch. We have to go back for it!"

Rachel had just merged onto the toll road that would take them toward Oklahoma City and the Texas border. She peered into the rearview mirror.

"Maybe Saul put it in the back."

Liam strained against his seatbelt to search the bed of the truck. "It's not there. We have to go back for it." His voice frayed with emotion.

"We've driven for twenty minutes already. We can't just turn around and go back." Saying goodbye a second time wouldn't be any better than the first.

Liam faced forward again, clearly overwrought. "We'll never find cedar in the city. I'll never whittle again." Averting his face, he hid the tears she guessed were in his eyes.

Rachel's heart ached for him. If the wood meant that much to him, why shouldn't she go back for it? It wouldn't inconvenience anyone but her mother if they arrived in Dallas one hour later than expected. Shannon would understand, especially once Rachel called her to explain. The last thing Liam needed right then was one more reason to hate where they were going.

"You know what?" Rachel put on her blinker and headed toward the upcoming exit. "Let's go back and get the cedar."

Liam wiped his face and regarded her hopefully. "Really?"

"Really. I want you to carve something special with it."

"Thank you." He sagged back against his seat, seeming relieved.

Rachel took in his solemn and resigned expression. Would he ever be as happy as he was at Saul's ranch? For that matter, would she ever be as happy, either?

What had seemed like an hour of driving in one direction felt like only ten minutes driving the other way. Rachel guided the old truck up the pitted driveway. She ought to have added "Fill the potholes" on her list of things to do. The rough track could turn away even the most intrepid buyers.

Mixed emotions gripped her at the prospect of seeing Saul again, if only momentarily. The trees gave way to grass. Peering over the tall blades, disappointment knifed through her at the realization his Camaro was gone. Saul wasn't home.

It's for the best. It would probably stress him out to learn they'd made no progress whatsoever in getting to their destination. As she slowed before the house, she spotted Liam's lump of wood sitting on the porch where they'd left it the previous afternoon. She could also hear Duke inside the house, barking his head off.

"Hop out and get your wood, honey." She pushed the gear into park.

"Why's Duke barking like that?"

"He probably knows it's us." The poor dog would so miss having her son around.

Liam pushed out of the truck, leaving his door open, and ran up to the porch to retrieve the lump. All at once, two young men came around the corner of the house, and Rachel gasped. Fear gripped her as she realized by their closely shaved heads they were likely members of the FOR Americans, here to collect their firearms. No wonder Duke was barking so insistently.

"Liam, get back here!"

He turned on the porch with the hunk of cedar in his arms. Spotting the men, he froze.

The twosome split up. One of them headed straight for Rachel while producing a handgun from his waistline. The other climbed the stoop toward Liam. By the time the first man wrenched her truck door open, the other had reached her son, forcing him to drop the wood.

"Don't touch him!" Rachel shouted as the tip of the barrel touched her head.

"Turn off the engine," the young man ordered.

She cut the ignition immediately. At the same time, the youth unfastened her seatbelt, grabbed her by the arm, and hauled her out of her seat. Keeping his gun pointed at her temple, he marched her toward his companion.

Rachel met Liam's terrified gaze. *Stay calm.*

"It's okay, Lee." At the sound of her voice, the dog fell quiet. "These men just came for their weapons."

Assessing them more closely, she realized neither one was a day over twenty. Their young age might be to her benefit. "Honestly, guys, I'm not sure if they're here anymore."

The tall youth holding onto Liam displayed his crooked teeth in a smile. "We can see that for ourselves, lady." He gestured to the new office window that gave them an unfettered view of the gun cabinet.

"Tell us where he hid 'em." The man prodded her with the pistol.

Rachel shot Liam a warning glance to keep him from mentioning the police. "I don't know. He didn't tell me."

"We need those guns, Timmy." The gangly youth holding Liam grew visibly agitated. "We were told not to come back without 'em."

Told by their leader, Rachel supposed.

Timmy, who held her arm in a bruising grip, thumbed off the safety on his pistol, in what was clearly an act of intimidation.

"Tell us where Saul hid the guns," he repeated more loudly.

They knew Saul's name. Rachel shook her head warily.

"I'm sorry," she stated with feigned sincerity. "I have no idea where the guns went. We were just visiting. We have people expecting us."

"Hey, I got an idea," cut in the tall youth next to Liam. "Let's take these two hostage. That way we'll be sure to get our guns back, and Will won't be mad at us."

Rachel's blood ran cold. *Oh, no, no, no. That can't happen.* She was supposed to be reuniting with her mother in a few hours.

"You know Saul is a Navy SEAL, right?" she asked Timmy, while painfully aware the safety on his pistol was still off. "He'll hunt you down and hurt you. You don't want to take us anywhere."

The instant Timmy's eyes narrowed, she realized her words of intimidation had backfired.

"Shut up. Will ain't afraid of a Navy SEAL," he added with forced bravado. "Where's your cell phone? You call him right now. Tell him we want our guns, or he'll never see you or your kid again."

Rachel's thoughts raced. As much as she longed to call Saul at that moment to apprise him of the situation, she needed to ensure her son's safety first.

"I don't have a cell phone," she lied. In fact, it was still in the cupholder between the front seats. "I had to throw it away," she added, as disbelief darkened Timmy's face, "so my ex couldn't follow me. But I have an idea," she inserted, before he could cut her off or go looking for it. "Take just me with you and leave my son here. He'll give Saul the message."

She could tell he was considering her proposal. Rachel transferred her gaze to Liam's stricken expression. "You can give Saul a message. Can't you, Lee?"

"S-sure," Liam stammered. "What's the message?" he added, forcing the skinheads to make a quick decision.

The tall one deferred to Timmy, who divided his gaze between mother and son.

"Fine," he finally agreed, resetting the gun's safety. Rachel relaxed one notch. "Tell Saul we've taken your mama to the old Reeve's place. He'll know where it is. If he wants to see her again, without a scratch on her, he'll bring all twelve guns that were in the cabinet and lay 'em on the porch. If he tries to be slick, to call the cops, or trick us, we'll hold on to your mama as long as we want."

The threat, whether hollow or sincere, made Liam pale. Unable to speak, he managed to nod.

"I'll be fine, honey." Rachel inwardly panicked. How was Saul supposed to give the skinheads their weapons when he'd already surrendered them to the police? "Just give Saul the message. He should be home soon." Saul would figure something out.

"Let's go." Timmy prodded her spine with his pistol. "Leave the kid there." As he impelled Rachel toward the corner of the house, his companion shoved Liam, sending him sprawling next to his dropped cedar, before he loped down the stairs after them.

Rachel kept her gaze on Liam until Timmy jostled her around the corner of the house. There sat the El Camino parked on the far side of the barn. If only she'd glimpsed it earlier.

Timmy stuffed her into the front seat, then went around to the driver's seat while the tall skinhead sandwiched her between the two of them. The engine revved, and Timmy backed the car from its hiding place. With a lead foot on the accelerator, he shot them forward. Rachel tried to send Liam a reassuring nod as they barreled past the front porch. He stood on the porch hugging himself in fear.

The words he'd told her in the family graveyard echoed suddenly in Rachel's head, drawing a shiver up her spine. *"Mom, you're not going to die too, are you?"*

~

Saul spotted the Ford F-150 the instant his Camaro emerged from the tree line.

What the heck? He asked himself, even as his spirits lifted, what could have caused her to return. Perhaps the engine had started sputtering, making her decide to turn around. Either way, Liam, who was sitting on the porch, jumped up and waved at him frantically. Saul searched for Rachel but didn't see her. Increasing his speed, he skidded through the turn in the driveway, trying to glean Liam's state of mind. The certainty something was wrong solidified as the boy ran off the stoop directly into his path.

Saul locked up the brakes to avoid hitting him. He threw his car into park and pushed open his door at the same time. "What's wrong?"

"The bad men took her!" Liam rushed up to him and grabbed Saul's T-shirt. "I couldn't call you 'cause I don't know my mom's password." He shook the cellphone clutched in his other hand. "They want the guns back!"

"What? Slow down. What men?"

The boy was trembling. "The men who want the guns! They said they were taking my mom 'til you give them back!"

Saul held Liam's shoulders firmly. "Take a deep breath in and hold it." He used the soothing pitch employed by his former master chief, Santiago Rivera, back in Virginia Beach. "Now let it out slowly and start over. Take the guns where? Where'd they take her?"

Liam exhaled harshly. "The old Reeve's place." His voice quavered. "You know where it is, right?"

Saul pictured an abandoned house not three miles away. It stood in the middle of a field without a single tree or outbuilding to offer cover.

"Sure, I know." He cursed inwardly.

"You can't call the cops. If the police come, they said they wouldn't let her go."

"Don't worry. I won't call the cops." Not only did he trust only himself to get the job done, he didn't want the police laying eyes on Rachel or her son.

"But you gave them the firearms already, didn't you?"

Saul glanced toward the trunk of his car where the eight rifles and four shotguns still lay.

"Not yet." He was struck by the serendipitous fact he still had them. "Don't worry." He squeezed Liam's shoulders. "I'll get your mama back. Come on." He pulled Liam with him toward the door. "Let's grab Duke and get going." He didn't yet mention his plan to drop them off at Tami Goodner's house.

"Get Duke. Why?" Liam eyed him suspiciously.

"Don't how know long this might take. He might need you to walk him."

"But I'm going to be with you." The boy jerked to a halt.

Saul sighed. "I'm taking you and Duke to my neighbor's house." The dog was coming, in fact, to give the boy something to do.

"No! I'm going to the Reeve's place to get my mom!"

Saul tugged Liam closer and lowered his face to reason with him.

"Listen," he said in his gentlest voice, "I understand how you feel. If I were you, I'd want to go to the Reeve's place, too. But you can't come with me, Liam. There's liable to be a shootout, and your mama would never forgive me if I let something happen to you."

Liam glared at him with the light of mutiny in his eyes. Wrenching free of Saul, he stamped up the stoop to get Duke.

Twenty minutes later, Saul left Liam standing under the protective wing of Tami Goodner, who had rushed out of her house to greet them. The boy had stern orders to take Duke on a long walk and to keep him from chasing Mrs. Goodner's cats.

"Should I call the police?" Tami had asked Saul as he prepared to pull away.

"I'll call them," Saul assured her, "afterward," he'd added to himself. First, he intended to teach Cyril's cronies a lesson in etiquette. It wasn't polite to seize innocent civilians and use them as pawns in their nasty little game of intimidation. It would cost Saul some valuable time to disable the components of the firearms he was giving back. He could only hope, in the meantime, the skinheads wouldn't get tired of waiting for him or harm Rachel while keeping themselves entertained.

The urge to say a prayer for her safety caught him off guard as he accelerated toward the Reeve's place. Between his devout former master chief and several other SEALs in his squadron, faith was a huge component of any operation they undertook. Saul himself never prayed. But he knew God looked out for His sheep. He trusted God to protect this particular innocent ewe until Saul could get to her.

Sitting in the front room of a dilapidated farmhouse, dark due to the boarded windows that blocked the late afternoon sunlight, Rachel hugged herself against the chill and marveled at her circumstances. She was supposed to be arriving in Dallas right about now. Instead, she sat on an upended crate next to a single Sterno burner. Its flame cast light onto the large Nazi flag pinned to the wall. It also reflected in the eyes of Will, leader of the FOR Americans, and deepened the hollows under his cheekbones.

In the time she'd spent in his company, she had heard Will's entire life story. While the youths who'd brought her there had merely made her wary, Will made her skin crawl.

"I was in the Army Rangers during the First Gulf War." He paced before her as he talked. "We comprised the ground assault, and the Marines came in right behind us. I've still got mementos from that war. Wanna see 'em?"

Without her saying yes or no, he crossed to a jar sitting on his makeshift desk and carried it over to her. "Know what these are?"

It took her horrified mind a moment to process what she was

seeing within the dusty glass container. Dear God, were those human teeth?

He grinned, exposing the fact that several of his own teeth were missing.

"My victims," he affirmed. "Took us two weeks to storm Saddam Hussein's palace." He returned the jar to his desk and picked up a framed photo. "If you don't believe me, take a look at this."

He brought her a photo of himself, lounging on a silk-covered chaise in a setting that had to be a palace. He hadn't changed much in almost thirty years. Whipcord thin, with leathery skin, he could have passed for forty, although he had to be pushing sixty.

"What's the matter?" he demanded, no doubt seeing the revulsion she found hard to hide. "You think I'm evil, don't you?"

Rachel swallowed against a dry mouth. "It's not my place to judge you."

"Why not? God gave us that ability, so why not use it? You think all people are the same?"

Unwilling to step into a trap, Rachel kept her mouth shut.

"Well, we're not. God made the white man in His image and other races with the parts left over. We were created"—he moved his hands as if molding clay—"to rule over the other races. They don't like that," he acknowledged. "But that's the way it's always been, and that's the way it will be. We will fight to keep our inheritance. You can't just tear down history like it never happened. You can't take down our flag. You do that and we'll hoist this one." He gestured to the Nazi flag hanging on the wall.

Then he whirled toward a box in the corner. "You see this?" He picked it up and gave it a gentle shake. "Grenades." Flashing an evil grin, he put the box back down. "That's not all, either. I've got shells for a FIM-92 Stinger. That's a surface-to-air missile that's being sent to me via UPS. You can shoot down helicopters with a Stinger. Why not? We gotta be prepared. These activists who claim we're all the same are just asking for trouble. We'll bring 'em trouble, all right, soon as we get enough weapons. We ain't givin' up what's rightfully ours. We shouldn't have to."

He resumed his pacing, growing more agitated by the moment.

"The Constitution guarantees us the right to bear arms. We'll bear them all right. We'll teach those liberal hackers it ain't right to take jobs from Americans and give them to Latinos, just because they'll work for cheap. That's un-American! We were here first, weren't we?"

Rachel squelched the impulse to point out that, actually, Native Americans had been here first, then the Spanish.

"You can't take away our livelihoods like that, like we don't count for nothing." He jabbed a bony finger at his chest as he paced. "We're the *only* ones who count." He swung around suddenly and glared at her. "What the devil's taking Saul so long?"

Rachel flinched at Will's raised voice. Timmy and Les, the name of the tall youth, ceased their bickering in the back of the house. They probably worried, like Rachel did, that Will was about to go ballistic.

"Um. I don't—I don't know," she admitted. Chances were, Saul didn't even have the guns anymore. But he wouldn't involve the police in her rescue; she was certain of that. She was also certain he would come for her, as he had done back in Virginia Beach.

Lord, please help him to hurry!

Will swung around with a sound of disgust and resumed his pacing.

～

The Reeve's house had been abandoned even when Saul was just a boy. Teenagers had used it as a place to escape their parents, to smoke and drink. It had fallen into serious disrepair since then. Like every tree in Oklahoma, it listed to one side due to the constant breeze. The sagging roof seemed as if it might cave in at any moment. The once-white clapboard siding had mostly peeled away, exposing old, dried wood beneath. With many of the windows broken or boarded shut, the house reminded Saul of a skeleton as he surveyed it from a distance of two hundred yards, beyond the scope of peering eyes.

Welcome to the headquarters for the FOR Americans, he scoffed inwardly. They used to be holed up in Cyril's office. This was a more fitting place for them.

He eyed the line of gray clouds surging closer. Should he wait for nightfall or get this exchange done now? Darkness would provide him a modicum of concealment. But Rachel was alone in there with men of questionable morals. He'd disabled as many of the firearms as quickly and as crudely as he could. The sooner he extracted her, the better off she'd be.

As much as he wanted to alert Andy to her abduction, he couldn't. Rachel's true identity would likely come to light. Then Andy would have every right to turn around and arrest Saul for abducting her.

Help me do this right.

Gathering his resolve, he checked that the magazine in his SIG was full before concealing it beneath his T-shirt. The K-Bar he carried in his left boot was his backup weapon. He could peg a man in the chest with the flick of his wrist. Cyril's small hunting rifle lay on the floor behind his seat next to his own Weatherby hunting rifle, which he'd grabbed out of his trunk in case he found himself in a firefight. He'd jammed all the other firearms with dirt and loosened their components before rewrapping them in the blanket, ready for delivery.

With his heart thudding swift and hard, Saul got behind the wheel and eased his Camaro out of the copse of trees and onto a rutted road. The warrior in him coalesced, heightening every one of his senses. He could feel every rock in the road through his steering column. The skylarks diving for insects over the fields seemed to fall in slow motion. And a cicada buzzed over the hood of his car, moving like a CH-46E Sea Knight helicopter.

By the time Saul pulled up before the clapboard farmhouse, the sky had taken on a bruised hue, with rain clouds sweeping closer. He eased out of his car, certain several pairs of eyes were watching. He rounded his car to the trunk, opened it, and reached inside to gather up the blanketed firearms. The skinheads wouldn't be happy when they'd learned what he'd done to them. By then, however, he would have gotten Rachel safely away from them—he hoped.

Prepared for every conceivable outcome, Saul marched with his load toward the sagging front porch. The boards bowed beneath his weight. He hoped they wouldn't cave in. Shifting his burden to his right arm, he freed his dominant hand and rapped with authority on the old, beveled door.

CHAPTER 11

*A*t the sound of Saul's knock, Rachel's heart leaped with relief, then clenched with fear as she envisioned what might possibly go wrong. Will, who'd been watching through a hole in the shuttered window, had hissed for Timmy and Les to join him in the front room and keep an eye on her while he negotiated with the SEAL.

"I'll handle this," he told the youths, who stood on either side of her. "She goes nowhere until I'm sure we got what's ours."

They nodded, all too happy to let him face Saul while they babysat the hostage.

With her pulse tapping on her eardrums, Rachel leaned forward so she could watch Will make his way into the foyer. He cautiously opened the door. As it creaked open, the old soldier tensed in recognition of another warrior. To Rachel's frustration, the door blocked her view of Saul.

"Those the guns?" Will inquired brusquely.

"Yep, all but one that was Cyril's." The sound of Saul's laid-back drawl eased a portion of Rachel's tension. He could handle these men, no problem, even Will who'd been similarly trained. "I'm holdin' on to that since he made me his heir."

Will's eyes narrowed to slits. "Cyril was a traitor. He promised us his land and his money years ago. Then he went and left it to some half-breed."

Rachel caught her breath at the insult.

"Careful," Saul retorted in a voice turned to ice. "I've killed many men like you. Might see it as my duty to kill one more."

Will's raspy chuckle suggested he found Saul's remark amusing. "Fine. I know which rifle was Cyril's. You can keep that puny thing, but the rest are ours."

"Take 'em," Saul invited.

"Put 'em down at your feet and take the blanket off."

"I'll need to see Angel first—unharmed."

For a tense minute, Will glared at his visitor. Then with a grudging smile, he glanced back at Les and Timmy and crooked his fingers. "Let that angel walk on over here."

"Go." Timmy hauled Rachel up from the chair—good thing because her legs had turned to rubber—and pushed her toward the door. As she tottered into Saul's view, the emotion that winged inside of her felt like the purest form of love.

Saul's gaze locked on hers, then traveled down and up as he inspected her for any sign of harm. "Give her to me. Then I'll show you the guns."

Looking to Will for his decision, Rachel found him aiming a pistol at her head. Her heart threw itself against her breastbone.

"Try anything slick, half-breed, and your girlfriend's gone."

Girlfriend?

Over the swoosh of blood against her eardrums, Rachel heard Saul say, "Angel, walk toward me."

At her unsteady approach, he bent over and gingerly laid the rolled-up weapons on the threshold, then tossed one end of the blanket off of them. The instant he'd freed his hands, he grabbed her wrist and hauled her behind him. "We'll be on our way."

"Not so fast." Will pointed his gun at Saul as he counted the firearms. "Eleven," he stated on a note of satisfaction. "I guess you're free to go."

Wordlessly, Saul backed up, impelling a stunned Rachel along with him. Had they actually made a peaceful exchange?

Keeping his body between hers and the building, he hustled her toward the passenger side of his car and stuffed her into the front seat.

"Keep your head down," he ordered before rounding the vehicle swiftly. He dropped into his seat and was backing down the driveway before his door was even shut.

Over her thudding heart, Rachel listened to the whine of his engine as they picked up speed. Saul found a place to spin them around, and they shot away from the farmhouse with an efficiency that left her breathless.

He didn't slow down until they'd driven at least a mile. All at once, he pulled off the lonely country road, threw the car into park, then reached over and pulled her into a fierce embrace, planting an equally fierce kiss on her lips. Rachel responded with a surge of passion. Saul groaned as if in physical pain and threw himself back into his seat. He drew several breaths before snapping on the interior light to inspect her.

"Did they hurt you?" he rapped out. His eyes shone with a possessive light.

She could feel the tension rolling off him. "I'm fine, Saul."

"Are you sure?" he grated.

"Yes." She reached for his hand and clasped it between her own. His fingers held a faint tremor as they curled around hers. "You were amazing. I knew you would come for me when Liam gave you the message, but I didn't know if you could get me away from there without causing World War III."

"God knows I wanted to," he said through his teeth.

"But you didn't. That's what makes you the good guy. Where's Liam?" she asked belatedly.

"At my neighbor's." Saul regarded their interlocked hands.

She found herself kissing his knuckles in gratitude. "I'm so sorry this happened. We shouldn't have come back, but Liam forgot his cedar, and he was so distraught."

Saul stared at his captive hand. "Not your fault."

Searching his hard profile, Rachel tried to guess what he was thinking.

"Wait, how did you still have the firearms? You went to the police to turn them in, didn't you?"

He averted his gaze. "Something came up."

She waited for him to elaborate, but he didn't. "The police need to know about this. I know you don't want them to see me, but that man you just met, his name is Will. He used to be an Army Ranger, and he acts like there's a war going on. He even has a surface-to-air missile being shipped to him. He's dangerous, Saul. You heard how he talked to you."

Saul dropped the back of his head against his headrest and stared through his sunroof at the dark clouds roiling above them. "If this was Mexico, I could take him out and his private war would be over."

The chilling words shocked Rachel into momentary silence.

"Okay, but this isn't Mexico, and it isn't your job to eliminate this guy. I know you're trying to protect my identity, but that's not as important as stopping Will from whatever he's planning."

Saul rolled his head to look at her. "How do you know he's planning something?"

"He said so. He said he was going to teach the liberal hackers a lesson for giving jobs to Latinos—his word, not mine."

"What is a liberal hacker?"

"I have no idea, but I got the impression he's planning to kill people to make his point. Why else would he need all those guns? Call the police, please. You don't have to mention me."

With an audible sigh, Saul reluctantly withdrew his hand from hers and took his cell phone from the compartment between the seats. Unlocking it, he dialed three numbers with his thumb.

"Nine-one-one, what's your emergency?" Rachel overheard.

In a concise message, Saul relayed the existence of a hate group called the FOR Americans, adding that they were holed up at the old Reeve's place and heavily armed. He made no mention of Rachel and how they'd held her hostage.

"And your name, sir?"

With a glance at Rachel, Saul replied, "Anonymous," and promptly hung up.

"Thank you." Rachel heaved a silent sigh of relief.

"Let's go get Liam." He put his phone away.

"He'll be so relieved." Rachel pictured Liam's terror as he'd witnessed her abduction earlier.

She was relieved, too—and grateful. A situation that could have turned deadly had been resolved without violence, proving to Rachel that God had been watching out for all of them, but Saul most especially.

～

Wide awake, Saul stared into the dancing flames of the fire in his hearth. The drum of rain on the roof of the house ought to have lulled him to sleep as it had the others, but Saul, who felt the ground was shifting under his feet, kept replaying the day's events and trying to pinpoint what made him feel like something inside him was changing.

When they'd pulled up to the Goodner's house, Liam had burst out the front door with Duke on his heels. Instead of running straight to Rachel, who jumped from the passenger seat to greet her son, the boy charged in Saul's direction and threw his arms around him.

"You did it!" he exclaimed with tears of relief streaming from his eyes. The boy fisted Saul's shirt and shook him. "You saved her!"

Now Liam's words brought to mind what Rachel had said earlier, *You were amazing.*

She hadn't known what she was saying. For more than a decade he'd done what no decent human being would ever desire to do. He annihilated people. He wasn't amazing or a hero.

He reflected on their dinner of fried chicken, where Liam had demanded a blow-by-blow recounting of what happened. Rachel had interrupted Saul's terse synopsis, elaborating for her son. She detailed Saul's refusal to let Will make the rules. She described the way he'd whisked her away like they were in some kind of action movie. Of course, she hadn't mentioned how he envisioned returning to the Reeve's house to wreak holy havoc on the men who'd taken her.

Why her glowing account had unsettled him, he couldn't say. It didn't matter anyway. In the morning, she and Liam would strike out for Dallas for good this time. Rachel's birth mother, who had been out of her mind with worry when Rachel and Liam never showed, had placed dozens of unanswered calls to Rachel's cell phone. She had even called Saul while his phone was shut up in his car. He could only imagine what Shannon thought of Broken Arrow, after having learned what her daughter had been through. Then again, their neighboring city, Tulsa, had a long history of racism, too.

Beyond the walls of Saul's house, thunder rumbled, reflecting his tumultuous emotions. He pictured the moment Rachel had lifted his hand to her mouth and kissed his knuckles. In the very next instant, he imagined her living in his house and fixing it with the money Cyril had left him. It was easy to envision Liam growing up the way he had, on fifty acres of unspoiled land. But then, disturbingly, he pictured himself living with them.

"That's crap," he muttered, furious with himself for imagining something so impractical. For one thing, he had a year left on his reenlistment. For another, he didn't deserve to have people waiting for him, especially not a little family—Blake's little family.

Pushing to his feet, Saul prowled into the kitchen, dark but for the light under the hood of the stove. He filled a glass with water, then chugged it while picturing the kitchen with the new cabinets, new counters, and stainless-steel appliances Rachel had suggested on her second list.

Was the twenty-five grand sitting in his bank account a sign that Rachel was meant to stay here and renovate his home?

Don't be stupid. Just because Rachel had kissed his hand didn't mean she cared about him enough to stay here. Why would she, when she was about to meet her birth mother. What's more, he'd spent his entire adult life trying to forget this place. Why would he want to keep it? It wasn't his job to protect Rachel and Liam forever. He already had a job, and it was waiting for him to get back and get busy.

With that self-directed sermon, Saul thrust the enticing vision of Rachel as his woman from his head, thumped the glass down on the blue Formica countertop, and made himself lie back down on the couch to close his eyes, hopefully, to sleep.

The following morning, with her suitcase repacked, Rachel ventured onto the front porch looking for Saul. The storm had moved on, drawing a clear cold front behind it. The changing weather urged her to get to Dallas swiftly so she could enroll Liam in school. According to Shannon, their new documents had arrived in her mailbox, making that feasible.

Expecting to find Saul under the hood of the truck as he'd been the day before, Rachel was surprised to see him dragging a plywood contraption across the tall grass toward the tree line. The wooden base cut a swathe through the heavy dew.

What is he up to? she wondered, even as her heart recalled the joy that had buoyed her heart when he showed up at the Reeve's place.

The screen door opened behind her, and Rachel glanced back to see Liam slip through it.

"Stay," he said to Duke. Joining his mother on the porch, they both watched Saul set the contraption upright, at which point the bull's-eye spray-painted on the flat surface became apparent.

"Target practice," Rachel guessed, as Saul headed in their direction.

"Mornin'." His gaze lingering on Rachel's face made her recall the sweet current that had flowed between them when they'd kissed by the stream, then again in the car.

All at once, he scooped up a rifle previously hidden in the tall grass

—the one belonging to Cyril, she guessed. Walking a few more paces with it, he turned and aimed it at the target.

Crack, crack, crack. Again and again the rifle discharged, until a dark spot replaced the white center of the bull's-eye.

"Whoa," Liam breathed, giving voice to Rachel's private reaction.

With his ammunition expended, Saul propped the weapon over his shoulder and walked into the middle of the driveway, his expression inscrutable.

"Your turn," he called to Rachel.

"Oh." She balked at the thought of firing a rifle. "No."

"Come on down," he invited on an implacable note. "You're not going to Dallas until you know how to protect yourself."

"From whom?" She knew her marksman skills were nonexistent. "The skinheads all live up here."

Saul frowned. "You know who." He flicked a glance at Liam.

From Ethan. She'd almost forgotten about him.

"I want to learn," her son piped up.

Rachel glanced over at him. "No, not yet. When you're older," she amended, reading disappointment on her son's face. "You don't want to be a hunter, anyway, do you?"

Liam rolled his eyes. "Saul's not teaching you to hunt." With those insightful words, her son marched back into the house, letting the screen door slam shut.

Rachel turned back to Saul and found him with a foot on the bottom step.

"I don't know why he's upset," she said apologetically. "He knows we have to leave. Shannon is expecting us, and she's got our new documents." She fell silent, half hoping Saul would suggest a reason to stay.

"Come on down," he said, instead. "You're not leaving until you know how to defend yourself."

Rachel stood her ground. "With that gun? You're giving it to me?"

Saul held it up for her to see. "It's a lightweight semiautomatic hunting rifle, small enough for a woman to handle. Cyril used to keep it mounted to the gun rack on the truck's back window."

He seriously expected her to drive a truck with a rifle mounted to the gun rack?

"Blake tried to teach me already," Rachel reminded him. "I'm telling you, I'm hopeless."

"No one is hopeless. You just need more lessons."

"It's not my thing to shoot people."

Saul's jaw hardened. "Are you sayin' it's my thing?"

She hadn't meant it like that. "Of course not."

"Look," Saul added on a growl, "I need to feel better 'bout sendin' you off alone so, please, indulge me."

When he put it like that, she really didn't have much choice, did she?

With a sigh of resignation, Rachel plodded down the steps in her jeans and a sweater once belonging to his mother. She crossed the driveway and joined him in the spot from which he'd shot eight consecutive bull's-eyes. The target seemed impossibly far away.

"Watch me for a minute," Saul instructed.

With her eyes on his tan, nimble hands, she witnessed him remove the empty magazine, then push it back in.

"Here, you exchange the old mag for a new one."

She had only ever handled a pistol before, but this much she knew. Without difficulty, she removed the magazine he'd exhausted and replaced it with the one he handed to her.

"Good," he said when she'd clicked it into place. "Show me the safety."

"It's here."

"Yep. You keep it on until you're ready to shoot. Step closer to me."

He turned her toward the target. With one hand on her right shoulder, the other on her left hip, he positioned her into a proper front-and-back stance. Startled by how good it felt to be handled by him, Rachel struggled to follow his instructions as he told her to brace the butt of the rifle against her shoulder. "Bend your elbows," he added in her ear. "Loosen up your shoulders. I don't want any tension in 'em."

His proximity was making her tense. The low timber of his voice traced a pleasant shiver down her spine.

"Okay now, sight down the barrel and center the crosshairs on the bull's-eye. You doin' that?"

"Yes," she said, shutting one eye and squinting through the lens with the other.

He put his ear against hers to inspect her aim, and the scent of cedar stole into her nostrils. She loved the way he smelled.

"Go ahead and release the safety."

His low-pitched voice gave rise to goosebumps.

"Squeeze the trigger."

Rachel flicked the safety off and crooked her finger over the trigger, then pulled it.

Boom! The rifle kicked, ramming against her shoulder and knocking her against Saul's larger frame.

"You didn't say it was going to do that!" She craned her neck to glare at him.

He chuckled at her outrage. "Now you know. Try again. I think you hit a squirrel. Remember, the safety is off."

With a groan for her shoulder, she readied herself a second time.

"Check your stance."

He nudged her left foot back, brushing her inner thigh with his knee. The electrifying contact short-circuited Rachel's brain for a second. Blowing out a breath, she sighted down the barrel again. This time she squeezed her eyes shut in anticipation of the rifle's kick.

Boom! She staggered against him a second time.

"You can't close your eyes, Angel," Saul chided with a smile in his voice.

Angel. Rachel's heart fluttered at the endearment until she considered maybe he was merely getting her used to her name.

"I can't do this," she said, not referring to shooting so much as feeling her body come alive for the first time in three years.

"Sure, you can," he countered, unaware of her private dilemma. He positioned her back in the proper stance. "This time keep your eyes open."

She blew out another breath, widening her stance before he could wedge his leg between hers, and peered through the scope to fire again. *Boom!*

"I missed."

"Try again."

Boom! "I think I hit something."

"Yep, the ground. One more time."

Rachel groaned. Her shoulder was going to be bruised by the time this was over. *Boom!*

"Maybe you need some help," Saul conceded, stepping closer.

With that scant warning, he fitted his body, front to back, against her smaller one.

Rachel swallowed the whimper that rose in her throat. Saul's heat enveloped her. Her focus tunneled, so that fixing her gaze on the distant target was impossible.

"I can't." She lowered the weapon that was suddenly too heavy to lift. She twisted helplessly to face him.

"Can't what?" His stubbled jaw was directly in front of her eyes. Returning his heavy-lidded gaze, she realized he was waiting for her to make the first move.

Rachel searched herself for feelings of betrayal, but none cropped up. With a sense this moment had been a long time coming, she caught the back of Saul's neck, rolled up on her toes, and pressed herself against him, from lips to thighs. A moan escaped her.

She was only vaguely aware of him plucking the rifle from her slackened grip and flicking the safety back on before dropping it at their feet. His hand went at once to the small of her back and pulled her closer. His other hand cradled her head, tilting it so he could kiss her more deeply.

Rachel submitted to the warm current sweeping through her. How could this be happening? Why now when she was poised to leave, when Saul himself was about to return to Virginia?

Stop it. Stop it now before you fall for him.

But it was Saul who lifted his head abruptly, tearing her from the lifeline of his kiss to gaze alertly over her shoulder. His entire body tensed against hers.

"Car's comin'," he warned.

She couldn't hear a thing over the thudding of her heart. But trusting his senses more than hers, she let go of him and ran toward the house on legs that jittered. Could it be the skinheads, bearing down with vengeful intent for his having compromised their firearms? Or maybe it was Tami Goodner, who couldn't get enough answers about Rachel and Liam to satisfy her curiosity the night before.

From the shadow of the porch, Rachel looked back to see a white police cruiser with blue and gold decals swing around the bend in the driveway. Alarm choked her throat. Most likely the police had figured out who their anonymous caller was the night before. She couldn't let them see her, let alone question her. Without the ID that was waiting for her in Dallas, her cover was too flimsy for scrutiny.

Ducking into the house, she was determined to find her son and hide.

CHAPTER 12

*S*aul snatched up the fallen rifle and, making certain Rachel was completely out of sight, approached the cruiser just as Andy parked in front of the truck and pushed his door open.

"Mornin', Saul." Andy stepped out of his vehicle wearing the same dark-blue uniform Saul had seen him in previously. Plucking off his sunglasses, he glanced from the rifle in Saul's hand to the distant bull's-eye. "I thought I heard gunfire."

"That's not illegal now, is it?"

"Oh, no," Andy rushed to reassure him. "You can shoot all you like on your own property. I'm here about the paperwork left by the FOR Americans. Bethany said you'd stopped by the station yesterday, but you were in an all-fire hurry to leave."

Saul ignored the implied question. "Thanks for comin' out so quick."

"Is this a bad time?"

"No, no, it's fine. Come on in." Saul searched the windows of his house, hoping Rachel would keep herself and Liam out of sight for as long as it took to load Andy up with stuff from Cyril's office and send him on his way.

"BAPD got a call last night," the detective volunteered as they approached Saul's porch. "Someone tipped us off about some skinheads holed up at the Reeve's place with a bunch of weapons. You know anything about that?"

Remembering Andy's skill for pulling information out of people, Saul determined it best simply to tell the truth, or at least some of it. "I might." He climbed the steps slowly to give Rachel time to hide.

"Figured you did," Andy countered smoothly, "'cause the boys we talked to last night said they got their weapons from you."

Saul stopped in his tracks. "Did they, now? Those were the firearms they left in Cyril's study. I disabled most of them before I gave them back."

"Good for you." Andy sounded unperturbed.

"Did you arrest them?"

Andy grimaced. "'Fraid I couldn't. In this state, there's no requirement to register firearms, plus you can own as many as you want. Only selling a gun to a known felon is illegal here. All I could do last night was write 'em both a ticket for trespassing, though technically, the Reeve's place is abandoned. Sorry, buddy."

"Both!" Saul pounced on the word. "But three of them were there last night."

Andy cocked his head. "I only ran into two—Timmy Olsen and Les Wright."

Saul sighed and shook his head. "They have a leader, someone by the name of Will."

"Never mentioned any Will." Andy's sharp gaze focused on Saul's face. "They did mention a lady friend of yours, though."

And just like that, Saul's plan to keep Rachel hidden went up in smoke. He froze with his hand on the screen door.

"She's just a friend," he said, correcting any conclusions Andy might have come to. "You want to talk to her?" he added casually.

"Sure." Andy masked his interest with an equally casual reply.

"All right. Come on in." Pulling open the screen door, Saul let the lawman into his house.

Andy let out a low whistle as he stepped into the living area. "This place looks a good sight better than the last time I was here."

"When was that?" Saul cast a surreptitious glance down the hallway. As long as Liam kept out of sight, the odds of Andy associating Rachel with an AMBER Alert flyer hanging on the BOLO board at work wouldn't be too high, especially with her hair cut and colored.

"I got called out once to break up a fight." Andy peeked into the kitchen.

"Not surprised to hear it. I'll go get Angel. Help yourself to the lemonade in the fridge. There's a glass in the cabinet over the dishwasher."

As Andy walked toward the kitchen, Saul hurried toward his mother's old room where Rachel and Liam both sat on the bed looking tense.

He shut the door quietly behind him.

"Just relax now," he told them in a low voice. "I went to school with this policeman. He was dispatched to the Reeve's place after my call last night, only Will wasn't there, just the other two, and they happened to mention you," he said to Rachel, causing her to gasp. "Naturally, Andy wants to ask you some questions. Just use your new name and stick to the facts."

"You want me to tell him what happened?"

"Yes. If he asks to see your ID, tell him the skinheads took your purse. Make sure he knows you're leaving the area."

Rachel nodded, but fear flooded her eyes as she slipped off the bed.

"Liam, you stay in this room and don't make a sound, okay?" Saul added to her frightened son. "It'll be all right. Andy's a good guy."

Escorting Rachel from the room, Saul shut the boy inside.

Keeping hold of Rachel's hand, Saul led her into the living area. At their entrance, Andy returned from the kitchen holding a tall glass of lemonade. Given his stunned expression, Andy either recognized Rachel right away or he thought she was cuter than all get-out.

"Well, hey there."

Definitely the latter. Saul was less relieved than he was annoyed.

"I'm Andy Cannard." The man approached with a smile, forcing Saul to release Rachel so she could shake the policeman's hand.

"Angel Johnson," she stated with commendable poise.

Andy regarded her more closely. "You're not from here, are you?"

"No, I'm visiting from Texas."

"Texas, huh? Well, how did you come to fall into the hands of those boys yesterday?"

With a glance at Saul for courage, Rachel stated she'd been staying with Saul, and just as she was leaving yesterday, two young men showed up and demanded to know where Saul had hidden their weapons. When she said she didn't know, they decided to take her as a bargaining chip.

"That must have terrified you," Andy said with genuine concern.

"Yes." She nodded several times.

Andy's brown eyes shifted to Saul. "How'd you find out she'd been taken?"

Saul had to think on his toes. He couldn't mention Liam, and phone calls were traceable.

"They left me a note. Stuck it to the door."

"I see." Andy turned his attention back to Rachel. "How long were you with these men, and what was that like?"

"Couple of hours. It was pretty scary." She hugged herself. "The young guys, Les and Timmy, seem fairly harmless, but their leader Will is not...right...in the head," she added delicately. "He collects weapons, including grenades and a surface-to-air missile, which he says UPS is shipping to him. He told me the white man has been at war with non-whites for centuries. Plus, I'm pretty sure he's planning something violent."

Andy cocked his head. "What makes you say that?"

"He said his group was going to teach the liberal hackers a lesson for giving jobs away to immigrants."

Andy frowned at Saul. "Any idea what that means?"

"No. I mean, obviously he's upset about jobs being given to people who'll work for less, but I don't know what he means by liberal hackers."

"Huh." The lawman focused back on Rachel. "Ma'am, would you like to press charges against these men for holding you hostage?"

Rachel licked her upper lip and glanced at Saul. "Well, I'm heading back to Texas today," she said apologetically.

Andy's disappointment was almost comical. "Can't you postpone for a few days? We could use your help trying to identify this Will fellow."

"Um." Rachel cast Saul an uncertain gaze. "I'm afraid I can't. I really have to get back."

"Well, that's a shame. I'd sure like to hold that man accountable, provided I can find him."

It was time to redirect the conversation. "Maybe we can learn something about him in the paperwork you came to see. Why don't you come on back?" Saul started to lead Andy away.

"Pleasure meetin' you, Angel." The lawman made a point of clasping Rachel's hand one last time while smiling warmly at her, clearly smitten.

"You, too. Are you done with that glass?"

"Yes, thank you." He put it into the hand he'd been holding, letting go with visible reluctance.

Saul stewed with annoyance. "You comin'?"

Tearing himself from Rachel, Andy turned and followed Saul toward the bedrooms. As he stepped into Cyril's office, he let loose with another low whistle.

"Sure is a lot of stuff in here." Moving from one pile of amassed media to the next, he assessed it with a discerning eye. He skimmed one of the FOR Americans' pamphlets and uttered an expletive. "You mind if I help myself to some of this?"

"Take it all. Especially this." Saul handed him the folder that explained the group's bylaws.

"I'll take what we can carry in one trip," Andy decided, "if you want to give me a hand."

By the time Andy pulled away several minutes later, the piles in Cyril's study had dwindled to more manageable proportions.

"Do you think he suspects who I am?" Rachel asked Saul as he returned to the house.

"No. Though he does wonder why you've got a burning need to get to Texas—nice job being unspecific there."

She smiled up at him. "Thank you."

Saul's gaze slid helplessly to the soft curve of her lips. With a stab of regret, he recalled the blissful kiss they'd been sharing when Andy showed up. Kissing Rachel might have been a lapse of judgment on his part, but he did not regret it, not for a second.

"Guess you should head out soon." He had to force himself to say the words.

She swallowed hard, dropping her gaze as she nodded. A beat of silence fell between them. She raised her head suddenly.

"I'll miss you."

It was all Saul could do not to haul her into his arms and kiss her again.

"I'll miss you, too," he mumbled. He had never in his life told a woman that—apart from his mother—because he'd never gotten emotionally close enough to make it true.

A sheen of tears slipped over Rachel's gray-green eyes. With a furrowing of her smooth forehead, she spun away and headed slowly toward the back room to fetch her son.

For the second day in a row, Rachel pointed the truck toward Highway 51 and the Muskogee Turnpike. If possible, her heart hung even lower in her chest than it had the day before. In the past twenty-four hours, her private assumptions and resolutions had been turned inside out by Saul's heroic rescue and by his unforgettable kiss.

When Blake died, Rachel had assumed she would never love another man again. Blake had been the love of her life, her soulmate, the only one meant for her. The mere notion of intimacy with anyone apart from him was unthinkable—until yesterday.

Seeing Saul at the door of the Reeve's place had been like an epiphany. Their kiss that morning had shifted the very earth beneath her feet. The memory alone left her breathless—until she contemplated never being kissed by him again, and then she simply felt cheated.

Even so, Saul hadn't proposed she stay at the ranch under the onus of fixing it up for him to sell, which meant he didn't want her living there. Of course, he didn't. He'd set out from the beginning to put the place up for sale, to go back to SEAL Team Six, and rejoin his band of brothers. Who could blame him? That was the life he'd made for himself and he was good at it—the best.

As for herself, she had a mother who was waiting to meet her after being apart for over thirty years, who was offering her a place to live. Rachel could start up her business slowly and not worry about where to live or how to keep Liam and herself fed. It made perfect sense to go to Dallas to live there. All the same, she kept an eye on her rearview mirror until the mailbox on Oak Grove Road fell away from view.

The old truck seemed to run better in the cooler weather. Rachel edged her speed up to sixty miles an hour. A fresh breeze blew through the truck's half-opened windows, bearing the scent of prairie grass she'd grown to love. There wasn't a drop of humidity in the air, so the sky above them stretched from one flat horizon to the other. It was an excellent day to put her plans back on track. Texas had always been her final destination.

And yet the farther from Broken Arrow they traveled, the more uneasy Rachel became. The leader of the skinheads was spreading his message of hate and plotting something—but what? If she'd helped the policeman identify Will, maybe that man could be apprehended before he got the chance to unleash some type of violent act.

But she couldn't involve herself in a police investigation when she herself was a woman on the run, as yet without identification. With a grimace of regret, she snapped on the radio and searched for a

Christian station. Locating K-LOVE at 95.9 FM, she raised the volume on King & Country as they sang *"step into a new day"* and glanced at Liam, who sat unmoving with the lump of cedar on his lap. He'd been carrying it around all morning, "listening to it," as he'd earlier explained.

To Rachel, her son seemed alarmingly depressed.

She tried to interest him in their surroundings. "Honey, check out the bulls."

They passed a dried-up pond with despondent-looking steer jostling for shade under a single tree. But Liam stared unseeing down the highway. His fingers moved over the wood's surface like a blind man reading Braille.

"Are you okay, Lee?" She used his new name intentionally. They would both have to get used to it.

"Sure," he said, although it sounded as if he were miles away.

Minutes later, he startled her by exclaiming. "Hah, I hear it."

"Hear what?"

"I know what to carve," he clarified with a hint of enthusiasm, the sound of which was a balm to her ears.

"Are you going to tell me?" she prompted after a minute.

"Nope, I can't." He turned his wood over to examine the underside. "Anyways, it's for Saul."

"Oh, honey." His words wrung her heart with grief. "We're not going to see Saul any time soon." *If ever.*

Liam flashed her a rebellious glare. "You don't know that. No one knows what's going to happen."

Except God, she agreed, disheartened by Liam's irritability. It couldn't be any more obvious he wanted to go to Dallas even less than she did. With the reminder that God alone knew what the future held, she gripped the steering wheel more firmly and surrendered her aching heart to heaven.

～

With buzzards circling in the cloudless sky, it seemed like an appropriate time to clean out Cyril's office. Rachel and Liam were gone. There were no distractions to prevent Saul from getting the unpleasant task over with. Nobody was going to buy his ranch with a room cluttered and the rug stained.

First Saul opened the new window he'd installed and removed the screen. Then he carried an empty bin from the barn and placed it right under the open window. Back in the office, he picked up armloads of old magazines, some of which dated back to the years he'd lived there, and lobbed them through the window straight into the bin. Later, he would take it to the recycling plant.

As with Rachel's first departure, the silence in the house unsettled him. The walls seemed to whisper snatches of conversations from his past and the sound of his mother grieving over the baby's death. It seemed like she'd wept for months, dying soon after. The memory of her depression made him think of Rachel, who had grieved so deeply after Blake's death, she almost died. For the first time, he realized the depth of a woman's love and the toll it took on them when their loved ones were taken away.

He, too, had lost loved ones. But instead of weeping, he'd turned his grief into something bitter and cold.

The insight so disturbed him he nearly walked out of the house to jump into his car and take off. But running from the source of his pain didn't make it any less real. And nobody was going to buy his house until he purged this room of its evil contents.

The more propaganda he discarded, the more he could feel the cold anger in him growing. Cyril had taken over the ranch and cast his shadow over all of them. What a hypocrite he had been, secretly loving a non-white woman while believing in the supremacy of the Aryan race. In fact, his stepdad and Will were no better than the terrorists Saul hunted and eliminated. If Will were a jihadist looking to spread radical Islam by killing westerners, Saul could finish him, and the threat would be over.

The conversation he'd had with Rachel about wanting to rain holy terror on the skinheads came back to him.

God knows I wanted to.

But you didn't. That's what makes you the good guy.

If that were true, then self-control was the only thing distinguishing him from the bad guys. And yet, the more terrorists he'd killed, the more evil he felt, probably because Puca had taught him never to kill what he couldn't eat and, clearly, he wasn't eating his victims. For the first time ever, Saul asked himself if terminating targets designated by the Joint Chiefs and Southern Command was the morally correct thing to do. He had always told himself that killing the bad guys ultimately saved lives. But did it, really? Or did it just provoke the enemy to retaliate, killing more innocent people? If that was the case, he was nothing more than an instrument for evil, a weapon to be deployed however the powers-that-be saw fit.

Good thing Rachel didn't see him that way. She'd called him a freakin' hero. The only heroic thing he'd done, in his opinion, was to get her and Liam away from her domineering brother. He wished she would just call him already and let him know she'd made it to Dallas. Then his private mission would be over, and he could forget about her. He checked his watch. She ought to have arrived there by now.

Only no call yet. That had to be the reason why his skin was crawling. What if something bad had happened to them on the way south? What if the old truck had broken down? Or they'd gotten lost? No, she had her cell phone to help with that. And he was fairly sure she would've called him if she'd run into trouble. No news was good news. It had to be.

Still frustrated, Saul hurled the last pile of magazines through the open window, and half of them fluttered open and fell outside the bin. He muttered a bad word. At the same time, the vibration of his cell phone made his tense shoulders relax.

He snatched his cell from his pocket, barely glancing at the screen. "Rachel?" he rapped out.

His greeting was met with momentary silence. "No, sorry, this is Andy."

Andy *not* Angel, which was the name he'd typed into his contact list. Saul perspired briefly. But Andy didn't know anything about Rachel and Liam's disappearance.

"Go ahead," he said, wondering what the man wanted.

"Okay, so I've been going through the stuff from Cyril's office." Andy's voice took on a note of excitement. "Turns out I don't need Angel Johnson to press charges. There's plenty here that constitutes a crime. Conspiracy to murder, for one thing."

"That doesn't sound good, but I'm glad the paperwork was helpful."

"Yes, it was. But there's more. I came across plans to make a sophisticated variant of ANFO with nitromethane as the fuel."

Saul nodded to himself. "That's what Timothy McVeigh used in the Oklahoma City bombing."

"Precisely," Andy confirmed. "According to the minutes from a FOR Americans' meeting three months ago, the group had five hundred pounds of fertilizer and fifteen liters of nitromethane. All they needed was a truck to put it in. Saul, there's mention of a plan to use it on Monday, Columbus Day."

Columbus Day. Saul was supposed to be back at Spec Ops the day immediately following.

"That's a week from today. What's the target?"

"I can't find that information. I still have some digging to do."

"Good luck with that," Saul said sincerely.

"Listen, I was thinking maybe you could help us out."

"Me? How?"

"One of Tulsa's Special Operations guys just pulled his back, putting them a man short. Any interest in filling his shoes for a while? This should all be over by Monday."

"Uh, no, thanks." Saul immediately pictured the flyer pinned on the BOLO board at the station. "I have to report back to work the day after Columbus Day, and it takes at least two days to drive home." At the same time, he remembered Lieutenant Mills telling him he could extend his time off if he needed to.

Andy uttered a word of disappointment. "That's too bad. We could use a man with your expertise. If you change your mind, I'm meeting with the SOT and my captain on Thursday afternoon, 4:00 p.m. You're the only one besides Angel Johnson who's laid eyes on the leader. His name is Will Davis, according to the paperwork you gave me. You know how many William Davises there are in this state? Over three thousand. We don't even know what the man looks like."

"It was dark. I couldn't see him very well."

"It's a shame Angel's gone," Andy lamented. "I bet she remembers what he looks like."

"What about the other two?" Saul wished he would forget about Rachel. "You could pick them up for questioning."

"They're laying low. Their own mothers don't know where they are."

"Sorry to hear that."

"Could you ask Angel if she'd like to work with our forensic artist to come up with a composite?"

"She's gone. You know that." Saul didn't want to talk about her, especially her absence, any longer.

"We could do it over Zoom or FaceTime."

True. "I don't know. I'll ask her." *If she ever calls me.*

Andy heaved a heavy sigh. "Well, if you change your mind, we could really use your help. You've got a lot more experience with terrorists than we do."

"I'll think about it," Saul promised.

"Fair enough. It was good to see you after all these years."

"Good seein' you too, Duck."

Saul hung up with a hollow feeling in his stomach. All at once his phone chimed. Rachel had just texted him.

We're here, safe and sound. Thank you for EVERYTHING.

The empty feeling in Saul's stomach spread to his chest. Sure, he was relieved to know she and Liam had made it to Dallas safely, but he'd been hankering these past several hours for the sound of her voice, and yet she'd chosen a far less personal form of communication. If that didn't convey their time together was over, he didn't know what did.

It's better this way. He put his phone away, deciding not to tell her about Will's plans or even Andy's request. She had removed herself from the realm of Broken Arrow. *And that's for the best. I can't begin to give Rachel what she deserves. I'm the Grim Reaper and the property of Uncle Sam.*

It was time he headed back to Virginia Beach to fulfill his obligations.

~

Ethan drove home from work on autopilot. He did some of his best thinking when he got behind the wheel. The name Shannon Johnson-Brown had been bouncing around in his head for some time, without his being able to identify her. All at once, as he cruised London Bridge Road through a downpour, he realized where he'd seen it.

The first two names, Shannon Johnson, were printed on the birth certificate filed directly behind his—Rachel's birth certificate.

Hah! He knew the name had sounded familiar. His thoughts raced as quickly as the windshield wipers beating a fervent tempo before his eyes. So, Rachel had reached out to her *birth* mother. How surprisingly clever of her. Yet, he was still the cleverer of the two for remembering the woman's name—unless he was misremembering. Laying a heavy foot on the accelerator, Ethan sped toward home to ascertain if he was right.

Minutes later, he guided his car into the garage, snatched up his briefcase, and hurried into the dark house, flicking on lights as he went. Anticipation pulsed through his veins as he made a beeline for his office.

He thrust his way through the door, flicked the light switch, and crossed straight to the tall mahogany filing cabinet. In the same drawer he'd recently opened, Rachel's birth certificate was sticking up a bit. He plucked it out and studied it.

He'd been right, of course. Euphoria raised goosebumps on his body.

Swiveling with the certificate in hand, his gaze went to Liam's framed photograph.

"Told you I'd find you, didn't I, son?" He regarded the certificate again and considered calling Mooney with his latest discovery. Or was this an interstate matter, now? Maybe the FBI ought to get involved.

Wait. His planning came to a screeching halt. If Rachel had been plotting with her birth mother, that meant she *hadn't* been abducted. The man with the beard had merely been an accomplice, enabling Rachel, under her own volition, to leave Virginia with her son and without a trace. It scarcely mattered Ethan had shared custody. Truth was, any lawyer apart from his old classmate at Washington and Lee would uphold Rachel's right to parent her son by herself. Nor would the card Ethan had played in court—that Rachel was emotionally and mentally unfit to parent—be used again. Her clever disappearance proved there was nothing wrong with her mind, apart from her documented dyslexia.

But what if she were to become mentally impaired, say through an accident or something? Then Ethan stood a chance of getting Liam to himself.

Possibilities wormed into his mind. He could hire a thug to bash her over the head—but no. Thugs for hire tended to get caught and, when caught, tended to finger the one who'd employed them. Moreover, Ethan trusted no one but himself to handle such a sensitive matter.

He sank into his comfortable leather chair to contemplate. First, he would have to find Rachel's birth mother. Then, assuming Rachel lived with the woman, he would have to surprise her when she least expected it, preferably in a place where there were no witnesses, no cameras.

Could he bring himself to disable her? Strangulation was simple enough and often resulted in an ischemic stroke. But how to do so without leaving marks? And how could he be sure he wouldn't kill her? It wasn't like he had any practice at strangulation.

Then again, would it be so bad if he did kill her? Perhaps that was a simpler solution. He wouldn't have to fret she might fully recover. He wouldn't need to find long-term care for her. Besides, she deserved to die, didn't she, for betraying him? She knew how much Liam meant to him, and still she'd taken him away. She might as well have stabbed him in the heart.

One death deserved another, he reasoned.

Reaching behind him to his credenza, he poured himself a glass of scotch, neat. Yes, she should die, and he would make sure of it. He had weeks of vacation time on the books, and thanks to several classes in criminal law, he'd learned exactly how to cover his trail. No one would suspect him. By the time law enforcement went searching for Liam's closest living relative, Ethan would be back at home from his vacation in New Orleans, a place he'd enjoyed once before. Getting a hotel there during the off-season would present no difficulty. No one would question him renting a car to get around. The hardest part would be leaving his cell phone in his hotel room while he took off for Texas.

With a plan solidifying in Ethan's mind, he turned his attention to locating Rachel's birth mother. It had taken Mooney days to get a court order merely to read Rachel's emails. It would take the detective at least that long to locate Shannon Johnson-Brown. By that time, Ethan, with his various contacts in the government, would have found the woman himself and would have eliminated his problem, once and for all.

He took a soothing sip of his drink. If he'd only taken Rachel out of the equation earlier, none of this nonsense would be necessary.

CHAPTER 13

*R*achel sat at Shannon's kitchen table poring over her Bible. The sun rising in the window next to her had gone from pink to gold as she looked up thirty-three passages related to fear and anxiety, in the hopes of combatting the churning uncertainties that had awakened her at dawn.

The creaking of treads betrayed Shannon's descent from upstairs. Rachel sent her birth mother a sheepish smile as she came into the kitchen in her robe.

"You're up early." The petite, pretty brunette cast a quizzical glance at Rachel's Bible.

"I hope I didn't wake you."

"Oh, no. I have to go back to work today." With a frown of concern, Shannon turned on the coffee pot, stealing glances at her as Rachel continued reading. "Coffee?" she inquired.

"No, thank you."

Seconds later, Shannon slipped into a chair opposite Rachel and studied her. "Is everything okay, honey?" she finally asked. "You seem troubled."

Looking up into a face that resembled her own, Rachel relived the awe and wonder she'd experienced upon meeting her birth mother for the first time three days earlier. They had bonded instantly and unconditionally, making them both lament the lost years they could have spent together. With Shannon only seventeen years older than Rachel, she seemed more like an older sister, however, than a mother.

On their first day together, Shannon had taken her and Liam on a tour of the city. Each subsequent day, they'd gone on long walks at a nearby park while Liam rode Shannon's ten-speed. Their easy relationship affirmed for Rachel that her decision to move to Dallas had been the right one. Her only continuing concern was Liam's withdrawn state. When they weren't all eating or exercising together, he isolated himself in the room belonging to Ryan, Shannon's son who was away at college, and carved obsessively at his piece of wood.

Then, just yesterday, the three of them had gone together to enroll Liam at the middle school he was zoned to attend. That was when doubts assailed Rachel, making her question her plan. Moreover, she had awakened at dawn with anxious thoughts that kept her from falling back asleep.

"I'm worried about Liam." Rachel pitched her voice low lest it carry through the ceiling to his room on the townhome's second floor. Her chest tightened as she explained. "When we went to enroll him at that school yesterday, the look on his face...he was so obviously terrified."

Shannon reached over and put her hand over Rachel's. "Most children are overwhelmed by the notion of a new school at first. Don't you think he'll get used to it?"

"I don't know." Rachel heard the doubt in her own voice. "Liam is pretty introverted. Plus, he loves the outdoors." Her throat tightened, making speech momentarily impossible. "I just want him to be happy," she managed to add, "the way he was in Broken Arrow. I hope that doesn't offend you," she added when Shannon stared back at her blinking thoughtfully.

"Of course, it doesn't," her mother assured her. "What about you?" she added with gentle inquiry. "Were you happier in Broken Arrow?"

A self-conscious blush heated Rachel's face. "Well, no. I mean...

maybe. There was so much open space there, so much peace. Not that it isn't lovely here," she qualified, loath to hurt her mother's feelings. But the townhome in which Shannon lived was right off the Beltway, where the traffic circling Dallas created a muted roar that never went away.

"But there's no Saul here," Shannon stated with a knowing expression.

Rachel's face heated another degree. "No Saul?" She pretended the statement puzzled her.

Her birthmother sighed. "Look, I may not know you as well as I wish I did, but I know when a woman has feelings for a man."

A confusing mix of emotions sluiced through Rachel.

"I guess I do." She cherished the memory of their last kiss.

"There's nothing wrong with that, you know."

Rachel swallowed hard. "I know. It just never occurred to me I might feel that way again for anyone."

"Why not? You're still young. You have your whole life ahead of you."

Rachel shook her head. "But Saul's not like Blake. He's a loner. Even if he has feelings for me, he's not going to attach himself."

Shannon cocked her head and raised an eyebrow. "Why not?"

"Because of his job, I guess. I told you he's a sniper, right? I think he feels like he's beyond redemption and doesn't deserve to be loved or to be happy."

"How much longer will he be a sniper?"

"At least another year. At that point, he can either leave the service or reenlist again."

"Don't you think he might have an incentive to leave if you're waiting in Broken Arrow for him?"

Rachel's hopes rose, only to tumble back to reality. "I doubt it. His plan is to sell the ranch and never go back—too many sad memories."

"So, that's it? You go your separate ways like falling in love happens all the time? Trust me, it doesn't."

Hearing the cynicism in Shannon's voice, Rachel guessed she was thinking of her divorce five years earlier.

"Why don't you call him." Her mother slid Rachel's cell phone toward her. "Ask if you can stay in his house in return for overseeing its renovation."

The possibility Saul might agree held Rachel in thrall momentarily. "But he would have to put up the money to renovate the place. I don't want to impose a financial burden on him. Besides, he's in a hurry to sell."

"You don't know if that's a burden until you ask him." Shannon patted Rachel's hand. "Don't underestimate your pull on him, honey."

The memory of their shared kiss rose in Rachel's mind a second time.

"If you won't do it for yourself, do it for Liam. I want to see him happy, too."

"But what about you?" Rachel asked as Shannon rose to her feet to give her privacy. "You've done so much to accommodate us. I'd feel like we're abandoning you."

Shannon's green eyes misted over. "What matters most to me is your happiness, just like Liam's happiness matters most to you. Plus, you can always visit me. Don't worry, I'm not letting you vanish from my life a second time. Call him." Sending Rachel a wink, she went back upstairs. A few moments later, Rachel heard the shower turn on.

Rachel's heart began to thump. Blowing out a nervous breath, she found Saul's number in her very short list of contacts, put the call through, and held her breath as she listened to the phone ring. She had never known Saul to sleep in, but what if she was calling too early?

Park Grove Cemetery stood deserted at that early hour. Dew quilted the thick grass, silencing Saul's footfalls as he wended his way through the maze of headstones and sepulchers, in search of Cyril Lawson's final resting place. All the while, Saul asked himself why he had come there. Maybe it was the fact that Cyril had held on to Saul's sculptures instead of throwing them away. Maybe it was the apology he had written in his letter. Something deep in Saul's gut was insisting he needed to acknowledge Cyril's decision to make him his heir before he started out on his long journey back east.

The names of the dead echoed in Saul's head as he read them— Morris, Vawter, Halperson. He remembered what Rachel had said about Blake their first night in the motel in Bristol. *"It just blows my mind that he's still alive—just not here, where we are."*

The same could possibly be said for these other souls. Saul pictured them still alive, in another place. A better place, he hoped.

He came across Cyril's marker suddenly. It was a simple granite plaque, placed at the foot of his grave. Two small American flags fluttered on either side of it. With a lurching of his stomach, Saul eyed the freshly covered site. Tiny blades of grass were beginning to sprout from the slightly mounded soil. His gaze returned to Cyril's name, etched crisply into the stone with the insignia of the US Army Rangers underneath it.

Something significant nudged his consciousness, but it took a backseat to his reason for being here. He hadn't sought out Cyril's grave solely to pay his respects. He was there to forgive the man. After all, it would be crass to cling to his hatred of Cyril when his stepdad had extended him an olive branch.

Looking back, it must have been hard for Cyril, if not impossible, to fill his father's shoes. Saul's mother had clearly only married him for stability or, perhaps, to give Saul another father—like that had worked out. And yet, while alleging to hate anyone with skin that wasn't white, Cyril had clearly loved his mother. The fact he'd left her room untouched suggested that was true. Perhaps, in his own rough way, Cyril had even loved his stepson. He hadn't touched Saul's room, either.

With an indrawn breath, Saul bent over to lay the flowers he'd picked off his property upon the marker.

"I forgive you, Cyril," he murmured. Even as the words left his mouth, he feared their unintended and far-reaching consequences.

His cell phone buzzed as he straightened. Plucking it from his pocket, his heart leaped to see the name Angel Johnson on his caller ID.

"Hello?" He could only guess she'd run into a problem.

"Hi."

The sound of her voice filled him with a painful longing to see her.

"Hi, yourself. What's up?"

"Are you outdoors? I hear birds chirping."

"I'm at Park Grove Cemetery. Came to pay my respects to Cyril before I head out of town."

"Oh." The approval in her voice was obvious. "That's great."

He could hear the question in her response. *Have you forgiven him, then?* Instead, she asked on a guarded note, "Are you planning to leave today?"

"Depends," he said, slowly.

"On what?"

On why you're calling. "How much I get done first," he lied. Truth was, he wouldn't accomplish half the tasks Rachel had written on her list. Without her around, he lacked the motivation to get them done. All he wanted to do was to pack up and leave.

"Ah. Well, I'm proud of you for visiting Cyril's grave."

It sounded as if she wanted to say something but lacked the courage. "Is anything wrong?" He turned toward his car and started walking. The sun had risen higher, burning the dew off the grass.

"No...but I do want to ask you something," she finally admitted, "and I don't want you to say yes just because you're an honorable man. You know you've gone above and beyond for us already."

Excitement bubbled up in him. "Ask me what?"

She drew an audible breath, then said in a rush, "I want to know if I can live on your ranch and maybe fix it up in exchange for shelter."

Questions careened through Saul's head. He paused in his approach to his vehicle. "Are things not working out with your birth mother?"

"No, it's not that. Shannon's been great. It's Liam—Lee. He's been depressed ever since we left and I just...I can't picture him attending the huge public school here. He was so happy last week in Broken Arrow."

The agitation that had been churning in Saul for days vanished suddenly. He couldn't believe he hadn't realized the reason for his turmoil until that moment.

He'd wanted Rachel to live on his ranch, safe from Ethan, all along. What's more, it was meant to be, just as the money Cyril had left him suggested.

"Of course, you can live on my ranch, angel," he replied, using the name as an endearment. "You don't even have to ask."

"Thank God." She issued a laugh of relief and then fell silent a moment. "Are you still heading east, then? Will I get to see you first?" she asked on an anxious note.

His plans to leave soon went right out the window. "No. I, uh, I need more time to work on that list you gave me. Lieutenant Mills said I could get another two days off if I need it." He decided suddenly that he *did* need it.

"Great."

He could tell she was smiling. For that matter, so was he. "When will you get here?"

"Is this afternoon too soon?"

His thoughts went to the nefarious intent of the FOR Americans, causing concern to mingle with his anticipation. "Of course not."

"Are you sure?" She had obviously picked up on his reservations. "I mean, we can wait a few more days, but I'm anxious to enroll Liam in school. He's missed so many days already."

Saul decided he would tell her about the hate group's intentions after she arrived. It wasn't like their plans would impact her and Liam's safety, anyway, so long as they remained at home on Columbus Day.

"This afternoon is fine," he assured her with an urge to pinch himself. He couldn't believe he would get to see her that same day. His spirits soared.

"Awesome! Liam will be so excited when I tell him we're going back to the ranch."

"Well, hurry on up, then," Saul said as casually as possible.

"Thank you, Saul. Thank you *so, so* much."

"Text me when you hit the road. That way I'll know when to expect you."

"I will."

"See you soon, then." He ended the call before something sappy slipped out of him. The last thing Rachel needed was to think she and he were going to be a couple now that she was living in his house. He needed to check his own expectations, too. Happily ever after was for other people—not for a dark horse like him. Rachel might be used to having a SEAL for a husband, but Blake, the Team navigator, rarely ever hunted down and targeted his victims the way Saul did, over and over again. That was Saul's burden to bear. And so long as he bore it, he could not, would not ask an innocent like Rachel to link her life with his.

～

Ethan guided his black rental car slowly up Piccadilly Street in Dallas, Texas, in search of house number 1335. A hot noon sun glanced off the hood of his vehicle, blinding him briefly. According to his contact in the National Security Agency who had tracked down all the Shannon Johnson-Browns in Dallas, only three of them were in their late forties, making them potentially Rachel's birth mother.

Two days ago, he had started his vacation to New Orleans by catching a direct flight from Norfolk International. At the airport in New Orleans, he'd rented the black Pontiac he drove now and driven it straight to the hotel where he had stayed once before while attending a convention. Checking into his room, he'd plugged his cell phone into the wall, hung the DO NOT DISTURB sign on the door, and left a message with the front desk that he didn't require room service.

Departing New Orleans, it had taken him just over seven hours to arrive in Dallas, where he'd located an auto detailing shop and paid to have all the windows of his rental darkly tinted. He had then picked over his dinner at a cheap restaurant, then tried to sleep on a rock-hard mattress at a motel that accepted cash in lieu of a card. The next morning, he'd begun his search for Rachel by visiting the three addresses supplied to him by his contact.

The first Shannon Johnson-Brown lived close to the airport in a mobile home with her hulking husband. When Ethan had knocked on their door, the man had taken one look at him and told him to get lost. Certain Rachel and Liam were not living with that couple, Ethan had been happy to comply.

The second Shannon Johnson-Brown had done better for herself, Ethan mused, scrutinizing the complex she lived in. The newly constructed townhomes were made to resemble Victorian-era townhouses in London, with gas lamps every fifty feet and dormered third-story windows. But they were crammed together within shouting distance of the Beltway. With just enough room out front to park two cars, none of them had more than a strip of grass for a yard.

Ethan squinted at the numbers mounted to the mailboxes as he drove slowly by. 1331. 1333. 1335. This was it. He braked abruptly and visually raked the unit's façade for any indication Rachel and Liam might be hiding inside.

Two cars were parked in the abbreviated driveway, a black Toyota Prius and a white Ford F-150. The truck seemed to indicate a man lived inside. With no desire to face another irate male, Ethan eased his foot toward the gas and continued up the road, feeling deflated. Perhaps he'd been too optimistic in his ability to find a needle in a haystack.

A glance into his rearview mirror had him braking abruptly. Was that Rachel? A woman had come out of unit 1335 with a suitcase, and she was hefting it into the bed of the truck.

No, the petite blonde couldn't be Rachel, for her hair was way too short and the color was like sunshine. But there was something about the way she moved. He glanced ahead again, ready to drive off before taking one more look in his side mirror.

He couldn't entirely dismiss the blonde. She was the right height, after all. With his heart beating faster, Ethan decided to double back and investigate. He pulled into the nearest driveway and executed a three-point turn. But by the time he passed the unit, the woman had gone inside.

With his curiosity roused, Ethan wedged his rental into a tight space alongside the curb and waited for her to come out again. He could see her suitcase still in the bed of the truck. She wouldn't just leave it there. The minutes crept by. Ethan freed the top button of his dress shirt and cranked up the air conditioner. Texas was so bloody hot, even in October. Why would anybody choose to live here?

The door at 1335 opened suddenly and, this time, three people filed out. Ethan craned his neck to peer at them. His gaze went straight to the boy, and a cry of relief escaped him.

"Liam!" Yes, it was him, even though his hair had been cut short and he wore unfamiliar clothing. The urge to leap out of the car and run up to his nephew made Ethan wring the leather-covered steering wheel. *Not yet.* He had to get his boy back carefully, craftily.

His gaze returned to Rachel, scarcely recognizable in youthful clothing, as she hugged a woman of similar stature. That had to be Shannon Johnson-Brown. Liam hugged the woman, too. It was evident they were saying their good-byes, but where on earth would they be going? Back home? Had Rachel realized what a mistake she'd made?

Ethan watched them with his heart in his throat. Liam, who appeared tan and healthy and wore a smile on his face, wrestled his own suitcase into the back of the truck next to Rachel's. Then they both climbed into the vehicle and slammed their doors. The motor kicked on. In the next instant, the truck pulled away while Shannon stood on her stoop waving and blowing kisses.

Ethan glared at her. She was little better than his father had been, giving her baby away.

As Rachel drove past him, Ethan shrank down in his seat, counting on the newly tinted windows to protect his anonymity. Then jerking upright, he shifted into drive and pursued the truck. Following Rachel through several city blocks, then onto a highway headed toward the Turnpike, Ethan racked his brain trying to guess their destination. Something told him he was in for a bit of a drive.

He concealed his pursuit by keeping a U-Haul truck between them, then switching lanes now and then to make sure the white truck was still in front of him. Triumph simmered in Ethan's veins mixed with fury. How dare Rachel drive across the country with his boy, like she had the right to take him anywhere? When the time came—and he would know when that was—he would exact justice, the same way he did in court, ruthlessly and effectively. Rachel didn't know it yet, but her days on this earth were numbered.

The familiar rumble of Cyril's F-150 doubled Saul's heartbeat. At last, Rachel and Liam were back at the ranch! He laid the roller carefully in the pan and took a moment to tamp down the lid on the gallon of paint, lest it dry while he welcomed back his guests. Duke, who was not so adept at hiding his emotions, barked and bounced with excitement, his tail swinging wildly.

Letting the dog out ahead of him, Saul paused on the porch as the truck drew alongside his Camaro. A glance at his watch told him Rachel had made the trip in just four hours and twenty minutes, which meant she'd pushed her ride as fast as it could go.

As their gazes locked across the space between them, a chord of desire strummed in Saul's gut.

Easy, there, hotshot. You're only giving them a place to stay.

As Duke sprinted toward Liam's opening door, Saul forced himself to walk slowly off the porch. Liam exploded out of the cab, dropped to his knees, and welcomed Duke's effusive greeting.

"We're gonna live here now!" he announced between doggy licks and assaults.

"I've heard that rumor." Saul's gaze went across the bed of the truck to the woman shutting her own door and grinning at him. Had he seriously once considered her unremarkable?

"You cut the grass," she noted with approval, "And you bought Adirondack chairs!" she cried, as her gaze went to the porch behind him.

"You like 'em?" He lifted both suitcases out of the back before she could reach for them.

"Very much." She admired the nautical blue chairs as she rounded the truck to join him.

"Come on in and see what else I got done," he invited, leading them inside.

He had just put a foot on the first step to the porch when the sound of a car froze him in his tracks. Turning his head sharply toward the sound, he spotted the front end of a black sedan—not the El Camino—sticking out of the tree line. He set the suitcases on the ground and reached for the gun he'd taken to carrying on his hip again.

"Who's that?" Rachel had stilled next to him.

"Liam, take the dog inside," Saul instructed. "You, too. Go on in." Reaching for Rachel, he urged her swiftly up the stairs toward the door.

The screen door banged shut behind the trio. Saul tried to guess the make and model of the car—Chrysler? Pontiac? The windows were darkly tinted, frustrating his efforts to identify the driver. Perhaps the car belonged to prospective buyers. He had yet to tell his Realtor he was taking the property off the market.

Seconds later, the vehicle backed out of sight. Rachel and Liam's recent arrival prevented Saul from jumping into his Camaro to pursue it. .

Feelings of foreboding pooled in his gut. Two things occurred to him at once. First, he couldn't leave Rachel living alone and defenseless in his house as long as the FOR American's leader lived at-large, which meant he really ought to take up Andy's offer and help the police stop the planned violence, whatever it was. Second, while he visited the police station, he needed to remove the flyer with Rachel's and Liam's pictures on it. They couldn't live anonymously in this town with their faces staring off the BOLO board for everyone to see.

With his thoughts thus preoccupied, Saul continued into the house, putting down the suitcases to shut and lock the inner door.

She stood waiting for him, literally wringing her hands. "Any idea who that was?"

He hastened to reassure her. "Probably some prospective buyers. I need to call my Realtor and tell him the property's not for sale anymore." He could hear Liam back in his bedroom, talking to Duke like they were old friends.

Rachel searched his expression. "I hope you don't regret your decision."

It took all of his self-control not to pull her into his arms and make it obvious exactly how glad he was to have her back.

"It's the best decision I've made yet, second to helping you and Liam leave Virginia."

Her gaze softened. She took a couple of steps in his direction. Saul could see it in her face. She wanted to hug him, maybe more. He quickly picked up the suitcases he'd put down and used them as an excuse to walk away from her.

"I'll put these away." The silence following him betrayed her chagrin.

It pained him to embarrass her. But the sooner Rachel realized her moving back didn't mean they were a couple, the happier she would be. She had known when she asked him if she could live here that she would be alone with her son. She'd known he couldn't stay. Those few blissful times they'd kissed didn't change that fact. Surely she already knew that, but in case she didn't, he would abstain from kissing her again.

Disappointment shackled him. Still, he resolved to keep his distance, not just for her sake but for his own. The affection Rachel showed him aroused feelings he'd never known he had. Feelings he could ill afford in his line of work. A sniper had to be cunning and ruthless, not soft and caring.

Rachel deserved better than a dark horse like him, anyway. She deserved a man like Andy Cannard, an upstanding and friendly man, who lived right here in Broken Arrow, who could love and protect her from this day forward.

Jealousy simmered in him. But facts were facts. Saul Wade, The Reaper, couldn't begin to give Rachel LeMere the love she deserved.

Watching Saul snatch up their suitcases and carry them to the bedrooms was a painful wake-up call.

Rachel walked blindly into the kitchen, put a hand on the counter to steady herself, and drew a deep breath before releasing it slowly.

Saul could not have made his intentions any clearer. Regardless of the unforgettable kiss they'd shared prior to her leaving for Dallas, Saul didn't want to be her life partner. Chagrin seared her heart. She could have sworn the gentle yet protective way he'd treated her meant he felt the same way she did. Clearly, she had been fooling herself.

Reliving the moment their gazes had met, just minutes prior as she'd pulled alongside his vehicle, she paused. Hadn't she seen her own delight mirrored in his face? Yes, she was sure of it. Saul Wade *did* have feelings for her; he simply didn't want to admit to them. What if it wasn't for lack of love that he distanced himself, but some other reason, like the fact he still had to fulfill his reenlistment?

What if she could convince him none of that mattered? She would wait for him to come back. Blake had taken off for months at a time, and she'd never once wavered in her love for him. Her commitment wasn't the issue. The real issue was whether Saul could walk away from the niche he had carved for himself. Did he really want to come back to a house he'd been so keen to sell? Or would he keep doing what he did best, leaving her to live here all alone?

That was a question only Saul could answer.

CHAPTER 14

*E*than had never staked out a property before. He'd viewed many a detective movie, however, and it didn't seem too hard. Just a lot of waiting and watching. Following another fitful night's sleep at yet another cheesy motel, this time in downtown Broken Arrow, he headed for the property where Liam and Rachel were now situated, purchasing a pair of binoculars along the way. He was pleased to discover a utility road that hid him from those coming and going up the driveway, which was on the other side of the street and down a ways.

He passed the entire morning watching for activity. What was Rachel doing there, of all places, and did she intend to stay? That likely depended on who the stranger was whom Ethan had glimpsed the previous day.

After three hours of nothing happening, boredom impelled Ethan out of his vehicle to walk around a bit. He was sitting on the hood of his car, batting at a pesky fly, when the blue car next to which Rachel had parked yesterday emerged, galvanizing Ethan into action. Sliding quickly off his car, he jumped into the driver's seat to follow.

As the Camaro dipped out of sight over the hill, Ethan raced to catch up with it, then fell back to follow from a distance. He believed he could see three people in the car, which meant Rachel and Liam were likely going somewhere with the stranger. Curiously, the license plates were from Virginia, which made Ethan suspect the man they were visiting was the same man who'd helped Rachel disappear. After trailing the Camaro several miles, it turned unexpectedly into Ernest Childers Middle School.

Shaken, Ethan drove past the entrance, then doubled back in time to see Rachel and the stranger escort Liam inside the building.

How dare she, Ethan raged. Rachel was enrolling Liam in this *public* school. The action suggested she clearly *did* intend to stay in Oklahoma. Moreover, it demonstrated she had no idea how critical it was for Liam to get a top-notch education. Of course, she wouldn't know.

Seething with helplessness, Ethan waited for Rachel and the stranger to emerge from school again. When they did so, fifteen minutes later without the boy, Ethan gave an exclamation of disbelief. They were leaving Liam to spend the rest of the day in a strange school, surrounded by ill-mannered public-school children?

Realizing he recognized the man, Ethan gasped and forgot about Liam's plight. Wasn't that Lieutenant Mills's teammate, the sniper who'd testified at Mills's court martial the previous year? Of course, the SEAL with a ponytail and a savage tan was singularly unforgettable, even with his long hair cut and his jaw clean shaven.

Ethan recalled trying to ruin the man's credibility by pointing out how he'd carried an unauthorized rifle onto the military base, the one he'd allegedly used to protect Jonah Mills when Commander Dwyer turned on him. Neither the judge nor the defense, however, had cared much about the violation. What was the sniper's name again? Wade, wasn't it? Yes, Chief Saul Wade.

To think that Rachel might have known the man even then was eye opening. But, of course, she likely would have. Blake would've been among the SEALs supporting Lieutenant Mills if he hadn't already been dead. How long had she been planning to betray her own brother with this sniper? Had she been in touch with Wade back then, using her helplessness as a means of enlisting his aid? Yes, of course she had. No wonder she'd managed to escape so cleverly. A nasty word found its way to Ethan's lips. She deserved to die for her deception. Wade deserved a similar fate, but Ethan knew not to tangle with a SEAL in person, especially not the nation's top sniper.

With his heart pounding, he watched Wade assist Rachel into his car, then drop into his own seat. As they left the school, headed in the direction of town, Ethan pursued them at a careful distance. All at once, the Camaro turned into the parking lot of the Broken Arrow Police Station. Panicking, Ethan squealed into a fast-food restaurant across the street, then veered into a parking spot. Had they noticed him tailing them? Were they reporting him to the police?

Snatching up his binoculars, he scrutinized the couple as they walked casually into the police station. They didn't behave as if someone were following them. Puzzled as to what they were up to and wondering if it was in some way connected to the nationwide Amber Alert, Ethan kept his gaze riveted on the entrance until his air conditioner started blowing lukewarm air. Abandoning his stakeout, he got out of his car and went inside Raising Cane's Chicken Fingers to purchase lunch.

His plans to eliminate Rachel had just gotten trickier. If that man was protecting her, Ethan would have a much harder time getting Liam back.

Saul led Rachel toward Andy's cubicle with his palms sweating. He hadn't wanted her to set foot in the police station before he'd removed her picture from the BOLO board. But she'd been adamant about helping the police identify Will Davis, especially now that she'd decided to live in Broken Arrow. Since Saul couldn't bring himself to tell her about the flyer on display there for anyone to see, it was up to him to remove it, ASAP.

The delight that lit up Andy's face when he caught sight of Rachel set Saul's teeth on edge.

"Angel!" Andy popped out of his chair to greet them. "I thought you went home to Texas. What brings you back?"

Rachel glanced at Saul and shrugged. "I decided Broken Arrow was a better place to raise my son."

Saul's breath caught. He hadn't expected Rachel to mention Liam quite so soon.

Andy's blinking eyes were the only indication of his surprise. "I didn't know you had a son."

Saul wiped his moist palms on his jeans while picturing Liam's photo next to his mother's, right outside the door.

"We just dropped him off at the school he'll attend so he can get his feet wet."

"Ernest Childers? That's a good school." Andy smiled at her warmly. "I'm so glad you decided to come back."

Saul wished the man would dial back his gladness several degrees.

Rachel clasped her hands in a nervous gesture. "Thanks. Me, too. Do you still need a description of Will Davis?"

"You bet I do." Andy glanced at his watch. "Come with me. I'll put you together with our forensic artist. Higgins can render a composite while Saul and I head to a meeting two doors down. How's that sound?"

"Great." Rachel raised her eyebrows at Saul in a look that meant, *Told you it wouldn't be a problem if I came along.*

Hah, if she only knew. Saul followed Andy and Rachel out of the Command and Control Room, past the BOLO board, toward the rear of the building. Andy was too busy staring at Rachel to pay notice to any one of the dozens of flyers posted there.

As they arrived at Higgins's office, Saul remained at the door while Andy introduced Angel to the forensic artist. The flyer, still visible out of the corner of Saul's eye, was turning his mouth dry. The sooner he took it down, the safer Rachel would be.

Realizing the hall was presently deserted, Saul muttered his intent to use the restroom and backed away. Neither Rachel nor Andy, nor Higgins paid him any heed.

A woman stepped out of the restroom, intercepting Saul's path. He changed course for the water fountain.

"Hey, Saul." Bethany breezed past him. It was clear she wanted to chat but was in too much of a hurry.

As the hallway emptied again, Saul searched the ceiling for signs of any camera. There was only one at the far end, focused on the lobby. Clear. All he needed was five seconds to make things right.

Five. He crossed from the water fountain to the bulletin board. *Four.* He reached for the flyer, grabbed it, and gave it a yank. *Three.* The pushpin popped out and fell to the floor. *Crap. Two.* Saul kicked the pin down the hallway and spun toward the bathroom, folding the flier as he went. *One.* He stuffed the flier into his pocket as he pushed through the heavy door. *Done.*

He went to wash his hands and let his tension ease. Apart from the pushpin falling, his execution had been flawless. Hopefully nobody stepped on the pin before Saul had a chance to pick it up. With that intent, he left the restroom and ran straight into Andy Cannard, pushing the pin back onto the BOLO board in the exact spot where it had been earlier.

Dang it.

Fortunately, Andy didn't seem to notice there was a flyer missing. "You ready?" he asked Saul.

"Sure."

"Let's go." Andy gestured and, together, they went past the artist's office, where Rachel was busy describing Davis, and into Conference Room B.

The door stood open. As they walked inside, Saul and Andy were the last to put in an appearance. Fifteen members of Tulsa's Special Operations Team sat around a long table in the company of an older officer. The SOT guys, dressed in dark-blue battle dress, reminded Saul of his teammates back home, all supremely fit and itching for action. They eyed Saul with a mix of respect and curiosity. Clearly, they'd read the same article in the newspaper Tami Goodner had mentioned the day they'd run into each other at the Neighborhood Market.

Andy introduced him. "Everyone, this is Navy SEAL sniper Saul Wade. I'm pretty sure everyone here has heard of him, since he's a legend. We used to call him Half-Breed back in high school, but I'm the only one who still gets to do that. Saul's going to fill in for Meekins, since you're a man short. Saul, this is Captain Lewis, head of our Operations Division."

The blue-eyed captain with a handlebar mustache came partway out of his seat to shake Saul's hand. "Privilege to have you with us, Wade."

"Thank you, sir."

Andy added, "And this is the team lead, Commander Boykins."

A bald and weathered man, Boykins could have been thirty-five or fifty-five. Nodding at Saul respectfully, he gestured with his head to the only empty chair. "Have a chair next to Robison. He's your partner."

Saul grasped the tall blond's extended hand as he dropped into his seat. Robison seemed pleased to have him for a side kick.

Saul focused back on Andy, who was writing **Fists of Righteous Americans** in bold black letters on the white erase board.

"They're a local hate group," Andy faced the group again, "with a history going back to the Tulsa Race Massacre of 1921, if you can believe it. They used to have hundreds of members, but this year they were only eleven members strong."

He took a folder off the podium and opened it, reading all eleven names out loud, including Cyril Lawson's.

"About six months ago, Lawson, who was Saul's stepdad, was their elected leader. When he got sick, a fellow named Will Davis took over. The group used to meet at Lawson's house. Since his death, we don't know where they're meeting, although they've been known to use the abandoned homestead locally known as the Reeve's place."

Saul suffered the scrutiny of every man at the table. It was obvious they were asking themselves how a racist like Cyril had ended up with a half-native stepson. Andy recaptured their attention by describing the recent confrontations between Saul and three of the group's members. He detailed how the group had left rifles and shotguns in Cyril's office, then bartered for their return by holding a friend of Saul's hostage.

"Her name is Angel Johnson," Andy continued. "You may get to meet her in a little while. She's working with Higgins right now to come up with Will Davis's composite."

Boykins interrupted, asking Saul, "How'd you get her back?"

Finding himself in the hot seat, Saul cleared his throat. "I just walked up to the place and knocked on the door."

Andy rolled his eyes at the humble reply. "First he jammed and rendered useless all the firearms. Then he negotiated Angel's release, using diplomacy instead of force. We all know what he could have done."

Saul's face heated as the SOT members studied him approvingly.

Andy continued with his spiel. "Now that you know the background of this hate group, let me clue you in on their plans. Minutes taken from their last meeting mention a demonstration on Columbus Day and the detonation of a truckload of ANFO, with nitromethane as the fuel."

Some of the men present muttered their dismay with colorful epithets.

"What the minutes don't say," Andy added, "is where this detonation is supposed to take place or what time of day. Furthermore, all ten remaining members of the group have gone underground. BAPD has been scouring the streets for them, to no avail."

"Put their faces on posters and offer a reward," Boykins suggested. "Someone knows where they are."

"We'll do that," Andy answered, gaining a nod of approval from Captain Lewis. "Another tactic is to arrest their leader, Will Davis, but we know virtually nothing about him. Miss Johnson says he told her he'd been an Army Ranger serving in the first Gulf War. We looked that up and, sure enough, there was a Willard Davis—not William—in the Ranger's division in the 1990s. That man was dishonorably discharged. After that, there's no paper trail. He might be our guy; he might not."

The realization that had occurred to Saul fleetingly while visiting Cyril's grave site crystallized suddenly. Cyril had been an Army Ranger also, which meant the two men might well have known each other when in service. He would investigate on his own watch, perhaps enlisting Charlotte's help. Her mentor, Special Agent Casey Fitzpatrick, had access to all kinds of records.

"Let's talk about potential targets," Andy suggested with a grimace. "And feel free to offer up any ideas you may have. According to Miss Johnson, Davis was upset about jobs being taken from Americans and given to immigrants. He said he was to teach the 'liberal hackers' a lesson. Anyone who knows what that means, I welcome your input."

The room fell quiet as everyone mulled over the words.

Captain Lewis volunteered a possibility. "There's an ethical hackers course taught in Tulsa every few months, but I don't see what white supremacists would have against computer geeks."

Andy spread his hands. "That's the problem. We have no idea what Davis meant. Obviously, we need to pull in members of the group and interrogate them, but first we have to find them."

A light knock at the door cut into Andy's statement. Excusing himself, he went to answer it and came back with his hand curled around the arm of a self-conscious Rachel.

"Everyone, this is Angel Johnson, and this is the composite of Davis she has helped to come up with." He displayed the computer aided composite with his other hand.

Saul found himself regarding a very good approximation of the man who'd greeted him at the Reeve's house.

"Has anyone seen this guy?" Andy finally let go of Rachel's arm.

All present shook their heads.

"We'll put that composite in Friday's newspaper," Captain Lewis suggested, "along with a modest reward."

Andy whispered something into Rachel's ear. She nodded and started out of the room, conveying to Saul, by tipping her head, that she would wait for him in the hallway.

Following a few more comments from the chief of operations about the importance of keeping the public safe, Andy informed the group they would meet again on Saturday afternoon, same time. He then ceded the floor to Boykins, who told the SOT members, including Saul, that they would train for a worst-case scenario on Saturday morning at zero-eight-hundred hours.

"Talk with me afterward," Robison, his partner, said from the corner of his mouth.

Saul nodded.

Captain Lewis brought the meeting to an end. The room emptied out except for Saul and Robison, who simply wanted to get to know Saul better. When Saul finally joined Rachel in the hallway, he found her talking to Andy, her cheeks unquestionably flushed.

Recalling his intent to lay no claim to her, Saul strode right past the pair, headed for the water fountain. There he took a sip and waited for them to catch up with him. He straightened to find Andy jutting out a hand for him to shake.

"Thanks for deciding to join us, Half-Breed. You're going to like working with the SOT. I have no doubt."

It was all Saul could do not to crush Andy's hand in a bruising grip.

"Angel." Andy smiled warmly down at Rachel. "Don't be a stranger."

Saul glanced at his watch to act like they were running out of time, although they still had an hour before they needed to pick Liam up from school. He decided to take Rachel to the bank first.

"We'd better go. Later, Duck." Putting a hand at the small of Rachel's back, Saul steered her lightly toward the exit.

Rachel glanced at him sidelong. "Duck?"

"We used to call him that in school. *Cannard* means 'duck' in French, except it's spelled with one *n*, and his has two."

"He's super friendly."

Saul clamped his jaw shut to keep from saying something distinctly *unfriendly*.

～

"Are you applying for a line of credit to do the renovations?" Rachel asked when Saul explained they were going to the bank before picking Liam up from school.

Saul stared straight ahead. "Here's the thing: I haven't been totally honest with you." He glanced at her briefly, then back at the road.

Rachel braced herself. "About what?" Had he sold the house right out from under her and not told her about it?

"I don't need to apply for a loan. Cyril left me money—twenty-five thousand dollars, as a matter of fact."

Rachel's jaw dropped with amazement. "Exactly twenty-five thousand?"

"Yep."

Something occurred to her. "How long have you known this?"

"Since my visit to the lawyer soon after we arrived."

The confession dismayed her. Saul had known all this time he could afford a total renovation, yet he'd never once mentioned his windfall. Why not?

She hardly noticed when he turned into the one-way entrance of a local credit union, glided into an empty parking spot, and put the car into park.

"Look, I should have told you earlier," he admitted.

"Why didn't you?" She hid her hurt feelings with difficulty. "I could have stayed at my birth mother's condo. You didn't have to say yes to my proposition. Clearly, you want to sell the place. So, do it. We'll go back to Dallas."

"No." Saul caught her hand unexpectedly and held on to it. "The reason I didn't tell you is because I'm a knucklehead. When you called me," he continued, finding his words with difficulty, "and you asked if you could come back...I knew it was meant to be."

"Really?" Relief replaced Rachel's disillusionment.

"Really. The money, the timing, everything. You and Liam belong here. It's fate."

Pleased that he'd decided her renovation was meant to be, she leaned toward him to plant a grateful kiss on his cheek.

Saul turned his head at the last instant. Their lips connected, then lingered. What ensued was a kiss that went from platonic to passionate in a heartbeat. Rachel's pulse raced. Her senses sang. She lifted a hand to caress Saul's hair, but then he caught it and, with visible difficulty, pulled himself away, putting her hand down on her lap.

"Sorry. That shouldn't have happened." He scowled with self-censure.

Rachel searched his taut profile wondering what he meant.

Saul sighed. "Don't look at me like that. This is the real world we're living in. We're not going to be together. I'm leaving. And I may never be back."

Dismayed by his gruff tone and chagrined by his rejection, Rachel started to assure him she would wait for him, but he cut her off.

"You deserve better than me, Rachel. I'm not the one for you. You understand?"

He seemed so serious, she realized he actually believed that. "What do you mean, I deserve better? There's nothing wrong with you."

"I'm a sniper. If the devil doesn't already own me, then Uncle Sam does."

"Only for one more year. And the devil doesn't own you, Saul. That's your conscience talking. If you feel unworthy, all you have to do is ask for absolution. There's nothing God can't forgive—"

"Enough." He cut her off. "Maybe I don't want God's forgiveness."

She gasped. "Don't say that."

"I'm saying it. I made my bed a long time ago. Now I have to lie in it." With those final and disheartening words, he pushed his door open. "Let's get this done so Liam doesn't have to wait for us."

Rachel responded automatically, stepping out of the car and blindly following Saul into the bank. Thirty minutes later, she had access to twenty-five thousand dollars, placed in a special shared account. What she didn't have was the hope Saul would give up his legendary reputation so he could be with her and Liam.

In silence, they buckled their seatbelts and headed back to Ernest Childers Middle School. Once there, Rachel went in by herself to fetch Liam from the office. The other students thronged the front hallway en route to their busses.

"How was it?" Rachel asked Liam as they stepped into the sunshine and crossed the parking lot to Saul's car.

"Not bad," he said with a dismissive shrug.

She hoped he wasn't lying just to make her feel better.

"Is that your schedule?" She indicated the paper in Liam's hand.

"Yep." He gave it to her. "They put me in the highest math class."

"I'm sure you'll be fine, honey. I doubt they're as rigorous here as they were at Norfolk Academy." Rachel opened her door and let Liam duck into the backseat.

"How'd you do, tiger?" Saul asked.

"Good." Liam's seatbelt gave a *click*.

Rachel got into her own seat and buckled in.

"I made a new friend," Liam added, as Saul drove away from the schoolgrounds, getting out ahead of the busses.

Rachel was delighted to hear it. "That's great, honey. What's his name?"

"Cody. He says he has a trampoline in his backyard, and he wants me to come over this weekend to jump on it."

"Well, that sounds fun. So, you're okay with starting school tomorrow? You'll have a three-day weekend right afterward."

"Sure, but I want to take the bus. Kids might think I'm weird if my parents come and pick me up."

Rachel's breath caught. Glancing at Saul as he accelerated, she could tell by his frown Liam's comment unsettled him.

On their short drive back to the ranch, Rachel asked herself how Liam was going to handle Saul's departure. Not well, she suspected. Her son had developed an attachment for their rescuer, as had she. If only there was a way to convince Saul to return to Oklahoma once his commitment to the Teams was over. She envisioned him turning down another four-year enlistment in order to return to Broken Arrow. An unexpected yearning gripped her heart. *Don't even think about it. Saul is free to do whatever he desires.* But having pictured Saul at her side in the years to come, Rachel acknowledged that was exactly what she wanted, what she needed, to be truly happy.

She would never admit that much to Saul, however. It wasn't her place to try and persuade him. If God intended for them to one day be a family, God would whisper into Saul's ear, transforming his thoughts and his plans for the future.

A sudden parallel encouraged her. In the Bible, Saul of Tarsus had been a chief persecutor of the followers of Christ. And yet, in an encounter with the risen Jesus on the road to Damascus, Saul had been transformed into one of Jesus' greatest enthusiasts, no longer Saul but Paul.

Wow! If the God of creation could transform Saul of Tarsus from an enemy of Christianity into an advocate for Christ, then surely God could transform Saul of Broken Arrow from a wandering warrior into a family man.

Resolving to pray for precisely that, Rachel glanced over at him and smiled.

"What?" Saul asked, with a frown of suspicion.

"Nothing," she said lightly.

Yet it would mean everything to her and Liam if her prayer came true.

CHAPTER 15

"I want Saul to walk me to the bus stop," Liam announced over breakfast the following morning.

Saul, who was polishing off a bowl of oatmeal, glanced from Liam to Rachel. Considering she had fussed over the clothes he was wearing and packed his lunch, Saul worried Liam's preference might hurt his mother's feelings.

Seeming surprised rather than upset, Rachel asked Saul, "Is that okay with you?"

"Sure." Perhaps he could use the opportunity to check Liam's expectations.

"Better hurry, then." Rachel glanced at the clock on the microwave. "He's supposed to be at the top of the driveway in thirteen minutes."

"I'm going to brush my teeth." Liam left his bowl in the sink.

Saul polished off his breakfast and followed Liam's example. The time had come for him to explain his obligations to Liam so he didn't nurse unrealistic expectations. Poor kid, he so obviously enjoyed the presence of a father-figure in his life. Blake's death had left a gaping void that Saul couldn't begin to fill, not as long as he was a member of SEAL Team Six.

No pressure. Saul headed to the bathroom to brush his own teeth. Telling Liam he couldn't be there for him held as much allure as being told he had to cross a mine field in order to fulfill his objective.

Five minutes later, they left the house to be greeted by an autumnal chill, the kind that stimulated the brain and made a body actually want to go to school. The morning sun lit the tops of the trees, setting them ablaze. As they started down the driveway, Saul summoned the message he wanted to impart to Liam.

Glancing over at the boy, he found him loping happily alongside him. Words of farewell stuck in Saul's throat.

"Not afraid or anything, are you?" he asked him instead.

"Nope." Liam shook his head. "It's not scary. The teachers are nice. Most of the kids are, too."

Saul caught himself about to say, *If anyone bullies you, just let me know.* Considering he wouldn't even be around, the words were pointless.

"There are things worse than school," Liam added, as they stepped under the trees.

"Like what?"

"Like my uncle finding us."

Saul's stride almost faltered. "He won't find you here." He cast the boy a reassuring glance.

But Liam, who was watching his feet glide in and out of shadows, didn't see it.

"I wish you'd stay," he said quietly.

The words pegged Saul right in the chest, although he was glad Liam had brought up the subject.

"You know I can't, right? I reenlisted three years ago, which means I owe the Navy another year. I have to go back, or I'd violate military law."

"The Uniformed Code of Military Justice," Liam replied, surprising Saul. "Uncle Ethan told me all about it." He sent Saul an appealing glance. "What about after that? Couldn't you come home?"

Home. It did feel like home now that Rachel and Liam lived there.

"Maybe." Saul hadn't planned on giving the boy hope, but the word popped out of him before he could stop it.

All at once, Liam shrugged off his backpack and unzipped the front pocket. His steps slowed as he felt inside it.

"I made this for you while we were in Dallas." He pulled out a palm-sized object and handed it to Saul.

What used to be a hunk of cedar had been whittled down into a miniature box turtle. Saul drew up short to examine the turtle's high, rounded shell with hexagonal markings painstakingly delineated. Liam had even remembered to carve out three toes on the rear legs.

"Wow," he breathed, touched by the gift.

"You said those were your favorite animals."

And the kid remembered that? A noose seemed to close around Saul's throat.

"You sure you don't want to give it to your mama?"

"I'm sure. It's for you."

Inexplicably moved, Saul cradled it in his palm. "Thank you."

"Turtles carry their homes on their backs," Liam added solemnly. "When you look at it, I want you to think about your home."

The words stitched through Saul's heart. "I will," he promised thickly. Then he glanced at his watch. "Better walk fast or we'll miss the bus."

They reached the head of the driveway just as the bus came into view.

"All right. Go get 'em, tiger." Saul gave Liam a gentle nudge.

Shooting Saul a brave smile, Liam stepped through the opening doors and climbed inside. Appearing at a window, he waved good-bye. With a pang of nostalgia, Saul remembered having done the same to his mother, year after year, until he was old enough to drive.

The feeling he was being spied upon pulled him sharply from his reverie. He scoured the empty country road, hunting for the cause of his sudden awareness. Birds twittered in the branches overhead. The ubiquitous wind stirred the yellowing leaves. But the road appeared deserted—unless someone was parked up the utility road. He asked himself if he was seeing a glint of metal through the foliage, or was that just a trick of the sunlight?

Hearing nothing to indicate a human presence, he backed slowly up his driveway. He'd been away from the field too long. He turned toward the house, his steps lagging as he remembered Rachel's express desire to go over her renovation plans with him. He reflected on the kiss he'd stolen in the car the day before. His actions had totally negated the message he'd been trying to tell her. He couldn't let that happen again.

Regardless of her pull on him, he shouldn't give her any reason to believe they would be together in a year's time, or ever.

Rachel had experienced true love. She'd had that with Blake. Saul, with his awful past and the present demons, told himself he couldn't begin to give her the kind of relationship she was used to. Like he'd told her yesterday, she deserved better.

What's more, he wasn't about to ask God to forgive him for everything he'd done solely so he could feel worthy of her, not when he would be called upon to kill again.

And yet that word *maybe* that had slipped out of him in response to Liam was stuck in his heart like a splinter he couldn't remove. Maybe he *would* come back when his debt to Uncle Sam was paid. But that was a long time from now, and Andy Cannard wouldn't waste a second of it before he asked Rachel out on a date.

Saul swallowed the bad taste in his mouth and resolved not to think about that. Puca used to tell him no man could see the future. *"Only the Great Spirit knows which way the wind blows,"* Puca used to say. Fretting over events he couldn't predict accomplished nothing.

As the front door opened, Rachel lifted her gaze from the sketch she was making of the new kitchen layout. The shuttered expression on Saul's face had her lowering the notepad.

"Did it go okay?"

"Yep. We got there right as the bus pulled up. We, uh, we had a talk on the way, so it took a little longer than it would have."

"Oh?" She hoped he would tell her he'd let her son down gently.

Instead, Saul approached her with something in his hand. "He gave me this."

Intrigued, Rachel took the item and inspected it. "Oh, my. This has to be the sculpture he's been whittling all this time."

"You haven't seen it until now?"

"No, he kept it hidden. He said it was for you. Gosh, it's precious." She handed it back while searching his expression.

The muscles in Saul's face tightened, suggesting he wrestled with something he wasn't sharing with her.

She observed him slip the gift into his pocket.

"Is this a bad time to pass my plans by you?" She showed him her sketch.

He glanced at her sketch of the new cabinet layout. "I trust you, Rachel. You don't need my approval on anything."

His words, meant to be supportive, made it clear he didn't wish to spend time with her.

"All right, thank you," she said, hiding her hurt, "but this is the first kitchen I've ever remodeled. Couldn't you just listen and give me your honest feedback?"

"Sure. But then I'd better finish painting the bedrooms."

Again, his words suggested he preferred to work alone. "Suit yourself." To her chagrin, the words came out sounding snarky.

Saul cast his gaze toward his feet and sighed. "Look, I think it's best for me to stay away from you right now."

Hope flared, chasing her hurt away. "Why?" Her question demanded honesty.

His eyes smoldered as he raised them to her.

"You know why." He turned and strode from the kitchen toward the bedrooms, growling over his shoulder, "I'll check out your plans later."

Rachel bit her lip against the urge to follow. Saul's searing expression filled her with a reckless urge to chase after him and experience the passion his caution suggested. But that would be a hollow experience. She didn't want casual intimacy. She wanted a lifetime of commitment—something she'd experienced for a decade with Blake. Saul deserved to know what that felt like. He deserved to have a family again, and she would do everything in her power to make that happen.

Ultimately, however, the choice to participate was his.

They worked in separate areas of the house all morning. Once, Saul strode into the kitchen for a wet sponge, and then promptly turned around. Rachel had finalized her plans for the kitchen and had started her design of the bathroom in the hallway, when her stomach rumbled. Overhearing Saul talking to someone on his cell phone, she approached the master bedroom, where he was rolling paint on the last wall, his back to her. He held his phone to his ear with one hand, the roller with the other.

"Thanks, Charlotte," he said, his voice rich with affection. "That's exactly what I needed. Yeah, I miss you, too. See you soon."

Rachel whirled away with sudden consternation. Did Saul have a girlfriend? Perhaps a woman waited with open arms for his return to Virginia. An awful empty feeling spread inside of Rachel, robbing her of her appetite.

With hands that shook, she put two ham-and-cheese sandwiches together for their lunch but only ate half of her own.

Rather than take Saul's sandwich to him, she left it on the counter, heading onto the porch with her tea to sit on an Adirondack chair and mull over her discovery.

The prospect for a future with Saul seemed suddenly much less likely. No wonder Saul had rebuffed her outside the bank when she tried bringing up the future. He already had a woman in his life—a circumstance that had never even occurred to Rachel, probably since he'd kissed her twice now. No wonder he had apologized and said kissing her had been a mistake.

She stewed for a moment, feeling betrayed, then decided her naiveté was to blame.

Of course Saul had a woman waiting for him. With his exotic features and dangerous air, he had to be irresistible to women. *What a fool I am.*

~

At the outset of their meeting Saturday afternoon, Andy shot Saul a peculiar look, then avoided making eye contact.

"Welcome back, everybody," Andy called out, bringing their meeting to order. "Before we get started, please join me in welcoming two bomb experts from Tulsa. Doug Flint and Nate Sievers are going to help us with the ANFO threat."

Saul joined the rest of the men in showing their gratitude. Having trained all morning with the SOT, Saul felt more like a valued team member than he had on Thursday. Somewhere between their two-mile run, followed by hostage rescue drills and target practice, the other men had started talking to him and cracking jokes at his expense. Andy, on the other hand, was making him nervous with his suddenly strange behavior.

The detective snatched a piece of paper off the lectern. "Let's start with an update. I managed to get my hands on Les Wright and Tim Olsen's state tax returns. Turns out they both used to do landscaping at Indian Springs Golf Course. I called their manager and he admitted, with some chagrin, that he'd replaced both of them in June with Latinos who worked harder and accepted lower wages."

Captain Lewis tapped the end of his pencil on the table. "Have we managed to pick those two up yet?"

"No, sir. According to their mothers, neither one is answering his cell phone. Matter of fact, all ten members of the group are still off the grid. They must be hunkered down somewhere. However, we've put up posters all over town offering a hundred-dollar reward per member and two hundred dollars for their leader, so I'm hopeful we'll be tipped off soon."

Captain Lewis cleared his throat. "What else have we learned about the leader? Where does he work? What makes him dangerous, apart from his military background?"

Andy grimaced and shook his head. "He's elusive, sir. I can't find a home address, and the rest of his military records are sealed."

"I've got something," Saul ventured as Andy fell quiet.

Nineteen sets of eyes swung in his direction, including Andy's narrowed ones.

"Who's your source?" Andy demanded, uncharacteristically rude.

"Sorry, can't say," Saul replied. Charlotte's mentor, Fitz, had made her swear she wouldn't reveal her source since, technically, he wasn't supposed to share classified data with a training candidate. "The suspect's full name is Willard Douglas Davis, born July 27, 1960. He was an enlisted Army Ranger and a teammate of Cyril Lawson's when they both served in the 75th Ranger Regiment in Iraq. While Cyril retired, Willard was dishonorably discharged for irregular behaviors, including pulling the teeth of his Iraqi victims. He returned to his home state of Arkansas in 2001, where he lived until his wife divorced him. In 2008, he came to Broken Arrow to reconnect with Cyril. He worked as a dishwasher at Indian Springs Golf Course—same place Wright and Olsen worked. And his paychecks have been going to a P.O. Box just up the street."

Captain Lewis sent Saul a nod. "Now we're getting somewhere."

"We still have no home address," Saul pointed out. "Davis has a history of renting properties, but he's never owned any."

Lewis gave a frustrated growl. "Why do I get the feeling we're not going to pick him up before Columbus Day? If we can't find these people and stop this thing, I want all of you here at zero-six-hundred hours on Monday, geared up and ready to roll at a moment's notice. We still have no idea what the target is, do we?"

Andy grimaced and shook his head. "Could be anywhere."

"Anything else, Detective?" Lewis asked him.

"Just watch your phones for updates. Otherwise, be here at the crack of dawn Monday."

Saul was the first man out of his seat. He didn't want to be badgered about his source, and Andy's change in attitude made him nervous. As he darted out the door, however, Andy called out to him.

"Hey, Saul, got a minute?"

Saul paused in the hallway and braced himself.

Andy gestured to the door at the end of the hallway. "Why don't we step outside a moment?"

Saul's stomach lurched. With a reluctant nod, he followed Andy out the fire exit onto the field where he'd trained with the SOT members earlier that morning.

"What's up?"

Andy squared off to face him. "Nice work in there, though I don't see why you can't share your contact."

Saul just stared at the man, and Andy gave up asking.

Instead, he said with a watchful gaze, "I know you removed that flyer from the board the other day."

Saul froze, too dismayed to defend himself.

"I hang up those fliers myself. Took me a while to figure out which one you'd taken, but I found it. Rachel looks nothing like her picture. Only her eyes are the same."

Saul flushed hot then cold as he tried to guess what action Andy was going to take.

"You don't strike me as the kidnapper type," the man mused, still watching him closely.

"I'm not," Saul bit out.

"Mmm." Andy gnawed on his bottom lip for several seconds. "Let me guess. Rachel's running from a jealous, possibly abusive husband. That's why she changed her name, so the jerk couldn't find her."

Saul couldn't tell if Andy was toying with him while still intending to arrest him, or whether he sympathized with Rachel's plight.

"Something like that."

"If that's the case and you're not her kidnapper, then you rescued her," Andy deduced.

Saul crossed his arms over his chest and deflected Andy's gaze without speaking. He wasn't going to say anything that might implicate him.

"What about her son?" Andy probed. "Did his father abuse him, too, or only his mother?"

"The kid is better off here; let's just leave it at that." Part of him wondered whether he should tell Andy the whole story. He didn't know, though, if Andy was bound by law to inform Virginia State Police where Rachel was.

The detective's expression softened abruptly.

"Yeah. That's what I thought. You're not the tough guy you make yourself out to be, are you, Half-Breed?"

"Don't call me that."

"Sorry." Contrition furrowed Andy's forehead. He dropped the interrogation altogether. "I'm sorry, man. I'm not trying to offend you or play mind games with you." He sent Saul a long, earnest look. "I just want you to know that *I* know who Angel Johnson really is. You must have helped her get her new credentials. Don't worry, though. I'm not about to rat you out or blow her cover. Angel, as I will continue to call her, doesn't deserve some dirtbag beating up on her or her kid. Her secret's safe with me."

Saul's legs went weak with relief. "Thank you," he said, profoundly grateful for Andy's decency.

"I've got one more question for you. Is she your woman now, or could I ask her out one day?"

Saul went from feeling grateful toward Andy to wanting to punch him in the nose. With great effort, he battled down his jealousy.

"She's not my woman," he stated through gritted teeth.

Andy cocked his head at Saul's tone. "Really?"

"I'm leaving for Virginia on Tuesday. I have a job to get back to."

"And then?" Andy's gaze remained watchful.

"I don't know."

But the *maybe* he'd given to Liam was still stuck inside his heart. If Rachel fell for the dimple-cheeked, confident detective who lived right there in Broken Arrow, Saul would have to yank that splinter of hope out for good.

Andy lifted his nose and sniffed. "You smell those chicken fingers?" He changed the subject.

Saul did smell them. The scent was wafting from Raising Cane's across the street.

"You want to catch a bite to eat?"

Saul appreciated the gesture. "Thanks, but no. I promised Rachel I'd paint another room before I leave town." He didn't want her up on a ladder painting the room herself.

Andy nodded a couple of times. "Understood. Well, I know I speak for all of us when I say we appreciate you pitching in while we're short-handed. And thanks for IDing Willard Davis for us. If he picks up his mail anytime soon, we can grab him and hopefully avert whatever he's planning."

"Let's hope he does. If not, I'll see you Monday."

Andy turned to the door and used his badge to release the lock.

"Take care, buddy. If we catch Davis and we don't need you on Monday, have a safe trip back."

Saul grunted, certain the man would sidle up to Rachel on the very day he took off.

Leaving Andy outside of the Command and Control Room, Saul hurried out of the police station and jumped in his Camaro. He sped home, intending to check the utility road for a vehicle that didn't belong there. That morning, he'd found fresh tire tracks in the dirt.

Probably just a work truck belonging to Oneta Power.

Apart from the possibility of the FOR Americans, it was unlikely anyone in Broken Arrow was watching his house. All the same, Saul considered leaving Duke at the ranch to protect them. Liam had forged such a bond with the dog, it would sadden both of them to be separated. The decision felt right.

~

Ethan wrung the steering wheel of his rental as he wrestled with the urge to act. The SEAL sniper had driven off that morning, leaving Rachel and Liam alone at the house. Rachel's vulnerability fueled Ethan's thirst for revenge. But Liam's presence in the house kept Ethan from acting. For what Ethan was about to do, there could be no witnesses, certainly not the boy who would one day call him Father.

School was out until Tuesday. Clearly, Ethan would have to wait until after that to punish Rachel for her treachery.

"There's no hurry," he assured himself. He still had plenty of vacation time to burn. His colleagues all assumed he was drowning his grief on Bourbon Street. According to Captain Spenser, who represented the SEAL from Team Six, Chief Wade would be back from leave the day after Columbus Day. In that case, Wade would be leaving Broken Arrow very soon. On Tuesday, Liam would return to school, and Rachel would be all alone in a house surrounded by nothing but grass and trees.

Her reckoning would come, then. Ethan merely had to bide his time.

As for the SEAL who'd aided and abetted her crime, Ethan countered the boredom of his stakeout by imagining ways to frame him for Rachel's demise. For that to happen, however, Rachel would have to die before the man's departure for Virginia Beach. Since that would likely happen on Sunday for the man to be at work on Tuesday morning, and since Ethan couldn't take action until Liam went back to school Tuesday, framing the SEAL wouldn't work.

Ethan gave up staking out the ranch and started his car. Rolling up his windows, he sealed out the breeze, then eased from his hiding place onto Oak Grove Road. As he accelerated up the hill ahead of him, Chief Wade's Camaro appeared over the rise in front of him.

A startled curse escaped Ethan's lips. Sweat breached his pores before he remembered, with gratitude for his own foresight, that he taken the time to get the rental's windows tinted, a liberty he would have to pay for when he returned the vehicle.

The SEAL's windows, on the other hand, were only moderately tinted. Ethan sensed the exact moment the driver noticed him. His deep-set eyes locked on to Ethan's car like heat-seeking missiles. The Camaro slowed abruptly, and Chief Wade strained to get a clear view of him.

Directing his own eyes straight ahead, Ethan fought the impulse to gun his engine and, instead, proceeded leisurely on his way. As the two cars passed, Ethan searched his rearview mirror, certain the SEAL was noting his license plate number and its state of issue. *No worries there.* Ethan's Pontiac might show up as a rental, but Hertz had to honor privacy laws. The SEAL wouldn't get any information out of them.

Blowing out a breath, Ethan grabbed up a napkin left over from his breakfast and mopped his damp brow. He couldn't wait for the Navy SEAL to head back East. The man's reputation alone made Ethan nervous.

CHAPTER 16

eeping his distance from Rachel that weekend proved easier than Saul had figured it would be. Either she was thoroughly engrossed in her plans to renovate the house, or she was avoiding him.

Between Saturday evening and Sunday morning, Saul and Rachel encountered each other only at mealtimes. While he worked diligently to cross off tasks on her short list, Rachel busied herself drawing plans for each of the bathrooms. With Liam's grudging help, Saul finished painting every room, stained the shutters outside, and was kneeling in the weeds beside the porch, applying channel-lock pliers to the leaking faucet, when Rachel and Liam stepped onto the porch. Clearly, they were headed somewhere.

Saul stared. Rachel had found a skirt and a matching top in his mother's wardrobe that made her pretty as a picture. The possibility she would set the town on fire had him pushing to his feet.

"Where are you two headed?"

She sent him a polite yet reserved smile. "I'm dropping Liam off at his new friend Cody's house. He's going to spend the night there."

Saul's stomach went into freefall at the realization he and Rachel would be alone that evening. Cutting his gaze to Liam, he noticed the backpack he was carrying was stuffed with what he needed for a night away.

"I thought we were going to sleep on the porch tonight and look for bobcats," he said to the boy. They'd discussed that plan while painting the hallway.

Liam scuffed his feet on the gravel. "I changed my mind."

It occurred to Saul that Liam might be pulling away emotionally and with good reason.

"I'm also going to Lowe's," Rachel added, "to buy some mums for the pots on the porch. Do you mind if I use money in the account for that?"

"'Course not. That's what it's for." The bank had provided her with blank checks while she waited for her debit card to come by mail.

"Do you want to come with me?" she added unexpectedly. "We could check out the kitchen cabinets and bathroom tiles."

Her offer tempted him, not because he wanted to help her shop, but rather to deflect the attention she was going to get from other men. Heaving an inward sigh at his pointless jealousy, he shook his head.

"No," he said, more tersely than he'd intended. "I have work to do here," he added more gently.

"You don't have to do everything on that list, you know. I can hire a plumber if you can't fix the leak." She gestured to the faucet.

"I can fix it."

Her shoulders sagged. "I'll see you later, then."

"Yeah." *Later*, with Liam out of the house, was what worried him most.

Rachel turned slowly away and walked to the truck. As she and Liam climbed inside, Saul kneeled back beside the faucet and listened to them drive away.

The memory of the mysterious black Pontiac sparked sudden nervousness within him. He could have sworn the vehicle he'd passed yesterday was the same one that had stopped halfway up the driveway the day Rachel and Liam had returned from Dallas. The tire tracks he'd seen on the utility road suggested a car could very well have been parked there, just out of sight, any number of times.

But who would be staking out the ranch? Maybe the skinheads had discovered that their firearms were disabled, and they were looking to get revenge. Leaving Duke with Rachel and Liam might be enough protection. He would have to ask the local police to keep an eye on the ranch. His mood darkened at the thought. Andy would be all too pleased to become Rachel's newest protector.

"You made your bed, now lie in it," he muttered, repeating what he had told Rachel the other evening. In a mere two days, Rachel would be living there without him. He couldn't protect her from a distance of thirteen hundred miles. He might as well get used to that idea.

As for what he would do that night to avoid the temptation she presented, he could only hope his integrity would hold strong. If Rachel made the first move, he wasn't sure he could resist her.

"Lord, give me the strength," he muttered, focusing again on the leaking faucet.

In the act of adjusting the channel-lock pliers, he froze. *Since when am I on speaking terms with God?* Rachel was obviously rubbing off on him. He frowned at the realization. Not that he minded or anything, but he couldn't have God in charge of his conscience. If he was going to do his job and do it right, he needed to cling to his rage, to be more machine than man.

Funny how his feelings for Rachel overshadowed those older emotions.

~

Pulling out of the driveway, Rachel followed the directions dictated by Waze and accelerated in the direction of town. Having communicated via phone with Cody's mother, she looked forward to meeting the woman, to making friends in her new hometown, and to putting down roots.

A cooling breeze wafted through the truck's lowered windows, suggesting Liam and Cody would have a fine time playing in Cody's backyard and jumping on his trampoline.

"Are you sure you want to spend the night, honey?" Liam hadn't done more than a handful of sleepovers.

"I'm sure," he said stoically.

"I thought you couldn't wait to camp on the porch with Saul."

Liam shrugged noncommittally, making Rachel suspect he cared far more than he was letting on. Saul's impending departure meant Liam needed to seek out friendships elsewhere. She could relate to that.

As they neared town, Rachel paid attention to her surroundings. This would be her hometown now. The sooner she learned how to find things without Waze, the better off she'd be. They passed Lowe's, where she would spend a considerable amount of time after dropping off Liam, and crossed town to enter a suburban neighborhood with neatly trimmed lawns and kids on bicycles.

After spending twenty minutes chatting with Cody's friendly mother, Rachel left Liam in a more positive frame of mind. She'd made a new friend and was confident her son would make it through the night without calling for her to come pick him up.

Pulling away from Cody's curb, she executed a U-turn that pointed her back the way she'd come. In her mirrors, she glimpsed a black sedan ease onto the road behind her.

After two hours spent in Lowe's narrowing down her options, Rachel spotted what appeared to be the same black car behind her when she left the parking lot. Alarm feathered her spine. She accelerated, watching to see if the car did likewise. To her relief, it fell behind. By the time she turned onto Oak Grove Road outside of town, the car had disappeared.

"Don't be paranoid, Rachel. You're safe here, remember?" She drove swiftly up the driveway, eager to show her samples to Saul. While he professed to trust her to the point of not involving himself in the renovation process, she was determined to draw him in. Maybe doing so would help convince him this was his home, too.

They would be alone that night, just the two of them, for the first time since he'd masterminded their escape. A mix of apprehension and confusion cycled through her. A part of her longed to cook him a meal he would never forget in the hopes of eliciting a promise he would return to Broken Arrow when his obligation to the Navy was over. Yet, she couldn't overlook the existence of another woman in his life.

Even if she managed to turn Saul's home into a place he would never want to leave again, who knew what kind of pull this other woman, Charlotte, had on him? She wasn't going to risk giving her heart to Saul if he couldn't do the same for her.

Tell me what to do, Father, she prayed as she slowed to a stop before the house. Saul would be gone in just forty-eight hours.

Ethan stood inside the tree line, camouflaged by the darkness, and stared. The Camaro, clearly visible in the moonlight, was still parked by the truck Rachel had driven into town. He'd witnessed her dropping Liam off at a friend's house and had deduced two things. First, she would be alone that night, keeping him from having to wait until Liam went to school to do away with her. And, second, assuming the SEAL had already departed for Virginia, Ethan could still frame the man.

But the Camaro parked in front of the house made it plain Wade was still here. He was cutting it awfully close, wasn't he? He would have to drive all the way to Virginia without stopping if he meant to put in a full day's work on Tuesday. Evidently, SEALs were as crazy as they were reputed to be.

Uttering a low growl, Ethan opted to postpone his plans. The visions of justice that had been running through his head would have to wait a little longer. The SEAL *had* to leave by dawn the next day if he meant to get back to his base in time. He hadn't made it to the rank of chief by being careless with his deadlines. *I'll come back then.*

Turning around, he melted into the trees, heading for his vehicle. He would return to his tawdry motel and try again in about eight hours, eager to witness the SEAL's departure. Timing was everything if he was going to make Chief Wade look guilty of killing Rachel.

Rachel stepped back from the kitchen table and bit her lower lip. Had she set too romantic a table? A tea candle she'd found during her cleaning flickered within the amber jar from a box in the attic. A dinner of shepherd's pie sat warming on the stove. All that was missing was Saul, who had disappeared into the hallway bathroom to shower. After fifteen minutes, she could still hear the water running. The tealight would run out of wax if he didn't soon emerge.

They'd been avoiding each other, that much was clear. For her part, she wanted to know what their relationship meant to him, whether he was attached to the mysterious Charlotte, or whether he might possibly return to Broken Arrow once his commitment was fulfilled. If he was avoiding her because he had a girlfriend waiting back home for him, then so be it.

Whatever his decision was, she could handle it. She had come a long way since Blake's death shattered her whole world. The faith she and Blake had discovered together before his death had given her a staff on which to lean whenever life got difficult. When Saul left, possibly never to return, she would lean into God's love and He would sustain her.

Saul emerged suddenly from the hall, dressed in jeans and a clean white T-shirt that emphasized his tan skin.

"What's this?" he asked, taking note of the flickering candle and the meal she'd made.

"Shepherd's pie," she said, although she suspected that wasn't the question he'd been asking. Ladling their dinner onto plates, she laid the larger portion before his seat, and they both sat down. As usual, Rachel said grace. They both dug in, neither one of them talking.

Rachel scrounged for the courage to bring up the other woman.

"Who is Charlotte?" she finally asked, in as casual a voice as possible. "I heard you on the phone with her yesterday."

Saul shot her a dry look. "She's my teammate Lucas's wife."

Relief flooded Rachel. She hid her reaction, staring down at her plate as she carved out another bite with her fork.

"She's training for the FBI. I asked her to help me find more information on Will Davis."

"And did she?"

"Yes, but it wasn't enough to help the police locate him. Looks like the violence is still going to happen tomorrow."

"Be careful," she pleaded, although she trusted Saul's training to keep him safe.

"I'll be fine."

Rachel focused back on Charlotte. "Does Charlotte know about me?"

Saul's mouth quirked with irony. "She suspected me of helping you the day you disappeared."

Rachel gaped at him. "How would she have known that?"

"Good instincts, I guess." He shrugged. "You would recognize her if you saw her. She attended Lieutenant Mills's court martial last year. Here, I have a picture of her and Lucas on my phone." He pulled the Android from his back pocket, thumbed through his pictures, then held it out for her to see.

Charlotte found herself regarding a very tall, very striking couple.

"Oh, yes." She recognized both the redheaded woman and the handsome man from the trial she'd been forced to attend. "I do remember them."

"They're hard to forget." With a faint smile, Saul put his cell phone away and went back to eating.

"I thought maybe Charlotte was your girlfriend," Rachel said quickly, getting it over with.

Saul sent her that same dry look. "She's spoken for."

"Right." After several seconds of silence, Rachel added, "So, you don't have a girlfriend back home, do you?"

"No." Saul rearranged the food on his plate and avoided eye contact.

Rachel struggled to get the rest of her words out. "I heard what you told me in the car the other day," she prefaced. "You have to go back to work. I understand that, and I can see why it would be distracting to think about me while you're...working. But don't you think you could come back here when your enlistment's over?"

Saul slowly put his fork down. A maelstrom of emotions reflected in his eyes as he met her gaze.

"Rachel," he said, through his teeth, "I don't want you waiting for me."

Her hopes went into free fall. "Why not?"

"For the reasons I told you before." His voice turned gravelly. "I can't be thinking about you when I'm working. I have to be completely focused on the target."

She forced herself to nod. "I understand." Tears pressured her eyes.

"Do you?"

She nodded. "Yes."

"I wish things were different, but they aren't." He reached for her unexpectedly, covering her hand with his and gently squeezing it.

The words gave her a modicum of hope. "What about a year from now?"

He shook his head. "I don't know. I can't think about the future, only the present. I'm sorry. I don't know where I'll be then."

He sounded so committed to his job Rachel didn't attempt to convince him otherwise. Her heart hurt for him—and for herself. Yet, in spite of his words, hope still burned in her. There was still a chance he would come home for good one day, to spend the rest of his life with her and Liam.

"Thanks for dinner," Saul said, finishing his last bite. Without meeting her gaze, he added, "I have to clean my weapon now and get to bed early. Supposed to report at the station at 6:00 a.m." ·

Rachel listened to him rinse his plate and put it in the dishwasher. He left her in the kitchen staring numbly at the flame drowning in the tealight's wax.

CHAPTER 17

*E*than shivered in his long-sleeved oxford and wished he had brought along a jacket. Sunrise had merely been a suggestion when he'd left his car parked on the utility road. Crossing Oak Grove Street, he followed the driveway until the trees began to thin. It wasn't quite cold enough for frost to have formed, but Ethan could see his breath when he exhaled. Putting his back against a tree and clenching his jaws to keep his teeth from chattering, he waited for the SEAL to depart on his journey home. He couldn't believe the man hadn't left yet.

As a nearby rooster crowed, he glanced at his watch. "Come on," he muttered. "Get the show on the road."

As if on cue, the SEAL came out of his house dressed in old fatigues and holding a coffee travel mug and nothing else. Questioning the man's fashion sense, Ethan guessed he must have put a duffel bag or suitcase in the trunk of his car the night before, as he had nothing but the mug with him. Moving briskly off the porch toward his car, Wade paused to gaze back at the building, as if wondering when he would see it again. Then he promptly ducked into his vehicle and left, having likely said his goodbyes to Rachel the night before.

Ethan's lips curled at the satisfying thought that merely a day or two from now, the SEAL would be arrested for Rachel's murder.

Ethan waited for the Camaro to pass near him before he concealed himself behind a tree. He glanced at his watch again. It was quarter to six. If Chief Wade didn't stop more than once or run into too much traffic, he would make it to Virginia Beach with a few hours to spare before reporting to work Tuesday morning.

Counting to one hundred, just in case the man had forgotten something and turned around, Ethan notched his gloves. With rising excitement, he struck out across the field toward the house, where Rachel slept alone inside. Liam was still at his friend's house.

The prairie grass, so unlike the zoysia growing on his own front yard, crackled under his loafers. They grew damp from the dew. His heart pounded. His fingers flexed. He had decided to strangle Rachel with a chokehold commonly used by Navy SEALs. Once she was lifeless, he would head straight to the bedroom, tossing items on the floor, breaking others, as if there'd been a fight.

Ethan was so caught up in the visions in his head, he didn't hear the dog barking in the house until he was nearly at the porch. He froze with sudden dismay. There was a dog inside?

How careless of him! Suddenly, he recalled seeing the dog come out to greet Liam the day he'd followed Rachel all the way from Dallas. It belonged to the SEAL, so why hadn't the man taken it with him? It sounded big and dangerous. Moreover, it was going to waken Rachel who, if she caught sight of Ethan, would call the police—and then what?

He spun around and ran. He would have to think of another tactic and soon if he hoped to connect the SEAL to Rachel's death.

∾

Saul, whose thoughts of Rachel weighed heavily on his mind, anticipated joining the SOT in quelling certain violence. First, the team geared up in the armory. Saul, who carried his own pistol and knife, was nonetheless issued a semiautomatic rifle, a load-bearing ballistic vest, pockets full of ammunition, a radio, and flash bangs. Apart from his Navy-issue desert digital cammies, he looked like the rest of the team.

The SOT gathered in the Command and Control Room, bristling with weapons, to watch the real-time video feed of key buildings in town. The hate group's target was still unknown.

Saul dropped into a chair between a window and a potted plant and watched Andy field phone calls. The populace, eager to collect the promised monetary rewards, had been calling in since Thursday evening, he'd been told. Yet the messages were all the same. Members of the FOR Americans had informed their loved ones they were going hunting over the long weekend. The chilling words suggested they planned to go through with their violent act of domestic terrorism. But who was to say it would even take place in Broken Arrow? By now, they could have made it to Washington D.C.

With few details beyond a vague reference to a lodge somewhere out in Wagoner County, the members of the group remained at large. It seemed the police would be responding to a threat that day rather than preventing one.

We have to be overlooking something. Thinking hard, Saul analyzed everything they knew about the skinheads. The two whom Andy had run into at the Reeve's place had lost their landscaping jobs to minorities. Davis had been a dishwasher at the same golf course. Had he been fired, too? If so, wouldn't their resentment be focused on their employer rather than some random target?

A suspicion propelled Saul to his feet. He crossed swiftly to Andy's cubicle, interrupting a tense conversation between Andy and Captain Lewis.

"Excuse me," he said as soon as their discussion ended. "I had a thought about the word *hacker*." He gestured to Andy's PC. "Check to see if it's possibly a golf term."

Andy stared at him for a second, then swung abruptly toward his keyboard, doing as Saul suggested. Captain Lewis waited, clearly intrigued.

"Oh, wow," Andy exclaimed a second later. He swung around in his seat and faced the men behind him. "We just got ourselves a lead. Hacker *is* a golf term. It means a bad golf player, like the word *duffer*. The answer was under our noses this whole time."

Lewis's blue gaze jumped to Saul. "Indian Springs Country Club," he murmured, clearly picturing it. "It'll be packed on a day like today." He swung around and caught the bald team leader's attention, waving him over.

"Listen up!" Boykins shouted seconds later. The SOT members eyed him expectantly. "We have a potential target: Indian Springs Country Club. Load up and head out. Let's stop this thing before it starts."

As Saul climbed into the SOT's armored van a minute later, he spotted Andy running toward his police cruiser. The man might be just a detective, but he wasn't about to let the SOT have all the fun. Saul's respect for Andy climbed, but he still wasn't good enough for Rachel.

Seating himself next to Robison, Saul put on the headset his partner passed to him. The doors clanged shut, and they were off. In the van's illumined interior, Saul and the others exchanged adrenaline-fueled glances. If the country club was the actual target, they had a chance of saving lives.

As the van sped toward Indian Springs, Saul's thoughts drifted back to Rachel. Today was his last full day in Broken Arrow. *Don't think about her. You know you can't love her.*

Saul frowned down at his knees. Truth was, he had loved her for a while now. That wasn't the point, though. The point was he had other obligations, just like his obligation right now to halt terrorism in its tracks. *Stay focused.*

The radio crackled in Saul's ear, returning him to the present.

"Heads up, everyone. We have a situation at the country club. We have hidden shooters taking potshots at golfers. No one's been hit yet. Golfers are running for the clubhouse."

Saul raised his eyebrows at the stunned looks he received, then focused on Boykins as he laid out their strategy. The snipers and scouts would fan out, flushing the course for shooters and apprehending them on sight. The five entry guys would sweep the area around the clubhouse searching for the bomb. Once located, it was up to Flint and Sievers to neutralize it. Everyone would pitch in as needed to herd golfers to safety and to unite the injured with the paramedics already en route.

Saul sensed exactly when the van veered off 131st East Avenue, turning into the long driveway to the clubhouse. Having caddied one summer back in high school, he pictured the layout. First, they would come to the tennis courts, then the circular driveway in front of the clubhouse and the appended swimming pool. The golf course lay beyond the whitewashed clubhouse, roughly in the shape of a figure-eight.

The van braked abruptly. Boykins flung the doors open, barking, "Go, go, go!"

Saul hit the ground running, with Robison right behind him. As a sniper/scout pair, they ran straight for the course, spreading out as they went. Pockets of hardwood trees provided only moderate cover, forcing the men to dart from one grove to another. Saul wished they were on the other side of the green where a forest of pine trees concealed the Arkansas River.

He and Robison hauled butt to the fourth tee and the reported casualty. As they closed in, rifle fire rang out ahead of them, followed by a woman's scream, then silence.

In his earpiece, Saul overheard the entry guys relay their findings as they cleared the area around the clubhouse.

"Team lead," one of them cried out suddenly. "There's a truck with no plates parked at the food services entry!"

"Roger that. Make sure the building is evacuated. Don't let anyone in. Send all civilians toward the tennis courts."

The threat of a bomb detonating kept Saul's pulse elevated. As they approached the fourth tee, Saul spied an elderly couple cowering behind their golf cart, their faces white with fear. The woman who'd screamed appeared uninjured. Her husband clutched her close while trying frantically to place a call on his cellphone.

The shooter had to be crouched within the grove of trees closest to the green. As Saul and Robison closed in on him, he fired again, causing the headlight on the golf cart to explode. Both men spotted the shooter by his shock of red hair. Before he could fire again, Robison dispatched a bullet, hitting the young man's shooting hand.

With a scream of agony, he dropped his weapon and fell to the ground clutching his injured extremity.

Saul was on him in an instant. He kicked the familiar rifle out of reach, then, ignoring the blood gushing from the youth's thumb, secured his wrists behind his back with a nylon zip tie. The youth yelled invectives at him.

Saul flipped him onto his side and stared him in the eye.

"How many shooters are out here besides yourself?"

The skinhead spat in Saul's face and called him a mongrel.

Saul dug his fingers into pressure points on the young man's shoulder and repeated his question.

"Nine!" the youth squalled. "Nine more."

"Where?"

"The first and last four tees. We're not trying to kill them."

"What do you mean?" Saul demanded. "Why shoot at them if you're not trying to kill them?"

The youth ground his teeth in agony and refused to answer.

As Robison passed the odd remark on to the rest of the team, Saul dug his fingers into the youth's shoulder and repeated his question. At the same time, several sniper pairs reported three more skinheads captured. None of the golfers being fired upon had sustained any injuries.

All at once, Saul realized why. "They're chasing the white players away," he barked into his mike. "We're looking in the wrong place."

No sooner were the words out of his mouth than one of the sweepers cried out, "Team lead, we just found six Hispanic employees and their manager locked in the kitchen pantry. They say Davis was just here."

"This is Flint," another voice cut in. "Sievers and I can't get to the truck. We're pinned inside the bay doors by a shooter we can't see!"

Saul exchanged a look of alarm with Robison.

Saul tabbed his mike. "That's got to be Davis. Permission to pursue and neutralize."

"Granted," Boykins answered.

Robison grabbed the skinhead and gestured for Saul to head for the clubhouse alone. He broke into a run, retracing the route he'd just taken.

With no trees between the first tee and the clubhouse, Saul sprinted into the open, then dived behind the low wall shoring up the building's rear terrace.

Using the wall to conceal himself, Saul scrambled on all fours around the back of the clubhouse toward the delivery entrance. Coming to the end of the wall, he peeked around it. The side of the building stood deserted. With the shooters apprehended, the course had fallen eerily quiet but for the screaming of sirens in the distance.

From where he crouched, Saul could see the back of the mysterious delivery truck, suspected to contain the lethal explosive. He couldn't see Flint and Sievers, but he could sense their fear and helplessness as their approach to the bomb was being frustrated. The bomb itself was likely to explode at any minute, killing not only them, but anyone else close to the building, himself included.

A mental timer started to tick in Saul's head. *Tick, tick, tick, tick, tick.* His heart beat twice as fast as he raked the manicured shrubbery for the shooter. In order to see over the truck into the bay area, he would have to have a bird's-eye view, wouldn't he?

Several tall oak trees cast their shade over the lawn. Saul's gaze centered on the largest one, flushing from green to gold. His pulse echoed off his eardrums as he hunted for Davis, praying he would spot the man before the incendiary device was activated, before he died in the devastating reaction with the volatile ANFO.

All at once a breeze caused the leaves of the trees to flatten, exposing what looked like a mesh-covered figure stretched along the length of a sturdy limb.

Heart pounding, Saul eased the point of his rifle over the edge of the wall and took another look through his scope. "Target acquired," Saul whispered into his mic.

"For God's sake, take him out," Boykins pleaded on a tense note.

Opting for expedience over finesse, Saul aimed at what he thought might be Davis's thigh. He spared three necessary seconds to factor in the distance between them, the angle at which he was shooting, and the effect of gravity on the bullet. With a slow exhale, he depressed the trigger.

What goes up, must come down.

A startled shout answered his rifle's report. Davis, rocked by the bullet's impact, scrabbled to retain his perch, then dropped. The green mesh floated off him as his arms windmilled wildly. He hit the ground at the same time as his rifle, which discharged harmlessly into the sky.

"Shooter down," the team lead announced. "Flint and Sievers, you are cleared to approach the truck."

Saul bounded over the wall. Keeping his rifle pointed at Davis, he approached the still figure cautiously. The man lay with his eyes wide open. Saul felt for a pulse. Nothing. Saul searched his pockets and came up with a cell phone. Likely, Davis would have trusted no one but himself to remote-start the booster. Saul passed the phone off to the team lead. Glancing back at the green, he spotted Robison speeding toward him with the skinhead they'd apprehended zip-tied to the back seat.

"Medic!" Saul directed a set of first responders to the golf cart while others rushed around looking for someone to help. Miraculously, nobody had been terribly injured. Andy Cannard stood in the parking lot consoling hysterical golfers and taking their statements.

It lifted Saul's spirits to have restored peace to a place that had nearly been ripped asunder by hatred, ending the lives of the unfortunate employees and the manager who had hired them. Helping himself to the emptied golf cart, Saul went to assist his new teammates in rounding up the remaining five skinheads.

~

Ethan was not content with his secondary plan. It required Rachel to leave the house—something she would have to do eventually if she meant to pick up Liam at his friend's. But too much time had passed since the SEAL's departure for that man to be held in suspicion.

Enraged that events were not panning out the way he'd planned, Ethan sat in his car, parked halfway up the SEAL's long driveway, and fumed. While counting on the shade of the trees to conceal him, he still had a clear view of the house's front door. Once Rachel stepped out of it, locking the dog safely inside, Ethan would speedily approach her. Not able to see who he was though his windshield, she would stand and wait for him. He would then spring out of the car and choke her right there where no one could see him, leaving her for someone to find.

Ethan would have to discover some other way to avenge Chief Wade for his involvement. This was not at all how he'd envisioned delivering justice, but circumstances were working against him, and his cover story could only work for so long.

The result would still be the same, he comforted himself. Liam would still end up orphaned, leaving his closest living relative to take him in and adopt him permanently.

~

Rachel locked the front door behind her and came off the porch, too lost in thought to appreciate the bright sun and the cooler weather. The emotional distance Saul insisted on keeping between them was compounded by his physical absence that morning. Perhaps by the time she returned from picking Liam up, Saul would be back, and they could at least share the second half of his last day in Oklahoma together without the strain that marked their communication the previous night.

A bark from within the house, coupled with the churning of gravel, pulled Rachel sharply out of her reverie. Her stomach lurched to see the same black car she'd spotted more than once now barreling up the driveway. As it rounded the bend, the tinted glass concealing the driver from view elevated her fear.

The chance to run back into the house came and went as the car blocked her path by pulling up alongside her. Recalling her run-in with the skinheads, Rachel opened her truck door and put a foot on the running board, lest she needed to flee.

The door of the Pontiac slowly opened. A polished shoe appeared, followed by a head of dark, thinning hair and a face she'd hoped never to lay eyes on again as the driver straightened.

"No." Fear galvanized Rachel. She jumped into her cab, locking the door with her elbow while struggling to insert the key in the ignition.

"Stop," he ordered, striding up to her door with a taut expression. "I only want to talk to you," he yelled through the glass as the engine roared.

She didn't believe him. He hadn't tracked her down—*how?*—merely to talk to her.

"Go away! I'm calling the police." With a tug on the shifter, she depressed the accelerator, spraying gravel behind her as she shot forward, profoundly grateful to have backed into her parking space on a whim the previous evening.

A fearful glance in her rearview mirror showed Ethan jumping back into his car.

Call Saul. Rachel felt inside Melody's old purse for her cell phone. Knowing where the worst of the potholes lay, she drove around them while speeding as she dashed toward Oak Grove Road. To her dismay, Saul's phone went straight to voice mail. He must have turned it off.

"Saul, call me!" she cried, leaving a message in the hopes he would get it soon. "Ethan found me. He's here." She glanced in her mirror again.

"Oh, God, he's following me!" Reaching the head of the driveway, she turned right and stomped on the gas to get up the hill in front of her. Ending her call to Saul, she divided her attention between her phone and the road as she dialed another number.

"9-1-1, do you have an emergency?"

"Yes!" Rachel tried to keep from sounding thoroughly panicked. How to explain her situation? "There's a man following me. He's chasing me in his car." She deliberately omitted their relationship. "Please help."

"Yes, ma'am. Can you describe your location?"

"I just turned off Oak Grove Road headed toward town. I think the name of this street is Kenosha. I'm going to drive to the police station." Did she remember how to get there?

"You're welcome to do that, ma'am. Would you like me to stay on the phone with you?"

"Yes, please stay!" Rachel put the phone on speaker and placed it in the cupholder. "He's right behind me," she reported in a panicked voice. "He's trying to pass me."

Depressing the accelerator, Rachel hoped to maintain her lead, but the engine sputtered in protest, and Ethan zipped past her, then cut immediately in front of her, forcing her to slow down. They were approaching the overpass for Creek Turnpike. Rachel made a quick decision. Pulling a hard right, she cut over to the ramp she'd just passed, driving through a grassy median to link up with it. Ethan, who was out ahead of her, had no way of following.

Relief flooded through Rachel's veins, making her feel strangely weak.

"I think I might have lost him," she stated, as she merged into the light traffic. "I'm on the Creek Turnpike now, headed west. Please, can you get a message to Saul Wade? He's working with the Broken Arrow Police this morning. I need him to call me."

"Ma'am, this isn't a messaging service. If you have an actual emergency, I can dispatch police to your location—though, honestly, most of them are tied up right now."

Rachel searched her rearview mirror for signs Ethan was still chasing her. There were no black cars behind her.

"I may have lost him; I'm not sure."

"All right, ma'am. That's great. I'm being bombarded with calls right now. If you don't have an emergency, I need to let you go." The dispatcher hung up abruptly.

Rachel put her phone down and glanced again into the rearview mirror. A football field or so behind her, a black vehicle merged onto the turnpike.

"Oh, God, please help," she whispered, fearful beyond reason. Unwilling to drive farther away from town, she bore left as the road forked, putting herself on the Muskogee Turnpike headed east. That would carry her in the right direction, wouldn't it? Another glance behind her showed Ethan surging closer.

The rational half of Rachel's brain asked if she wasn't overreacting to his presence. Apart from the few times her brother had pinched or bruised her during childhood, Ethan's cruelty had always been more verbal than physical. But an image of the dead cardinal kept flashing through her mind. Maybe God was trying to tell her something.

As the toll road stretched before her without a single sign for downtown Broken Arrow, it dawned on Rachel she was still driving *away* from the police station, not toward it. A sign that read Wagoner, twenty-five miles, stood on the side of the road, causing her fear to mushroom.

Even if he got her message, Saul would never reach her in time to help her. She had to turn around, but the fortified railing dividing the two sides of the highway meant she couldn't execute an illegal U-turn. Her best bet was to get off at the next exit, go under or over the turnpike and get back on it, headed the right way. Thanks to the PIKEPASS device on her windshield, she could blow through the toll booth. Ethan, she hoped, would be hampered by the levered bar.

Licking the salt from her upper lip, Rachel edged her speed higher. A nervous glance in her mirror showed Ethan on her bumper, where he remained, clearly trying to intimidate her.

By the time the sign for the next exit appeared, the muscles in Rachel's neck and shoulders ached from tension. She gave no indication she would take the exit. At the last second, she veered toward the ramp. Ethan immediately gave chase. As she hurried through the toll booth, he followed right on her fender, slipping through before the arm even lowered.

Terrified, Rachel blew through the stop sign and squealed into a left turn, intending to drive under the turnpike, then right back on it, headed in the correct direction. But to her dismay, the exit wasn't on her right but on her left.

As she went to change lanes, the Pontiac drew up alongside her, blocking her escape.

"Let me go!" she cried, threatening to ram Ethan's car. Before she got the chance, he braked and zipped behind her again. Terrified, she eyed the road ahead of them. It was an older four-lane highway divided by a grassy culvert and stretching over flat, desolate terrain comprised of nothing but harvested wheat fields, telephone poles, and a grain silo.

"Oh, help," she cried. Snatching up her phone, she speed-dialed Saul again with a trembling hand.

CHAPTER 18

*A*s the chaos died down, Saul became aware his cell phone was vibrating. He recalled having felt it earlier, only he'd been too busy rounding up skinheads and uniting the injured with the paramedics. Tearing his gaze from the sight of Willard Davis's body being bagged, he glanced at his caller ID.

Concern edged aside his sense of accomplishment. "Hello?"

Andy, who stood farther down the sidewalk, glanced over at him.

"Oh, thank God."

The quaver in Rachel's voice put Saul on alert.

"What's wrong?"

"He found me. Ethan found me," she said, with panic in her voice. "He's following me. I think he wants to kill me."

Adrenaline surged back into Saul's veins. "Let me guess. He's driving a black Pontiac."

"Yes. How did you know?"

"Never mind that." He wanted to shoot himself for thinking the car belonged to the skinheads. "Where are you?" he rapped. Andy, who had overheard him, now faced him and was listening alertly.

"I was on the turnpike headed the wrong way, toward Wagoner, so

I tried to turn around at Coweta, but Ethan cut me off, and now I'm on Highway 51, I think. There's nothing around us but farmland. Wait, I just passed a sign for Wagoner, so I'm headed either south or east."

He couldn't begin to fathom how she'd gotten so turned around.

"Stay on the phone with me." Saul walked up to Andy. "I've got Andy here. We're coming to help."

Andy regarded him a second, then said, "My car's over there. Let's go."

Saul tried to catch Boykins' eye to tell him he was leaving, but the bald man stood with his back to Saul, watching Davis's body get wheeled away.

Giving up, Saul gestured to Andy, and they sprinted together toward Andy's cruiser.

"Let me guess," the policeman yelled as he ran. "The crazy ex just found her."

"Crazy, yes. But he's her brother, not her ex."

"Brother?"

"I'll explain later."

They jumped into the hot car and buckled in. As Andy pulled away, he hit a switch that made his lights sparkle. In deference to Saul's being on the phone, he kept the siren off.

"We're coming after you," Saul said to Rachel. To Andy he added, "She's headed to Wagoner on Highway 51, and he's right behind her."

"How the heck did she end up there?"

Saul did not relay the question. "How much gas have you got?" he asked Rachel.

"Um, just a quarter tank."

"Quarter tank of gas," Saul conveyed to Andy, then put Rachel on speaker so he wouldn't have to repeat everything she said.

"She might make it to Wagoner on that," Andy said, his dark eyes intent. "I'll alert the police there. They'll get to her faster than we will."

Snatching up his handheld radio, Andy summarized the situation as a high-speed chase with an assailant intent on bodily harm. At his

250

questioning glance, Saul nodded. To his relief, the Wagoner police dispatched two patrol cars.

"Wagoner police are on the way," he said to reassure her.

"Saul, I'm scared I'll never see my son again."

His blood ran cold at the portentous statement. "Don't say that, angel. You'll see him again. Just stay on 51. Don't stop driving until the police pull you over."

"Cody's mother is expecting me to pick up Liam. She probably thinks I'm taking advantage of her."

"Don't worry about Cody's mother," Saul soothed. "You can explain later."

"I can't believe I'm so far away from town. I lost my sense of direction."

"That's not your fault. Just keep driving."

"He's right on my bumper," she alerted him a minute later. The quaver in her voice told him she was terrified.

"Just hold your speed steady. Try to relax. The police are on their way, and we're coming, too. We'll be there soon." He prompted Andy to accelerate. Traffic on the turnpike parted for them, making it possible to scream down the turnpike at a hundred miles an hour. The speed kept Saul's adrenaline cycling.

"Please hurry," she begged him. "Oh, no. Not this."

"What? What's wrong?"

"The engine is stalling."

"Clogged carburetor," Saul breathed, even as his mind fast-forwarded to the potentially deadly consequences of Rachel breaking down in the middle of nowhere.

"I can't go any faster. He's pulling into the left lane to pass me."

Saul realized at once what she had to do. "That's good! Listen to me, Rachel. This is important. Your truck outweighs his car by a thousand pounds. You need to drive him off the road. How fast are you going?"

"Sixty-five. Sixty. I'm losing speed. He's right next to me!"

"Don't wait for him to cut you off. Do it, Rachel. Veer into him and push him off the road. Don't be afraid. Keep your eyes open and stay on the asphalt."

"I can't. I'm frozen."

"You can. Do it for Liam. Do it *now.*"

~

With a cry of pure terror, Rachel wrenched the steering wheel sharply to the left. It took all her strength not to squeeze her eyes shut as metal grinded against metal. Ethan's passenger-side mirror popped off, and his tires squealed as his vehicle swerved off course.

"Pull back!"

Reacting automatically to Saul's voice, Rachel hauled the steering wheel the other away. She gaped as the Pontiac moved past her, spinning in slow motion. One instant, she was looking at the rear fender, and the next, the underbelly of the car as it slid into the ditch. In the same instant, her own engine sputtered and cut out completely. She guided her truck onto the shoulder just half a football field away. Glancing back at Ethan's vehicle, she found it upside-down in the median, its tires still spinning,

"Rachel, Rachel, talk to me." Saul's controlled urgency grounded her.

"I'm here. I'm okay. I did it."

"I knew you could, angel. What's the status of his car?"

"It's upside-down. I can't see inside because of the tint. Do you think I killed him?"

"Doubtful. Look around. Do you see any police headed your way yet?"

"No. The road is empty. There's no one out here."

"Okay. Just sit tight. The police will be there soon." She heard him bark some muffled words at Andy before he spoke to her again. "We're getting closer ourselves. I'll be there any minute."

A suggestion of movement drew Rachel's attention back to the sedan. To her horror, the driver's door cracked open. Ethan's white sleeve appeared first. Then his shoulder and head as he shoved against the door to open it wider. He began squirming out of it, looking for all the world like some demon being born.

"He's getting out! He's glaring at me."

Blood streamed from a cut on Ethan's eyebrow. His teeth were bared in either a grimace of pain or rage. Climbing from the wreckage on his hands and knees, he started up out of the ditch.

"Rachel, take the rifle off the gun rack."

She had forgotten all about Cyril's old hunting rifle. Without a second thought, she reached back and seized it.

"He's coming toward me."

"There's ammunition in the box behind the seat. Grab a magazine. Get out of the car and load it quickly. Hold the rifle like I taught you. Shoot him if he gets too close."

In her worst nightmares, Rachel had never envisioned what was happening. With Ethan practically upon her, she groped for a magazine, finding it in a basket next to a bottle of engine oil and a can of carburetor cleaner. Next, shaking off her seatbelt, she pushed her door open and leaped out. Then she loaded the rifle and whipped it up, pointing it at her brother.

Ethan froze with an incredulous expression in the middle of the empty road. His angular shoulders rose and fell as if his lungs were bellows feeding a raging fire.

"You took my son from me," he accused through his clenched teeth.

Had the blow he'd taken to his head scrambled his brain?

"Don't come any closer," Rachel warned him, amazed her voice was as steady as it sounded. "I won't hesitate to shoot."

"You would shoot your own brother?" Ethan countered, undermining her assertion.

"Yes," she lied. Even with a loaded rifle at her disposal, she doubted she could bring herself to maim him—provided she could hit him in the first place.

The thin smile he sent her chilled her to the bone. "No. I know you wouldn't." He continued his approach.

Terrified, Rachel hurled the rifle at him. He batted it aside, arms extended, and seized her by her clothing.

"Saul!" Rachel screamed, hoping he could hear her over her phone's speaker as she scrambled into the truck for safety.

Ethan grabbed her by the ankle. She kicked him, clinging to the seat and steering wheel to keep from being pulled out of the truck where he could hurt her.

"Fight him, Rachel." Saul's voice, coming from her cell phone, seemed like it was coming from her own head. "Kick him. Claw him. Use anything within reach to hurt him!"

Ethan let go of her leg and ducked into the cab, seizing her throat with both hands. Rachel kicked him in the diaphragm, and his hold on her slipped. Recalling what she'd glimpsed behind the seat, she groped for the spray can as Ethan's hands closed around her throat a second time.

As he pulled her out of the cab by her neck, she popped the lid off the can, pointed it at his face and sprayed it, squeezing her eyes shut to avoid seeing his reaction. Ethan gave a roar and released her to wipe his streaming eyes.

Enraged, he called her despicable names, then lunging for her again, he succeeded in dragging her out of the cab. Swinging her around so he stood behind her, he wrapped an arm around her neck. Her feet left the ground. Within the vise of his elbow, he squeezed her trachea. Her lungs convulsed, desperate for air.

This can't be happening. She'd promised Liam she wasn't going to die.

All at once, Ethan stiffened. Rachel heard it, too, the blessed sound of sirens. Amidst the black spots obstructing her vision, she could see the blue lights of a police car closing in on them.

All at once, Ethan released her. Rachel crumpled, too weak to stand up. He glared down at her, furious.

"You've ruined me," he accused, his eyes bloodshot. "All I wanted was for Liam to come home."

Rachel lifted her chin, then dragged herself off the pavement. "It's over, Ethan. I'm backing away from you."

Two police cars braked practically on top of them, officers springing out of both doors, pistols drawn. Pointing them at Ethan, more than one voice yelled, "Step away from the female."

Ethan glanced desperately at the rifle lying not too far from her. She promptly kicked it beyond his reach.

"Put your hands in the air!" barked the largest of the four cops as they all bore down on him.

Ethan's face contorted with helplessness. He slowly raised both arms.

"Turn around and place your hands on the truck."

As he turned around, Ethan impaled Rachel with a glare that would have made her cower if he weren't being apprehended right in front of her.

As three male policeman clapped hands on Ethan, patting him down and cuffing him, a female officer helped Rachel to her feet.

"Ma'am, why don't you step over to my vehicle?"

"Just a second." Making a grab for her cell phone, Rachel let herself be led toward one of the two Wagoner police cruisers.

"Are you hurt?" The woman looked her over carefully.

"No. I'm...I'm okay."

Glimpsing another car bearing down on them, she recognized the Broken Arrow Police logo. Before it had even stopped near the other cruisers, the passenger door flew open and Saul vaulted out of it.

With a cry of relief, Rachel abandoned the policewoman to run toward Saul.

They met each other halfway. As their bodies collided, Saul pulled her against him and encircled her in the shelter of his arms.

"You're okay," he choked out.

She buried her face in the crook of his neck, locked her arms around him, and burst into sobs.

He swayed, murmuring gently, "He can't hurt you now." He smoothed a hand up and down her spine.

"I thought I was going to die," she admitted with a shuddering breath.

"But you didn't. You held him off long enough for the police to reach you. You were amazing, Rachel, freakin' amazing."

Hearing the gruff emotion in Saul's voice, Rachel pulled back to find tears rimming his hazel eyes. Despite what he'd said the previous night about not knowing what the future held and not deserving her, she could see it in his face. He loved her, too.

A peaceful wind blew through her heart. Regardless of her fear, she had emerged alive and unharmed. Ethan, on the other hand, had just ruined his prospects of ever getting Liam back by legal means. She couldn't imagine any judge agreeing to give him custody of her son, not after the police had caught him strangling her.

"It's over," Saul assured her.

The word *over* reminded her of his imminent departure. Sorrow threatened to steal her peace away, but she stopped herself from going down that path. Only God could see what happened after tomorrow. Because He knew her needs, she had nothing to fear.

"Ma'am." The female officer reclaimed her attention. "The paramedics are on their way. Could you step this way, please?"

"Of course." With regret, Rachel stepped from Saul's arms and followed the woman to her cruiser.

With the days growing shorter, dusk had already fallen beyond the closed blinds in the kitchen by the time their supper was ready. Wanting Rachel to relax after her taxing experience, Saul had taken it upon himself to cook their dinner of chicken and broccoli with a side of rice.

"I didn't know you could cook," Rachel commented as the three of them sat down to eat. "This smells amazing."

"Thank you." There were a lot of things she didn't know about him, and that was probably for the best.

"Let me guess," she added, with a sad tilt to her lips, "there aren't any restaurants in the places you go."

He realized she was repeating back to him what he'd once said about there being no barbers in the places he went.

"Pretty much." He didn't bother to add that most of the time he ate Meals-Ready-to-Eat from sealed packages instead of cooking. He couldn't even light a Sterno, let alone a fire, lest he give away his concealment.

Turning his attention to Liam, he asked, "What'd you do on your sleepover last night?"

Liam blinked over at him, clearly sleepy. "We jumped on his trampoline until dark, and then we watched a cool movie about a kid who pulled King Arthur's sword out of a boulder."

"That does sound cool."

Liam went back to forking his broccoli.

Realizing he wasn't going to get much more out of the boy, Saul waited for Rachel to tell Liam what had happened that day. Her son knew nothing yet about Ethan's appearance, nor the high-speed chase that had nearly ended in his mother's strangulation. All Liam had heard was the story she'd told Cody's mother about getting in a car accident as an excuse for picking up her son so late. The crumpled metal on the side of the truck lent validity to her tale.

Saul could appreciate Rachel's wanting to protect Liam from the truth, but the boy was old enough and mature enough to handle it. Besides, it would all come out in the newspaper, as would the results of Ethan's eventual trial. He was being held, without bond, at Wagoner County Detention Center.

Saul waited for Rachel to eat most of her meal before he said, "Interesting day, huh?"

Her gaze flew to his, then swung toward Liam, then back to him.

"Do you think what happened today means an end to the FOR Americans?" She steered the subject in a different direction than Saul had intended.

He'd already recounted the events at the golf course after they'd arrived back at the ranch.

"Hope so. Willard Davis was their ringleader, and he's gone. Les Wright and Timmy Olsen will be serving several years for attempted murder, as will the other members."

"Thank God the bomb didn't go off."

"That would've been bad," Saul agreed, but he still thought she ought to come clean with Liam. "Do you want to say more about your accident today?" he asked, raising his eyebrows.

Liam swung an expectant gaze toward his mother.

"Things are going to change," Saul added, when Rachel kept quiet. "And this is a small commu—"

"Okay," she cut him off. "I'll tell him."

For the next few minutes, Rachel described her nightmarish experience. Liam listened with growing horror as she relayed how his uncle had evidently tracked them down, then engaged her in a high-speed chase. When she added how she'd run him off the road, Liam cheered, only to pale and fall silent when she described how Ethan had crawled out of his overturned vehicle and proceeded to strangle her.

Saul marveled anew at how resourceful she had been, spraying him in the face with carburetor cleaner. That small act might well have saved her life, postponing Ethan's strangulation long enough for the police to intercede.

Watching Liam's face grow paler by the second, Saul offered reassurances.

"Your uncle's going to be locked behind bars for a long time. You don't have to worry about him anymore."

"What about afterward? He's going to come looking for me."

"You'll be an adult by then," Saul stated.

Liam turned back to his mother. "You actually drove his car off the road?" he said with disbelief.

Rachel nodded. "Yes. It was terrifying."

"Your mom is braver than she gives herself credit for," Saul said.

Shaking her head self-consciously, Rachel pushed her chair back.

"You cooked so I'll clean." Watching her gather up dishes and take them to the sink, he could tell by the stiff way she held herself she was emotionally overwrought by everything that had happened, not to mention his own imminent departure. If it wasn't enough that Ethan had found her, now Saul was leaving her to face her brother in court by herself.

It wasn't like he had a choice. He would have to leave at dawn and drive for two ten-hour days in order to report back at Dam Neck on Thursday morning. That reminded him.

"Hey, I was wondering if you two could do me a really big favor," he said into the quiet.

Rachel turned from the sink with tear-bright eyes. Liam, who was pushing his chair in, paused.

"I'd like to leave Duke here with you." Saul studied their reactions. "I'm sure I'll be sent overseas sometime this year. Leaving him here would save me from having to impose on other people."

Liam's face brightened. He sent his mother an imploring look. "Can we?"

Rachel considered the dog who lay with his head on his paws and his eyes on their plates in hopeful expectation of some dinner scraps. A fond smile touched her lips.

"Does that mean you're coming back for him in one year's time?"

Her slightly defiant tone meant the vague answers he'd given her the previous night hadn't satisfied her. She had to know he wouldn't leave his dog with them forever.

"Sometime." He kept his answer unspecific.

Given her nod of acceptance, *sometime* was better than his previous answer. Was it enough to keep her from falling into Andy's arms over the next twelve months, though?

"Then, yes," Rachel agreed. "We'll watch Duke for you while you're away."

"Thank you." Saul got up, avoiding eye contact. "I've got to make some preparations before I go." He snatched up his car keys and let himself outside to check the fluid levels in his Camaro.

As he envisioned his long ride home, followed by his return to the Team, followed by complex and dangerous operations, the armor that had always encased his heart before his journey with Rachel began to form again. He welcomed the emotionless, detached feelings that arose in him. There were hostages to liberate and drug lords to eliminate. He couldn't afford to lose his focus by thinking of the little family living in his childhood home, miles and miles away from whatever hellhole he might find himself in.

Even so, the unarticulated hope that Rachel would be waiting for him when his obligation ended was tucked inside his heart like a keepsake.

∼

At the sound of the Goodner's rooster crowing, Rachel's eyes flew open. The sun was just beginning to paint the wall of her bedroom a soft peach hue. She paused mid-stretch and listened. While Saul was always quiet, she intuited, without needing to check first, that he had left. She could *feel* his absence.

Closing her eyes again, she let sorrow rise inside her, spreading like the roots of an insidious weed. The emotions were all too familiar. But she wouldn't let them overtake her as she had when Blake died so suddenly. She would lean on God for solace and for strength.

Clasping her hands together, Rachel pleaded, "Father, give me strength to get through this day. To find joy even in my sorrow." She repeated her favorite fortifying verse three times, "'I can do all things through Christ who strengthens me.'" Then she tossed back the covers and went to wake Liam up for school.

An hour later, Rachel, with Duke on his leash, escorted a chatty Liam to the bus stop. Leaves twirled before them, blown from their branches by a brisk autumn breeze. It was heartening to hear her son express enthusiasm about returning to his new school. He seemed to have accepted that his uncle was out of the picture for a long time, anyway. They waited barely a minute at the head of the driveway before the school bus appeared. Liam climbed aboard, took a seat by the window, and waved good-bye.

The bus took off, leaving Rachel all by herself. Loneliness curled around her until Duke gave a sad whine.

She gazed down at him and stroked his broad head. "We're not alone. We still have each other, Duke. Come on. Let's go home. I have a lot of work to do today." She listed her chores aloud as if the dog understood every word of what she was saying.

They were approaching the bend in the driveway when the sound of a vehicle coming up behind them had her whirling with alarm. She huffed out a breath of relief as she recognized the now-familiar form of Andy Cannard's police car.

"It's okay, Duke," she said to the dog who faced the interloper with his fur bristling. "It's a friend this time."

Andy slowed beside her and rolled down his window to run his appreciative gaze over her plaid shirt and jeans.

"Mornin'," he said with a slow smile. "Takin' a walk?"

Rachel imagined many a woman had gone weak in the knees when Andy flashed his dimples at them, but only Saul had that effect on her.

"Sort of. We just put Liam on the school bus."

"Ah, I wanted to talk to you about that. Did Saul take off yet?"

"This morning." What had he meant by wanting to talk?

Andy's smile faded as he focused on Duke. "He left his dog here?"

"Yes." The reminder of Saul's eventual return cheered her.

"Huh. I'll meet you up at the house." Andy gestured with his chin.

As he rolled up his window and pulled away, Rachel continued on foot. He waited for her at the steps to the porch, clasping a printout of some kind. "This is going to show up in Friday's newspaper." He handed it to her.

She realized she was reading a police blotter. Ethan's name was circled, along with the charges he was facing: malicious wounding, attempted murder. The realization she was going to have to face him in a courtroom, yet again, made her swallow hard.

"I thought you'd be pleased."

Rachel grimaced. "Ethan's a good lawyer. I'm afraid he'll beat these charges and walk free."

"Not going to happen. We found evidence in his car and in his motel room that he was stalking you. The Wagoner police witnessed your brother with his arm around your neck while you dangled in the air, and you've got a doctor's report to back that up. He'll do time; don't you worry about that."

"How much time, though?" Rachel looked up at him. "And how do I know he won't try to kill me again when he gets out?"

"We'll extradite him back to Virginia and take out a court order forbidding him to return to this state."

As if a court order would stop him.

"Don't worry," Andy repeated, reading her mind. "I won't let anything happen to you."

The implication he would be her new protector wasn't lost on her. Rachel decided to level with him.

"Thank you, but you should know I'm waiting for Saul to come back when his enlistment is over."

Andy cocked his head. "You sure he will? He told me you weren't together."

The words nearly undermined Rachel's confidence until she remembered what Saul had explained to her on Sunday evening.

"The thing is, he can't be thinking about me when he's on assignment. It would interfere with his work. But that doesn't mean he's not coming back. He is."

Andy hid his reaction by bending over Duke to pet him. He straightened with a determined gleam in his eyes and another grin.

"I'm still going to give it my best shot."

She could only smile and roll her eyes.

"In all seriousness, though, Angel—Rachel." His smile faded. "I'm here for two reasons. The first is, you could face charges yourself for enrolling your son in school under a false name. The second reason is, the press is going to be all over this story. I think if you get out in front of it, you could elicit the sympathy of the school board and avoid getting into trouble."

Her stomach cinched with anxiety. "I didn't realize using a fake birth certificate was a crime."

"Like I said. People will overlook that once they know the reason."

"But how do we tell them?"

"We take your story to the press. I'm friends with one of the editors for *Tulsa World*. That's our local newspaper, with a section in it just for Broken Arrow. He said he'd be happy to meet with you and to write up your side of the story. It'll be in the paper by Friday, same day the blotter is published. I can take you into Tulsa this morning if you're free."

Rachel's plan to place orders for the new kitchen cabinets and backsplash took a backseat to this more urgent matter.

"I guess I'm free." Andy's helpfulness in avoiding humiliation and potential charges stirred her gratification. "Once the truth is known, can we go back to using our real names?"

"Yes. You could and you should. My friend says he can meet with us at a café in Tulsa at ten o'clock." He glanced at his watch. "That means we need to leave now."

"Oh." Relieved she'd already showered upon waking and was dressed for the day, Rachel glanced down at Duke. "Let me put the dog inside. I'll be right back out. Come on, Duke."

They dashed up the steps, leaving Andy outside to wait for her.

Rachel's thoughts raced before her. What a relief it would be to go back to using her real name and not have to hide who she and Liam really were! Shannon would be so relieved for her. And speaking of parents, she could even call Mom and Pop and tell them—what? That their older son had terrorized their daughter, forcing her to flee?

No, she would have to make up some story to explain her disappearance and Ethan's subsequent incarceration.

But at least she could be herself now. Maybe by the time Saul returned to Broken Arrow, she would have established her business, along with a reputation among home sellers.

And if he doesn't come back to stay? asked an insecure voice in her head. *After all, he'd merely said he would return some day to collect his dog.*

Rachel banished the cynical inner voice. Whenever doubts and uncertainties ambushed her, she would imitate Duke who, like her, waited patiently and without complaint for Saul's return.

CHAPTER 19

*P*rajuk Somchai, the leader of the notorious Golden Triangle, was hard to kill. He slept in a high-rise apartment in Bangkok, the tallest building in the vicinity, a circumstance that prevented Saul from setting up a long-range rifle on an equally tall or taller building and firing at the man as he walked by the window.

Moreover, Somchai's apartment had no balconies, which meant the SEALs couldn't rappel from the rooftop and enter his apartment through a sliding glass door. Last but not least, he was surrounded by a rash of bodyguards, who kept constant vigil over him. It wasn't any wonder SEAL Team Six had been sent in to eliminate him—or more specifically Six's top sniper, Saul Wade, and his three teammates, who were there for logistical support.

Theo Baker, a weapons expert, sat on their balcony at the Embassy Suites hotel, watching Somchai's apartment through a pair of binoculars. Subject to the oppressive heat, car pollution, and the tantalizing aromas of exotic food, it was all Theo could do to stay attentive and not to doze.

When Somchai stepped out of the building's front door, Theo nearly fell off the chair he was sitting in.

"Chief!" he cried.

Saul, who had stepped inside to polish off a bowl of spicy green papaya salad, snatched up his sniper rifle, joining Mr. T on the balcony.

"Somchai just left the building *alone.*" The black man pointed down at the crowd moving along the sidewalk.

"Where?" Saul couldn't see him.

"In the navy baseball hat and sunglasses right there. See him?"

Saul raised his rifle, peering through the scope for a better look. The baseball hat caught his eye. "You sure that's him?"

"Positive. I ID'ed him by his tattoo. He must have given his bodyguards the slip."

"Okay, let's go get him." Rushing inside, Saul exchanged his sniper rifle for a silenced 9mm, which he slid into the waistband of his khakis, concealing it with his loose flowered shirt. The Nikon camera looped by its strap around his neck transformed him into a tourist, as did Theo's LA Lakers jersey sporting Kobe Bryant's number 8. Both men were a little too fit to resemble real tourists, though, but they blended as best they could.

Riding the elevator to the lobby, Theo texted Lucas and Bambino, who were still asleep, having watched Somchai's apartment all night. Lucas, the officer in charge, texted back giving his permission to pursue the target. They'd been in Thailand for a week already, and this was their first chance to fulfill the objective.

Check in with a sit rep every half hour, Lucas added, requesting a situational report.

Saul and Theo skirted the lobby and exited the hotel via a fire exit. Walking at a near run in order to catch up to their quarry, they jostled more than a few pedestrians coursing the busy sidewalk. Pursuing a hostile in broad daylight wasn't Saul's first choice, but coming on the heels of his last botched assignment, it fit the mold.

They'd traveled three blocks before Saul glimpsed Somchai's hat again, weaving through the crowd along the opposite sidewalk. The four-lane, congested Sukhumvit Road stood between them. Turning to catch Theo's eye, Saul realized his partner had been cut off at the last side street by a vendor selling iced tea in plastic bags. Saul conveyed with a gesture that he had eyes on the target. Theo signaled for him to keep a visual on the target.

Nodding, Saul looked back at Somchai just in time to see him slip into an alley between two buildings.

Risking life and limb, Saul crossed all four lanes of slow-moving traffic. A minivan blared its horn at him as he darted in front of it. Thanks to his athleticism, he arrived on the opposite curb unscathed. Saul followed Somchai into the alley, discovering it to be a crooked passageway filled with discarded bottles and reeking of trash.

Was he being lured into a trap? Surely Somchai wouldn't bait his enemies without his bodyguards around to rescue him. Lifting his camera like he was taking pictures, Saul skirted puddles and stepped around broken glass to keep it from crackling under his soles. He passed several dumpsters and came across a young boy sitting disconsolately on an overturned banana crate.

Saul pretended to take the boy's picture, gave him a twenty-five baht coin, and gestured for him to leave. The kid bowed gratefully over his hands and scampered off, passing Theo who drifted up the alley in Saul's direction.

With a nod at Theo, Saul turned and continued his hunt. Plumbing the shadow-filled alleyway for any sign of his quarry, he rounded a dumpster in time to see Somchai opening the rear door of some unknown establishment. The man glanced back at him, and Saul ducked back behind the dumpster, signaling to his teammate that he had eyes on the target.

When the drug lord disappeared, Saul and Theo pursued him. The first to reach the door, Saul held his breath and slowly pulled it open. The door gave access to a deserted stairwell. Sounds overhead had him withdrawing his silenced pistol even as he handed off the door for Theo to close. They ascended the stairs on rubber soles. A cold sweat formed a layer between his shirt and his back. He never used to perspire like this.

Then again, he'd never doubted himself or his purpose until his previous assignment. He had only managed to injure the infamous Colombian arms dealer, Joaquín Emilio Díaz, last month, after surprising him on his yacht in the Gulf of Mexico.

At the top of the stairs, they were greeted by the sound of music coming through the walls. They eased through the door and found themselve in a dimly lit corridor lined with semi-private alcoves all draped with beaded curtains. The humid air, perfumed with incense, suggested they'd entered one of Bangkok's infamous massage parlors via the back door.

But where was Somchai?

It was still early afternoon, and the alcoves all stood empty, except for the very last one from which the sound of whispers floated. Leaving Mr. T to guard the door, Saul pressed his back to the wall and sidestepped closer. A peek through the beaded curtain revealed Prajuk and a woman in a passionate embrace.

Oh, joy. Saul would have to wait for the drug lord's tryst to end. He wasn't about to kill the man in front of his lover. Peeking one more time at the couple, he realized with a sinking sensation the woman was pregnant.

Startled, he glanced at her face. It was the wrong thing to do. Her gentle smile made him think of Rachel.

Focus. It was his job to protect the interest of his country. The Golden Triangle exported hundreds of thousands of pounds of heroin annually. Hundreds of Americans died from overdoses. Without Somchai at the helm, The Golden Triangle would disintegrate due to infighting. The leader's death was the easiest means of crippling the operation. It was that simple.

Deciding to wait for his target to come back down the stairwell, Saul signaled to Theo they should retreat. At the bottom of the stairs, they shared a brief whispered exchange. Then Theo slipped through the exit to guard the door from unsuspecting visitors. Under the second run of stairs and behind a pile of boxes, Saul hid himself and waited. The stairwell was an oven.

At long last, when Saul figured he was going to die of dehydration, the door upstairs swung open. Someone, presumably Somchai, started down the steps, whistling contentedly. Saul's heart began to hammer. He clutched his 9mm in a sweat-slick hand and waited.

The man finally stepped into view, heading for the door. Making a positive ID from his distinctive tattoo, Saul double-tapped him. *Floop. Floop.* The force of the bullets flung the target against the far wall. He slid down it, leaving a trail of blood and brain matter.

Saul shoved his pistol back under his shirt, stepped over one of Somchai's sandaled feet, and moved swiftly toward the exit. Theo looked relieved to see him. They hadn't gone thirty feet up the alley when they ran into the boy to whom he'd given the coin. The kid had bought dried, sugar-covered plums, and he wanted to share.

With a shake of his head, Saul pushed past the boy, dismayed by how lightheaded he was. *I'm just dehydrated.* Theo slanted him a sidelong frown.

The detachment Saul had been famous for was gone? Racked with shivers, in danger of losing his lunch, he followed Theo into the crowd surging along the sidewalk. Together they headed for their hotel.

As they pushed into the air-conditioned lobby, Saul muttered to his teammate, "I'll be in the bar. I need a minute." Lucas, their OIC, would want to debrief him. Saul wasn't up for that. He needed a beer to rehydrate and to steady his nerves.

To his relief, Theo let him go without comment. The bar was empty. Saul ordered a tall can of Singha, found a booth to hide in, and gulped it.

The very thing he'd been afraid would happen if he forgave his stepdad had, in fact, happened. The anger he had carried with him up until then no longer fueled him. It was gone. He couldn't use it like a shield to deflect the protests of his conscience. In its place was an empty, nagging feeling that felt like a stomach ulcer. All at once, he came up with a name for it—guilt. The horror of twenty assassinations was consuming him from the inside out.

A waitress sidled up to his booth, and he ordered another Singha. Her pitying smile made him think of Rachel. Everything made him think of Rachel. Had Andy Cannard made his move yet?

Saul reached into the pocket of his cargo pants and pulled out Liam's turtle. He put it on the table in front of him.

"What is with that thing?" Theo had asked him a few days back.

"Makes me think of home," Saul admitted. He asked himself what he ought to do next. One thing he was sure of.

He could not, would not, kill another man, whether ordered to do so or not.

Rachel's advice sounded in his head as surely as if she were sitting there next to him. *That's your conscience talking. If you feel unworthy, all you have to do is ask for absolution. There's nothing God can't forgive.*

She had been right about his forgiving Cyril. She was probably right about this, too, although it seemed too simple to be true.

Staring down at Liam's turtle, Saul addressed the Great Spirit the way Puca had taught him.

I have no right to ask this, Holy One, but please forgive me for all I've done.

"Hey, buddy, mind if we join you?"

Startled out of his meditation, Saul glanced up to find Lieutenant Lucas Strong looming over him with Theo and Bambino in tow. The former tight end for the Dallas Cowboys wore a baseball cap over his light-brown hair and a frown of concern mirrored by the men behind him.

Saul groaned inwardly. "Have a seat." He scooted over to make room. Lucas crammed his six-foot-six-inch frame in next to him as Theo and Bambino, the super-young Italian American, slid onto the opposite bench.

Lucas searched Saul's profile with his worried gray eyes. "Did you fulfill the objective?"

Clearly Theo, who'd reported their adventure, wasn't sure the deed was done.

Saul smothered a burp. "Yes, sir. He's out of the picture."

A long silence ensued with Saul staring at his beer can and lots of meaningful glances between his teammates.

"Are you okay, Saul?" Lucas finally asked.

Saul considered the question. "Nope."

The silence grew thicker.

"You can talk to us, Saul," Lucas assured him. "What's wrong?"

Saul dragged in a breath, then let it out again. "I've hit a wall. Can't do this anymore."

Hearing himself talk was like listening to someone else. At the same time, his confession eased some of the pressure in his chest.

"Are you talking about your specialty," Lucas asked delicately, "or being a SEAL?"

Saul traced the Singha logo on his beer can and said, "Both."

"And you've got what—a year left of your reenlistment?"

"Ten months." In his head, he pictured Andy Cannard doing everything in his power to win Rachel's affections. "You think I could get a bad psyche eval and be medically discharged?" he quipped.

Theo clicked his tongue. "Come on, Chief. You're not crazy."

Bambino, who was wise beyond his twenty-one years, said, "Maybe he's crazy in love."

Saul scowled at the Tony Danza look-alike, even though he'd hit the nail on the head. Then he shrugged.

"Yeah, that's possible," he confessed. No need to hide it from his brothers.

"Have you told her?" Lucas had obviously been tipped off by his wife that Saul had a thing for Rachel.

"Not really." Saul stared at the tabletop, wishing he'd asked Rachel to wait for him, after all.

"Told who?" Theo and Bambino asked at the same time.

Saul told them. "Rachel LeMere."

Their eyes widened in identical expressions of astonishment.

"Blake's widow?" Theo's deep voice came out two octaves higher.

Lucas locked an arm around Saul's neck in a modified man-embrace.

"Hang in there, Chief. In a few days, we'll be stateside. I'll talk to Lieutenant Mills, who's tight with the new CO, and see if we can't find a sniper to take your place."

"Thanks." Saul wasn't going to count on that happening. After what he had just done, depriving a baby of ever knowing his father, he didn't expect or deserve any kind of special treatment.

"Come on." Lucas tossed down two hundred-baht bills to cover Saul's tab. "Let's go upstairs and tell Lieutenant Mills the job's done and we're ready to go home."

"Hooyah," Theo added, acknowledging Lucas's words with the SEAL battle cry.

Saul returned Liam's turtle to his pocket before scooting out of the booth. Going home didn't mean to him what it meant to the others. He had ten more months to serve before he really got to go home.

With arms folded against the December chill, Rachel waited with bemusement as Andy backed his cruiser toward her porch steps. It was obvious he was delivering the live Christmas tree that stuck out of the partially open trunk. She had told him countless times already to stop bringing her unexpected gifts. No matter how much he tried, he wasn't going to win her heart. That belonged to Saul.

Moreover, she didn't need a Christmas tree. She and Liam were planning to spend Christmas with Shannon in Dallas, at which time Rachel would get to meet her half brother, Ryan. But Andy popped out of the driver's seat with such a determined expression the words never reached her lips.

"You can't have Christmas without a proper tree," he declared, tugging at the rope that kept his trunk half-closed. Dainty snowflakes landed on his police jacket and glinted in his dark hair as he lifted the lid of the trunk and put his arms around the strapped boughs. He carried the small tree up the steps and propped it against the side of the house.

"Figured you didn't own a tree stand," he said, heading back to his car, "so I bought that, too." Reaching into his trunk, he pulled out a bright metal stand.

"Thank you, Andy," Rachel said, touched by his thoughtfulness and despite having found three rusted tree stands in the barn. "Why don't you come in and have some cocoa?" Liam's presence inside would keep Andy's flirtation in check.

"I wish I could. I have to get back to work."

Taking in Andy's unusually solemn expression, Rachel's concern rose.

"What's wrong?" The Andy she had come to know would have whipped a sprig of mistletoe out of his pocket by now and angled for a kiss.

"I have bad news." He put the tree stand down, then closed his trunk.

Rachel's stomach went into free fall as her memories flashed back to the lieutenant up at her doorstep three-and-a-half years earlier, wearing the same expression and saying the same thing.

"No." She took a backward step and bumped her hip on the porch rail. "Not Saul," she breathed, certain Andy was going to tell her Saul had been killed and she would never see him again.

"No, no, Rachel." Andy stepped toward her and caught both her arms. "This isn't about Saul."

Her knees buckled with relief. Andy caught her from falling. He pulled her unexpectedly into his arms and hugged her close. Rachel couldn't bring herself to chide him. When he set her at arm's length, she could tell something was different about him.

"I just realized how much you love him," he stated on a strange note.

Rachel nodded.

"You would wait a lifetime for him, wouldn't you?"

"Yes." She regretted the disappointment she could see in his kind brown eyes. "What's the bad news, Andy?"

He dropped his arms slowly to his sides. "Your brother." He paused, clearly struggling to find the words. "He was found dead in his cell this morning."

"What?" Dizziness assailed Rachel a second time.

"He strangled himself with his bedsheet. Wagoner police are sick about it. They never pegged him as a suicide risk."

Rachel pressed a fist to her stomach. "It's my fault. He told me I'd ruined him."

"Stop that." Andy lifted her chin with his gloved hand. "It is *not* your fault. He was psychotic. That's what the psychiatrist who tested him said. His defense council was going to plead insanity. Did you know his Russian mother took off and his father abandoned him at an orphanage at the age of three?"

Dazed, Rachel stared at Andy. "He was the one from Russia!" she marveled, thinking back to the lies he'd told her when she was young. She pictured Ethan as a toddler, crying for his father as workers at the orphanage carried him away.

"Poor, Ethan." Perhaps his obsession with her son stemmed from his lost childhood. Had he seen his younger self in Liam? Had he been trying to rewrite history?

All at once, she realized the trial she'd been dreading, slated for the sixth of January, would never take place. In killing himself, Ethan had spared her the torture of testifying against her own brother.

Overwhelmed by emotions, feeling both relief and grief, Rachel covered her face with her hands.

"I can feel you shaking," Andy said with sympathy. "Come on, let me take you inside."

"I'm okay." Rachel dragged her hands from her face and managed a smile for him. "Thank you for being the one to tell me." She went to embrace him and took comfort from the strength of his arms. If only Saul were here to do likewise.

They both stepped back and let their arms fall at the same time.

"Merry Christmas, Rachel. I hope you hear from Saul soon," he said, sounding sincere.

Me, too. Her heart gave a pang. "Merry Christmas, Andy. Don't work too hard."

"Tell that to the guy who just stole fifty thousand dollars from his employer," Andy quipped, as he headed for his car door.

"Thank you for the tree," she called, glancing back at it. With a week to go before Christmas, it wouldn't hurt to put a tree in the window, even if they wouldn't be there on Christmas Day.

"Holler if you need me." Andy ducked into his car and pulled away. The flurries had turned into snow showers, falling so thickly they obscured Andy's cruiser before he'd even disappeared beneath the trees.

Rachel picked up the tree stand and carried it up to the porch. Instead of going inside, she sat in the nearest Adirondack chair, ignoring the cold, needing a moment to come to terms with Ethan's death.

In the ensuing quiet, she could make out Liam's voice inside the house as he praised the dog. She had left him trying to teach Duke how to roll over. A sound resembling the rush of waves onto the shore made her realize she was hearing snowflakes hit the ground. She'd never known snowflakes made a sound before. Movement near the family cemetery drew her anxious gaze. She was amazed to see an eight-point buck trek cautiously across the open field. Something about the buck's lurching gait reminded her of Ethan.

Tears sprang to her eyes. "I forgive you, Ethan," she stated quietly.

Lowering its head, the buck paused to nibble at the grass that was fast disappearing beneath a quilt of white.

I wish Saul could see how beautiful it is right now.

Closing her eyes, Rachel inhaled the crisp air and relived her relief at being told it wasn't Saul who had died.

"Protect him, Lord," she whispered, repeating the same words she had prayed every day since his departure. "Bring him safely home."

CHAPTER 20

*O*n the heels of a sixteen-hour flight routed through Germany, the four-man SEAL squad exited the C-17 Globemaster transport plane at a quarter to midnight. As they crossed the dark and frigid tarmac headed for their vehicles, Lieutenant Strong put a call through to their command, letting Lieutenant Mills know of their return to the continental US. After two weeks in the tropics, Saul savored the bite of cold air.

"The CO and the XO want to talk with us," Lucas said to Saul as he put his phone away.

Saul's foggy brain had trouble decoding the message.

"Now, sir?" He glanced at his watch, realizing he had yet to reset it.

"Apparently, yes. Good night, guys," Lucas called to Theo and Bambino, who stayed behind to oversee the unloading of their weapons.

The men waved back, too tired to talk.

It occurred to Saul the untimely meeting meant he was going to be reprimanded for the poorly executed job on the yacht in the Gulf of Mexico.

"Isn't it Christmas Eve?" Saul asked, consulting his mental calendar.

"It will be Christmas Eve *day* in fifteen minutes," Lucas corrected him. "You're still on Pacific time."

Even so, neither the XO nor the CO ought to be waiting at the Team building to debrief them, not at that time of night.

"You want a ride?" Lucas asked him as he headed for his black F-250 pickup truck, about fifteen years newer than the one Rachel drove.

Will you ever stop thinking about her?

"I've got my Harley." Saul gestured to his Street 750 hidden under a protective cover.

"You're going to freeze," Lucas warned. "It's thirty degrees out here."

"It'll wake me up." Given the new CO's no-nonsense reputation, he would need to be incredibly coherent, or the man would string him up by his toenails.

By the time Saul motored through the gates of Dam Neck Naval Annex where SEAL Team Six operated, his face was numb from the cold and his ears ached, but his brain was wide awake. Stowing his biker's gloves, he strode toward the halogen lights glaring over the entrance to the Team building. Lucas, who stood directly inside the door, gazed through the glass insert and pushed it open for him as he approached.

"They're waiting."

With butterflies in his stomach, Saul followed Lucas down the hallway into the new CO's office.

Both Commander Monteague and Lieutenant Mills were in the room. Notably absent was Master Chief Rivera who'd retired a year ago while Saul was in Mexico. This was Saul's second encounter with the CO, who'd taken Dwyer's place after he'd been hauled away in cuff's at Lieutenant Mills's court martial.

Monteague sat behind his desk wearing an inscrutable expression. The utilitarian desk lamp cast an unkind light on the scarred half of his face, a reminder to Saul he was standing before the sole survivor of the worst disaster in SEAL history. One would never suspect

Commander Monteague once had a reputation as a playboy. His poker face gave no hint of what Saul was about to face.

In complete contrast, Lieutenant Jonah Mills stood behind Monteague resembling the cat who ate the canary. Saul, who knew Jonah as well as if they were brothers, relaxed slightly at the gleam in the man's gold-green eyes.

"Evening, sirs." Saul and Lucas greeted both officers at once, snapping them sharp salutes.

Saul was painfully conscious of his rumpled civilian clothing and windblown hair.

"At ease, Chief, Lieutenant." Monteague waved them both toward the chairs in front of his desk. "Have a seat. You must be crusty after such a long flight."

Saul sat stiffly in the farthest seat, grateful for Lucas's reassuring presence. Lieutenant Mills crossed to the window and swiveled the blinds to keep anyone from seeing inside. Meanwhile, the CO drummed a large-knuckled hand on his desktop and frowned down at some paperwork. Saul strained to see what he was staring at. Was that his personnel file?

"You've been a sniper for, what, sixteen years?"

"Close to fifteen, sir."

"And in that time, you've racked up twenty kills. Is that right?"

Saul's stomach wrenched. It ought to have been twenty-one. "Yes, sir."

"What happened with Joaquín Emilio Díaz?" The CO lifted his gaze and stared at Saul through narrowed eyes.

Saul swallowed against a dry throat. "His kids were sleeping in the cabin with him, sir. One of them woke up and spotted me."

"So, you fled without completing the objective."

"Yes, sir." He wouldn't apologize for what he'd known was the right thing to do.

"The man went after you and, in self-defense, you injured him when you could have finished him. Why didn't you fulfill the objective, Chief? Could the kids still see you?"

Saul, who had given his reasons for not pulling the trigger, had an answer.

"I lost my father at a young age, sir, and it wrecked my childhood. I couldn't do that to his children."

Monteague made a scoffing sound. "You had no such compunction about the target in Thailand."

"I did," Saul confessed. "He's the last man I hope I ever kill."

"The last?" The CO's tone was slightly incredulous. "Are you telling me you're undeployable?"

Saul grappled with his pride, then replied through his teeth. "As a sniper, yes, sir. I will not shoot to kill again." He fought the urge to squirm as Monteague studied him like a bug under a magnifying glass. His thoughts flashed to Liam and his cricket. *Focus!*

"Thanks to your brothers on the Team," the CO finally said, "now you don't have to kill anyone."

"Sir?" Saul looked from Jonah to Lucas and found them both trying not to smile.

"You tell him, Jonah." The CO gestured for Lieutenant Mills to explain.

"Ever heard of Camp Gruber in Oklahoma, Chief?" Jonah's gaze was far warmer than the CO's.

Startled to hear the name of his home state, Saul sat up straighter. "Of course, sir. It's a training base, about an hour's drive from Broken Arrow."

"Correct," Jonah continued. "It trains National Guardsmen and law enforcement personnel primarily. They're searching for an active-duty field-artillery expert to instruct the trainees. You've been granted a humanitarian assignment to train them until your enlistment is over. You'll start just after the New Year."

Shocked into silence, all Saul could do was stare first at Jonah, then at Lucas. The room seemed to fill with sparkling dust as he realized not only had he been transferred from sniper duty to instructor, but the source of his heartache was gone. Working at Camp Gruber meant he could live in Broken Arrow and commute to work for the last ten months of his service.

Tears of joy rushed into his eyes, and he had to bow his head a moment with gratitude. As soon as he had his emotions under control, Saul raised his head again.

"Thank you, sirs. I don't how you managed this," he choked out.

Jonah gestured to Monteague. "You can thank the CO, Saul. We don't have that kind of pull."

Saul abandoned protocol, coming out of his seat to extend Monteague a grateful handshake. To his relief, the man accepted it, his grip firm but brief.

"Look for your orders coming via email, Chief. If we're done here," he stood, "I'd like to get home."

"Yes, sir," his XO assured him. "Thank you, sir. We'll lock up behind you."

They waited for the CO to don his peacoat and stalk out of the office. As soon as the outer door clanged shut, Jonah threw his arms wide. With a growl, Saul rushed at him and lifted him off his feet, then went to hug Lucas, only to find the man holding out an envelope.

"Merry Christmas, Saul."

"What's this?" Not his orders. They were coming by email.

"Open it," Jonah urged. "All the guys in the Team pitched in."

Bemused and intrigued, Saul opened the envelope and pulled out the single sheet inside. It took him a moment to decipher what it was.

"It's confirmation for a round-trip plane ticket with my name on it," he stated with astonishment, "to Tulsa International." He noted the date and time of departure. "I'm going home today?"

Lucas grinned at him.

"Just in time for Christmas." Jonah glanced at his watch. "You can still get a full night's sleep before you need to head to the airport."

"Oh, God." Saul stared up at the ceiling momentarily overwhelmed by the realization this was what it meant to receive grace. Whether in exhaustion or humility, he was confounded by the fact that what Rachel had told him had come true. Not only had he forgiven Cyril, but he had asked God to forgive him, and then he'd been blessed. What else could explain such an unexpected and miraculous turn of events? He sank in abject gratitude to one knee.

Fighting back tears of joy, Saul sensed Jonah and Lucas approach him. Their hands, warm and comforting, landed on his shoulders, causing his heart to swell with emotion. If Master Chief had been here, Saul was certain he would have uttered a beautiful, spontaneous prayer.

Too choked up to speak, Saul wiped his leaking eyes and let his teammates help him to his feet.

Lucas thumped his back. "Come on, Saul. Leave your Harley here. I'll take you home. You've got a big day ahead of you tomorrow."

"Yeah, let's hope it doesn't snow tonight," Jonah muttered, as they all moved toward the door.

Saul had bigger concerns than whether it would snow. He had to wonder if Andy Cannard had made inroads into Rachel's heart while he was away. *I should have written her. I should have asked her to wait for me.* Then again, he could never have anticipated the yoke he'd carried for such a long time would be lifted from him so unexpectedly.

Fourteen hours later, Saul thanked the Uber driver who'd picked him up at Tulsa International and stepped out of the car at the head of his driveway on Oak Grove Road. It was 8:00 p.m. on Christmas Eve. Several inches of snow quilted the ground and magnified the luminous moon, so Saul could see through the naked trees as he plodded toward his home.

Having come from the other side of the world within the last thirty-six hours, he had to wonder if he was hallucinating. Was this really happening? The crunch of snow beneath his cowboy boots and the glow of a doe's eyes suggested it was real. He was actually back home!

But would Rachel even be here? She might have gone to Dallas for

Christmas, he considered for the dozenth time since heading to the airport at noon, Eastern Standard Time. Worse still, he might find her in Andy's arms. That man's ability to get what he wanted out of people could not be underestimated. More than once, Saul had started to text her, only to change his mind.

If they were meant to be together, God would make it so.

Stepping out of the tree line, his hopes rose abruptly. A lit Christmas tree twinkled in the picture window and the old truck sat parked out front. Smoke curled from the chimney, letting him know for certain someone was inside. He marveled at how much his perspective of the place had changed. The grief and turmoil he'd associated with the ranch had given way to a deep sense of belonging.

With a burst of confidence, Saul hefted his duffel bag higher and doubled his stride. Anticipation, repressed for the past fourteen hours with fear of disappointment, swelled suddenly in his chest, prompting him to break into a run.

Playing Christmas music through the YouTube app on her cell phone, Rachel lounged against one corner of the sofa and stared wistfully into the fire dancing in the hearth.

Her gaze dropped to Liam and Duke snuggled up together on the rug, basking in the fire's warmth. A smile tugged at her lips. It wasn't so disappointing, after all, that the snowfall had delayed their drive to Dallas. Shannon hadn't wanted her daughter and grandson driving on a slick highway in an old truck. She'd asked them to drive down on Christmas Day instead, when the snow was predicted to melt and the roads would be free of traffic. Then she wouldn't have to worry.

At first, Rachel had been disappointed. But staying home had allowed her and Liam to attend a children's Christmas service at her new church in town. They'd come home and made Christmas cookies, eating them in front of the tree Andy had given her. The previous week, she and Liam had decorated it with ornaments found up in the attic. Hanging decorations that would have been familiar to Saul made him feel nearer, somehow. Nevertheless, sorrow stitched through her unexpectedly.

Would he be spending Christmas with them next year? Or was she putting too much stock in her belief he would return to Broken Arrow? Ten months still to go felt like an eternity.

Duke lifted his head abruptly and pricked his ears. The telltale sign he'd heard someone or something outside brought back memories of Rachel's run-in with the skinheads, not to mention the horrible incident with her brother. The dog stood suddenly, prompting a murmur of protest from Liam, before Duke went to look out the window.

"Woof!" Duke's entire body began to wag.

Rachel and Liam eyed each other before jumping up to see what the alert was about. A lone figure, with a full beard and a duffel jiggling on his back, was running up the driveway toward the porch.

"That's not Santa Claus," Liam stated with sudden excitement.

"Woof!"

Both Liam and Duke headed for the door.

Afraid to believe what her eyes were telling her, Rachel put her nose to the window, staring. The figure caught sight of her and slowed. There was no mistaking, even with fifty feet between them and her breath fogging up the pane, Saul's rare grin. He raised a hand to greet her.

"Saul!" she cried.

Liam was already unlatching the door. Duke nosed his way past him and shot outside. Rachel joined Liam at the threshold, flicking on the porch light in time to see Duke assault his owner at the base of the steps, then abandon him to run in frenzied circles in the snow.

Liam ventured onto the porch with bare feet in order to greet Saul as he came up the steps.

"You're here!" He threw his arms around Saul's neck.

"You've grown." Saul scrubbed his knuckles on Liam's head as he hugged him back. All the while, his damp gaze was fixed on Rachel.

Unmindful of getting her socks wet, Rachel walked toward him in a state of disbelief.

"Are you on leave? Are you home for Christmas?"

"Yes," Saul said, releasing Liam and climbing the last step so they stood eye-to-eye. He caught her face in hands that were bare and icy cold. "I'm on leave, but I'm never leaving again, except to rent out my house in Virginia Beach."

His message was too much to take in. "You're half-frozen. Come inside." She stepped back and opened the screen door.

Saul stamped his feet and followed her inside while Liam hopped on the icy steps, barefoot, calling the dog in.

Unable to tear her gaze from Saul's tan, bearded face, Rachel watched him drop his bag on the floor and shrug out of his lined jacket. Hanging it on the mounted hook rack behind the door, he then turned and examined every detail of the living room, including the fire, the large mirror over the hearth, and throw pillows on the couch. With an expression of approval, he stepped past her to peer into the kitchen.

"Wow." He took in the results of her labors.

Rachel blushed with pleasure at his obvious approval.

"You like what I've done so far?"

"I love it," he said, then turned around, locking eyes with her. "And I love the genius behind it." He gestured for her to place her hand in his.

Saul had just told her he loved her. It made her giddy. Giving her hand willingly to him, she couldn't help enjoying the feel of his callused yet tender grasp.

He studied her a moment. "You've changed your hair."

"I had it styled. I'm doing highlights instead of coloring it all."

"I like it."

She flushed at the desire in his eyes. "Thanks."

He tugged her closer. "I have something to tell you." Hooking his arm around her waist, he whispered, "I missed you."

Rachel floated on a cloud of contentment. She was only vaguely aware of the dog rushing back into the room, followed by a grinning Liam.

"I missed you, too," she said. "More than you know."

"I was afraid I'd find you curled up next to Andy."

The vulnerable-sounding confession tugged at her heartstrings.

"No, I don't love him."

"Who *do* you love?" Saul prompted.

Liam, who came up next to them, eyed his mother expectantly.

"I think you know who," Rachel countered, playing Saul's game. "Who do *you* love?" she demanded.

He had just suggested he loved her, but she wanted him to bare his heart completely.

Saul released her to stroke his beard thoughtfully. "Well, I love lots of people, and some things, too," he added, clearly procrastinating.

"For example?"

"For example, I love my teammates, who went to bat for me."

Rachel cocked her head, wondering what that meant.

"I love my dog." Saul bent over to call Duke. The dog went up to him and got a thorough scrubbing.

Saul looked up and caught Liam grinning.

"I love this kid right here," he said to Rachel as he gave Liam a friendly push, "because he reminds me of Blake."

Liam's blue eyes grew shiny. Then Saul reached for Rachel again and pulled her closer.

"But most of all, angel, I love you for believing in me. You mean the world to me."

Melted by his words, Rachel looped her arms around Saul's neck and rewarded him with a heartfelt kiss. Finding his lips still chilled from the outdoors, she lost herself in warming them.

With a sound of disgust, Liam wheeled away and went to stoke the fire.

When their kiss finally ended and Rachel's heels returned to the floor, she brought up Saul's earlier remark.

CRY IN THE WILDERNESS

"What did you mean when you said you're not ever going back? Don't you have ten months left?"

"Well!" Saul smiled and shook his head. "You're never going to believe it. I got a humanitarian assignment to teach artillery at Camp Gruber. It's only an hour away, so I can commute from here."

Rachel gasped and Liam spun around expectantly.

"Are you serious?" Rachel breathed.

"Yep. And when my ten months are up, I've decided to join the Tulsa Special Operations Team, if they let me in."

Rachel rolled her eyes at him. "Of course, they'll let you in."

"So…are you two good with me moving in with you?" Saul divided his attention between them.

"It's your house," Liam pointed out.

"Yeah, but I want it to be *our* house," Saul replied.

Rachel's pulse ticked upward.

"In other words, is it okay with you, Liam, if I marry your mom?"

As Rachel reeled at the implied proposal, Liam returned the poker to the tool stand and walked back to them, his expression thoughtful.

"Okay," he finally said, as if their getting married was entirely up to him. "But don't expect me to call you Dad."

Sorrow briefly cast a shadow on Rachel's happiness.

"I wouldn't want you to do that, tiger." Saul reached out to put a hand behind Liam's neck. "No one could take Blake's place in this world. No one."

Liam nodded. "He's an angel in God's army now," he stated definitively.

Rachel remembered telling Liam those words well over a year ago, on the day she had sworn to him they would escape Ethan's tyranny. Never in a hundred years could she have imagined how completely God would answer her pleas for help.

"That's right, he is." Saul gazed down at Rachel. "Cat's out of the bag," he said with a grin.

She feigned ignorance. "I don't know what you mean."

"I can't propose right now. I have to find the ring—my mother's engagement ring my dad gave her. Or would it bother you to wear something used?"

Rachel pictured the ring Saul was referring to. She'd found it in a box full of keepsakes inside Melody's dresser.

"I would be honored to wear your mother's ring."

Saul swiped a hand over his eyes as if suddenly overwhelmed.

"What's the matter?" Rachel asked, suddenly anxious.

He opened his eyes and smiled at her. "Nothing. I just never believed I could be this happy. You were right, Rachel. Everything you told me about forgiveness and asking for pardon—that's all it took. I'm in a completely different position than I was two months ago. Only God could have done that."

Stepping closer, Rachel pressed her ear to his heart as she hugged him.

"It's nothing short of a miracle," she agreed.

EPILOGUE

FOUR MONTHS LATER

*J*t took an entire week in April for Rachel to settle her brother's estate. With their adoptive parents too old and infirm to act as executors, Rachel had volunteered to undertake the responsibility. Besides, her parents still didn't know the circumstances surrounding their son's untimely death.

Rachel, Liam, and Saul, who'd wanted to check on the renters occupying his little bungalow, had taken advantage of Liam's spring break to fly back to Virginia while the Goodners took care of Duke for them. They weren't just there to dissolve and disperse Ethan's assets— most of which went to Liam—but also to get closure on a brief but troubling period of their lives.

"Thank you, Saul." Rachel took in all the household goods he'd boxed and bagged and then stacked in the foyer to be taken to Goodwill. "I could never have done this without you."

"Sure, you could've. Would have taken you about a month, but you could've done it," he said with certainty.

289

She loved the faith he had in her—so different from what she'd grown up hearing from her brother. "This was good for all of us. Especially Liam."

Her son, having been so abruptly uprooted from Virginia Beach, had benefited most from going back. Not only had he gotten to reclaim his belongings, but he'd also made peace with Ethan. His body had been shipped home courtesy of his colleagues at JAG, and buried at Colonial Grove Memorial Park, close to NAS Oceana, where he'd worked. Liam had laid flowers on his grave just that morning and talked to his uncle's spirit, while Rachel and Saul took a brief walk.

All three of them had also stopped in at the Virginia Beach Police Department Headquarters and spoken with a detective named Mooney. The man hadn't seemed the least bit surprised to hear Rachel's reasons for taking her son out of the state. The AMBER Alert naming them as missing had been stricken from the record.

"Work's done," Saul declared, approaching her. "It's time to head to the Team's get-together."

Rachel looked down at the grubby jeans and long-sleeved T-shirt she was wearing. "Please tell me we have time to change first."

"Five minutes." Saul swatted her playfully as she raced up the stairs.

Half an hour later, Rachel smoothed the pleats in the skirt she'd found hanging in her former closet as Saul rang the doorbell at Lieutenant Strong's upscale condominium. Given the number of cars parked in the short driveway and along the curb, the get-together to which they'd been invited was well attended.

A tall, redheaded woman opened the door. Although Charlotte's hair had grown past her shoulders, Rachel still recognized her.

"They're here!" she shouted over her shoulder before she hugged Saul first, then surprised Rachel with an equally fierce embrace. She stepped back to run a frank gaze over her. "You look great." Then Charlotte stuck out a hand to Liam.

"And you must be Liam."

"How do you do?" Liam said politely.

Charlotte threw her head back and laughed. "Better now."

As she drew them into her foyer, Rachel noted with interest the lovely antique furniture visible in both the living and dining rooms. She wanted to comment on Charlotte's taste in design, but shyness kept her quiet.

"Where is everybody?" Saul asked.

"In the backyard. Follow me. The drinks are out there."

They trailed Charlotte through a high-end gourmet kitchen toward the patio door. With a twinkle in her cherry-brown eyes, Charlotte opened the door and motioned for them to precede her.

Rachel, Saul, then Liam stepped out onto a large deck, only to startle back as at least two dozen people jumped into view from beneath a raised deck where they'd been hiding. "Surprise!"

The deck railings and the fence surrounding the backyard were festooned with white and gold ribbons, while matching balloons drifted in the cool April breeze.

Saul was the first to recover. "You gotta be kiddin' me," he exclaimed with a grin. "Is this party for us?" he asked the tall man, whom Rachel recognized as Lucas, though he'd joined the Team shortly after Blake's death.

"Of course." Lucas turned his attention to Rachel. "You must be the love of Saul's life," he said, causing her face to heat.

"I hope so." She laughed self-consciously as Lucas, who, like his wife, greeted her with a friendly hug.

For the next ten minutes, Rachel was welcomed by the very people she had known as Blake's wife. She already knew Jonah Mills and his blonde wife, Eden, a fitness instructor. Their teenage daughter, Miriam, pulled Liam aside to tell him something. Rachel's attention was diverted as Theo Baker, a hulking dark-skinned man with a robust laugh, greeted her next, followed by a swarthy young SEAL she didn't know named Tony Caruso.

"But everybody calls me Bambino," he admitted with an accent straight out of Philadelphia.

Next, she got to reunite with Master Chief Rivera, a man Blake had always raved about. Rivera, who was carrying a ten-month old baby, introduced her to his slim, brunette bride, Nina, who carried the first baby's twin.

"That one is Esme," Nina said, about the gorgeous dark-haired baby girl in Santiago's arms. "She prefers her daddy to me, for obvious reasons. And this is Rodrigo, named after Santiago's father. As you can see, he's very serious." Rodrigo studied Rachel with gravity.

"Twins," Rachel marveled, wondering wistfully if—once she and Saul finally carved out the time to get married—she would ever have Saul's child. "They're so beautiful."

Charlotte joined their little knot. "I hear you two got engaged." She glanced from Saul to Rachel.

Rachel showed off the understated ruby-and-diamond ring on her left hand.

"Oh, that's sweet," Charlotte said sincerely.

"It used to be Saul's mother's," Rachel volunteered.

"So, when is the wedding?" the redhead asked.

"Oh." Caught off guard by Charlotte's forwardness, Rachel managed a casual shrug. "Sometime. You know, Saul's been busy with his new job."

"Yep," he agreed. "And then Rachel got tasked with handling her brother's estate."

"Sounds like you haven't had much time," Charlotte said, with a sympathetic grimace. "What would you say to getting married right here, right now?"

"Oh." Wide-eyed, Rachel met Saul's eyes and found him watching her reaction.

"What do you say, angel?" He didn't seem the least bit surprised by Charlotte's suggestion. "Would you like to get married, right here, right now?"

Rachel looked around to find every guest waiting for her answer. She also noticed, for the first time, a white trellis standing to one side of the deck and a three-tiered cake on the dessert table.

"Wait a minute," she said, her heart pounding faster. "Did you know about this?" she demanded of Saul.

"It was Charlotte's idea," he said, promptly receiving a punch in the arm. "Ow!"

"Don't throw me under the bus, you cad." Charlotte laughed.

"She twisted my arm," Saul insisted, continuing their game. But then his smile faded and his expression grew serious. He caught up Rachel's hand, brought her knuckles to his lips, and kissed it. "Please marry me. It's the only way all of my friends can witness our wedding."

With a thought for her birth mother, who would understand, Rachel glanced at Liam and caught him smirking. "What do you think?"

"I think you should," Liam agreed holding up something in his hand—a pair of wedding rings.

Saul *had* been planning this all along. She faced him, amazed.

"Is there a justice of the peace here, or a priest, or something?" She gazed around at all the faces she'd been introduced to.

"That would be me." Santiago Rivera lifted a hand, as if volunteering. "I was recently named associate pastor at my church. So, I can legally marry you, if that's what you want."

Taking in the crowd of smiling faces, the clear spring sky, and the warmth of the sun, Rachel realized this was meant to be. In her heart of hearts, she was already married to Saul anyway.

"I wish I'd worn something nicer." She glanced down at her white blouse and flowered skirt.

"I'm in love with your heart, not your wardrobe," Saul assured her.

His schmaltzy reply drew a chorus of exaggerated "awws" from his teammates.

"Fine," Rachel finally agreed, betraying her delight by beaming at him. "Let's do this."

So, they did. And they never, ever regretted it.

RISING FROM ASHES

ACTS OF VALOR, BOOK FOUR

Opal backed down her porch steps to admire the life-sized scarecrow that she'd just stuffed. It guarded her front door from a lawn chair, a festive reminder that Halloween was less than a week away. All she needed now was a cornucopia of gourds and several pumpkins to complement the chrysanthemums that graced each step.

"We need to talk."

With a gasp, Opal whirled to find her neighbor standing less than a yard away. Heavens, where had he come from? She put a hand to her pounding heart, aware that its beat was not subsiding beneath his glare. Sober and in the light of day, he looked ten times more dangerous, more forceful, and more appealing than ever.

The memory of his kiss warmed her like a ray of sunlight.

"Of course." She forced a smile. Questions whirled, like just how much of last night did he remember and what, exactly, did he have an issue with? "Why don't you come in?"

With several neighbors working in their yards, Monty nodded in favor of the suggestion.

Opal led the way inside, guiding him through her foyer to the kitchen. "Would you like a cup of cider?" She hoped desperately to put their talk on a friendlier level.

"This isn't a social call." He crossed his arms and planted his feet.

Opal drew a breath and met his gaze. Monty stood a foot taller than she. His frown put a crease between his eyebrows. It was all she could do not to appear as intimidated as she felt. "Okay, then. How can I help you?"

"You broke into my house last night," he accused, his expression grim and watchful. "How'd you get in?"

"You keep a key under one of your flowerpots." And when she'd left, she'd put it right back where she found it. "I could tell by listening at your door that you were hurt, sir. I'm sorry for entering without permission." Since he didn't want to be neighborly, she fell back on military-speak.

His eyes narrowed at the intentional formality. "Did it ever occur to you that I would rather have been left alone?"

Opal considered whether that was true. "With all due respect, sir, you weren't in any state to know what you wanted."

Anger flashed in his golden-brown eyes. "Whatever state I was in, in my own home, is none of your business, *lieutenant.*"

Really? Did he have to emphasize her inferior rank like that? "Correct, Commander." She swallowed her intimidation. "But your physical wellbeing is my business, as is the wellbeing of any serviceman or woman," she added, impersonalizing the incident.

His hot glare should have incinerated her. "If you tell a soul about last night," he warned, on a low growl, "then you can kiss your career goodbye. Is that clear enough?"

What on earth was he afraid of? Opal wondered. Did he think she would accuse him of indecent behavior? Did he even remember kissing her? "Crystal, sir." Indignation that he would think her so indiscrete emboldened her to add, "Perhaps you'll tone it down next time, so that I'm less privy to your business."

A dull blush highlighted his cheekbones, and she felt a little better for it.

"I don't know what kind of game you're playing." Both his words and his scowl conveyed confusion. "But whatever it is, you're wasting your time."

"I don't play games."

Her answer made him hesitate. She could see him struggling to understand her.

"You cleaned my rug," he said, his tone still accusing.

"Yes, I did."

"Why?"

Did he really want an honest answer? "Because the blood would have stained it otherwise, and I thought you'd been through enough already."

His frown became ferocious. He took a step forward, and Opal took a cautionary step back. "Leave me alone," he said through his teeth. "I don't need a nosy neighbor prying into my business."

The words 'nosy' and 'prying' stung too much for her to make a reply. Uncertainty chased across his face in the wake of his anger, before he pivoted, stalking toward her front door. It closed quietly behind him.

Five seconds elapsed before the silence was broken by the crescendo of running feet. "Oh, my God!" Ruby burst into the kitchen, her face a reflection of outrage. "Was that our neighbor?" She seized Opal's arms. "Who does he think he was, talking to you like that?"

Opal blinked away her numbness. Consternation rose up in its place as she realized Ruby had just overheard every word Commander Monteague had said to her. "Don't worry about it." She held up a finger. "He wasn't threatening me; he was protecting his privacy."

"What do you mean, he wasn't threatening you?" Ruby propped her hands on her jean-clad hips. "I heard what he said. He implied that he was going to ruin your career. And for what? All you did was patch up his cuts and clean his carpet."

Opal had explained why she'd slept until ten that morning. "I said, forget it," she repeated. "He's been through enough, okay? He didn't mean to threaten me. If he really knew me, he wouldn't have bothered."

"Oh, come on!" Ruby stared at her in disbelief. "There's no excuse for him talking to you that way! He's the one who got drunk last night."

Opal copied her sister's stance. "You need to forget about that, too."

"What?"

"Stories like that can damage a man's career. He's hurting inside. Try to be sensitive to that, and forget the rest, okay?"

Ruby slapped a hand to her forehead. "I can't believe you're just going to let that pass."

"Yes, I am." Opal nodded emphatically. "He's grieving." She wondered if perhaps he'd watched his man die and even tried to save them. He'd been hit by shrapnel, he'd said, implying that there'd been an explosion.

Ruby's eyes widened. "You're crazy about him," she accused. "You have to be. Otherwise, you would never let him talk to you that way."

Opal wanted to deny the truth, but she'd never been good at lying. "I admire him for his commitment to this country." She crossed her arms over her chest. "Now, leave it alone, Ruby. I don't want to talk about this anymore."

Thoughts glimmered in Ruby's jewel-like eyes. "Whatever," she said, airily.

That wasn't the reassurance Opal was looking for. "I mean it, Sis. Don't even look at him if you see him again."

"Okay. Gosh." Ruby pushed past her to raid the kitchen cabinets.

With a sigh of mistrust, Opal went to fetch her purse. "I'm going to the store to pick up pumpkins," she said, expecting her sister to tag along. Ruby had developed a habit of shadowing her lately. "Are you coming?"

"No, I don't want to miss *The View*," came the unexpected reply.

Opal sighed and headed for the door. "Why don't you work on your résumé?" she tossed over her shoulder.

"I'll think about it."

Thinking about it was all Ruby had ever done with her degree in journalism. "I'll be back in an hour." Opal shut the door behind her, scanned the street as was her habit, to make sure that Eric wasn't stalking them, and hurried toward her powder blue Toyota Matrix.

Backing out of her driveway, Opal snuck a peek at her neighbor's house. He'd closed the blinds in all his windows. Now he was blocking the world out, hiding in his lair.

What secret was he harboring? she wondered. She couldn't dismiss the question, any more than she could stop Monty from hijacking her thoughts.

Available in Paperback and eBook from Your Favorite Bookstore or Online Retailer

ABOUT THE AUTHOR

Rebecca Hartt is the *nom de plume* for an award-winning, best-selling author who, in a different era of her life, wrote strictly romantic suspense. Now Rebecca chooses to showcase the role that faith plays in the lives of Navy SEALs, penning military romantic suspense that is both realistic and heartwarming.

As a child, Rebecca lived all over the world. She has been a military dependent for most of her life, first as a daughter, then as a wife, and knows first-hand the dedication and sacrifice required by those who serve. Living near the military community of Virginia Beach, Rebecca is constantly reminded of the peril and uncertainty faced by US Navy SEALs, many of whom testify to a personal and profound connection with their Creator. Their loved ones, too, rely on God for strength and comfort. These men of courage and women of faith are the subjects of Rebecca Hartt's enthusiastically received *Acts of Valor* series.

RebeccaHartt.com

Sign up for the Rebecca Hartt Newsletter Here

https://rebeccahartt.com/contact